The Beckett Cypher Series

Book 3 – The Politicians

Lee Cunningham

The Beckett Cypher Series – Book 3 – The Politicians takes the reader through a fictional rollercoaster ride involving realistic corruption often corresponding to current world events. Fascinating characters bring to life a terrifying look at the evil that lurks in the shadows of our modern day government and society. Readers will discover and delight in the unfolding series leaving them wanting even more pages to turn and enjoy.

The Politicians is a thrilling novel of suspense, intrigue, mystery, corruption, and passionate romance, built on the continuing investigation that undercover operative Shane Beckett began in **The Beckett Cypher Series – Book 1 – The Case**, and continued in **The Beckett Cypher Series – Book 2 – The Committee.**

Shane began his investigation in **The Beckett Cypher Series – Book 1 – The Case**, working undercover for the Carson City Sheriff, investigating an organized crime syndicate involving drug cartels and corrupt politicians. Shane discovers his father's massive investigation, dubbed **The Case**, concealed and encrypted on a military grade flash drive.

For more than a decade, the flash drive had preserved and protected one of the only remaining copies of the California Department of Justice investigation that led to his father's and mother's murders, the California Attorney General's assassination, and the killings or disappearances of nearly all members of the task force. Detailing more than a year of high-level, intensive investigation, **The**

Case is now protected by an advanced encryption system known as **The Beckett Cypher**, updated and modified by a surprise ally.

As Shane maneuvers through his dangerous assignment, he becomes the target for assassination as he meets the woman of his dreams. Shane begins to fall in love with the mysterious beauty, only to discover that she and her family have monitored his actions for years, and are much more than he first imagined. Shane craves to run headlong into a romance with this lovely, intriguing, woman at the same time his instincts caution him to slow down or not proceed at all.

Shane's choices lead him to discover missing pieces of his father's case file and the final key that will unlock its secrets, **The Beckett Cypher**. Working with his new ally, Shane's cyber team uses the powerful new cypher system to expose the mysteries of the past, present-day crimes, and planned deadly schemes yet to come.

The Case investigation leads Shane and his team to discover **The Committee**, a secret political organization seizing power in preparation to establish a one-world government. As Shane's operation focuses on this expanding, far-reaching conspiracy, he learns **The Committee** is nearly ready to test their new algorithm system in preparation to launch their Primary Objective.

Shane must again rapidly expand his team to further develop **The Beckett Cypher**, racing against the clock, to understand **The Committee** structure and identify their members. As his investigative team chooses needed alliances, they must also carefully guard against discovery or risk destruction by forces from **The Committee**, drug cartels, and corrupt government agencies.

While **The Committee** plan threatens personal freedoms in all free governments of the world, Shane finds more enemies motivated by greed, sex, power, and money, at almost every turn. Corrupt politicians, foreign agents, drug cartels, and internal betrayal further complicate Shane's life and choices when he risks his teams' safety to save a Committee member's life and family. The rescue requires that Shane create an elaborate plan, dependent on people with questionable loyalties working together.

In **The Beckett Cypher – Book 3 – The Politicians**, Shane's cypher team incorporates advanced technology developed by a new group of collaborating ingenious team members, who create a nearly unstoppable Beckett Cypher Artifical Intelligence Spy System, known as *BaCayse*. Once perfected, Shane's cyber-weapon becomes capable of bypassing cybersecurity barriers and simultaneously controlling multiple enemy operations at remote locations around the world.

BaCayse also discovers and penetrates cybersecurity barriers concealing social media and government spy sites working *together* to gather data on all people worldwide. Combining the massive intelligence, BaCayse provides Shane and his team with the most advanced information system in the world.

In their quest, Shane and his team uncover scandal and corruption in federal government leading to the office of the President of the United States. The Beckett team must partner with a member of the President's own administration and solicit help from a foreign ally in order to battle the most powerful man in the world.

Readers will be captivated by surprise twists and turns as the exciting plot unfolds, detailed characters develop, and Shane Beckett and his team push headlong toward their final conflict.

Watch for the next novel in the storyline, **The Beckett Cypher Series – Book 4 – The Prophet**

Dedication

I dedicate this book to our country's guardians and first responders. They are the heroes who daily fight the good fight and keep the faith in the system, even when it fails.

The men and women serving in the armed forces of the United States of America are some of the bravest and most selfless people alive. They protect us and assist others in many nations all over the world.

Inside our communities, our country's hundreds of thousands of law enforcement officers and firefighters work around the clock, risking their lives, as they patrol and stand ready to respond to any threat to public safety or health.

Collectively, all of these brave men and women represent our first line of defense, protection, and safety against all enemies foreign and domestic. They work tirelessly against crime, oppression, natural catastrophes, illness, disease, and injury. They protect our nation's borders and autonomy.

We owe these brave souls our respect, support, and gratitude. I thank these fine Americans and their families, for their service.

ISBN: 978-1-7320055-4-9

Table of Contents

Chapter 1

"Politicians can be your worst enemies because you can never be certain of their loyalties. Their loyalties are moving targets, changing with the winds of influence and opportunity. And the winds come from the most unusual directions."

Shane Beckett sat in a brown camping chair placed at the top edge of a meadow filled with lush grass and wildflowers. The long, narrow field sloped downward toward the edge of a cliff overlooking a broad and deep river canyon, which fell some 2,300 feet to the rushing water below. Shane absentmindedly studied a cottontail rabbit nibbling grass 50 feet away. As he gazed at the peaceful scene, he struggled to focus his thoughts but failed to contain any one consistent subject. His mind filled with random details that carried conflicting worry, joy, love, hope and plans, all mingled together, making no sense, leaving him frustrated.

Another 100 yards past the big cottontail, the brush suddenly moved aside, and a man appeared, wearing a light green large-brimmed Australian bush hat, khaki shirt, jeans and brown hiking boots. The man looked down as he moved steadily toward Shane as if watching the ground, while lost in his thoughts. The man had a familiar form that Shane knew but didn't immediately place. He walked purposely, yet effortlessly, carrying a camp chair that perfectly matched Shane's.

As the man approached the rabbit, the chubby cottontail refused to move. Rather than rushing off to safety, the bunny sat quietly munching a purple wildflower stalk as though the man didn't exist, or

1

posed no threat. And as the man walked close by the rabbit and approached Shane, a strange calmness overcame Shane, even as he was consumed by the desire to know the man's identity. Unusual for him, Shane also felt no threat.

Once he had journeyed several feet beyond the unmoving rabbit, the man looked up and smiled at Shane, revealing his face. It was Shane's father...not as Shane remembered seeing his dad the last few times, but as his father had appeared during Shane's earliest childhood memories.

Patrick Beckett arrived and stood next to Shane. The two men stared at each other as if in expected, but still shocked disbelief. Shanes' father unfolded his chair and sat at his son's right side. He took Shane's hand in his and stroked it with his thumb, hungry for his oldest boy's touch.

Patrick said, "I've missed you so much, Shane...I can't even begin to explain the hole in my heart created by my death, and absence from your life. Not being with both of you boys is almost too much to bear."

He added quickly, "But then, I believe you also know that hopeless feeling of loss and emptiness as well as I do!"

Shane nodded silently until he cleared the forming lump in his throat. He said softly, "Dad, I have *needed* to talk to you about so many things that I don't know where to begin. Heath told me about his dreams and how he pleaded to talk to you, while you walked away. We *both* want your advice about the important decisions we need to make and all our current challenges. I've tried several times. I'm reluctant to start now. But, if I do ask...will you promise to stay awhile and answer my questions?"

Patrick looked at his son inquisitively, smiled and stroked his hand. "I'll do everything I can, Shane. But I don't understand why you can't talk to me. You see, I'm always there for you." He nodded for Shane to begin.

Failing to understand, Shane explained, "Dad, in my dreams, I used to come to the campfire at the Valley of the River to sit beside you so we could talk about important matters. But, I could never get all the questions out, so the answers never followed. You always left me alone. It's the one thing in my life that seems unfair, that I still can't get my head around. I don't have you and Mom, your love, your presence, and your counsel. The older I get, the more I need you both in my life!"

Patrick smiled at his son as his face softened. He said, "Both you boys always have your mom and I...just differently now. You talk, and we *will* help you find your answer...on your own. Just know that it seems as unfair to us, not being able to be with you, since our deaths. We can't give you career advice, plan vacations, participate in your lives, or watch all your relationships with others grow. For us, there are no weddings to plan and enjoy, and...no Grandkids for us to hold." Emotion shaped Patrick Beckett's voice, while tears welled in his eyes.

Trying to control his own emotions and lighten the moment, Shane asked, "What's it like...there? Can you tell me where you are, Dad? Are you with Mom...safe and happy?"

Patrick Beckett smiled and stroked his son's head. "About that, I can't tell you much. It *is* so different I can't explain it. But I can tell you to stick to your roots, believe in God, lead a good life, and keep doing the right things...and we will all be together again. But now, I don't have much time in your dream, so I need to tell you some things quickly."

3

Shane nodded, encouraging his father to continue, realizing his suspicion was correct. This experience was, in fact, a dream.

Patrick said, "So much has happened in your life since I left." He smiled. "You graduated from the police academy and began your law enforcement career. And I was so proud to watch your brief, but stellar career with DEA. I'm so sorry it ended the way it did when the cartel killed your partners, and then you discovered that cartel corruption destroyed your case's prosecution. But you bounced back so quickly. After you chose to leave DEA, you became a world-class undercover operative."

"And your work discovering The Case that led to your mom's and my murders was outstanding! Meeting Walter and Kate and falling in love with Kate has given you the hope you needed and the family you missed so much! Pete has stepped up and become as good a father to you boys as any person could want. He loves you and your brother as if you were his own, and now you two *are* his boys! And finally, you've discovered the Beckett Cypher, which has led you to The Committee, one of the most organized political threats that the world has ever faced. You've done remarkable work to get to this point. But, now I fear the worst is in store for you and those you love. Of all the things you've done, you're finally in the most danger of your entire life!"

Patrick Beckett looked shaken. He paused, and gazed into his son's eyes, needing to say more, not knowing where to begin.

Shane searched his father's gaze for any sign that would help him understand. He finally asked, "What is it, Dad? What can you see? Can you tell me?"

4

THE POLITICIANS

Patrick looked intently at his son as if imparting a momentous warning, as he said, "I *can* tell you that of all the enemies you and the world face, the worst, and the most dangerous are the politicians!"

Shane stared at his father in disbelief. He blurted out, "Politicians?"

Patrick nodded, drew in a deep breath, sighed and looked down. He said, "Your mom and I died…along with many other good and honest people working The Case because a few who worked with us betrayed our team. And I couldn't see it coming. None of us could. We didn't recognize the evil in the bureaucrats and politicians who smiled and encouraged us while they planned our demise. It wasn't just Franky Magadinno and his drug cartel goons who killed us. Bureaucrats and politicians planned and arranged our murders. Franky and his crew just did their dirty work."

"You see, Shane, unlike the enemy on a battlefield, wearing an easily recognized uniform, or a tattooed, cartel gang member flashing gang signs, who stands out in a crowd, these lethal politicians, and government administrators are nearly unrecognizable."

"People enter every office of local, county, state and federal service, all appearing as normal unthreatening people. And most are just that! Most go on to work for years or decades…maybe even their entire adult lives in government service, just doing their jobs. They help move humanity forward. They provide a service to the people who pay their salaries, the people they serve."

"But others, growing exponentially in number over the decades since World War II, enter public service with a hidden agenda or are turned to their political hot button once they begin to serve. They

5

navigate their agency through their work to a place not sanctioned by mainstream Americans. Within all government, this is becoming more and more commonplace."

As his father spoke, a group of deer crashed through the brush at the far edge of the meadow. Two bucks emerged following a small herd of does. They didn't seem to notice the people sitting and talking more than a hundred yards uphill. Shane marveled at the colors bursting forth in the late morning sun from the green emerging grasses and the substantial numbers of yellow, white, purple and pink wildflowers on display in the scene. Shane glanced at his father and realized Patrick Beckett had blurred in his vision. His father's words were now nearly inaudible. Shane focused on his father.

"Shane! What I'm telling you is so important! You've already experienced corruption that blocked a federal prosecution of major dope dealers and the evil men who murdered your fellow field agents. You now understand that there is every manner of corruption imaginable present in government. You and many Americans now distrust their government to act fairly, impartially, or even tell them the simple truth. Distrust born of government corruption and abuse of power is now so commonplace in our country that society has come to accept it as the norm."

Patrick continued. "You see, we citizens have come to expect the worst from our politicians and government employees. Think about the VA scandals or visit the average DMV. You have to look hard to find honesty, good service, and consistent, fair treatment. But as bad as the incompetence, laziness, and abuses are, that's not what has become dangerous for the rest of us!"

Shane studied his father's eyes intently as Patrick continued. "The real danger is organized, focused corruption, obstruction, and misdirection."

"Shane, Americans used to think that organized crime was the Mafia, or top union bosses pillaging retirement accounts, or making payoffs to officials to acquire a government contract. But, in today's world, organized crime is much more politically sinister and evil, and not just about profit. Now, along with money, it's politicians in bed with arms dealers, drug cartels, sex traffickers, foreign governments, or all of the above. And those in power now often abuse their authority, colluding quietly as they focus the collective power of many government agencies to achieve a political goal."

"Shane, small groups, operating together within the government, are committed to disrupting and misdirecting their organization's mission. These officials accomplish their goals *while* they eviscerate and discredit their organizations! They have become the shadow government."

"People hate that term because they aren't sure how to define it and they don't want it to exist. But, the shadow government does exist, from politically appointed positions and directed hires in every office in government, to activist judges, intent on changing the law and freedoms from the will of the people to *their* political point of view and agenda."

"The shadow government resists and obstructs the voters will through politically coordinated and directed movements! These organized secret groups re-direct policies and target citizens, remove freedoms, and even even destroy lives. And what makes it worse is that they believe so strongly in their political views, that they believe those who disagree don't deserve their freedoms or their lives."

Shane knew what his father said was true, based on his own experiences. He thought back to the DEA team and his most important case. After working for four years together, his team grew to be tight, and the members had become his closest friends. But some of them were now dead, due to leaks in the government, purchased with drug money. And even worse, after a cartel lawyer bribed a judge and paid off two corrupt DEA administrators, all the cartel suspects were not only free but protected from future prosecution. It wasn't right. And it wasn't fair. But this was just one example of organized lethal corruption at work.

The corrupt system's failure had convinced Shane to resign from the career he had loved. Shane's fellow agents and friends had died. He now often wondered what all the training, preparation, work, time and effort had accomplished.

Suddenly, Shane saw a large porcupine waddle into the scene from a thicket of small pines off to his right. He watched the pudgy mammal's quills sparkle purplish-brown in the sunlight. Above the slow-moving porcupine and grazing deer, a light wind moved the tops of the tallest trees along the canyon rim. Shane felt the brush of the wind on his cheeks and suddenly realized his dad was talking. He again focused, disappointed that his concentration had once again wandered.

"You see, Shane, as the political parties moved further apart, their radical fringe members have become activists for every opposing position you can identify. Activists often believe so strongly in their position that they think if you oppose them you're ignorant, unworthy of life, and need to die and go away. And if you don't, they *are* willing to help you. Look at groups we would think of as benign and good, like environmentalists. Their radical fringe activists morph into ecoterrorists, people willing to kill people they don't even know over whales, or owls, or trees, or a vanishing species of insect."

"Both radicalism and terrorism have grown to the point in the world that they are now accepted as part of everyday *normal* life. They exist everywhere and represent nearly every hot political topic you can think of."

"Once radicals organize, the Internet becomes their most lethal tool. They advertise, recruit, spread their propaganda, grow in number, and influence the mainstream, while they spread their hatred for whoever or whatever. These radical groups impact civilized nations to the point that their destructive actions are constantly in the daily news. They even flaunt identities that would never have been accepted decades earlier by Americans: Anarchists, Socialists, Communists, Racists, Terrorists. And they flaunt their commitment to violence and destabilization."

"The result is that citizens trying to live a regular life are uneasy, nervous, unsettled. To compensate, many good citizens now isolate themselves in a growing number, withdrawing from society, pretending not to notice. They take no action. They don't even want to talk about societal problems."

The wind surprised Shane, blowing a hot gust that enveloped him, fanning his face and raising his neatly-combed brown hair. He quickly re-focused on his father's words.

"Radicals and gangs seize the opportunity to fill the void and infiltrate society more deeply. Extremists now boldly march about calling for the destruction of this or the death of that part of American society, as they disavow our nation's history, purpose, and direction. Some Americans now see screaming radicals as the voice of America! We are witnessing the death of the rule of law! And the result is the destabilization of our systems of legislation and law enforcement."

"Destabilization in Western nations also affects third world countries. Foreign wars have become so frequent, that somewhere everyday innocent helpless people are dying in staggering numbers while some despot or terrorist group subjects people to unspeakable terror and oppression. Western nations now do little or nothing other than sending food shipments and medical staff to treat the aftermath."

Shane recalled the images of the many all-boy street gangs he had seen during a trip to Bogota, Colombia. The scenes were now images Shane could never seem to completely dislodge from his mind. As he recalled, he realized how much he hated the misery and hopelessness the boys faced each morning. And he loathed that these groups of *lost boys* were a by-product of street prostitutes controlled by drug cartels.

On that trip, Shane learned that these prostitutes produced a constant supply of babies. Girl babies were raised to be servants to the cartels. The cartels eventually forced most of the girls into prostitution. The prettiest ones were sold on the dark web to buyers around the world or housed in cartel-owned brothels in nearly all major metro areas. Girls as young as seven years old commanded high dollars with the cartel's pedophile clientele.

Boy babies were given to homeless gangs to be raised, toughened-up, and used. The roughest teenagers were forced to become soldiers for the cartels. Other weaker boys were rounded up for competitions between the corrupt Colombian National Police and their paramilitary counterparts. Both groups protected the wealthy drug cartels.

A group of heavily armed men would bet who could shoot one of the boys at the furthest distance as the boy ran through a long field. The longest shots won the biggest prizes. Bets increased as competitors drank more alcohol. There was no choice. Armed captors gave the boys the option to die where they stood, or try to reach the safety of the jungle before they were shot in the back. These competitions occurred more frequently when the street gangs grew too large, or the Ministry of Tourism received too many tourist complaints.

Surviving boys lived in horrible poverty and hunger. Street gangs used babies to beg for money. Older boys placed a tourniquet to stop the blood flow on a baby's arm and then chopped a hand or lower arm from the infant. Once the arm scabbed over and healed teenage street thugs thrust these baby's stubs through open car windows as they walked up and down the highways in stop-and-go downtown traffic. The babies made sympathetic begging tools, allowing the older boys to collect money from motorists. It was this money they used to feed their small homeless groups.

Shane hated that the atrocious situation was born of Americans buying cocaine. He wished every user had to spend a month on the streets, living in cardboard shacks in alleys, struggling to survive with the lost boys, or being used as street whores by whoever paid a few dollars. Shane fumed as the vivid scene overpowered his dream. And then, a mighty wind gust blew grains of dirt onto his face, breaking the memory. The Bogota scene abruptly vanished as he heard his mother speaking.

"Tell him, Patrick! Help him understand the threat, so he and Heath stay safe, and survive The Case! Please, Patrick. Hurry!" Annie Beckett sounded pleading and frightened, even as she spoke in her usual soft, sweet, reassuring tones.

Shane asked, "Mom, where are you?"

When no answer came, Shane again listened intently to his father.

Patrick smiled at Shane, and asked, "So how does this affect your investigation? You discovered that The Committee was formed to force all nations into a committee-run, one-world government, to control the fundamental conflicts infecting civilization, stabilize life for all people, and to keep the peace. But in the process of creating *one* governmental plan to control *all* people, nearly all freedoms that give rise to differences will have to be stripped away by Committee planners."

"To be successful, the Committee must time their inception of the Primary Objective, to coincide with essential world social, economic and financial chaos and destabilization. They must control key positions in governments to assume authority. And over decades, they have recruited, taught, and placed politicians and administrators in all necessary positions to give them that authority. But, Shane, remember when you deal with them, that they are in fact, *politicians*. They can harbor any numbers of secret loyalties, and as you know, be influenced by money, sex, power, control, title, fame or threats. They all aspire, and they all have weaknesses. And *most of them* can be manipulated or even controlled."

Patrick continued. "Shane, always remember that it is the politicians and administrators who control the alphabet soup of

12

agencies at all levels in all countries, and none of these agencies can be automatically trusted to do the right thing anymore! In the United States, the FBI, CIA, DEA, NSA, IRS…you name the alphabet, even within local, or state agencies…they can all ruin or end your life with little effort from any small well-organized group within these agencies. And they do it free of charge, funded by the taxpayer's wallet!"

"We have seen these cohesive groups of politicians and bureaucrats chastise, oppose and threaten the voters, the Congress and even The President of The United States. And not just oppose and threaten, but obstruct and flaunt their power as they attempt to destroy the government the people created. Small organized groups within basically good agencies abuse their power and trust by attacking the citizens they were sworn to serve. They misdirect investigations, conceal crimes or ignore their responsibilities."

"They even attack their bosses and oversite committees when it serves their purpose. And, they have grown in number and assumed power they were never intended to possess, to the point that they are completely out of control. Unfortunately for you, and all of humanity, many of these people are now Committee members."

"Just as the Founding Fathers feared, our once cherished government has become our biggest enemy, our worst nightmare, and our greatest threat!"

Patrick stared hard into his son's eyes. He said, "Remember, Shane, politicians can be your worst enemy because you can never be certain of their loyalties. Their loyalties are moving targets, changing with the winds of influence and opportunity. And the wind comes from the most unusual directions. Be careful as you venture into their world, Son!"

Patrick paused, and then added, "And protect your brother, Heath. He *has* grown a great deal since prison, but he is still easily influenced. His judgment has never been as good as yours. Protect yourself, Kate, Walter, Pete…all those you love. You have to be on guard with all your cunning, intelligence, training, good character and will!" Patrick looked deep into his son's eyes, searching for a sign of complete understanding.

Shane gazed back at his father in silence. He nodded, thoughtfully. As they sat in the peaceful meadow, a large shadow appeared on the ground, approaching both men. They looked up at the same moment and beheld a giant golden eagle, with a wingspan of at least eight feet, soaring effortlessly overhead as it rode a thermal upward. Patrick Beckett immediately stood up and began to fold his chair.

He said sadly, "I have to go now, Shane!"

Shane protested, "Not yet! Dad, please! I have so many more questions!"

Patrick shook his head and said, "I love you more than you know, Shane. But, this is *your* time, and this is now *your* fight. That has to be all for now. But, do me one favor?"

Tears formed in Shane's eyes as he nodded.

"Hug Pete for me…and kiss your beautiful Kate on the cheek." Patrick Beckett added as an afterthought, "And kiss Masai on his muzzle. What a cute puppy! I'm so glad you finally found the dog you've always wanted. You're happy now. And genuine happiness like yours makes a father smile."

Shane smiled back at his father through his tears. He asked, "You *have* seen Kate and Masai then?"

Patrick smiled, and said, "I never stop watching, smiling and crying...right along with your mother." He stepped forward and hugged his son long and hard, and then stepped back and pulled down the brim of his hat. Patrick Beckett turned and walked toward the end of the field, making his way slowly to the rabbit, in silence. Once there, he paused, turned and motioned goodbye by raising his free hand. Shane returned the gesture, tears streaming down both cheeks.

"Goodbye, Dad. I love you...and Mom!" Shane spoke quietly, almost inaudibly.

The rabbit swallowed one last wildflower stalk and then followed along a few steps behind Patrick until both were out of sight. The eagle's shadow again appeared, now heading the opposite way on the ground near Shane, in the direction his father had left. Shane looked up to see the huge bird pass one last time before it disappeared over the brush and the hills below. And just as the bird vanished, an unusually bright beam of light shot from the eagle's wingtip directly to Shane's eyes, causing him to startle.

"I just wanted to tell you I love you one more time, Dad!" Shane shouted in the silent forest, not knowing if his father could hear his words. Looking at the scene, he noticed that the deer and porcupine were gone. He now stood alone in the beautiful meadow, his chest heaving with emotion. Tears streamed down both cheeks to his muscular jawline, where they fled him in silence as they fell to the ground. The forest remained still, void of any animal or weather sounds, seemingly intent on listening to and watching Shane struggle with his sorrow. He felt utterly alone, but oddly close to Kate.

"Shane!" Kate called as she shook him by the shoulders, in their bed. "Shane, wake up! Honey!"

Shane moved slowly, raising his hands first to feel and then wipe real tears from his eyes. He said, "I know it was a dream. But the experience was so real I wanted it to be true. Dad even told me it was a dream, but it was still so good to see him! God, I love my parents so much, Kate! I wish we were able to see them."

Kate took Shane's hands in hers and kissed his lips. She slowly kissed the tears from his cheeks as he roused from his deep sleep. She said, "I know. I want to see my parents, too. And I want to meet your parents someday. But you were dreaming again. I guess your dreams are back for a while. That's the second dream about your parents so far this week!" Kate kissed the last tear stain from Shane's face and stopped to gaze into his eyes.

Shane smiled as he studied Kate's ruby red lips, the mouth he instantly longed to kiss. He was mesmerized by her stunning blue-green eyes, that quickly filled with brilliant light from the morning sun. Shane realized the sun must enter the windows each morning to search for Kate, just to illuminate her incredible beauty. As he gazed at Kate's perfect mouth, parted lips, flawless skin, and thick, luxurious hair, Shane felt the stirring of arousal. He quickly pulled Kate down to him and kissed her passionately.

Kate melted into Shane, their bodies adjusting as they found that one position where they could move perfectly together as their lust grew. Shane yearned to get lost in Kate's firm, beautiful body, feel the warmth of her skin, smell her fragrance, and lavish her gorgeous firm breasts with kisses. He longed to taste her essence and experience the brush of her fingers running through his hair. Shane brushed his fingertips along the skin on the back of Kate's thighs. He thrust his tongue into Kate's mouth and felt her tongue respond with erotic french kisses. Shane could almost feel himself making love to Kate, slowly, passionately, without a care or concern other than their love.

But today Shane had dreamed about his parents and had a conversation with his father. At this moment, his mind still held memories from the dream, and Shane knew what he must do to preserve those memories. As much as Shane wanted to make love to the woman of his dreams, he paused and pulled Kate to his chest, held her tightly and focused his thoughts. And after a few moments, as was their custom now, Shane recounted to Kate every word and every scene he could recall from his dream.

When he finished, Kate remarked supportively, "It was probably a dream in response to all the briefings we've had over the last few days. All this information coming from The Case has been exhausting. So many people identified, and the dozens of plans outlined by the Beckett Cypher...sometimes it seems so much it almost becomes unbelievable. Can we really have that many people involved in that much corruption in America? It's been an awful lot to digest. Some of it seems surreal."

Shane added, "But not surreal. Just real. Real crimes. Real people dead, or injured or missing. Real corruption, and real plans to interfere with our way of life. To think that while all the politicians were squabbling over Russian interference in our elections going back to the 1920's the evidence suggests that decades ago some of our politicians on both sides of the political aisle were doing far more to impact the outcome of all of our elections than foreign enemies! And then, once elected, they were lying to us about what they were doing *to* us, and planning *for* us!"

Kate said, "It's so disappointing to think we can't trust *our* own people. But right now we have to focus on The Committee, what they're planning; and figure out a way to stop them. Or at least we need to figure out a way to slow them down until someone can stop them!"

Recalling something his father had said, Shane felt suddenly energized. He said, "Agreed. Let's get dressed, join the team for breakfast and see where we are today!"

Kate vaulted out of bed with her usual grace and mighty agility. She raced to the bathroom ahead of Shane, who remained in bed, taking in the sight of Kate's luscious body, bouncing in all the right places. When he didn't follow, Kate stopped and turned to him.

"Not coming today?" She teased Shane by twirling her hair in her fingertips as she arched one foot off the ground on her toes, tightening her calf and thigh muscles. She swayed her body from side to side, allowing her large, firm breasts to swing back and forth as she cocked her head and pursed her lips forming a subtle, yet sexy, pout. The incoming sunlight continued to accentuate Kate's flawless beauty, as it played along with her teasing, highlighting her ruby red toenails and fingernails that perfectly matched the lipstick on her full, inviting lips.

Shane felt the swelling between his legs and the blood surging in his veins, as his heart's pace quickened. He groaned and smiled even as his face contorted in apparent pain. Shane shook his head, rejecting the inferred opportunity. Kate feigned disappointment, and turned to leave, walking in model-like strides to the bathroom. Her small red bikini panty accented a perfectly formed butt that Shane couldn't stop watching. Each step Kate took sent shock waves through her tight muscular body. And each shock wave brought about corresponding surges within Shane.

Before she could close the bathroom door, Shane called out, "I never tire of seeing that in the morning you know…the incredible way you look and move!"

"I know!" Kate replied. "That's why I do it!" She looked back, threw a kiss through the open door and then quickly closed it behind her.

After showering and dressing, Shane and Kate walked into a buzzing kitchen. Walter, Lee, and Pete greeted them and invited them to the dining room for a breakfast meeting. Shane and Kate began to fill plates with their choices of smoked ham, extra thick, crispy bacon, pork chops, varieties of eggs, Belgian waffles, homemade blueberry muffins, yogurt and fresh fruit in plum wine marinade, courtesy of Jesse and Juanita's most recent collaboration with new recipes. The scents in the kitchen made Shane salivate before his plate was half-filled. Juanita provided caramel lattes just as Kate and Shane adjourned to the dining room.

Once everyone was seated inside, Tom closed the door. After receiving a nod from his half-brother Lee, Tom said, "Thanks for coming in so quickly. Lee and I would like to explain what we have proposed to Pete and Walter." Shane and Kate glanced about the room inquisitively. Lee, Walter, and Pete all met them with excited faces bearing approving smiles.

Tom continued. "This investigation has become so large and time-consuming that we have decided to add additional resources. A few months ago Lee and I were approached by a nationally renowned competitor, an investigative firm owned by a family we know, trust and have worked with in the past. The other company asked us if we would consider buying them out so they can pursue other opportunities. Lee and I approached Walter and Pete with the idea of your family joining in partnership with us, forming a new LLC to own the combined investigative firms."

"We have also agreed that we would jointly fund this investigation. The additional resources would give us access to hundreds of investigators around the country, who could do a great deal of background for us on this case, along with taking over responsibilities on other pending cases. Walter and Pete asked Spenser Pinetta to look into both the other firm's profit and loss statement, and our profit and loss statement, to prepare a recommendation to your family. Spenser is standing by for a conference call, but Walter and Pete want to speak to you before we continue. I might add that we would like Pete to coordinate legal matters for both firms, and Kate and Shane to consider working on high profile investigations other than this one, once we finish this case." Tom sat down abruptly and sipped a black coffee.

Walter nodded to Pete. Pete said, "Walter and I believe this is a natural progression for our developing long-term business plan. Lee and Tom's investigative firm already does a great deal of the background work on our acquisitions and mergers, and The Case has already cost an estimated $11,000,000 to pursue. The expanded LLC would be run primarily by Tom and Lee, just as it is now, with financial oversite by Spenser and Margie Pinetta. Going forward, the six members in the LLC would have equal shares, with the four of us, Pete, Kate, Shane and I each adding 3.2 million to the business and Lee and Tom each adding 2.1 million to the business to accomplish the merger with the competitor…and, of course, reassigning their current business assets to our new joint LLC."

Walter asked, "Kate, Shane, what do you think before we call Spenser?"

Shane looked at Kate and grinned. She spoke first. "If this is good for all of us and all of our family, I agree." She smiled back at Shane, who nodded, approvingly.

Walter looked relieved and pleased. He immediately reached for and pushed the speed dial button on the conference phone. Spenser came on the line after the first ring.

"Good morning! Spenser and Margie Pinetta are here. How are you all?"

After pleasantries circled the room, Walter asked, "Spenser, what have you for us this morning?"

Spenser said routinely, "After we met with the attorneys and the paperwork was approved, with minor corrections, we again reviewed the entire financial process. I have just emailed the numbers to each of you for your approval. The bottom line estimate is, after the initial investment, considering a conservative projected business growth rate of 6.2% per year, adjusting for projected costs, the total initial investment should be recovered by year four. I could bore you with a guestimate of the rate of return on investment by each quarter, but with your permission, I won't! Although this estimate is subject to the economy and other factors, it is fairly conservative, considering the number of government contracts held by both investigative firms. In short, this looks like a good deal for everyone!"

After fifteen minutes of discussion, the deal was wrapped up, everyone in the room shook hands, and final plans were made for paperwork to be signed. Margie and Spenser said their goodbyes by phone. Lee and Tom agreed that Lee would meet with the California and New York office managers over the next week, while Tom remained with the team to manage security details at the ranch. Lee and Tom left the family in the dining room.

Shane asked, "I assume that Heath won't be part of this LLC, due to his past?"

Pete said, "Correct. There is nothing we can do about that. But, we have included Heath in everything else."

Shane said, "I understand. And I'm fine with that." Shane stood up and walked to Pete, as Pete and Walter stood to leave. He said, "Dad asked me to give you a hug!" He hugged Pete tightly, adding, "In a dream last night." Both men smiled, as they hugged.

✱✱✱

As the group exited the dining room and walked around the corner, Tom came bounding down the stairs, taking two at a time. Shane marveled at the big man's dexterity. It was the second time he'd seen Tom move so quickly, and quietly.

Tom rushed up to the group, and said, "There has been a shooting. Heath, Angie, and Tasha are alright, but there are multiple suspects down. FBI Special Agent in Charge Bryan Holland just called and relayed the message. We need to call him back now!"

Shane asked quickly, "Where are Tasha, Heath, and Angie? I just saw them all at dinner last night!"

Pete answered, "They went to La Grande this morning. They wanted to shop and sight-see on the way. And I asked them to pick up some items we can't buy here in the county."

Shane wrinkled his brow.

Pete said, "They took some time off to recover, be ordinary people for a day, and unwind. They left early to drive the scenic highway to the Old Emigrant Road Interpretive Center. I thought a break would do them all good."

Shane stared at Pete, waiting for more explanation.

Pete continued, broodingly, "Heath and Angie just arrived back from their last trip to Carson City a week ago. Angie completed the sale of her vet practice to her colleague, picked up her pit bull, Bruiser, collected the remainder of her belongings, and leased her home to her friend Beth. Now that she and Heath are together as a couple, Angie insisted she contribute as a functional member of our team."

"Without any break, Angie dove right into collating and organizing Committee flowcharts and timelines, assisting Tasha. She took over the lion's share of the tedious work. They've both been at it non-stop, taking short breaks to eat and sleep. I think the job has taken a toll on both ladies. All the sinister plots, murders, and corrupt schemes would ravage any normal mind, trying to fit the pieces together in an understandable chart!"

Shane frowned, questioning the decision.

Pete added, "Angie and Tasha wanted to be tourists for a day. They read about this old Oregon Trail museum that explained the westward migration of the 1800s. Thousands of wagon wheels ground ruts in surface bedrock as wagon trains made their way west, carrying pioneers and their belongings. They wanted to see the ruts, old photos

23

and one of the Conestoga wagons at the site. And they wanted to drive the backroads through forests where they could visit salmon spawning grounds and see herds of elk and deer. They wanted to feel alive…normal."

Pete looked down as his shoulders slumped. He said, "I suggested they go. And they thought it would be a fun break from all the cloak and dagger details coming out of cypher briefings. I guess not so much, now."

"And Heath took them out of the county without a security detail?" Shane asked.

"Heath wanted a detail to go with them. Tasha refused it. She wanted to be free from guards to prove to herself that it would be…could be…all right. I agreed to her terms, not Heath." Shane nodded his understanding.

The small group made its way back into the dining room and dialed FBI Special Agent in Charge Bryan Holland on speakerphone. Holland answered immediately, out of breath, having run to his office desk phone.

"They're all okay, Tom! Char took them down before they could take the car!"

"Before who could take who?" Pete asked.

Bryan recognized Pete's voice, took a deep breath and began again. "Sorry, Pete. I thought it was just Tom again. No offense, Tom. I mean I didn't know I would be talking to all of you so quickly after Tom and I just hung up. He must have run to get you all together so quickly. Let me start over from the beginning."

SAC Bryan Holland stood in his secret FBI office, located in a mostly vacant building in Washington D.C., one of dozens owned by the federal government. He walked to the door and checked the hallway to ensure privacy before closing and locking the door.

He returned to his office chair, sat down quickly and said, "Okay, here's what I know so far. Very early this morning I received a call from Vice President Crawford. He had just spoken with British Home Secretary Walcott, who had received a tip from her Russian contact in The Committee. The Russian said that the Chinese and North Koreans had posted a reward on the dark web for information leading to the identification and capture of those possessing the cypher, your cypher."

Holland took another deep breath and continued. "The cypher is worth two hundred and fifty million U.S. dollars to them."

Walter sat back in his chair. A worried look overcame him. Pete placed a hand on Walter's arm.

Bryan added, "Several days ago, at Crawford's insistence, I placed a team about an hour from you, in La Grande and tasked them with advanced planning for an attack on the ranch, or...attempts like this. We thought you were all there at the ranch or at least in Wallowa County. I called my team to place them on alert after I spoke to Crawford this morning."

"An hour later I received another call from the Vice President informing me that the Home Secretary spoke to him again. He said that a North Korean military interdiction team stationed in the U.S. identified and tracked a cell phone from your group. Fortunately, the Home Secretary received the targeted cell number from her Russian contact and gave it to Crawford, who provided it to me. I tracked the number and sent my team to intercept."

Holland said, "The number belongs to Tasha McKnight. Her phone signal wasn't scrambled, so the North Koreans were also able to track it. I notified my team as we began to monitor the phone. My units positioned themselves ahead of Heath, Angie, and Tasha driving in their SUV, along a remote location off Hwy 203, the Medical Springs Hwy. It's a roundabout route to a historic site, scenic, but remote. That may be why they drove that direction."

"Anyway, about the time I was ready to call you, my team spotted the North Korean team. We barely had time to set up and neutralize the North Koreans. The North Koreans had staged to block the road and tried to swarm your SUV. Three of the North Korean's are dead. One is wounded, in custody, and being interrogated before surgery."

"Where is the North Korean now?" Shane asked.

"Bryan answered, "On a helicopter. And I can't reveal any more about her location, or our activity with her at this time."

"Understood," Shane said.

"Where are our people?" Pete asked.

"On the way back to you, with Char driving, and part of my team bringing up the rear, working countersurveillance. Tasha's phone has been turned off, placed in a lead-lined box, and will be driven by one of my team to the Special Agent in Charge at the FBI office in Portland. He's a good man, a member of my inner circle. He'll have his team scrub the data, clearing the phone of all information. And then the phone will make it's way to a homeless person downtown. We'll put out some disinformation about the phone and change all the cell records to reflect calls to hospitals, drug dealers, and homeless shelters. No evidence will ever be discovered to the contrary."

Shane smiled. "Excellent. But the question remaining is, where is the leak? No one knows who has the cypher. By the way, what are they calling it? The cypher, I mean."

Bryan laughed. "They call it the 'Mayfield Cipher,' after the California Attorney General who started the old case investigation. They use the American spelling of cipher, not the English version: cypher. And you should know, The Committee wants it just as bad as the foreign players. But, to your first question, there is only one possibility to explain the leak that makes sense. My team."

"Your team?!" Shane nearly yelled.

"My team," Bryan repeated. "At Vice President Crawford's request, my team had a briefing day before yesterday. We covered all the known possibilities of a foreign team finding your team. We came to dead ends. I gave one of the tech guys working in my unit the list of all phone numbers for every person on your team and asked him to check signal tracking. I tasked him to verify none of the numbers were trackable, and notify me today if there was a problem. He didn't show up for work this morning. I went to his desk, and found Tasha's number written on his notepad."

"That son-of-a-bitch!" Pete said. "Where is he?"

"Hold on. I sent a team to his apartment twenty minutes ago. They're just calling in." Pete picked up his work cell phone and answered, "Holland." After a lengthy pause, he said, "Okay, you know what to do."

After a period of silence, Pete asked, "Bryan?"

Bryan Holland said thoughtfully, "He's dead! The team leader said someone tortured him and then put two small-caliber bullets into the back of his head. It's not pretty."

Shane asked, "So back to your team, your bosses, your contacts. Who knew about your involvement with the cypher? Who could have been the source of the leak?"

Bryan answered slowly. "I've thought this out in advance trying to do some preplanning for any possible future scenario. There are very few possibilities that make sense. The Vice President authorized and set up this entire FBI operation, and from my experience with him, he's about as closed-mouthed as politicians come. And I believe he's a good man. He even called a few days ago to make sure I had my best team stationed close by, ready to protect your people. That's why I put Char in charge."

Walter smiled and added, with pride, "Bob Crawford is a good man and a dear friend."

Bryan paused and then continued. "My old boss has been doing some snooping around in the higher echelons of the Bureau, trying to discover where I've been re-assigned and why. He's mega-political and a control freak, but I don't see the espionage connection. It just doesn't fit him. He's a patriot, albeit *very* political."

After another pause, Holland said, "That leaves the Assistant U.S. Attorney General." Holland stopped.

Shane added, "And the Beckett Cypher identified him as a Committee member. But how is he connected to North Korea? How could North Korea be in The Committee?"

Walter added, "Maybe they aren't *in* The Committee. And maybe our Assistant U.S. Attorney General is involved with *more* groups than just The Committee. After all, he's a politician, and who knows where his loyalties reside now! He's been critical of Vice President Crawford for years, and even more critical of the current investigation into the President's sordid arrangements with Russia, and his *questionable* activities with China."

Shane said, "Good point. Dad told me that a politician's loyalties are moving targets that change with the winds of influence and opportunity. And the winds comes from any number of unusual directions. I think he was right!"

Pete asked, "When did he tell you that, Shane?"

"Last night," Shane said solemnly, "we had a conversation."

Pete smiled.

Kate asked, "So, where does that leave us with this threat? Someone tortured Bryan's team member for information. At this point, all we know is the dead agent had Tasha's phone number. And if it was the Assistant U.S. Attorney General behind it, why did he do it and who is he working with, or for?"

Bryan added, "There are even more questions. How did someone know this agent in my team would have information? What information were they trying to find? If the North Koreans already had the cell number, who else was searching for it?" Bryan sat back at his desk and pondered the answers to his own questions.

Shane said, "Logically, if the wrong people knew that *you* possessed the cypher team's identity and location, why didn't they take you? The dead agent is our clue. Who did he speak with during the last two days? What did he tell someone that led to his own murder."

Bryan said excitedly, "Right you are. I'll look into that. In the meantime, you all should think about moving until we get this buttoned up. I have another call." Bryan hung up. There was silence in the room as minds raced.

Finally, Pete asked, "What are you thinking, Shane?"

Shane raised his eyes to meet Pete's and said, "Among other things, Heath is coming back with Tasha, Angie, and Char. It should be an interesting ride for my brother with those three women in the car. I wish I could hear the conversation."

Kate looked sideways at Shane and said, "I'm just glad they're all safe."

Shane answered, "I am too, honey. But all the same, Char being in the mix with the way she feels about Heath, still concerns me."

As the group stood to leave, the phone rang again. Walter answered the speakerphone. Bryan Holland said, "I think you should know three more pieces of information that just came in through my agents. Initial reports are that Char took out all three would-be kidnappers, and then intentionally just wounded the fourth, a woman, so that we could interrogate her. Char's team believed the woman was the North Korean team leader based on her hand signals to her team. Oh, and by the way, the report is that Heath bolted from the SUV, knocked the female NK agent to the ground, and cuffed her just after she was shot. He was just a few feet away when Char nailed her before she could..."

"Shoot him," Shane finished.

Bryan Holland continued. "Right. A ballsy move, I might add. Secondly, my tech here today just confirmed that my dead agent made or received seven phone calls from the Assistant U.S. Attorney General over the last 24 hours. Most interesting is that there were no phone contacts between them before that, going back for more than twelve months. The phone calls began with the Assistant USAG calling my agent."

"And lastly, initial IDs on the dead bodies indicate these are freelance agents, who have all done dirty work for the Chinese, North Koreans, Iranians, and Russians in the past. A great deal of info is coming in from my CIA contact now, so I may have more to report soon. We're running the North Korean's phones now, to see who they were communicating with, so we can generate a communications map. Talk later." Bryan Holland hung up after his cell phone rang in the background.

Pete looked hard at Shane, and asked, "Your thoughts, Shane?"

Shane started methodically. "First we need to debrief our people and Char when they arrive back here. Then we need to ask everyone at the ranch if they're willing to continue with this case, considering the risks. Then, for all who are willing, those on the cypher team need to leave under guard and relocate somewhere new. I would recommend somewhere not traceable to any of us or anyone in the government."

Shane stood and began to pace as he spoke. "The rest of us need to figure out how best to proceed to the next phase of our plan, which is to break into The Committee's California Center for Information Extraction. We have the As-Built drawings and other information we obtained from the Carson City Sheriff, taken from the flash drive Carson detectives retrieved from the suspect's girlfriend at the end of their stolen car chase."

Shane continued. "And lastly, we need to figure a way to see what all is now inside Yucca Mountain. We have the As-Builts and records Hector took from Franky's car and gave to Heath, along with the old information The Committee spy *Armistead* has provided through the Beckett Cypher. The Committee's Yucca Mountain stronghold holds the key to their plans, their influence, and their workforce throughout the world."

Shane added, "One final thought. We need to use the cypher to cut down on our use of manpower so we can spend our limited resources wisely and swiftly at changing targets."

One by one, Walter, Tom, Kate, and Pete nodded in agreement.

Tom added, "Until Bryan figures out how this happened on his end, we need to be careful about what we communicate his way. I guess it's no longer surprising when the leak comes *out* of the FBI, but it is sad and disheartening just the same. We may not be able to count on government resources to fight the initial battles…maybe not any of the battles."

Jesse appeared outside the door, knocked, and said from the other side, "Char just called Tracy to report they plan to arrive back here in an hour and a half. She figures you all want to set up a briefing room?"

Tom walked to the door, opened it and said, "Please join us, Jesse." He turned to Walter, Pete, Shane, and Kate, still seated at the table and asked, "Where do you want to do this?"

Walter looked around at the group and said, "How about the hangar. Everyone on our team needs to hear this!" They all stood up in agreement.

✱✱✱

Char stood at the smart board in the large hangar, with Bryan Holland's team of agents flanking her on both sides. She briefed the group of nearly forty people on the events that led to the attempted kidnapping, and her team's interdiction of the enemy force. Her briefing was professionally concise, informative and impressive to all who attended. The accompanying federal agents fielded follow-up questions about their actions only. At the conclusion, those agents left to return to their hotel rooms in La Grande and await further instructions from SAC Bryan Holland.

When they had gone, Char explained that the three agents accompanying her were members of a secret off-the-books unit known to only a few within the Bureau. They had been assigned by Vice President Crawford and the FBI Director to work directly under Bryan Holland, taking directions from him only during this investigation. Char said she trusted the agents completely.

Shane studied Char carefully as she spoke, and then again when she returned to the group and sat next to Tasha and Pete. He read nothing in her actions. Shane watched Heath closely for a reaction. He could detect nothing when their eyes met. Angie sat next to Heath, holding his hand resolutely through the entire briefing. When Angie looked at Char, both women smiled and nodded.

Walter, Pete, and Tom each spoke briefly about the need to move to a new location for all those who wished to remain on this investigation. No one requested to leave the team. When the briefing ended, the cypher team broke off for a meeting about equipment and resource needs. The security detail departed to attend their own conference to prepare proposals for splitting their resources.

In a private conversation between Walter, Angie, and Heath, Angie advised Walter she planned to remain with the family permanently, at least through the end of The Case, if he agreed. Walter was obviously pleased and requested she attend all future family gatherings. Walter immediately asked the family to meet with Tom and Char in the dining room in thirty minutes.

As the group filtered out of the hangar and back toward the main house, Tasha grabbed Kate and Juanita by their hands and requested they remain to speak to her alone. Her look was serious and determined.

Once they were by themselves, Tasha said, "I need to speak to you both before I speak to Pete." The three women sat down and pulled chairs close together around a small table.

Tasha said, "I can't do this any longer. I thought I could be stronger, but I can't. I'm not like the two of you." She placed her head in her hands and began to cry.

Juanita covered one of her hands and said softly, "You've been through a shock, Tasha. It's only natural. It *will* be alright. We're all here for you!" Kate leaned in to provide comfort and placed a hand on Tasha's back.

Tasha shook her head and said, "That's just it. I can't be there for any of you, Pete, or even myself. I'm terrified of things like this happening. And now, what I feared could happen, actually happened right in front of us. We could have been taken as prisoners and ended up in North Korea or some other foreign country, tortured and eventually killed. I can't be a part any of this cloak and dagger work anymore. I have to leave and go back to a normal life, where I'm not afraid that some rogue mercenary or foreign agent is coming for me!" She began to cry harder.

Kate asked, "Why don't you go to bed to rest awhile upstairs and think about this later after we make some plans? You love Pete. And I know how much he loves you. Maybe you and Pete can even leave for a while and forget about all this?"

Tasha smiled at Kate through her tears. She said, "You're both so sweet. You've been such good friends. But Pete can't and won't leave the boys and all of you. And I couldn't ask him to leave. If I did ask, and he did leave, and something happened to any of you, neither of us could ever forgive ourselves."

"No, Pete needs to stay with you. And I can't drag him down and put you all in more danger than you already are. I need to leave. I think I've known it for a long time, and I've just been too stubborn and afraid to admit the truth to myself!"

Gathering strength from her resolve, she stood quickly and began to walk away. Tasha hesitated, turned back and said, "I'm going to say a brief goodbye to Pete and leave as soon as I can get a driver. I can't give him the time to try to talk me out of my decision." She forced a weak smile through tears and began to walk away.

Kate stood up and said, "Wait, Tasha! Let us drive you to the airport!"

Tasha raised a hand to wave goodbye behind her, and said, "Having to say goodbye to both of you again would make it harder for all of us. I'll get someone on the security detail to drive me, so no one can try to change my mind." She left the hangar quickly.

Juanita and Kate sat and held hands. Juanita said, "I respect her decision. I have fears, too. But the family is everything to me. All of you are so important to me and necessary to my happiness. I couldn't be happy if I tried to live without you all in my life. How will she go on without the man she loved for the last twenty years? Doesn't she love him too much to leave him?"

Kate said, "I think for Tasha, it isn't that she loves too little or can be happy without him. I think it's that she knows she can't live happily with him when she fears each day something may happen to him. For her, the worries of life have consumed her ability to be happy. She can't suppress the worry to allow the happiness and hopefulness to rise and fill her life. I feel sorry for her and Pete. But I know Pete, and he can go on to find happiness. I doubt that Tasha can do the same."

Juanita looked down and said, "Tasha and I were sharing so much and growing so close. But she never let on to me these feelings were torturing her soul. I'm so sorry I couldn't help her overcome these tormenting fears."

Kate took both of Juanita's hands and said, "Do you remember what you told me when I used to cry about my mother being gone when I was a little girl?

Juanita smiled and said, "I told you a great many things back then. Which one do you mean?"

Kate looked up as she recalled. "I said I was afraid because my mother was dead and in Heaven. And because I couldn't talk to her, she was never going to be there to help me stop being afraid." Juanita smiled as she tried to remember.

Kate squeezed Juanita's hands as she said, "You said that my grandfather and you would always be there to help me and protect me, while my mother watched from Heaven, where she lived with God. You said that God loved both my mother and me and He would always put people in my life to love and protect me until I could be with my mommy." Juanita smiled as she began to recall.

Kate added, "And then I asked if you would be my mommy until I could see my real mommy again." Juanita blushed and smiled as she recalled the conversation.

36

Kate said, "And then…you asked me what I would do with two mommies. And I answered I would love them *twice as many* as one mommy."

Kate smiled wider than before. "I've never forgotten that conversation. And I did…love you just as much as I could love any mother. And I still do, and always will, love you. That's what family means to me. Especially after you told me you *would* be my mother all those years ago."

Tears formed in Juanita's eyes along with a lump in her throat and a tightness in her chest that made it nearly impossible to breathe. She was silent.

Kate said, "I never thanked you properly for being my mother after my other mother died. I couldn't have had a finer, more loving mother than you. And I thank God for you every day!"

Speaking through tears, Juanita answered, "Nor I a more wonderful child than you!" Both women hugged tightly with tears in their eyes and love in their hearts.

The door suddenly flew open as Walter entered, and asked, "What's going on? Tasha walked by me ten minutes ago crying, waved me off and is now sitting in one of the SUVs with Pete asking her not to leave. Now you're both in here hugging and crying. Why am I always the last one to know anything important about family around here?"

Kate motioned for her grandfather to join them, and then kissed Juanita on the cheek. The ladies smiled at each other and then at Walter as he sat beside them and waited for an answer.

Kate was the first to speak. "Tasha is telling Pete her goodbyes. She can't stay with him."

Walter looked incredulous. He said, "That's absurd. She loves him, and he loves her. They can't be apart!"

Juanita countered, "She said she loves him so much they can't be together!"

"But that doesn't make sense! How can you love and not want to be together if you love so much?' Walter looked bewildered.

"Sweetheart, she's afraid of losing him, or something bad happening to him!" Juanita reached for Walter and took his hand in hers. "I think I can understand that now. Can't you?"

Walter began thoughtfully. "I guess I can understand it a little. But I also know that I would be more worried if I left, not knowing what was happening. And if something did happen, I could never live with myself, having left!"

Juanita smiled and squeezed Walter's hand. "Sweetheart, we're all built a little differently. Tasha isn't strong in the way you are, or I am. She has fears that control her and are too difficult for *her* to overcome. For Tasha, I believe she can worry less if she doesn't see the truth. She can no longer deal with the briefings, and confront the possibilities of death or injury on a daily basis."

Walter shook his head, having difficulty understanding.

Juanita continued, trying to explain something Walter didn't want to believe. "But she isn't alone. Many people don't want to hear about the real evils in the world anymore. They entertain themselves with stories of vampires and werewolves because these threats aren't real. It's just entertainment for them. The real threats like gangs, drugs, and terrorism are real, and the *reality* scares them to death. So some people don't want to know about it or think about the truth. We have to respect that in Tasha. Lord knows the threat we're dealing with is among the worst in the world I know about!"

Walter sighed. "I know you're right. But this is going to kill Pete! He loves her, and needs her."

Sounds of the SUV leaving as it drove by the hangar brought the conversation to a sudden close. Walter jumped up, saying, "I must go check on Pete! We should all go!"

They all walked out together. Walter, Kate, and Juanita searched the ranch house until they found Pete in the library, standing alone as he gazed out the window, sipping a full glass of scotch.

Walter asked, "Do you mind if we join you, my boy?"

Pete turned and smiled, as he said, "Family is always welcome! I wouldn't have it any other way!"

Kate asked, "Are you okay, then?"

Walter and Juanita walked to the bar to fill three more glasses.

"Better than I expected, and to be honest, quite relieved!" Pete turned to meet all three inquiring faces with a smile.

"Not the response I expected, Pete, but if you're serious, then *I'm* greatly relieved." Walter walked to Pete and placed a hand on his shoulder. "Are you truly okay?"

"I am," Pete said, as he motioned for them to take seats. "You never know what goes on in the quiet alone times, when a couple is by themselves in the bedroom, or off on a walk. For me, it was…" Pete paused, and then added, "wearing!" He looked up at looks of shock and disbelief.

He continued. "Don't get me wrong. I do love Tasha. But she worries about everything so much that she can't enjoy anything. Going for a walk in the woods, she worries about the unseen bear behind the brush. On a bike ride in the city, she worries about cars jumping a curb and crashing into us. On a boat, she worries about something happening causing everyone to drown. It never stops because she can't turn it off."

"I blame myself for the failed relationship. I knew obsessive worry was Tasha's tendency when we got together. I was tired of being alone, and I've always been attracted to her. In truth, I think I had fallen in love with her years ago. But I soon realized I was in love with the person I thought she could become, and not with who she was! That was a colossal mistake, and dragging her into this dangerous investigation was an even greater mistake."

Pete added, "It's better to break it off now, and hope we both find someone to be happy with and enjoy. Life is too short to live in a self-imposed, tortured existence! I don't want to spend the rest of my life worrying about what she is worrying about and trying unsuccessfully to find a way to help her stop so she can be happy. Because she can't stop. And I understand now, that she can't allow herself to be happy. I need and want so much more in a relationship!"

Walter said, "I am truly sorry, my boy, but maybe when this is all over, and things are calmed down, it will be different."

Pete smiled. "I love you all. But my time with Tasha and her time with me is over. We don't fit together in some of the most important ways. I am always holding a glass half full, thirsting to sip the essence from every last drop of elixir, while she is always holding a glass half empty, worrying about dying of thirst. I thought I could transfer enough of my strength to her to allow her to overcome her nature and change to what I wanted."

"But, you can't change the spots on a leopard. And even if you could, you'd still have a leopard. Tasha is a worrier afraid to embrace the passion of life, drowning in misery and worry *she* creates. I'm a lover of life searching for more passion, refusing to leave space for misery and worry. As much as Tasha and I can love one another, we make each other miserable. And that is how we left it. And *that* is how it needs to end!"

Pete smiled and released a great sigh of relief. He raised his scotch into the air and said, "I propose a toast to our wonderful friend, Tasha, a beautiful lady who came into our lives and shared our love and joy. May she find happiness and peace!"

Kate, Juanita, and Walter raised their glasses, and said, "To Tasha," in unison. Each took a sip of scotch. Juanita looked sad and disappointed, even as she sipped her drink.

Walter added, "To Pete, my son, may you find joy, true love, and lasting companionship!"

Kate and Juanita lifted their drinks into the air and repeated, "To Pete!" They all sipped their scotch again, as Pete joined them.

✸✸✸

Vice President Bob Crawford sat in an overstuffed wicker swivel chair on the expansive, stained wooden deck overlooking a large pond at his heavily wooded Virginia estate. He sipped a large glass of cold sweet tea as he held hands with his longtime love, British Home Secretary Barbara Walcott, who sat in a matching chair next to him. Barbara smiled at Crawford and took a sip of her tea.

She pulled the cold glass away from her lips, looked at the condensation dripping from the outside, and said, "It's still difficult to get used to tea served cold in the States. Ours is just as sweet at home, with two lumps of sugar. But, it's always served piping hot, ready to perk you up, and push you off to a running start!"

"Ours is made this way to sip and enjoy while slowing down to *relax* and enjoy life!" Crawford quipped back with a smile.

"You know, I *am* getting used to the *enjoying* part," Walcott confessed with a grin, as she shot a coy smile at Crawford. When her smile faded away, she added, "The conflicts created by Brexit, Islamic terrorism, Russian assassinations, an out-of-control press, and a country overrun with displaced foreigners took its toll on me these past few years. Not to mention the constant political wrangling and scheming to seize power."

"Wrangling and scheming to seize power by you and yours, or from the others?" Crawford chided with a smirk.

Walcott chuckled. "Stop it, Bob! You know exactly what I mean."

Barbara squeezed his hand and clarified, "I'm tired of the bullshit bombs constantly thrown by everyone with an ax to grind. It's become a constant onslaught from enemies of the state, foreigners trying to change our culture, politicians lying to the voters to get elected, a press corps committed to sensationalism rather than truth, and the shadow government maneuvering to resist the government, *after* officials were lawfully elected and placed in power to lead the country."

As she reminisced, Barbara Walcott began to feel the fire that continually re-fueled her passion for politics. But she was also growing to detest her career choice.

She added, "You can never relax and concentrate on finding solutions to problems confronting the kingdom! You're always defending yourself against imaginary demons, lies, and trumped-up charges of wrong-doing. And if things start to settle down, and you begin to focus on the reasons you were elected, some radical blows up a group of tourists and all the crap turns over again as a fresh cycle of the same old thing begins anew."

Walcott closed her eyes tightly, drew in a long breath of fresh mountain air and released an equally long sigh. She confessed, "I'm exhausted, Bob. And I'm even more tired of the bullshit!"

Bob Crawford squeezed Barbara Walcott's hand a little tighter, and laughed, saying, "I would normally think you were referring to the problems we have in the United States, and not England, if I didn't know better!" They both smiled, as Barbara opened her eyes and nodded.

Walcott looked over the manicured grounds and pond to the line of trees and hills in the distance. She added thoughtfully, "It all wears you down, darling. Not to mention this Committee business; trying to help hold the Middle East together; and now, keeping the Chinese, Russians and North Koreans away from our cypher!"

"Not quite *our* cypher yet!" Crawford commented with raised eyebrows. "Without the cypher team that possesses and understands what the cypher has become, we might be years away from using it. We need those people more than ever, and we need them intact!"

"Still…" Walcott trailed off as her gaze affixed on several merging families of ducks floating in the picturesque pond.

She shook her head to focus on the conversation, and continued. "Still, with or without the *people*, the *cypher* must be ours. The good guys must control the technology that controls the masses. Not the bad guys, ever."

Crawford looked pensively at Walcott, and nodded in agreement. He stroked her hand just as his cell phone rang. He placed

43

his tea on the table to his right and picked the phone up with his free hand. Still caressing Barbara's hand, he answered the phone calmly, "Crawford."

SAC Bryan Holland said, "Sir, this is Bryan Holland. We have had an incident. I need to brief you on the phone quickly. Can you speak freely?"

"I can, Bryan. My communication is safe. I'm on my secure scrambled line, alone, outside."

Holland briefed Crawford on the incident involving Heath, Tasha, and Angie. He then outlined the details on his dead FBI agent.

When Holland finished, Vice President Crawford said, "I am so sorry to hear about your agent, Bryan, but relieved to understand we have a bad guy to debrief, and everyone else is safe! Will the inquiry be conducted by our inter-agency friends as our partners requested?"

"Yes, sir. The enemy combatant is on the way to the pre-arranged meeting location now. She should arrive in less than two hours. I'll let you know as soon as I hear anything."

"Excellent, Bryan. Thank you so much!" Crawford hung up. He smiled at Barbara Walcott.

"Sounds like our plan worked perfectly. Does anyone suspect anything?" Walcott asked.

Crawford took another sip of tea and answered, "Not yet, or Bryan would have asked the delicate question. But I don't like that it seemed so obvious when we placed a heavily armed team near the cypher just in time to get set up and intercept an enemy force we knew was coming. I don't like that we had to use my friend's family and the cypher team as bait to lure the enemy team out of hiding. I don't like that we had to be less than transparent with my FBI team. I especially

44

don't like that our plan resulted in the torture and death of an FBI agent."

Crawford looked out thoughtfully over the neatly trimmed lawns, lavish gardens and colorful flower beds that led to the pond, now shimmering in the morning sunlight. He beheld the beautiful grounds he never tired of studying, as his mind raced through several political scenarios that may come to pass.

He finally agreed with Walcott's prior calculation, saying, "But you and your secret MI6 agent were correct in your assessment, and we finally have the head of the enemy team in custody. So now we learn and bargain…and buy more time. So, in the end, it *was* worth it. We *must* have more time. But, now we live with another death on our hands. And the dead man is one of *our* agents! I am truly so sorry for his family. I'll need to compose a commendation letter and meet with his family soon."

Crawford looked down at his lap, overcome with the emotion of his burden, as he suddenly looked ten years older. Walcott leaned over and kissed Crawford on the cheek. She paused to hold and stroke his hand in both of hers.

She said softly, "Honey, you are vastly more sentimental than I am, and I love you all the more for that quality! But, the truth is, one dead FBI agent is an acceptable sacrifice for us to make if it means we acquire one of North Korea's most highly trained assassins and team leaders. Think of it! She is in *our* custody! We've been trying to capture her for more than a decade! The intelligence reports from her debriefings will be more entertaining than the best mystery novels! And they'll serve a phenomenally loftier purpose than mere entertainment."

Walcott became excited as she spoke. She added, "That one 'NiK' agent may be the key to us discovering the North Korean and Chinese plans in so many critical areas. We don't have a clue about the number of teams they have sent to your beloved country to steal the cypher. We don't know the location of the dirty nuclear devices our intel confirmed were smuggled in and placed in Europe *and* The United States. She may know about the planned cyber attacks on western nations' financial systems or the truth about the Chinese development of a drone-delivered electromagnetic pulse generator, And, sweetheart, that's just the start!"

Walcott breathed a sigh of relief, followed by a wide grin. She mused aloud, "She may be the key to all of it!"

Crawford frowned. "But an important question remains, my dear. What do I tell my good friend and schoolmate, Walter O'Leary? If his team ever discovers *we* unscrambled Tasha Mcknight's cell phone so it could be tracked, and then fed the probable location and cell number to the Russians to give to the Chinese to provide to the North Korean team, he'll know I gambled with his loved ones to locate and capture an enemy."

Barbara quickly countered, "And he'll realize you did it to help buy *his* people more time, my dearest. The FBI *will* discover the phone records of the Assistant U.S. Attorney General calling Holland's dead agent over the last few days…if they haven't already. And besides, our technicians are highly capable, my darling. No one should be able to discover or prove anything."

Walcott looked up with an after-thought, and added, "And, in the event something is discovered, you are a very polished and skillful politician. And you and I follow the rules of political speak. We don't answer direct questions directly; we deflect subjects to the agenda we desire to speak about; we never tell the whole truth unless it fits in our sound bite, and we never let the bastards see us sweat. If anyone challenges us, we discount them as lunatics or act outraged. And then, we challenge back with some outlandish exaggeration! *We* will be just fine!"

Crawford cringed. He mused, "Having journeyed through this modern political life for decades, I can safely say that none of us ever come out the other end of our political life, 'just fine.' We're all tarnished. In fact, most of us become tarnished beyond recognition."

Walcott scoffed. "As are most people, regardless of occupation, sweetheart! No one is a saint. Not even dear Mother Theresa. She conveyed her frustrations and sinning nature openly to the world! And besides, my dear, *we* aren't like the North Koreans or Chinese. The difference is we have a respectable and honorable agenda, my love!"

Crawford frowned. He said quietly, "I know we try to do what we determine is best at the time. And I know we think our motivations are in the highest interests of humanity. I wonder though, how many other politicians before us thought they had humanity's best interests at heart, but were later judged by society to be abusers of their people, or even worse…monsters?"

Crawford looked intently at Barbara Walcott. He lifted her hand to his lips and kissed it gently. He said pleadingly, "Let's agree to be careful, so we don't end up on the wrong side of history, sweetheart."

Barbara Walcott nodded gravely, as the excitement faded from her face. She looked back toward the grounds and pond. The two lovers sat in silence, holding hands, as they gazed out over the gorgeous scenery, while the late morning sun danced on the water around a mated pair of wood ducks. The fates of both politicians and their world swirled through their minds, as they sipped their cold sweet teas.

Chapter 2

"A secret is no longer a secret once more than one person knows about it."

Heath walked toward an old wooden bench positioned to take advantage of a spectacular mountain view, placed beneath a substantial old-growth pine, not more than 100 yards from the ranch house. Char had just arrived at the bench and sat to observe him. As he approached, Heath glanced repeatedly at Char, seated there anxiously waiting. She smirked at him coyly, as she studied his advance. Heath knew this conversation would be awkward at best. Unsure of what he would say, he slowed his pace to buy more time.

But as the distance between them steadily diminished, Heath felt his insides begin to churn. He reluctantly acknowledged he did have feelings for Char. But those feelings, he asserted to himself, were vastly different from the *love* he had developed for Angie...a love that had begun the first day he met his beautiful Angie and her canine pack.

Still, Char *had* saved Heath's life by placing a bullet neatly into the North Korean team leader's forearm, just as she raised her pistol and took aim at his chest. The shot's impact had knocked his attacker off her feet and sent the handgun flying from her hand. Heath had been less than three feet from the North Korean assassin when Char's saving round found its target...and spared his life.

Now, in the space of a minute, the incident replayed as clearly in Heath's mind as if he were watching a social media video post in high-definition. He now realized that after the shot, within the tiny space of one more heartbeat, he had crashed into the NK agent, rolled her over on the ground and handcuffed her. After he fought the woman and lifted her to her feet, she spit in his eyes to distract him, and then quickly head-butted him.

The killer's momentum sent Heath recoiling backward, allowing his assailant to bite his neck. She attacked him savagely. The painful bite ripped flesh and drew blood as Heath pulled away. He was so enraged he pulled his fist back to pummel the attacker, but stopped at the last second, as he quickly recovered. He could feel Angie's eyes watching him closely and suddenly felt shame at his anger and loss of self-control.

While his neck throbbed and bled, Heath placed the enemy combatant into a wristlock, twisting her arm as hard as he could. She screamed in pain and immediately submitted. Heath released some pressure and led the assassin back toward the bulldozer, road barricades, SUVs, and pick-ups, all still parked askew, completely blocking the highway.

In the scene now replaying in his mind, Heath noticed four FBI agents running from various positions to help him, while three others checked the bodies, all dead North Koreans or assassinated highway workers. Heath also saw FBI agents in vans placed 1/3 mile down the road in either direction, turning traffic around on both sides of the roadblock. He was stunned he hadn't noticed anything until the chaos erupted directly in front of his vehicle.

As he approached the first FBI vehicle now, Heath recalled meeting Angie's eyes. She smiled at him reassuringly as she nodded. Angie stood outside the front passenger door of their SUV. She had never moved to the driver's side to drive away and escape as Heath had instructed. Angie's smile relieved Heath of some of his shame and embarrassment. He then noticed movement, and saw Tasha, crying in the rear seat, as she shook her head in disbelief.

And then, for the first time during the attack, Heath saw Char in the distance, as she moved toward the vehicles from her position above and beyond Angie. Char jogged swiftly down an embankment above the highway, still scanning left and right for more threats. She continued methodically and deftly down the hill, through the timber, carrying her sniper rifle at the ready, pointing it toward possible hostile locations, as she worked her way toward the car stop.

Heath looked down at his captive's black jacket and noticed the oozing blood soaking through the rain-resistant material. He observed the neat bullet hole in the fabric. Trickling blood made its way down the killer's arm to her hands. He sensed the sticky wet blood as it met his skin, and quickly confirmed the telltale sweet metallic scent in his nostrils.

Heath felt the assassin's arm carefully as they arrived at the first FBI sedan. He detected broken bones where the bullet had shattered them on its way through the flesh. When he moved the enemy agent's broken arm, the woman screamed again, in agony.

Heath realized now, that with his adrenaline pumping, and his focus narrowed to charge the hostile agent in an attempt to save the women in his SUV, he had never heard the rifle shot. He had never seen the FBI vehicles. Heath had not recognized the clues to the roadblock that could have warned him of the pending ambush.

He admitted to himself now that he had not been focused or prepared. The enemy trap was nearly successful due to his failure. If he had been cognizant of his surroundings, he could have evaded the roadblock.

Heath arrived at the old wooden bench beneath the majestic pine, just as Char's cell phone rang. The incident replay flashed out of his mind. Char deftly removed the phone from her jacket pocket and hit decline, without looking at the display. Heath sat down beside Char in dead silence. Her eyes never left Heath's, and he had to look away to begin to thank the woman who loved him for saving his life. Heath felt oddly embarrassed that he was with Angie when Char's team rescued him. He had been a failure in front of both women who loved him.

Heath mustered his courage, looked directly into Char's emotionless gaze, and said, "I can't thank you enough for saving me back there. It was very close."

"It was very foolish!" Char crossed her arms over her chest and recoiled from Heath as she said the words. "What were you thinking? Where was your gun? Did you actually think you could outmaneuver a bullet? Or, did you bother to think at all? You could have avoided their trap and all that chaos!"

Her expression was more severe than he had ever seen. But it was Char's words that cut Heath deeply as he began to understand all the implications.

He said, weakly, "I thought I could get them off of our SUV so Angie could drive away. I thought I could be the target, the distraction that allowed the escape! I…" Heath recognized the foolishness of the ill-conceived attempt, and stopped as Char stared at him in disappointment.

"Let me ask you a question, *my love*," Char said mockingly. "If that had been me in the car with you, instead of Angie and Tasha, would you have acted the same way?" Char cocked her head and studied Heath's response.

He answered immediately, even though he recognized the bait she had placed. "Of course not. You and I would have shot it out with them!" Heath smiled. "You would have taken three to my one, maybe, but we could have won the battle!" He added a misplaced grin.

"Exactly my point," Char chided.

She shook her head in anger, and rattled off quickly, "You didn't even think about reacting appropriately with the others because they can't take care of you the way I can. Those women are of no use in a firefight. And you had to know that eventually you and your family would be pursued at some point in this crazy case, by the cartels, The Committee, foreign governments or *your* government. So, if you know you're a target, why weren't you prepared and why didn't you have a plan? Where was your security detail? Where is the man I fell in love with, rather than killing, as I was originally instructed?" Char leaned back and unfolded her arms from her chest. Her eyes flared, and her cheeks burned red with anger.

Heath looked down in defeat. He had known from the start the trip was unwise, especially without a security team in tow, and a workable plan in place. He also knew he had made a dangerous error, taking a chance that everything would be alright, rather than counting on a probable attack.

But both he and Pete had wanted to get Angie and Tasha away from the constant intrigue and stress long enough to allow them to catch a collective breath. Heath knew he had taken a chance to let them *feel* normal. That chance had almost cost them their lives. Heath now recognized that as part of the team investigating The Case, Tasha and

Angie were no longer *normal*. They were always in danger. To assume anything else was idiotic.

Heath raised his eyes to meet Char's large accusing, yet alluring, eyes. "You're right, of course. I have no excuse," he offered, feebly.

Char took a deep breath, released a long sigh, and took Heath by the hand. Her voice softened, as she said, "Look, Heath, I love you with all my heart. And I know you are *with* Angie. I even know you think you love her. I can tell by the way you look at her and hold her hand. And, as hard as it is for me…"

Char struggled to control her emotions. She looked down briefly and then resolved to continue, as her eyes again met Heath's expectant gaze. Char said firmly, "Still, I need you *both* to be safe. You see, Heath, if you and Angie work out, then I lose your love. If you and she don't work out, then I have a chance at love, with you! But, if you and she die, I have no chance at love, and I'll never know if we could have ended up together."

Char's eyes glistened. Heath softened. She immediately avoided his eyes. "So, for now, I'll try my best to keep you both alive. But, damn it, you need to try, too!" Char released Heath's hand and stood up abruptly.

Before she could leave, Heath rose and gently spun Char around to face him. He hugged her firmly, and said, "Thank you for being there. I won't make that mistake again."

Char looked away. Heath reached for her chin and gently moved her head to meet his eyes. He said softly, "And if anything happens to Angie and me…if we don't work out…"

Before he could finish, Char covered his lips with two fingers. She said sweetly, "Don't talk about the what-ifs until they're a possibility. If that happens, there'll be plenty of time then for talk and hope. For now, always remember, your life is just a struggle to survive! Nothing more."

Heath nodded. Char leaned in and kissed him seductively on the cheek, allowing her lips to linger, as she breathed in Heath's scent, and left him with hers.

She stepped back, smiled coyly, and said, "Remember my lips and that kiss, my love. But for now, it's back to work for both of us." She turned to walk away, took a few steps, stopped and turned back to look at Heath again.

Char added, "And remember to take care of Angie. I don't want my chance to come to me the wrong way, the easy way, with no competition!" She smiled half-heartedly and turned to leave. Char walked seductively, appearing confident and elegant. Even so, Heath detected a strange sadness in her form. She disappeared around the deck.

Heath returned to the bench and sat on the warm wood. He gawked absentmindedly over the countryside, studying the valley below and the dry hills to the east. As a dust devil swirled upward from the furthest dry hill, Heath heard running footsteps steps behind him. When he turned quickly to his left, Jago vaulted into view, soon followed by Masai, struggling to keep up. Heath reached down and petted both dogs as he detected voices in the distance. Jago cocked his head to check Heath and then sniffed him, detecting Char's scent.

Angie called out, "He's checking to see how much scent she left on you when she hugged you!"

Heath looked up to see Shane, Angie, and Kate coming into view as they hiked down the trail that led to the small creek and waterfall higher up on the hill to the west. He saw Angie was smiling. Shane looked serious. Kate offered no readable tell.

Heath yelled back, "She didn't hug me. I hugged her, to thank her for saving my life, and yours. She kissed me goodbye, on the cheek, too," he teased.

When no response came, he thought better of his teasing remark, and quickly added, "She told me she wants us all to be safe, especially you and I, Angie!"

"That's because she doesn't want to have another chance at you just because something unfortunate happens to Angie," Kate added. "She could never revel in the conquest that way!"

"Ouch! That's not helping, Kate," Heath countered.

"She's just telling it like it is!" Shane added, somewhat sarcastically. "I'm not a fan of having Char mixed up in this. I've never thought it was a good plan, and I don't mind saying it."

Shane looked even more serious as he spoke. He said, "Having someone in love with you, stalking you from afar, while they're holding a sniper rifle and watching you love their competition was never a good idea in my book!"

Jago cocked his head and looked at Heath questioningly, as Masai jumped up and down bouncing off Heath's leg, struggling for attention. Jago's expression seemed to reinforce the comments from his people.

Heath lifted his hands upward in submission as he looked at Jago. "Not you, too! Are we mano a mano now? I thought we were buds!"

Angie laughed as she reached Heath and threw her arms around him. "Well, just so you know it, I, for one, am glad to see you. And I'm happy Char killed the kidnappers or assassins, or whatever they were! But, Shane makes a good point. I'm keeping you for myself. And Char *is* in love with you, has lots of guns, is very skilled with her weapons, and lurks in the bushes wherever we go. It could give a girl a complex, you know. Or even be hazardous to my health!" Angie smiled at Heath, satisfied that she had conveyed her teasing message appropriately.

Angie then pressed her luscious lips against Heath's mouth and kissed him deeply, repeatedly, lingering with her tongue. She pushed her firm voluptuous body into Heath, and whispered, "And just so you know for sure, I'm not afraid of Char *or* the North Koreans. Dad raised me to be a lot tougher than that! Thank you for trying to save us, but I couldn't drive away and leave you there…so please, don't ever do that again!"

She kissed Heath again, on both the lips and the cheek, taking her time to replace Char's scent with her own. And as she did, Jago leaned in and pressed against Heath's outside leg.

Masai immediately ran back to Shane, and then continued to run in tight circles around his legs. Shane grabbed at Masai, missing twice. He finally managed to capture his puppy and lift him up to cuddle and kiss. When he lifted him to his face, Masai quickly lavished Shane with wet kisses. Shane laughed and then sputtered when Masai's puppy tongue parted Shane's lips, drawing a laugh from Kate.

"My territory, Masai!" she laughed.

Kate and Shane walked to Angie and Heath. Shane said, "In all seriousness, I don't feel one hundred percent comfortable with Char involved in our protection, but she *has* saved your life. So, I'm okay for now, leaving our arrangement the way it stands. But let's not give her a *next time* to prove her loyalty again! I don't think we should always depend on Char to do the right thing. I'd like to reserve that requirement for our immediate family!"

"Amen!" Heath quickly added, "No more trying to be normal until this is over!"

The couples each walked hand-in-hand toward their scheduled family meeting, with Shane carrying his frisky puppy, while Jago walked obediently next to Heath, checking the bushes along the way for threats.

Char watched from where she stood in the library above, as the small group approached the ranch house. She remained inside the room and far enough back from the large window that no one on the ground below noticed her studying the group from the second story library. When they walked out of sight, Char moved to the wet bar and poured a glass of her favorite Kentucky bourbon whiskey. She took a healthy mouthful, swirled the liquid in her mouth, swallowed slowly and enjoyed the burn moving slowly down her throat. She looked at the label on the bottle and said aloud, "Someday, I'm going to Loretto, Kentucky and tour your birthplace, my friend! You and I will become even closer then!"

✳✳✳

Joshua Walker, Hunter Murray, Helena Thomas, and Tracy from the cypher team joined Walter, Juanita, Kate, Shane, Pete, Heath, Angie, Char, and Tom in the dining room. They sat at the large walnut table, built to seat up to twenty people. Without Tasha seated next to Pete in her usual place, the table seemed oddly off balance, and, ridiculously, too large for the current group. Char and Shane both seemed to notice the anomaly at the same time.

Walter dialed FBI Special Agent in Charge Bryan Holland at his D.C. office. Once Bryan was on the phone, and a secure private connection was confirmed, the group began discussing the logistics of separating the main body of investigators from the cypher team.

The team struggled to choose a site to place the cypher group, considering ease of access using multiple routes, safety, privacy, security, and fast and reliable Internet service. The ensuing discussion quickly excluded all proposed locations with a link to anyone on the investigative team, including family or close friends. The group agreed that no government property should be considered. After an hour, no viable place suggested satisfied all requirements.

Char finally spoke and said, "I know of one possibility. There is a house in North Carolina, located on a property the U.S. government seized from a Colombian cartel lieutenant many years ago. The drug cartel used the property to store cocaine for distribution throughout the Eastern United States. The house has seven bedrooms, five baths, a huge office with two desks, a large formal dining room and an equally massive great room. It sits on a large private tract of land, some sixty-five acres, if I recall correctly."

"There are outbuildings, a five-bay attached garage, a shop with a hydraulic lift, a small airstrip about 1/3 mile long and a large barn used to store boats and ATVs. And, there's a hangar for the helicopter the cartel owned. The current owner's Airbus corporate five-passenger helicopter is in the hangar and goes with the property. The ship is up-to-date on inspections and maintenance and has about 600 hours total time."

Walter and Pete looked at each other and then nodded, encouraging Char to continue. Char stood, and began to pace as she spoke. "The government held the property vacant for about four years until the courts authorized the sale. A millionaire from Asheville bought it for a fraction of its value at that time. He was a custom home builder who had made his fortune in residential and commercial construction. He had the foresight to get out of the business before the recession of 2007-2009. The builder spared no expense when he updated the property. He remodeled it into the turnkey retirement home his wife always wanted."

There was silence in the room as interest in the property peaked. Masai yawned widely and rested his head in Shane's lap as he drifted back to sleep. Jago sat obediently between Heath and Angie, his massive head resting on Heath's knee. Heath stroked his loyal friend's ears as Char continued to pace.

She said, "A week after the last remodel was complete, the owner was preparing to fly his wife in to see his final surprise, an outside brick pizza oven he had just finished. That morning she died of a heart attack at a friend's birthday party. He never moved in, and no one has lived there since the feds seized it in 2003. It's in perfect condition, isolated, yet close to maintained access and towns. *And* both the land and house offer multiple escape routes."

Shane asked, "How do you know so much about the property, Char?"

Char looked from Pete to Heath, and then back to Shane. She said, "Sometime ago I decided to prepare an exit plan from my work. I wanted to try living a quiet life. And I decided to start somewhere no one knew me, where I could pursue a happy, simple existence, and…maybe even have a real relationship." Char struggled to avoid glancing at Heath.

She said abruptly, "I started looking for property in Kentucky and Tennessee. A friend of a friend had seen this property with her aunt when the owner first decided he would sell. He never listed the home. I think he wanted to sell it himself to avoid crowds of people walking through his wife's dream home. And he was moving slowly, not overly anxious to part with his life's work and his ultimate masterpiece."

"So, I called him, arranged for a showing and fell in love with the property at first sight. After a great deal of thought, I decided I was interested, called him after the showing, and told him I planned to come out again and see it one more time before I made an offer. He liked me and said he wouldn't advertise it anymore. It's available. I spoke to him recently."

Char walked to a different seat to balance the room. She looked at Shane to see if he noticed, and realized he was studying her intently.

Shane whispered to Kate, "Finally a tell. She has a preoccupation with symmetry. She's been staring at that seat off and on for an hour, and it was driving her crazy! She's slightly OCD!"

"You're correct, honey!" Kate whispered back, barely moving her lips.

"You knew? How?" Shane asked.

Bryan Holland began to speak.

"I'll tell you later. I have a few questions. And we need to think about air access. Maybe we should use a different airplane for this property or find someone who can fly a helicopter."

Shane answered, "Right. Maybe we should locate a small six-passenger single-engine plane registered to someone else, and bury the purchase or lease in a holding company."

Shane looked at Kate briefly, and then focused on Bryan Holland's questions, when she nodded her agreement.

Bryan ended with a quick barrage. "How far off a major access road is the location? Considering your knowledge of the location, how would you prepare an assault? What's the downside? Are you positive it's still available? How do you propose we purchase it?"

Char sat in the seat to balance the room, glancing at Shane as she did. She answered, "First, regarding availability, I called the owner a few weeks ago when I was sure I wanted to go through with my planned career change. I called him again three days ago, and I have the property if I want it. We've even agreed on a cash price. He's just waiting for my call to meet for the final walk-through inspection and sign a contract for purchase."

"But to answer your first question, now that we know the location is a possibility, access is off a two-lane highway, about six miles from a four-lane North Carolina State Route. There's a full mile of roadway to the gate-guarded restricted-access driveway, which continues about 1/3 of a mile to the house. All outbuildings are positioned behind or to the side of the house, away from the runway and hangars. There is a 4-strand barb wire fence surrounding the property."

Char stood again and began to pace back and forth on her side of the table. She said, "The grounds feature manicured pastures and stands of trees placed strategically around the house to maximize the view from three sides. All sides of the property, the interior of the house, and all outbuildings are monitored 24/7 by a sophisticated system of 36 hard-wired security cameras that report to three 12-port DVRs. An additional array of night-vision cameras report to a fourth DVR, covering all approaches to the house. The owner placed motion sensors at all outside camera locations."

She looked up and met Kate's grin. She added, "The cartel installed the original security equipment, which the owner modified and updated." She smiled at Kate.

Char had taken six steps to the far side of the table, turned and paced six steps back before she turned again.

"Definitely OCD," Shane whispered to Kate.

Kate smiled as she nudged Shane under the table and whispered back, "Shush!" The nudge barely roused Masai, who raised his wobbly head, yawned, and again fell asleep on Shane's knee. He began to snore.

"An assault would be tricky, but most likely successful, if a team accessed the grounds close to the house via a high altitude low open, or HALO, parachute jump. A longer ground approach and alarm activation would be unwise. The assault team would gain access and suppress interior security using flash-bang stun grenades, smoke, and tear-gas. A capture team would use a combination of rubber bullets and police-style stun guns. A kill team would back up the capture team with standard weapons to minimize losses from any armed resistance."

Char turned at the end of her six-step slow march again. She said, thoughtfully, "I see no downside, compared to any other property I know of, absent the availability of a hard target…maybe a heavily armed secret bunker. And a location such as that, if available, would be much more complicated considering access and escape. Bunkers are, in fact, underground prisons."

"Considering property acquisition, I propose I rent the location with the option to purchase. I know a discreet attorney in Charlotte I've used before who can prepare the contract. I'll give the owner half the purchase price down, with rent of $10,000 per month for each month I fail to complete the purchase coming out of the down, for a maximum rental of one year. If I default on either a full year of rent or the purchase, he can keep the money. Whether I complete the purchase or not, he'll be happy because someone he likes, who loves the property, is enjoying it. *And*, he'll be paid very well for its use if the lease doesn't result in a sale."

Char ended her march at step six, sat in her chair and leaned back, crossing her legs. "To your unasked questions about links to any of us or the government, I propose that the property remains in the owner's name. The seller and I will agree that my attorney can hold the unrecorded lease option contract in a secure, locked envelope in his office safe. Only the owner and I will have copies of the agreement, and the owner will default if he records the contract, resulting in forfeiture of the property. Also, the attorney and the owner only know me by one of my untraceable aliases...courtesy of Uncle Sam!" Char flashed a coy grin at Pete.

She added, "And if anyone is wondering, the friend of the friend who looked at it before I did, has no idea I was even interested in the property. Her aunt ended up in a condo in Sarasota, Florida. No connections back to any of us. So, unless I've missed something, I think this property would work out perfectly!"

Walter leaned over to whisper to Pete.

Kate asked, "Char, would you really want our team to be in the property you found for your retirement and restart?"

Char smiled at Kate. She explained, "My future has always been up in the air, from one case to the next. It looks like this may be a long investigation and probably my last assignment. I have plenty of time to pursue other places, or I can land there when this is finished, not complete the sale and move on, or finish the purchase and settle down there…" Char trailed off as she glanced at Heath and Angie, and then finished the sentence with, "…depending on future developments." Char smiled at Kate.

Kate smiled back and nodded, and then glanced nervously at Shane.

Shane met Kate's eyes and whispered, "Freaky!" He barely moved his lips, as he did his best to disguise the comment. Char smiled at Shane from across the table.

Helena whispered to Joshua, who quickly asked, "Where is this property located?"

"East of Asheville," Char replied.

"Can you be more specific?" Joshua queried.

"Southeast nearly to Spartanburg, South Carolina. I can send everyone here the coordinates, address, and an interactive aerial map of the property. Why do you ask?" Char answered, appearing uneasy.

"Internet concerns," Joshua answered. "We need high-speed Internet. Helena may have the answer if we are clear to use our AI modified Beckett Cypher. Helena?"

Helena sat stoically, her luxurious blond hair pulled back, and thick-framed black glasses perched studiously on her adorable button nose. The geeky glasses highlighted her full, luscious pink lips, as they also accentuated her sculpted, high cheekbones and delicate jawline. All eyes in the room fell on the blond beauty, compounding the uncertainties she felt with public speaking.

Helena exuded a sweet, shy, reserved demeanor. But her rapidly beating heart, quick shallow breathing, and flushed complexion called attention to the fact that she yearned to be kissed by the man talking from the other side of the speakerphone…her secret lover, Bryan Holland.

Everyone in the room had noticed her excitement each time Bryan spoke, when Helena glanced at the speaker in the center of the table, fidgeted with her hands, and occasionally touched the necklace that dangled at her ample chest. The locket was a gift from Bryan, presented in their suite over champagne at their last rendezvous. A picture of them holding each other romantically was securely attached and hidden on the inside of one half of the locket. Bryan had the other side engraved. It read, "To my one true love, Helena, from your Bryan,"

Helena's shyness accentuated her natural beauty, just as her intellect gave her the courage to speak boldly and bluntly, even when she was nervous. Bryan Holland knew his lover well and recognized the awkward silence, even from three thousand miles away.

He asked, "What are you thinking, Helena? Is it about Bradenton Meadows?"

Helena replied softly, blushing crimson as soon as Bryan mentioned her name. "Yes. Yes, it is about the project there."

Seizing the opportunity to help Helena gain confidence, Kate asked, "What is the project, Helena? Are you free to speak to us about it now?"

Helena smiled and folded her hands together, garnering strength from the conversation. "The project," she began, "is a government-funded, high-speed Internet spy system that is manned by three groups occupying different floors. One group is comprised entirely of social media company contractors working for the government. They use all social media systems to spy on foreign nations *and* American citizens suspected of having ties to foreign entities identified as Enemies of the State. But their primary task is to monitor *all* U.S. based social media their algorithm identifies as significant."

"The other group is made up of government employee technicians. They monitor foreigners within America illegally, or legally on Visas, suspected of having ties to Enemies of the State. They track subjects using social media, email, phone call or text messaging data sent from other government locations. They create files on American citizens suspected of aiding or abetting Enemies of the State. They also monitor all American citizens who reside or travel outside of the country."

"Both groups forward all suspicious activity to investigators on a separate floor, the third group, who evaluate the information, assign a threat level and re-assign the files to appropriate intelligence agencies. I can only tell you that much because a social media staffer who once worked there blew the whistle on the project to a blogger, who blogged about it repeatedly. Bradenton Meadows is now known to the small segment of the general public who read the blog or reposted the material on other sites. The blogger is in custody, and his blog has been taken down. Investigators scrubbed most of the re-posts from public view, and continue to check for leaks. The details of the project itself are highly classified."

"And that helps us how?" Shane asked.

Helena smiled widely as she explained. "The project servers are very sophisticated and formidable, but entirely vulnerable to the AI modified Beckett Cypher."

She looked from Joshua to Hunter to Tracy, and each person nodded and encouraged her to continue.

"You see, I worked on the project and understood the system's vulnerability. Much of the spying that takes place there would be illegal, absent the presence of a search warrant, so the government *legally* cannot be involved. The illegal work is farmed out to the social media contract employees occupying the site, while government employees conduct the rest of their work from a different floor. Investigators occupy the private top floor in the structure. The servers that store all significant data for the all groups occupy the entire seventh floor. That set of servers has a backdoor entry *I* wrote, and only *I* can activate…at the direction of my boss, of course, Special Agent in Charge Bryan Holland. I can enter the server system from off-site, but it's also vulnerable to our cypher. If I enter, my entry may leave a trail, but the AI augmented cypher system will leave no trace of its presence!"

Helena smiled at Hunter, Joshua, and Tracy, and then at Bryan Holland, through the speaker. All eyes then moved to the speakerphone.

Bryan explained, "For classified reasons, I can't elaborate, but the back door authorization came from well above me, I assure you all."

Shane asked again, "So how, specifically, does all this help us?"

Joshua said, "You've asked us to keep the geek jargon simple for the non-techies in our meetings. So let's recap events."

"Some fifteen years ago, DEA Supervisor Kent Murray ran a task force that compiled a massive drug case involving drug cartels working with politicians. At the same time, California Attorney General Scott Mayfield created a task force that amassed corruption cases on some of the same politicians. That investigation, dubbed The Case, was given to your father, Patrick Beckett, to review for prosecution. Patrick worked with the task force for about a year, and eventually, he and Kent Murray shared information and discovered The Committee was directing both drug distribution and corruption through the same politicians. They protected their respective case files on a series of heavily encrypted flash drives using an advanced military cypher."

"The Committee discovered the investigation and severely injured Kent Murray in an attempt to murder him. Then, Shane, they murdered your mother, your father and some of Mayfield's task force. The Committee also murdered Attorney General Mayfield and stopped the investigation. But Patrick Beckett and Kent Murray had already hidden copies of their encrypted flash drives for their young sons to later discover."

"Motivated by his father's injuries, Kent's son, Hunter, became one of the most gifted cypher experts in the world and did groundbreaking work advancing the Beckett Cypher far beyond anything available today. Helena became an expert programmer and code writer and worked on the high-speed Internet system the government uses in North Carolina. Jesse and Tracy became computer experts for the U.S. military, specializing in military-grade cyber security. And my mentor is one of the world's Artificial Intelligence geniuses. Together, he and I created a groundbreaking AI spy system."

"So, when we all came together in your team, we combined Hunter's Beckett Cypher with my sophisticated and stable Artificial Intelligence Spy System, adding Helena's knowledge of the experimental secret government spy programs and Tracy's experience in military-grade cybersecurity."

Joshua grinned, saying, "The result is a stable military grade Artificial Intelligence Spy System capable of penetrating any known cybersecurity barrier, decrypting all the encrypted data inside the host, evaluating and collating data, and then sending any useful data out of the system. A few advanced techies might try to describe the system as an MDAI 3-dimensional military grade smart cypher with internal skeleton keys. But I'm here to tell you that this system is so much more. That simplified description would be totally inaccurate!"

Joshua and his team all grinned with child-like excitement.

Most of the table returned blank stares that expressed a total lack of technical understanding.

Joshua said, "Sorry. Okay, so most importantly, the AISS can access all data in infiltrated systems. It can *live* inside these systems indefinitely, and send intelligence reports back to us, all undetected. In short, we can use the Bradenton Meadows system to launch our missions and store our data, leaving no trace back to us here! Neither the social media spy team nor the government spy technicians will ever discover our system is even present…let alone living in, and conducting business from, *their* highly secure site!"

"What happens when we want to retrieve some of the data? How do we get it out?" Pete asked.

"Great question, with an easy answer that's also very exciting!" Hunter said, with a wider grin, "We merely piggyback out on email strings or a series of social media messages. We *cyber-hitchhike*, completely undetected. The AI component of the new spy system works by breaking the data up into nonsensical bits, attaching it to a dummy carrier, programming it with a secret rendezvous location, and instructing the pieces to track with their other components as they travel to the home destination. The AI breaks the data segments off its carrier en route and reforms the body of the data when it reaches home base."

Helena smiled and nodded vigorously, to a sea of still uncomprehending faces.

Joshua added, "The data will literally appear before our eyes just like our computer was writing a document or painting a picture, once the information arrives safely home."

Kate said, "And how many times can we send the AISS out to work for us? Maybe more specifically, can it work on more than one target at a time?"

Tracy said, "The real beauty of the AISS is it isn't one soldier fighting one battle. It's an unlimited army fighting in as many battles as we send it to, one at a time or all at once."

"Why is the location in North Carolina important? Couldn't we do this from anywhere in the country that had decent speed?" Shane asked.

Helena jumped in uncharacteristically, saying, "Yes and no. We want to use the social media and government site for more than just ultra high-speed. They have a building, roughly the size of a football field, crammed with massive servers, collecting data from all over the world, 24/7/365. While we do want their crazy high-speed, we also want access to the data they've already mined. We want to sift through and analyze everything, and then send back only what we need. *And,* we want to hide out there while our AI-enhanced Beckett Cypher works its magic."

"Our system will be the proverbial needle-in-the-haystack, logging and scrutinizing every piece of hay while it remains invisible! And it will only collect the intel that is important to us!!" Pleased with herself, Helena sat back, erect, perky and confident in her chair.

Helena grinned at the speakerphone, knowing that 3,000 miles away, Bryan was smiling and proud of her. More importantly, he was proudly in love with her.

Kate nodded at Helena when their eyes met. She asked, "What's the risk of discovery?"

Helena looked at Joshua, as they both grinned. They answered simultaneously, "Nothing!"

Pete confirmed, "Totally undetectable?"

Joshua answered, "Yes. In layman's terms, the AISS is fast and fragmented, evolving and adapting to any potential discovery. It reconfigures itself to avoid detection and captures and neutralizes detection software probes. At present, we are confident AISS is invisible, undetectable, and unstoppable."

There was silence in the room and on the speakerphone.

Finally, Walter asked, "If no one has an objection, I think we should go ahead with the proposal and move the cypher team to the property. Objections?"

Silence fell onto the group as individual thoughts raced to consider the consequences of this advanced technology.

Walter finally asked, "Char, what do you need from us, besides a helicopter pilot to check out the chopper, and money to cover the lease?"

Char answered, "The money is appreciated, especially if I buy the property. I guess the rent will be my retainer!"

She flashed Pete a coy smile, and said, "I am proficient in the helicopter, but we should have at least *two* more pilots, due to my security role."

Tracy said, "Jesse is a licensed instructor and very experienced in a multitude of helicopters. He would likely remain with the cypher team, so that leaves us wanting only one more pilot."

Tom nodded in agreement.

After a moment of silence, Angie offered, "I think that should be me. Now that I'm part of this group, I need to earn my keep with more than filing and building display charts, around this family!"

Silence overcame the room again as every eye rested on Angie. She smiled back at all the inquiring faces. Walter looked overjoyed.

Bryan eventually asked, "You are licensed to fly helicopters then, Angie?"

"Yes, I am. I took my first flight lesson when I was eleven. My birthday present. Dad taught me to fly an old Cessna 152 he owned. He was a nut for flying, hiking, mountain climbing, and competition archery. Dad and I were very close, so those became all my hobbies when I was young."

"I have my private pilot license with multi-engine, helicopter, and glider add-ons. But Dad couldn't get enough of helicopters, so I've flown nine different makes and models with him. I logged about 700 hours in choppers, and my license is current. Like Dad, I enjoy helicopters more than fixed wing. Choppers may not be as fast as the King Air, but they're a great deal more useful in demanding terrains."

Heath and Shane both slightly frowned as their minds raced, considering the possibilities. Both looked stunned as their eyes met. Heath and Shane gazed at each other until Shane raised his hands in submission.

Angie studied their expressions, as she looked from one to the other. She added, "No one ever asked if I had any talents other than veterinarian work, except Kate!"

Kate chuckled. "If you gentlemen can recall, I told you both you'd be surprised at Angie's talents, the first day I met her. And neither of you bothered to inquire as to what those talents were. So, I suggest you look around the room at the women seated here one more time, and realize, we're all a great deal more than just pretty faces!"

Kate, Char, Juanita, Tracy, Helena, and Angie all laughed at the men's expense, while Shane and Heath looked uncomfortably embarrassed.

Char said, "Well then, I propose that Jesse and Angie accompany me to the property as soon as possible so we can meet the owner and check out everything first, and then move on to the chopper. If all is satisfactory, I'll take the owner to town to sign the lease option, while the remainder of the team comes in behind us to look the place over and finalize your approval. You can phone me to confirm before I sign."

Heath stared at Angie, realizing she was enjoying his discomfort as he considered her being alone with Char.

Shane did his best ventriloquist whisper, uttering "Holy shit!" to Kate.

Kate nudged Shane under the table again, just as Walter said, "Then, let's do it, people! We'll pack up and leave tomorrow. Pete, Tom, Tracy, Hunter, Helena, Char, Shane and I can remain for a brief meeting to work out a proposed site for the remainder of the team, while the rest of you work out a transportation proposal. Bryan, do you have anything else?"

Bryan was silent for a moment, and then replied, "I think it best that you all keep in contact with me through one person for now, without me knowing any details of your locations until we're positive there are no more leaks from my house. Just let me know how I can help. I made no notes about the proposed site Char discussed. So, I'll say goodbye for now. God bless, and take care!"

Walter ended the call as Helena smiled at the phone and touched her locket again.

Half the team at the table stood up to leave, just as Char said, "I have one more thing."   Everyone sat back down, eager to hear more.

"Knowing there was a leak in the government that led to the attack on our people, I didn't think it wise to give enough detail to Bryan that he or someone in his office could do some digging and identify the exact property I proposed. I trust him implicitly, just not the leaky walls that surround him!"

"So, to be transparent to *this* team, my only team now, the actual estate is about 40 miles north-west of where I described the location. Its 1,390 acres, not 65 acres. The owner's wife didn't die of a heart attack. Her husband died in a car crash a year ago. The property is nine bedrooms and seven baths and was never seized by the government or owned by the cartel. It is all new construction. The builder was not from Asheville. He was from Atlanta."

"The runway is a half-mile long, not one third. The security system is twice as expansive and more sophisticated than I indicated. There is already high-speed internet installed there, albeit not as high speed as Helena described. The chopper is real, but it's a Bell 430 twin turbo, ten-seater, completely up-to-date. I assume you both can fly that one?" Jesse and Angie nodded.

Char smiled, and said, "Good. A few more details are different and will work to our advantage. Then, for now, that's all I have to add."

"Smart lady!" Walter shook his head, impressed with Char's ability to think on her feet.

Kate laughed. "Char, I particularly appreciated your skill in misleading Bryan with the seizure story. You couldn't help but smile, knowing he'd be interested in a law enforcement story, while it took his focus off the property. And he couldn't see your face! It was a masterful performance!"

Kate glanced at Helena, who also smiled. Helena was happy Bryan didn't know the site location so that he couldn't be a target. But, she was also sad they wouldn't be talking for a while.

Char laughed, and half-bowed as she raised her arms. She said, "Better not to worry about trusting a second time after someone has already disappointed you."

Shane looked at Kate and grinned. He whispered, "You knew *while* she was lying?"

Kate leaned toward Shane and whispered, "I did, and that's why *I* need to manage Char! I can read her better than anyone else on the team."

Shane whispered, "You'll get no argument from me about that!"

The group began to filter out of the room. Angie walked by Char, took her by the hand, and said, "Thank you for everything today, Char. You are a fantastic woman. I'm genuinely looking forward to working with you." She smiled an open smile of proposed friendship.

Char squeezed Angie's hand firmly, and responded, "I wouldn't have imagined it before now, but I'm looking forward to working with you, too. I'm sure there's a great deal more to learn and appreciate about the veterinarian from Nevada than meets the eye!"

Heath walked anxiously up behind the two woman still shaking hands in mutual admiration. He asked, "Everything good?"

Angie said, "Everything is just fine," at the same time Char said, "Yes, it really is good!"

The groups parted for separate meetings, as Shane muttered under his breath, "Freakier and freakier!"

Kate chuckled softly.

✳✳✳

Bob Crawford and Barbara Walcott had taken time to enjoy an afternoon glass of wine after a light lunch. They had celebrated their romance by making love just as they had done when they first fell in love almost fifteen years earlier. Uncharacteristically, today they had made love twice, spoken to each other in whispers about their future together, and fallen asleep in each other's arms, unrushed by any political event or duty.

Vice President Crawford was sound asleep in bed, dreaming that he and his 5-year-old daughter were sailing their small sailboat on a lake some thirty years ago. In his dream, he was laughing so hard his eyes began to water when Barbara Walcott rocked him roughly side-to-side by the shoulders as she tried to rouse him to consciousness.

She said, "Honey, Sean just called. The Committee has tasked *him* with finding the Beckett Cypher. This development is even better than we could have hoped. We thought he could get close to the team charged with locating the cypher, but we never dreamed he would *lead and hand-select* the team!"

Crawford grunted, "Just when my little girl was about to steer the boat using the rudder for the first time, too. She was nervous and asking questions so fast I couldn't keep up with them. It was really quite funny! Before that day she had always tried to guide us using her little plastic toy paddle. That was a fond memory, and a better time for the entire world, from decades ago!"

Bob Crawford grinned at the picture in his mind as he scooted back in bed, coming to rest against the headboard with a pillow supporting his back.

Crawford rubbed his face briskly with both hands in an attempt to wake quickly and take control of his senses.

He finally said, "This MI6 agent of yours, Sean, or 'Odysseus,' as we should call him using his code name, has quickly become much better connected with The Committee's upper echelon than we planned. No one in The Committee should know *you* are the secret head of British MI6, our equivalent of the CIA. No one should know your agent possesses the spy talents he does. The Committee courted Odysseus specifically to take over the West Coast drug cartels and manage Franky Magadinno's businesses after they killed the poor devil. So I wonder why this quick change of direction and elevation in status? Your Russian friends, you think?"

"I certainly hope not!" Barbara exclaimed, "I would like to think *no one* knows my MI6 agent's identity but a handful of us in

British intelligence, and a couple of key figures like me, at the highest levels in our government, and possibly…" She trailed off, failing to complete the thought aloud, as she focused on all the possibilities.

"And me, and whoever else the others who knew told, and those people told, and so on, as usual," Crawford scowled, as he finished her sentence. "It's not just us in The States who can no longer keep a secret. I should have paid more attention years ago when my very wise grandfather told me that a secret is no longer a secret once more than one person knows about it. How many people in your government know about your MI6 agent, Odysseus?"

Barbara Walcott, the beautiful, politically battle-scarred, cunningly-tough stateswoman, known for her quick wit and sharp cutting tongue, scooted back against the headboard and remained uncharacteristically silent.

Crawford recognized the look of pensive fear emerging through her lovely eyes and stoic facial expression. He said, encouragingly, "Before we panic, let's plan some damage control. It may be nothing, and if that's the case, we don't have to worry. But if the Russians tell the Chinese, and they broadcast it to the Iranians or the North Koreans... Well, you see the problem, love. These days everyone seems to blab as they maneuver toward something they want…or while they inflict damage on an enemy."

In a weak attempt at self-righteous defense, Walcott snapped, "Bob, this is *my* turf. It's British MI6 we're talking about, not your American State Department or FBI that both leak classified material like a sieve leaks water!"

Crawford scoffed. He said, "And before the world heard about a *British* spy and his fake dossier, and learned such spies could be hired by the highest bidder to create fictitious intelligence, the spy world was a more credible place. But today, my love, Russians assassinate their own double agents in Mother England, and English spies hired by American political parties conspire with Russians to discredit American elected officials, and then accuse those elected of collusion."

Crawford added, "I'm afraid that in today's world of me-first at everyone else's expense, no one can be trusted to keep their mouths shut *or* to tell the truth. We must prepare for the worst, and create a list of possible scenarios our enemies may have already planned! And likely, we're *already* behind a dangerous curve, my dear. So, we need to get to it!"

Walcott sighed and conceded that Crawford was correct. She said, defeatedly, "Oh, I know you're correct in your assessment, Bob. So much for our vacation alone, celebrating our love at long last. We were just getting it all back again!" Barbara looked down in silence, obviously disappointed.

Crawford took her by the hand and said, lovingly, "We'll still be celebrating our love with each passing moment, dearest. We'll just need to work a little at protecting your man, Odysseus, while we celebrate!"

Crawford smiled and squeezed her hand. They left their bed together.

As Barbara Walcott and Bob Crawford donned robes and walked to the kitchen to hit the power button on the coffee maker, a senior North Korean diplomat called his second sleeper cell team stationed near Langley, Virginia. He gave them the name of their target, "Odysseus," and a possible location at a Committee member's home in Boston.

The North Korean team packed and readied for the drive to Massachusetts. They were on the road in less than an hour. The assassin team leader notified his handler in Canada as soon they were en route. An intelligence officer came on the phone and warned his group to take counter surveillance precautions, reminding them that the other cell team stationed in the United States was still missing. The lieutenant advised his team leader they must take Odysseus alive and sent a text with the MI6 agent's photograph and physical description.

Bob and Barbara sat at the 4-person wicker table, with etched glass top, on the estate's back deck, drinking coffee and dunking biscotti, as they created a flow chart of probable people in all governments who could know about Odysseus. When they finished some two hours later, there were thirty-seven names on paper, with risk assessment rankings and notes accounting for possible leaks or disloyalty, next to each name.

They made plans to assign SAC Bryan Holland further assessments on the names listed if the person was present in the United States, while one of Barbara's trusted MI6 regional directors would investigate all persons listed if they were outside the USA.

There were four exceptions to the planned investigation. The President of the United States of America and the Assistant United States Attorney General would both be investigated further by MI6, while the militant Trotskyist leader of the socialist movement in the House of Commons and a past Director of MI6 in England, would be investigated by Crawford's trusted CIA contact.

By early evening Barbara and Bob had managed to make all necessary phone calls and still take time to enjoy a leisurely walk through the grounds. Crawford's Secret Service detail remained inconspicuous, affording them the privacy they had requested for the week they were scheduled to be together at the estate.

As they sat to toast their love over their evening drink, Barbara commented, "Bob, I've said it before, and I'm repeating it now. I'm tired of all this. I want out of politics once we finish this mess. The day after we end it, I'm resigning. I want to pursue a simple, unencumbered life with the man I love. And I don't want my man involved in politics. I don't *ever* want to attend another political rally or endorse a candidate, or even attend a party meeting. I want relaxation, flowers, holding hands, a walk by the pond at this estate, and I want..." Barbara left her last thought hanging in dead air.

"You want what? You didn't finish." Crawford chided.

"You know what I want, Bob."

"Then you need to make it official, Barbara."

Bob looked at her nervously and abruptly stood upright, stretching his distinguished six-foot frame. He reached in his jacket pocket and pulled out a sparkling platinum engagement ring with two small diamonds perched below and on each side of the 1½-carat center stone.

Bob Crawford got down on one knee, took Barbara Walcott's left hand in his, and said, "Barbara, my love, I bought this ring more than ten years ago. I was going to ask you to marry me then, and I didn't, for all the wrong reasons. I can't ever let you go again."

"Will you, Barbara, love of my life, be my wife? Will you spend the rest of your days and nights loving me? And, will you do me the honor of allowing me to love you as much as I possibly can, as your husband?"

THE POLITICIANS

Barbara Walcott sat with her lips parted and chest heaving, as she glanced from Bob Crawford to the ring and back again, unable to fathom that the moment she had dreamed about for so many years had finally arrived. She slowly reached for the ring as her head nodded. She was unable to speak. Bob took Barbara's trembling left hand and kissed it gently. He slipped the ring on her left-hand ring finger. It fit perfectly.

As tears came to Barbara's eyes, she said only, "Yes, Bob, yes, and yes! We can finally be happy together!" She leaned forward and sobbed, as Crawford held her.

Thirty minutes later, at precisely 6:40 P.M. Eastern time, Walter O'Leary called Bob Crawford, as Barbara and Bob clinked glasses and sipped dry vodka martinis, each made dirty with olive juice and a pair of sizeable Spanish Queen olives. Crawford hesitated before he answered when he saw the caller ID.

He showed the display to Barbara and said, hesitantly, "Here goes!"

Crawford hit the speaker on the phone when he answered, and asked, "Yes, Walter, how are you all doing after the incident? Everyone is still okay, I trust!"

"We're all alive and well, but one of the hens has left the roost. It was too much for Pete's Tasha. She's packed and gone, and I'm sad to say their love is no longer in bloom, old friend," Walter answered sadly.

Walter added, "But, that's not the reason for my call. At our friend Bryan's suggestion, until we figure out where the information is leaking from, we're all packing and moving out of town, heading in different directions, to parts unknown. We'll keep in touch with Bryan, but the incident forced us to admit we must drastically tighten security to survive. I just wanted you to hear it from me, and thank you for everything you've done, my friend."

There was silence on the phone, as Crawford contemplated a response.

Walter continued. "And, I wanted to tell you that Judy called me and broke the news about you two splitting up. I'm sorry about that. I imagine there are some deep wounds after a lifetime spent growing up together, and raising a family. If you ever need to talk, Bob, I'll be there for you, and so will Juanita."

"I appreciate that, Walter. You were always a better friend to me than I was to you. And I mean that sincerely. I have always, much too quickly and too frequently, let my career get in the way of relationships, with both family and friends. You were much better at managing both sides of life than I! And, I suppose Judy told you about her doctor friend and wanted you to meet him at some point?"

Walter sighed. "She did, Bob, but..."

Bob Crawford interrupted. "No worries there, Walter. I have a *friend* of my own I'd like you and Juanita to meet at the appropriate time. We'll set it up when this craziness ends. You'll like her, of course! Just don't try and debate her. I warn you. You won't win!"

Crawford laughed, drawing a chuckle of relief from Walter. Barbara grinned slyly as she sipped her martini.

Crawford said, "I'll check in with Bryan tomorrow to make sure you're all safely tucked into your new lair. Please, don't hesitate to reach out to me for any help you think wise, 24/7, Walter. Promise me! You know this is far from over, my friend!"

"You have my word, Bob. Talk soon."

Walter ended the call, looked at the rest of the family all seated at the dining room table with him, and asked, "Well, you all heard him. What do you think?"

Shane said, "Joshua, Tracy, Jesse, and Helena said they're all convinced it was our government that unscrambled Tasha's phone. They are 100 percent sure the phone was scrambled and secure before. In my experience, the most obvious answer is also most often correct. I think the person responsible for the attack is probably someone on the inside with knowledge that we were working with Bryan. I trust Bryan with my life. I don't know Bob Crawford. But Crawford gave you a hint, maybe a hint from shame, when he told you he couldn't manage to separate family and friends from work."

Shane quickly added, "And only a few people have more power than the Vice President of the United States. My guess is it was Crawford, and if not, the President of the United States, who we all know is a card-carrying Committee member. I believe the possibility that the Assistant United States Attorney General so quickly corrupted an FBI technician he didn't appear to know a week earlier, is far-fetched."

Walter sighed and slumped down in his chair. "Bob Crawford's been my friend for most of my life. I want to believe it's CIA, FBI, NSA, the Assistant United States Attorney General, the President of the United States of America himself, or anyone other than my old friend. But, we can't chance being wrong by guessing. No, I agree with your advice, Shane. We won't let Bryan Holland or Bob Crawford know where we are."

"Telling Bryan would put him in a very awkward position when we also ask him to withhold information about us from his Vice

President. But, that also means Char has to work with us and for us, *and* she needs to be totally off the books with the FBI. Who will manage her and her security detail if Bryan is out?"

Kate said, "I will, working with Tom. And I'll need four of Tom's best people along with a counter-surveillance detail and relief teams. I've already worked out the details of the proposal."

Shane glanced quickly at Kate. She explained, "I can read Char, and I think a female is the best fit to manage her."

Walter and Pete looked at each other and nodded.

Shane quipped, "And what's *my* assignment?"

Kate pretended not to notice Shane's slight irritation. She said, "This has always been first and foremost, your case. I think you need to direct the sequence of the investigation and work with Bryan's FBI team to acquire any logistical support you think wise. We have too many constantly changing responsibilities now. Someone needs to be in charge of the big picture. One person needs to decide how we coordinate cyber attacks on The Committee's California Center for Information Extraction and Yucca Mountain stronghold. One person must evaluate the information coming in from the cypher and plan each move in the investigation. That can't be me. I don't have those case-management skills. I think it needs to be you, Shane. We need *one person* to keep us moving in the right direction, working toward the correct goal."

Shane said, "But..."

Kate interrupted and said, "And, Shane, you know Bryan best. He's been your friend for a long time, and you brought him into this. You need to manage that friendship, use it to our advantage, and track his activity."

Shane nodded in agreement, knowing that Kate's logic was correct. When he looked back up, everyone in the room was also nodding. He met Juanita's eyes, and when she smiled, Shane said, "Okay, I agree. But all that is more than I can handle alone, so now I have a proposal."

"You and Tom manage the security for our cypher team. We need a leader for the team we decided earlier we would set up in Montana. We need another leader to brief us on incoming intelligence from the AISS. We need another leader to collate and manage all intelligence so we can all easily refer to it, see it and understand it. And we need one lead to manage and run outside investigations. We need to set up and choose roles quickly, and then I need a communication schedule from all team leaders."

Pete asked, "Shane, can you suggest a lead for the structure you suggested?"

Walter interrupted, saying, "I'll help where I can, but Pete and I have family corporate responsibilities starting very soon that are going to take us off this case."

Pete nodded, and added, "Lee is gone setting up the new Investigation LLC and meeting with department heads. Maybe Tom should handle all outside investigations."

Kate stood to stretch. She said, "Sorry for standing. I've just been sitting too long this morning. What if Char, Jesse and I run the security in North Carolina, with Jesse and Char on different shifts, and Char and I together?"

Shane was transfixed as he followed Kate's every movement, noting her back arch accentuating her chest more than usual. He was instantly mesmerized as he followed each syllable formed by her luscious lips. Kate's beauty captivated his thoughts, making it nearly impossible for him to concentrate. He felt the stirrings he sometimes found untimely, but still yearned for, and he thought only of making love to his gorgeous Kate.

Kate said, coyly, as she stretched one last time, "Shane? What do you think?"

Saving face, Shane offered, "I was…wondering how the helicopter pilot assignment would work if you and Jesse managed the security shifts using Angie and Char as pilots. How do you see that working?"

Kate grinned, knowing where Shane's thoughts had been lurking. She sat back down, pulled her shoulders back to continue the torture, and answered, "Jesse and Char have the best security minds of the four of us. Char should fly on my team, and Angie on Jesse's crew, if we need to move to a 24-hour security schedule for pilots."

"When we first arrive, I think Angie and Char should train together, and then Jesse and I, in the chopper. He's a certified flight instructor. I want him to instruct me on the helicopter, so I can get certified while we're there. A week or so of intense instruction will provide us with four pilots, on two 24/7 shifts, and makes more sense in the long run. Plus, we'll all be familiar with the helicopter if we have to bug out or travel. And, I think we need to bring the second plane in, just in case.

"We have a second plane?" Heath asked, totally surprised.

"We do," Kate answered. "It's in Scottsdale."

Pete spoke up. "Part of an acquisition Walter and I agreed to last week, with the purchase of a shopping center. We did a little horse trading with one of the owners of the mall."

Heath asked, "What did we trade and what did we get?"

Pete smiled, "We traded a collector 1965 *Shelby Cobra* we never drove, to a car nut, to get the *Beechcraft Bonanza G36 Normalized Turbo* his wife bought him as a birthday surprise. He never flew, and he's been trying to trade it for a Shelby for a year. Turns out he had a fear of heights and flying, and kept it a secret from her for years." Pete laughed. "We seriously out-traded him!"

Shane said, "Finally, an airplane even I can fly without supervision!" He laughed. "So, along with Kate's and Pete's suggestions, let's begin with Tracy and Helena in charge of AISS intelligence briefings; Hunter and Joshua in charge of preparing the two cyber attacks; Angie in charge of collating all briefing intelligence; Juanita in charge of setting up first aid; and Heath in charge of communicating with the Montana team. That team can choose their group leader."

One by one all the participants agreed.

Kate and Shane strolled toward their bedroom, hand in hand, as Kate asked, "Enjoy my stretches, did you?" He grinned as they both hurried to the bedroom.

✳ ✳ ✳

At 4:00 A.M. Eastern time, the North Korean cell approached their target, a substantial two-story, colonial-style residence in an affluent neighborhood near West Roxbury, Massachusetts. An hour earlier, the team leader confirmed that a subject matching their target's photo had entered the home. After some conversation with two other men and a woman in the living room, the group inside had drawn the drapes and turned off the downstairs lights, as they all prepared for bed.

Thirty minutes later all the lights were out, and the North Korean team received the final green light to commence their assault.

Six members of the team exited the white van bearing magnetic signs identifying it as First Choice Plumbing Company, with a phone number that rang to a burner cell phone. The commercial van displayed recently stolen Massachusetts license plates that had not yet been discovered missing by the owner.

Two additional foreign agents, both trained snipers and assassins, remained in the vehicle as outside cover for their comrades. They peered through the darkness, occasionally using night-vision goggles. They watched activity on all sides of the van through one-way glass windows on the sides and rear, and via a periscope, disguised as a vent, directed to the front of the vehicle.

Precisely sixty seconds after the last North Korean team member entered the house three shots rang out from inside the house. Twenty-five seconds later, as the two outside cover agents ran into the living room, the entire house exploded. The house burned to the ground before responding fire department personnel managed to extinguish the blaze, partially due to a water main problem, eventually discovered a half-mile from the location.

An investigation later revealed that a computer software anomaly had turned off the valve supplying the closest area water main, ten minutes before the explosion. All hydrants in the area lacked water pressure.

Before the Fire Marshal investigation unit arrived, a rapid response task force took control of the scene. The specialized group included special agents from the FBI, Homeland Security, and the

NSA. An unidentified MI6 agent, referred to as a "British diplomat," accompanied the FBI Special Agent in Charge.

The four resident occupants who perished in the fire were identified two days later to the media by the Fire Marshall, who read a press release written by the FBI Public Affairs Unit. The statement identified one American and three British citizens, all employees of the British Embassy, as victims of a faulty natural gas line explosion. The group was reportedly on vacation at the residence, owned by the American, further identified as a retired college English professor. There was no mention of the eight dead foreign nationals from North Korea, or the van with stolen license plates impounded by the FBI.

As the press release began to air on television channels on the East Coast, the Russian Deputy Minister of Defense called Barbara Walcott, just after she ended a phone call with her undercover MI6 agent, Odysseus.

Barbara looked at the display, and answered, "Deputy Minister of Defense, how are you? It's been too long since we last spoke."

In a strongly overplayed Russian accent, the Deputy Minister of Defense said, "Da, Madam Home Secretary, I am fine. And I know you will be better when I give you the news. Madam Home Secretary, now that you *owe me one,* as you English say, should I call you Barbara, so you refer to me as Sergej?"

"Titles have never been important to me, Sergej, but I wasn't aware you did me a favor. Can you explain?"

"I can, Barbara. You just received a call from your MI6 agent, Odysseus, and he is living due to my efforts on your behalf."

Barbara Walcott was well-seasoned and used to being blindsided by politicians and bureaucrats. She never hesitated in her response. She quickly retorted, "And *if* I knew what you were talking about, and *if* what you say were true, how could you find out so quickly that I spoke to this person, Sergej?"

"I would like to be direct now, Barbara, and I think you should be open with me also. Now that we are on the same team with this Committee business, I used my position in the Committee sixth tier to have my Foreign Intelligence Service agent in The Committee, assigned to Odysseus to help find our cypher. So, I suspect your agent just called you, because he left his Committee team room to call his, 'Mother.' And that Mother would be you, I suspect."

"So, Sergej, if all this is correct, how did you save this fortunate man?"

"The Russians and Chinese share a great deal, to combine forces and stabilize the world from Western aggression."

Walcott roared with laughter. "Sergej, if you and I are to be close friends, we have to quit teasing each other with nonsense like that!"

The Deputy Minister of Defense boomed with laughter, in return. He said, "As you wish, Barbara. I shared the information about your MI6 spy with my Chinese counterpart, knowing he would share the information with the North Koreans. I even provided the Chinese with an address where the agent was staying, along with a photo of your man to confirm their target."

Walcott's heart skipped a beat. She looked at the door to the bathroom, hoping Bob Crawford would come out quickly so he could hear the call on speaker. The door didn't open.

She asked, "And you're calling me now to warn me about your plan, so that this agent can do what?"

Sergej said, "He must do nothing. Both you and he can relax and enjoy the world as it remains for us, Barbara. I took care of the problem."

"Okay, so now you have me very intrigued, Sergej. May I ask what you did to solve the problem you created?"

The Deputy Minister of Defense took a long sip of vodka, and laughed aloud again. "You tease me now, my friend. No, the problem was nothing I helped create! I was your solution, my new comrade! You see, the Chinese and Iranians got help from *your* French *allies*. The French would have discovered your man's identity in a matter of days using one of their double agents working in MI6. No, Barbara, I helped solve the problem by giving them the identity first, and steering them to a false target, a different man of my choosing."

"I see. And what target was that, my new best friend?"

Sergej answered, "Turn on the American evening news tonight, and watch their coverage of the explosion in Boston. The American FBI will say they located and identified only four bodies in the house that exploded and burned, due to a faulty gas line. But they will lie. They removed twelve bodies, Barbara, my friend. Eight North Koreans assigned to kidnap Odysseus, three British Nationals who were Embassy employees, and one retired English Professor who worked for your British Embassy in America."

Walcott was silent, as she contemplated the loss of one of her agents and good friends.

"Your Mrs. Livingston will be missed, I'm sure, at different times and in different ways by both Russian and British intelligence units. How long did she work as a spy, supplying you with information about the United States and Mother Russia, Barbara?"

Walcott replied slowly and calmly, as she raised a finger to her lips to silence Bob Crawford's approach, "Mr. Deptuy Minister of Defense, *if* I knew what you were talking about, you do realize I couldn't answer that question, right?" She turned the phone on speaker as Bob Crawford sat down quietly beside her.

"Ha!" Sergej laughed. "Not too trusting yet, comrade? Then, in a show of good faith, I agree to go first. But then you owe me two favors, and you must play the game too! Mrs. Livingston worked for us for twenty-one years. We fed her information to give to the Americans through you, their close ally, and I think she worked for you for ten years, at least. Now, it's your turn. Tell me I am correct!"

"Sergej, just because I think you're cute and I truly am enjoying this banter, if I were to tell you this person could have worked for us for twenty-two years, and we may have used a double agent of yours, now unfortunately deceased, to acquire her, so we could feed information back to you, what would you say?"

Uproarious forced laughter came from the phone. Sergej took another healthy swig of vodka as he tried to control his anger. After a moment he said, "That I could believe. And it is why someone killed him. He disappointed too many people, I think. But, I must admit, Barbara, I love playing these games with you!"

Barbara seized the opportunity to ply Sergej for information, knowing she had made him angry. She asked, "Sergej, now that we are friends, I must ask, why did you go out of the way to save this agent you think is my man and who did you, or the North Koreans, kill in *his* place?"

"Okay Barbara, I think you already know part of the story, but I will tell you because I need the favor back from you now. I sent them a picture of a low-level attaché´ assigned to your Embassy. He was a little piss-ant. You won't miss him. He saw himself as a big-time spy, in his small clerical position. He wasted our time. You don't need him anyway. He made a most excellent dummy target to save your Odysseus. And now, the Chinese and the North Koreans have to start over from the beginning, or they will believe your spy-man is dead. Either way gives you more time to find our cypher."

Walcott laughed aloud. "The attaché lured you into an attempt to turn him. You thought you could learn what secrets he would provide, only to find he knew nothing! Oh, Sergej, you're a dangerous man to try to fool." Barbara said the compliment flirtatiously.

Sergej bragged, "He was a foolish little man wasting our precious time. I did you a favor with him, also! But now, my good friend, I need you to help with the Americans and the Euros."

"In what way can I help you, my resourceful new friend?" Barbara inquired cautiously, still overtly flirting.

Sergej grinned, and said, "We have finalized an agreement to supply Germany with oil. We plan to grow our alliance with them quickly. In the future, we will provide many other goods and services, and also reach out to other European neighbors. Our American friends will oppose this, as will the treacherous French. The Iranians are working with the French along the same lines, and as you know, the Iranians are even more difficult to control than the North Koreans. So, I ask you to talk to your government and help us with the Americans and the European nations who would oppose us."

There was silence on the phone as Barbara and Bob gazed at each other in wonder, contemplating all the Russian Deputy Minister of Defense had said.

Barbara said, "Sergej, I will turn on the news now, and think carefully about what you have said! We should talk soon Mr. Deputy Minister of Defense. And I thank you sincerely, for the call, and for any trouble you have gone to for me, and my country."

"Barbara, my lovely lady, remember one more thing. In doing you this favor, I gave you access to my Committee agent's identity. Another show of good faith. And now, I will drink a toast in Russia to your beauty *and* your efficient use of political tactics. Madam Home Secretary, I think when you next come to Russia, we should have dinner!"

After a brief silence, Sergej added, "And let's see what happens as we discuss our political futures late into the night! Oh, and Barbara, my friend, please tell Vice President Bob Crawford I would like to meet him someday! Udachi!" He abruptly ended the call.

As soon as the line was dead, Crawford asked, "What the hell was all that about?"

Barbara mused, "Saying, 'udachi,' is like saying, 'good luck,' an informal way of saying farewell or goodbye for now."

"I don't mean that, damn it, and you know it. We're engaged to be married, and some half-drunk, oversexed, hairy-chested, bear of a Russian man calls you at my home to flirt with you and fantasize about what the late night may bring after dinner!"

Barbara smiled and leaned back in her chair. Admiring her attractive image reflecting in the far window, she accentuated her chest by pulling her shoulders back as she tossed her thick hair to the side and stroked it.

She asked, "How do you know he has a hairy chest if you haven't met him?"

Before he realized she was playing to his jealousy, Bob Crawford answered, "Intelligence photos, that's how." Crawford looked down in disgust as he considered the political ramifications of the conversation, in between thoughts of anger and rage that burst into his ordinarily calm and methodical mind.

Barbara laughed and said, "Bob Crawford, I do believe *you* are jealous."

Crawford crossed his arms over his chest as he struggled to focus clearly. He was silent, allowing Barbara to collect her thoughts. Barbara's friend and deep cover agent, Leslie Livingston, was dead. Barbara had recruited and trained Leslie more than twenty years ago after Leslie went to work at a private college where many American politician's children attended school, along with Russian children from embassy families. They had kept in contact and met frequently, nearly every time Barbara had been to the United States. And over the years they had shared many good times and bad times, becoming more like sisters, as they chatted on the phone for hours each week.

Barbara focussed her thoughts on her agent, Sean, code-named Odysseus. He was safe but closely monitored by a Russian double-agent, working inside The Committee. Sergej knew far more than she and Bob Crawford knew, and Barbara Walcott was angry and frightened. Barbara realized she had to discover what Sergej Petrov actually did know. And she had to move fast.

Barbara finally said, "Bob, let's watch the news and do some checking! This Committee business has become far more complex than we planned."

As Barbara turned on the news, Bob Crawford's Secret Service detail made the rounds outside the estate's principal residence. And while Barbara flipped through the cable network channels to locate the report on the Boston explosion, the junior agent assigned to the detail, monitored her from the shadows through the nearest window. He quickly dialed the President of the United States.

When the President answered, the agent said, "This is Christian, sir, calling with your nightly report."

"And what activity was there today, Christian?"

"A few hours of phone calls for the Vice President and the British Home Secretary, sir, and an equal amount of time spent on their computers and work together. Other than that, they have still received no visitors. They spend most of their time being a...couple, sir."

"Very well, Christian. Call me tomorrow unless something changes."

"Yes, sir. Goodnight, sir."

The President ended the call, and immediately called the Assistant United States Attorney General. He said, "I just got the report, and I don't like it. Something's going on with those two, other than love. See what you can find out in the morning. You might have to make a trip out there. Think of some excuse. Come up with a plan."

Before the Assistant United States Attorney General could respond, the President hung up, angry at not knowing.

Chapter 3

"Misrepresentation, exaggeration, omission, spin, and outright lies now infest our society to the extent that a person rarely finds the whole unaltered truth, even after an exhaustive search. And if the truth is finally located, uncertainty forces the finder to question its integrity. Unfortunately, by then, few people will fight for a truth no one really wants to hear."

(Daniel Lee Holub)

Barbara Walcott and Bob Crawford sat on the couch late into the night, discussing Barbara's conversation with her new-found friend, Sergej, the Russian Deputy Minister of Defense, or *Deputy Minister of Defence of the Russian Federation*, as it was spelled and titled in English, within Russia.

Crawford had calmed and reflected on his jealousy. The incident reconfirmed how vital Barbara had always been to him, even in the years they maintained a distance, during his marriage. Bob also realized he would fight and die for Barbara, motivated by love, passion, and duty, not just responsibility. He admitted to himself that Barbara made him feel ten times as strong as he had felt before, even as she made him weaker with need. But right now, Bob felt alive, virile, powerful, and protective, in ways he had forgotten possible.

Barbara asked, "Bob, when did the world become so unbalanced? I don't remember all the cloak and dagger, double-dealing, murder, lies, division, hate and corruption infecting political life back when we started in government."

Bob thought for a moment, and said, "I can't answer that question with other than an opinion, dearest."

"Then, I would like to hear your opinion. I'm struggling with what I should do next, and I value your judgment, honey!"

Barbara waited patiently for a response, as she gazed at one of the few people in the world she considered an unbiased political mentor.

Crawford sighed, took Barbara by the hand and looked down. "I find myself conflicted about modern day life, especially with politics. On the one hand, I want to focus on family, friends, country, and love. I want to be upbeat, fighting the good fight for what I believe is right, enjoying each day as it comes, able to maintain a positive outlook on life. I want to do good for my country, freedom, and justice. I don't want to be swept up into the political evils the system forces us to be involved in, if we wish to be successful within it. But, truth be told, I'm working in the scummy swamp right alongside all the other evil creatures."

Bob glanced at Barbara, somewhat ashamed of himself. "I think our ideals of honesty, integrity, responsibility and government service to our electorate were all possible before the two World Wars. People back then were concerned about family, friends, and community, as well as their reputation, jobs, and responsibilities. They didn't divide and isolate themselves to the point of hatred and cruelty to those who were different. People were calmer, more caring, more polite, respectful, and gentler."

"Those World Wars changed everything in my book. People became more mobile and began to question, criticize and devalue their culture and heritage. They developed identity politics and justified hatred and brutality. People moving to new lands refused to assimilate into their new culture. Instead, they imposed their ideas on people they didn't know, to whom they had no allegiance, and shared no history. Society devalued life and accepted death and destruction as normal. In some places, people who seized power even practiced genocide."

"And all this didn't just happen in third world countries. Here in the United States, families drifted apart. Lifelong friendships became rare. People moved to the big cities, and metro areas got too large. People began to identify themselves by their viewpoints, instead of their character and goodwill. People *became* their agenda, their career, their desires, and their opinions. They only chose friends with similar views."

"The media moved away from facts and truth, and preached failed leftist ideas the World Wars had just defeated. Journalists chastised readers and viewers with daily doses of political correctness in opinions and editorials. Eventually, the media edited *news* to the point that it became fictional propaganda. Reporters assassinated reputations and ruined lives as they fed the fire and fanned the flames of hatred and division. When people began to disrespect and hate everyone who disagreed with them, they officially lost their humanity and their souls."

Barbara asked, "Is it as bad as all that. How do you mean?"

Bob said, "I'll tell you a story that illustrates my points. When I lived in Oregon, I had just won the election to become a State Representative in my district. In those times the environmental groups' fringes had gone to war with loggers, and it had become violent. Some of these radical activists harassed, hurt, and even killed loggers. And loggers fought, injured and killed environmental activists."

"I didn't understand how this could happen among civilized people in the United States. When I attempted to discuss the problem with both sides in the room, the discussion always degenerated into name-calling and screaming."

"I wanted to understand both sides, so I interviewed some logging company owners and employees. And then I went to a prison to speak with a young black woman convicted of running a logging truck off a Forest Service road, causing a crash that killed two loggers in their truck, as they headed home from work."

"This woman had been in custody for a little more than a year when we spoke. During her trial, activists staged protests outside the court where she was tried and convicted. Those demonstrations continued for a short time near the prison after she was incarcerated. They started back up about the time I arrived, after a court denied her appeal. I couldn't understand how someone like this young woman, who had come from a normal, well-educated background, could do something so blatantly wrong. So, I met with the lady, and we talked for a long time."

"I asked her how she got involved in a movement to, 'protect Mother Earth,' as she described it. At first, her speech, talking points, use of phrases, and terminology belied the fact that her heritage was African American, and that she was from Portland."

"The young woman had become angry with how logging destroyed the environment, and that became her cause. I took notes and tried to understand how the process happened. She was a 23-year-old college student, majoring in economics, with a promising future ahead of her, now locked up in prison for murdering two people she thought she had never met."

"She told me that her viewpoints on life, and her purpose in the world changed once she attended college. She was excited and encouraged by two professors, who challenged her to become a new person and act on her ideas to force a positive change in the world."

"So she searched for her *cause*. She began going to rallies and protests and eventually met a Native American young man, who introduced her to an earth movement group committed to stopping logging in national forests. The group's stated mission was to protect old-growth trees and the endangered Northern Spotted Owl."

"The young lady learned the terms, the talking points, and even participated in chaining herself to trees with the group. She began blocking logging roads. She dressed like the movement members, wore their buttons and green striped bandanas, and helped them recruit more students. She still went to school, but economics was no longer significant. Her life became about stopping logging, using the most extreme of measures to force public attention to the forest."

"One night, she and her boyfriend set up a large mirror on a tight downhill curve on a specific logging road, so the mirror would be in the path of trucks driving out in the darkness. They waited until the right moment, when a truck was approaching. On her boyfriend's signal, she drove a van around the corner on the high side of the road with her bright lights on, just as the logging truck rounded the corner, and the driver saw both her lights and his own lights in the mirror, coming directly at him."

"The driver believed he was about to crash head-on into two oncoming vehicles, so he veered sharply off the road, rolled down the long, steep embankment, overturned several times, and crashed. The truck burst into flames, and the son burned to death as he screamed for help, unable to free himself from the cab. The died from his injuries at the scene."

Barbara Walcott grimaced and said, "Oh, my God, Bob, what an awful story! But, I don't see how..."

Bob interrupted, saying, "I haven't finished!"

A strange sadness came over Crawford. He continued. "At first, the young lady in prison didn't think she knew either one of the men she killed. After the arrests, her *boyfriend* made a deal with the prosecution and testified against her. As it turned out, she discovered that the younger man she killed had attended college with her, and was in one of her graduate-level economics courses. She knew him fairly well!"

"His father, the driver she killed, apart from owning a small family four-truck logging company, was a youth pastor at a local church, and had donated a great deal of money and his life to disadvantaged minority youth groups in the area. Also, he and his son were the primary care providers for his wife, who was dying, in the final stages of breast cancer."

"These men were great people. The father and husband was a pillar of his community. His son was following in Dad's footsteps. And this young, misguided, college student killed them both! And all for what?!"

Crawford was angry, just recalling the incident. Walcott sat further back in thought, trying to picture the people involved.

Bob Crawford said, "At trial, protestors outside the courthouse screamed and chanted, accusing the dead men of raping the earth and killing Spotted Owls. But inside, the prosecution pointed out that the logging contract the dead man had been assigned in this forest, was to remove bark beetle-damaged trees that were infecting healthy old-growth trees in the woods. These two men were helping the forest remain healthy."

"In prison, at the end of our conversation, when the young lady spoke about all she had learned since the incident, she finally broke down in tears and admitted she was remorseful. As I watched her sob, I began to see a young, frightened, college-educated woman, sorry for her mistakes, and once again concerned about her future. She told me she was learning to release her hatred to free her soul, and become herself again. I couldn't help but hug her and wish her the best of luck before I left. She asked me to come back again and talk to her, so I agreed. I asked her to call my office when she was ready."

"Six months later she wrote me a letter and asked for my help. So I met with her again. She told me that in researching the endangered Northern Spotted Owl, she learned that logging was not the only factor in decreased owl habitat and the bird's declining numbers. She read research that proved that as logging decreased in northwestern national forests, fuel built up in unmanaged woodlands. Fires in unmanaged timber had become unstoppable, partially due to the abundance of fuel. Millions of acres burned, destroying everything in the fire's path."

"Also, the young lady learned that another owl species, the Barred Owl, had interbred with, killed and forced out the smaller Northern Spotted Owl, slowly replacing the species in many areas."

Walcott asked, "So what did she want you to do, Bob?"

Crawford said, "She asked me to write her a letter of support for an idea she gave her lawyer about a reduced sentence. She discovered the concept in the prison law library."

Barbara scoffed, "Reduce her sentence based on what? She murdered two people!"

Bob Crawford smiled and said, "Based on the research that allowed her to discover these simple additional truths, and a legal principle. She told her lawyer that she believed the environmental group intentionally fed her partial truths, isolated facts with critical omissions, exaggerations, misinformation, and propaganda that inflamed her passions, while concealing the *whole* truth."

"She learned that legally, the earth movement group was equally responsible for the deaths of the men, once the leaders *encouraged* her to commit the criminal act *and* provided her with the plan! She wanted her lawyer to request those leaders to be arrested and tried as co-conspirators, so she could testify against them, just as her boyfriend had done at her trial."

Walcott said, "Good for her! What happened?"

Bob said, "Her lawyer liked the idea, and told her he would approach the prosecutor with the idea of a Rule 35 Motion."

Barbara sat forward on the couch, and said, "Okay, you'll have to explain that one. I'm English you know!" Barbara smiled.

Crawford said, "The idea is that a convicted person makes an agreement with the prosecutor to assist bringing other people to justice who were also responsible for the crime committed, and the prosecutor, in turn, files a motion to reduce the convicted person's sentence."

Crawford sat back, shook his head and smiled.

"Well, how did it all end, honey? What finally happened?"

"Unfortunately, nothing. I wrote the letter, as requested. The young lady's attorney went to the prosecutor, who researched the evidence and precedents and presented the offer to his boss, the County District Attorney. The DA called me and asked my opinion. We talked for about an hour. At the end of our talk, he told me the young lady's assertion was correct, and he could charge and prosecute the co-conspirators. Then he told me he wouldn't touch the case with a ten-foot pole."

Barbara asked, "But why, Bob, she had a good point, if her assertion was true."

"And that's precisely *one* point of the story, dear. What is true, what can be proven to be true, what truth people are willing to fight for, and the truth people are willing to accept, are not often all the same thing."

"When the District Attorney gave me *his* reason for not pursuing justice, he also told me that misrepresentation, exaggeration, omission, spin, and outright lies infest our society today to the extent that a person rarely finds a whole unaltered truth, even after an exhaustive search. And if the truth is finally located, uncertainty forces the finder to question its integrity. He also said, that unfortunately, by then, few people are willing to fight for a truth no one really wants to hear."

Crawford added, "And then he admitted that the entire logging and owl controversy was such an emotional issue for voters, he wouldn't shed light on the truth *if* he could prove it."

Walcott recoiled, saying, "But Bob, that's just wrong, especially coming from the elected legal guardian of the county!"

"Of course. I agree it was wrong, dear. But it's also the nature of our political world today, which is the second point of the story. Public opinion in our new world often demands that the loudest or most emotional voices must be perceived as truthful to some degree even when they're wrong. And if someone questions the integrity of their claims, those inquiring for truth are presumed to be ignorant, hating, *phobic-ist* bullies. And that is precisely what the prosecutor feared."

Crawford asked, "Can you imagine the political suicide the DA would commit if he investigated and prosecuted an environmental group for spreading propaganda and encouraging their followers to commit crimes against the publically perceived corporate villains that society believes pillage Mother Nature? Especially after the tree-sitter was killed."

"Tree sitter? Walcott looked surprised.

Crawford said, "Some activists would climb up into tall trees marked for harvest. They sat in the trees to prevent loggers from cutting them down. Several tree *sitters* were injured. At the time I spoke to the DA, one had just been killed, when a cut tree fell into him, causing the sitter to fall to his death. And before you ask, murder couldn't be proven, so the incident was ruled an accident. The timber company settled a lawsuit for damages brought by the sitter's family many years later. But, the incidents kept repeating, and the division between the groups grew wider."

Walcott leaned forward, looked down with a scowl, and asked, "Whatever happened to the young college student?"

"I don't know, dear. The prosecution proved premeditation when the young lady placed the mirror at the most dangerous location on the curve, waited for hours for the right opportunity to cause the crash, and drove around the dangerous curve with her high beams on, blocking the dead men's only possible escape route. And then, there was the strong testimony from her co-conspirator and other witnesses. Even those who encouraged her to commit the crime testified against her. She was serving two consecutive sentences of 20 years each for second-degree murder. I lost track of the young woman while she was still in prison, about fifteen years after we last spoke."

Barbara shook her head and asked, "What happened to the dead man's wife, the young man's mother?"

Crawford said softly, "She died about four months later at a local hospice. Some nurses, later interviewed by the small town paper, said she cried herself to sleep every night after her son and husband were killed, until she was no longer conscious."

"And logging and the spotted owl?"

"Much of it is still a controversy that is too emotional and divisive to talk about, dear."

"Bob, now I'm too invested in the history. I do want to know the end of the story, so please *enlighten* me."

"Okay, but as usual, the truth is not always on par with the general public perception. This subject has never been a popular topic." Crawford drew a ragged breath.

"Please, Bob!"

"Okay. It was true that many unethical companies maximized profits using aggressive logging techniques to harvest timber. Those companies destroyed watershed, damaged riparian areas, and decimated habitat for many species, not just the owl. And it's also true that many other timber companies practiced sustainable forest management, reforested as they cut, and improved the habitat for great numbers of trees, plants, and wildlife. The best companies even left many old-growth trees."

Barbara asked, "So how did you resolve the problem?"

"Not using our heads, yielding to the growing emotionally-charged public pressure, I'm afraid we didn't resolve it at all. Clubs and environmentalist groups sued and harassed both timber companies and the government. Eventually, both the U.S. Forest Service and Bureau of Land Management became riddled with kids out of college pursuing their lifelong ambition to stop logging, mining, and other legal uses of public lands they considered destructive. And, while in some cases, they were *correct* in their assessment, in many others, they were not."

"Activists and self-appointed guardians of Mother Nature packed committees and commissions, introduced skewed statistics, and eventually shut down more than 90% of logging on public lands. Thousands of people in every rural logging community lost their jobs and homes, as did people working in the service and retail sectors the logging families supported. Entire towns folded up overnight. It was horrible for a great many people for decades."

Barbara asked, "So, is it pretty much over now?"

Bob said, "Not really. Activists continued fighting about timber, grazing, mining, water rights, and finally camping and general public use. Hundreds of thousands of miles of roads on public lands were eventually barricaded, destroyed, posted and closed. It became an arrestable offense to drive off-road in many areas. More and more acres are still designated as National Monuments each year or pushed into The National Park system, where citizens have even less access to and use of their public lands. And when activists went after water rights, they dried up the farms and ranches that feed us, in favor of fish."

THE POLITICIANS

"So, Bob, what's the real downside of all the closures and restricted use?"

"Well, each year we've seen more and worse wildland forest fires decimating our unmanaged forests, killing all area wildlife, burning up old-growth and new-growth alike, and damaging riparian areas, sometimes beyond repair. We now import much of our timber from Canada or South America. A great deal of our fruits and vegetables come from places like Mexico. Some of our meat comes from Austrailia and New Zealand, at a much higher cost I might add."

"Even many small California wineries have been forced to shut down or be bought out by mass producers, due to the high cost, and limited supply of water."

"We only succeeded in sending our problems to third world countries that now supply our needs. Those problematic balls are bouncing in their courts now! Maybe they can solve the challenges using real science, negotiation, partnerships, and common sense."

"But, honey, all of this sounds so short-sighted on so many levels. Shouldn't the facts always lead us to the truth, even if we don't like the truth we discover?"

"Honey, we just settled the debate by agreeing that the facts and the truth are no longer always discoverable, relevant, or even desired by many people in our current world. That's one reason we're all in the mess we're in today, with pretty much everything! And, that story was just one example about one area of political division. There are thousands of incidents in every area of political division, all fueled by hate born of hidden agendas. The positions on both sides are riddled with misinformation, exaggeration, critical omissions, and outright lies. I'm afraid the world is in a real mess, sweetheart!"

✳✳✳

The weekend arrived two days later. Barbara and Bob enjoyed morning coffee as they snacked on fresh-cut fruit and bagels on the deck, overlooking the freshly mowed grounds. The resident ducks became particularly noisy on the large pond as an enormous flight of Canadian Geese set their wings to glide in for a landing.

Bob scoffed, "Here come the Canucks. Each year they fly over the border for free room and board!" He laughed at his joke, as Barbara rolled her eyes.

"They're entitled, Bob. They're allies from the Commonwealth," she quipped. They both chuckled.

The small Wood Duck family Barbara loved to watch numbered ten, counting both parents, although the father seemed frequently absent now. But he was present today, and Barbara studied both parents as they began to escort their ducklings toward the safety of their favorite cove. When a straggler duckling made a break for open water, the mother quacked until she got no response and then half-flew and half-swam to intercept the errant youngster.

As the mother splashed down in front of the duckling, it appeared startled and hurried to turn around. Mom escorted her little duck, scolding it all the way back to the family. At the same time, while the father took the lead with the other seven young ducks, he glanced back frequently, as if irritated at the offender, who now paddled even faster to catch up. Barbara giggled. Bob looked up from his phone at the disturbance in the water.

He asked, "Bringing the little tyke back to the flotilla?"

Barbara answered, "With some difficulty today. The young one seemed intent on asserting his or her will. Neither mom nor dad seems pleased with the challenge!"

Bob mused aloud, "Typically, that problem will escalate until the little one is grown and gone from home!" Bob smiled, recalling memories of his young children asserting their wills.

While Bob and Barbara chatted and enjoyed watching ducks, further south at the newly acquired estate in North Carolina, Pete's cell phone rang. He looked at the display, but didn't recognize the number and let the phone call go to message. A minute later Pete listened to the voice message and heard Tasha's voice, asking him to return her call. He quickly carried his phone and coffee to the back deck, where he sat alone in a new wooden rocker, with his feet up on a covered ottoman. Tasha answered on the fifth ring.

"Pete, hello, how are you?"

"Fine, Tasha, I'm fine. Thanks for calling to give me your new number. It's good to hear your voice and know that you're safe. Are you settled in there with your mom, and all calmed down from the incident?"

There was silence on the phone.

Pete asked, "Are you alright? Are you happier, away from the investigation?"

Tasha answered, "Oh, Pete, I don't know. I sleep better at night knowing North Korean killers aren't coming for me. But I miss you and wonder if I made the right decision. I can't seem to be happy and content there with you or here without you. I don't know what to do with myself, alone. I wondered how you felt. What do *you* want, Pete?"

Pete paused, and collected his thoughts, his fears, and his feelings.

He finally said, "Tasha, what I want most is for you to be happy with yourself, and for me to be happy in the life I have left. You know, after you left, I thought back to all the times, before and after Claire died, that worry overcame you. I always thought that someday my resolve to be content with what I have would rub off on you. I hoped you'd grow to be content with your life and appreciate every day you draw breath. But you were never content before we became a couple, and it only got worse afterward."

Pete sighed and admitted, "I don't know if you can *be* happy, Tasha. A person can't buy happiness, because there's always more or newer or bigger or better. A person can't find it in someone else, because no one can get inside us and make us feel better about ourselves. Happiness has to start on the inside, with each of us. And I've discovered that in you, what I've always known and refused to believe, was true. You won't allow yourself to feel happiness and contentment. And don't take that wrong. You can be happy with a distraction that lasts for an hour or even a day, just not happy and content day after day, with life."

Tasha said, "I'm sorry you feel that way, Pete. I didn't realize I was so awful!" She began to cry.

Pete drew in a deep breath and released it slowly. He said softly, "That's not what I said, and you know that isn't what I meant. We've talked about this so many times. It's just that we can't relax and enjoy life together. You always have to be doing something, cleaning, re-organizing, going somewhere, or planning the next purchase to make the house or office even better than it already is. You struggle to make life perfect, never enjoying the imperfections in life that are both the reality, and the attraction."

"Tasha, it's okay if there's a scratch on the office desk or a small dent in the car. I don't need another new shirt I won't wear. I'd rather wear my favorite slightly-faded shirt, work on my scratched desk, and ride around in my old dented car, enjoying the day. But you can't do that. You can't just let life happen and be happy. And it's not because you're bad or awful. You aren't satisfied with who *you* are, or who anyone else is. You're not content with yourself or with life!"

Pete paused, frustrated at repeating a conversation spoken many times in the past. When there was no response, he said, "The bottom line is what we've admitted a dozen times before. We love each other, but we make each other miserable, and we shouldn't be together. That's why you left!"

Pete again paused for a response. There was none. Suddenly he heard a doorbell chime and a door open. Tasha screamed, and Pete overheard quick footsteps, voices and a loud thump. He heard rough dragging sounds followed by more rapid steps and a pop, like the sound of a silenced revolver.

Pete called out to Tasha several times before the phone went dead. He ran back inside to notify his team and call the police.

In Virginia, Bob and Barbara sat discussing the Wood Duck's habitat. Barbara commented, "I read that their proper name is Carolina Duck," as her cell phone vibrated. She read the display and raised it for Vice President Crawford to see. It read, "Russian Deputy Minister of Defense." Bob Crawford nodded.

Barbara Walcott answered cheerfully. "Good morning, Sergej! You're calling bright and early. Is everything alright?" She hit speaker on the phone.

"I hope you will forgive my early call, there in Virginia, Madam Home Secretary, but I fear you will soon discover a development you will not appreciate, and I must apologize in earnest for the problem before it happens."

"Sergej, I am even more impressed than before," Walcott said flirtatiously, trying to use her feminine wiles to disarm the Russian.

"Now, you predict the problems and warn me *before* they happen! Would this be another problem you plan to solve before you create it?"

In a somber tone overlaid with an unusually thick Russian accent, Sergej said, "This problem was an unforeseen development, but my solution will both impress and convince you, even more, to help me with my last request, my friend!"

"Please, go on," Walcott said coyly.

"Excuse the delay, but I am receiving my confirmation now. Yes, ah, there is the picture of the lady and the message. So, to continue, you will soon learn that *possibly* one of your cypher team's people has gone missing."

There was silence as Barbara looked at Bob. Crawford shrugged his shoulders indicating he had received no information from Walter or Bryan about any problem with the team.

"Sergej, what have you done?" Barbara attempted to sound officially outraged without sounding demanding. Her voice no longer dripped seductive, feminine tones.

Sergej said unapologetically, "Not me this time, Barbara. No, this was my Chinese comrades. With the Iranians and the North Koreans, they hacked into the American's Operation Cobalt Eagle Eye system and discovered an email from a Tasha McKnight to her mother about a Committee cipher."

Barbara interrupted. "Sergej, you're losing me. I'm not familiar with the person or the American system you mentioned."

Sergej said, "Da, my apologies, my friend. I forget sometimes that we spy on the Americans and learn more than you British learn from being their ally *and* spying on them!"

Sergej laughed loudly, irritating both Walcott and Crawford as they sat silent. Neither commented.

Sergej continued, saying, "So, I will tell you that this Operation Cobalt Eagle Eye is a cyber spy network our American friends built in Canada that collects data from all phone calls, text messages and emails sent through all servers in North America. Their very impressive system searches for keywords like terrorist, bomb, dynamite, Jihad, radical, attack, and so on. Algorithms locate these words, scan the text of the conversation for possible threats and send suspicious data to an investigator, who reviews it and assigns it a threat level for further consideration. It's a good system! We use something very much like this one."

Barbara asked, "Sergej, are you pulling my leg? If you're telling me the truth, I have two more questions. If this system is so good, how did the Chinese team use it so easily? Also, if it belongs to the Americans, why would they build it in Canada?"

Sergej said, "Ah, excuse me again. I was distracted. This lady Tasha is so pretty, and a blond! So, first, I would love to pull on your beautiful legs sometimes, my friend Barbara! But I am not pulling one of them now!" Sergej loudly sipped his vodka and then laughed uproariously, as Crawford silently fumed.

When Barbara made no flirtatious comment in return, Sergej cleared his throat and continued. "Our Chinese comrades stole the software from its developer, in the American Silicon Valley. The Chinese, Iranian and North Korean computer specialists worked hard for three long years to steal the software. Once they had the technology, it took them more than six months to hack into and search the Cobalt system."

"Last week they searched to find the keywords 'committee' and 'cipher' together in the same emails or texts. They found this Tasha's email to her mother, saying she was coming to her mother's house in California to visit because she couldn't work on the committee cipher any longer. So, they sent a team to take her from her mother."

"Sergej, if this is all about to happen, shouldn't I ask you to speak with Vice President Crawford? He might perceive this as a great favor, coming from you directly. He could have his people prevent a kidnapping on American soil!"

Crawford nodded, encouraging Barbara Walcott to continue as he listened, seated next to her on the deck.

Sergej boasted, "No need, my friend. As in our past, I have already solved this problem for you both, just as I did before. My team has taken the lady and neutralized the Chinese plan. Unfortunately, there were losses."

Walcott asked, "Losses for the enemy team?"

"Yes, of course. Another North Korean team is now missing…so sad."

Sergej added, "But the loss for the Americans is the pretty lady's mother. She would have been a problem for everyone."

"And this lady, Tasha?" Walcott looked at Crawford, who suddenly seemed nervous.

"We have her, of course, and will keep her safe until you have our cipher and we can all be happier and less worried about all these small details!"

There was silence. Barbara maneuvered to buy more time to think.

Walcott asked, "Now Sergej, it's not like you to avoid a question! So, can you explain why the Americans would build a spy system in Canada?"

"My apology, Barbara. I hesitate to embarrass your friend, the Vice President. You see, the U.S. criminal justice system and congressional oversite committees have no jurisdiction in foreign countries. The American spies don't have to admit what they are doing in Canada, and your Canadian colleagues get free information about terrorist activities in their country. The Americans even warned *us* once about a planned terror event in Moscow. They discovered the plot using their Cobalt system. But, Barbara, I think you tease me again. You must know all of this!"

The crafty Home Secretary said, "Sergej, my friend, I have one more question. Since the Chinese are your allies and supply you with the information they find in the system, why would you tell me now, knowing I will warn my American allies? The Americans will figure out a way to stop the Chinese hacker team. It seems you are helping to stop the flow of information that benefits Mother Russia!"

As if on cue, Sergej's military cell phone suddenly sounded and played a ringtone of the first portion of the Russian national anthem from where it sat on his desk.

Sergej said, "Ah, I am out of time, my friend. I must report to my superiors. But a quick answer is…tell the Americans they now owe me a favor! A big one! We will talk later, Barbara. Udachi!" Sergej ended the call.

Crawford and Walcott sat in silence as the geese honked and ducks swam and flew to a safe distance from the boisterous newcomers. Barbara and Bob struggled to answer all the questions that sped through their collective thoughts.

Finally, Barbara asked, "What do you think we should do first, Bob?"

Crawford said resolutely, "First, I think I want to shove a fist full of 'udachi' down that cocky Russian's throat, my dear! And then, I need to make some phone calls to various directors of intelligence."

✳✳✳

Pete paced and nervously rechecked his watch after he made a call to the police department in the small West Coast town where Tasha had gone to stay at her mother's home. Twenty-four minutes after receiving the welfare check request, responding police units entered Marlene McKnight's modest home, through the unlocked front door.

The police officers found everything neat and tidy, except Marlene, who sat slumped over, dead in her rocking chair. Oozing blood from the small caliber bullet hole in her forehead had stopped flowing and already begun to dry on the 83-year-old lady's face and blouse. There was no bullet exit hole on the back of Marlene's head, and less than a pint of blood had soaked her shirt and drained down to her lap, seeping under the blanket that covered her legs. It appeared she had died instantly.

Police were unable to locate Tasha in their subsequent search of the home and neighborhood. Residents recalled seeing two white electrical service company vans parked on the street in front of the residence, but no one remembered observing anything unusual. Patrol officers sealed off the small home, as they awaited the responding forensic evidence team, detectives, and the coroner.

A full 48 hours later, detectives had generated no leads in the case, and no one had yet reported a single tip to the local tip line. The investigation grew cold. No motive or accompanying crime had been discovered. When detectives began to focus on the only possible lead in the case, the person who called to report the disturbance, Pete Harrington, they just as quickly received assurance from FBI SAC Bryan Holland, that Harrington had an ironclad alibi.

Pete had reportedly been at work on the East Coast at the time of the murder and possible kidnapping, witnessed by another FBI employee, Helena Thomas. Within an hour Thomas had written and emailed a formal statement to that effect to the lead investigator on the McKnight case. Both the murder and the possible kidnapping were unofficially filed as cold cases by the third day, even as investigators occasionally continued to search for clues, conduct neighborhood canvasses, and advertise on television and social media. Anonymous donations to establish a reward for information totaled more than three million dollars by the fourth day, and still produced no credible calls.

During the same period, both Bryan Holland and his team, and Pete and his team had failed to locate any information about Tasha. No one had received a ransom demand. It was as if she had vanished from the face of the earth.

As a last resort, Walter reached out to his lifelong friend, Vice President Bob Crawford, and left a voicemail requesting that Crawford call him with any news about Tasha. Ten hours later, Bob Crawford had not returned his friend's desperate call.

Crawford stood on the tarmac at the Charlottesville-Albemarle Airport. Crawford's Secret Service detail and cars positioned themselves a respectable distance from the private jet that would take British Home Secretary Barbara Walcott on the first leg of her journey toward home. Barbara had scheduled multiple meetings en route back to the United Kingdom, one of which was in Nova Scotia, between Walcott and her French counterpart.

Walcott planned to inquire about France's plans to import more oil, goods, and services from Iran, a known sponsor of Hezbollah and other terrorist groups. World governments knew that Iran supported Islamic Jihad, the Popular Front for the Liberation of Palestine – General Command, Houthis in Yemen, and many other Islamic extremist organizations.

Even after the ill-conceived Iranian nuclear deal, co-approved by the Europeans, the magnitude of France's planned support and investment in the known terrorist state had been deemed unwise by British Intelligence. The new, expanded French plan with Iran made the situation even worse.

Moreover, Walcott had received a recent report that Iran had conspired with Chinese radicals and agents of the fundamental Socialist Movement in France, to execute formidable cyberterrorism attacks on European and American targets. These reports were Top Secret, and only recently distributed to a handful of people in Great Britain. And Barbara Walcott had been the first person to read the dossier.

From her position as British Home Secretary, Barbara Walcott was the perfect diplomat to be the secret head of Britain's Secret Intelligence Service, MI6, of which she had been an agent for most of her adult life. She was literally hiding in plain sight as she interacted with politicians on the world stage.

Vice President Bob Crawford, Barbara's fiancé, was one of a handful of people in the world who knew Barbara headed the spy agency. But even he wasn't aware that Barbara planned to attend a secret shadow meeting with the Russian Deputy Minister of Defense, in Nova Scotia, after she met with the French entourage. Barbara wanted a chance at interviewing Sergej in person, and alone. She had already ordered all she needed to complete her elaborate plan.

Although Sergej knew Barbara by her reputation as a skilled negotiator with a cunning personality and a quick wit, he didn't realize that she was one of the U.K.'s most experienced and successful interviewers. The Russian who planned to interview Barbara Walcott would be thoroughly unprepared to be questioned and conquered in the little time they would spend together. Barbara Walcott could be brutal.

But today, on the Virginia airport tarmac, buffeted by increasing wind gusts and an off-season chill that cut to the bone, Barbara hugged her fiancé, Vice President Bob Crawford. She held him for a long time, and then kissed him on the cheek.

She said, "You be very careful with everything on your plate here, my love. And remember, we *will* meet soon next month. I'll make sure this works. We can't mess *us* up, now that we've finally taken steps to be together. And please, let me know what you plan to do about the Tasha affair. I promise to help if I can. I'll do some quick digging through my sources."

Crawford smiled as he said, "You know, love, as tough as I always imagined I was, I think, in many ways, you're even tougher. With my boss being who he is in The Committee, I have to move so carefully to help Walter find Tasha that I'm useless. I feel my hands tied behind my back."

Bob said, "And I can't risk putting the Beckett Cypher in jeopardy by making a wrong move. But, through my plan with the North Koreans, I'm ultimately responsible for the Iranians and Chinese finding Tasha and leading the Russians to her. If I didn't know better, I'd think this was all your new best friend Sergej's, plan all along. He either used me or my error, and I'd like to kick his hairy Russian ass for it…but I can't, at least not right now!"

Walcott leaned in and kissed Crawford deeply on the lips. She lingered longer than usual with her kiss, and then whispered, "Double crosses and playing both our enemies and our friends are so common in our business, we must always assume it will happen. It's as much my fault for not seeing it coming as it was yours. And the plan was half mine. You hang in there, my love, and together we *will* get Tasha McKnight back for your friend!"

She kissed Bob Crawford one more time, placed her arm on his, squeezed it, smiled, and said, "I need to go now, love. I'll call you soon."

As she began to walk toward the plane, Crawford called out, "So what did you decide about the important question, dear?"

Barbara Walcott turned and asked, "Which one, Bob?"

"What are you going to tell your aggressive British tabloids when they notice the new ring on your left hand?"

Walcott grinned and said, "I'm going to tell them I met a wonderful man I plan to marry the day *after* I leave office. And on that day, *if* they're still interested, I'll tell them his name!" She smiled and chuckled as she walked to the plane.

As Barbara Walcott winged her way toward Nova Scotia, a pretty blond assistant approached her carrying a briefcase and a small, rolling carry-on bag. The young lady placed both on a seat next to Barbara. Barbara opened the black metal briefcase first and found multiple files and a little red pouch. She flipped through the data and confirmed all the reading material she had ordered was present.

The dossiers included a lengthy treatise on Sergej Petrov, and the identities and synopsis on the entourage and security officers who would accompany him to the site. Barbara quickly scanned the profiles on the French contingent and found everything to be correct.

Barbara next opened the suitcase containing all the specialty items and garments she had earlier requested, which included a pair of 3½-inch red high-heeled sandals.

Barbara smiled and murmured, "Sergej, I'll make you feel like the rock your namesake suggests. And when I finish with you, Sergej 'The Rock' Petrov, you won't remember a thing!"

Barbara's aid smiled and sat beside her. She asked, "How do you want to handle it, ma'am?"

Barbara said, "Let's keep it simple. He has the vodka spiked with their new truth and date-rape drug. We have the same bottle, spiked with our more effective interrogation enhancing truth serum and sexual stimulant. He'll send the bottle to my room, with chocolate and a note requesting a private visit after our dinner meeting. You'll be in the adjoining room with your team."

"On my way back from dinner, I'll text you the signal. You switch bottles. I'll have the red velvet bag on the nightstand on your side of the bed. Petrov will drink the vodka. I'll take the antidote before, at dinner. I'll start the interrogation. When I'm ready, I'll get him warmed up for you."

"When Sergej's ready and submissive, I'll tell him I have a blond surprise. I'll describe you. He loves blonds. When I text, you come in and play your part. Use the condom just as we planned. He'll wake up the next morning. We'll all be gone. He'll be covered in red lipstick and have two pairs of panties to add to his private collection. But he won't remember a thing! And we'll have everything we need."

Walcott's assistant was a pretty, late-twenties, classy-looking young lady with long, straight blond hair, medium size breasts, deep blue eyes, and long legs, nearly as perfectly curved as Walcott's.

The young woman smiled, and asked, "And his security forces?"

Barbara smiled. "Sergej's method of seduction is to drug women, using a combination of stimulant dissolved in alcohol that also contains a powerful date rape drug. Our intelligence reveals that this drug removes inhibitions, excites desire and blocks long-term memory. The drugs never affect Segej because he takes the antidote before the session begins. Sergej never allows his security forces to witness his abuses on women. We'll have complete privacy. And by the way, his antidote doesn't work on our drugs!"

The young lady admitted, "I've never used our drugs on someone else before, other than in training."

Barbara took her assistant by the hand, and said, "We're dealing with one man on a quest to sexually abuse and conquer as many pretty women as possible before he dies. His ego has already defeated him. We have all the advantage we need. He loves my legs, your blond hair, and the thought of controlling and abusing both of us at the same time. And best of all, once you fit him with our condom, our combined drugs will render him helpless. The hypnotic will slowly put him to sleep after we finish our interrogation. No worries, agent. Just slide the condom on when I nod. Then kiss him, when I stop, and sixty seconds later, he'll be ours."

Walcott added, "And if he refuses the condom, get up to leave. Tell him you're married and trying to have a baby. He wants no long-term DNA evidence."

The young agent smiled, stood up, tugged her sweater down sharply, and said, "Yes ma'am. I've got it!" She began to walk back to the rear of the airplane.

Barbara Walcott said, "Deidre, don't forget, this mission is about far more than one kidnapped woman. We need specific information we know he has on The Committee and Russia's plan to steal the cypher. And we need to know where his true loyalties lie as we fight The Committee, with him as an ally. We have a good chance to accomplish everything in one short assignment!"

Deidre had stopped and turned to meet Barbara Walcott's eyes. She answered, "Yes ma'am, I completely understand. You can count on me. I'll be ready!" She smiled, turned back and continued walking with purpose in her step.

In North Carolina, the cypher team prepared for their morning briefing. Their plan proposed a simultaneous cyber attack on both The Committee's California Center for Information Extraction and their Yucca Mountain Facility. The Beckett Cypher had retrieved and organized all information in the flash drives recovered from Patrick Beckett and Kent Murray.

Char, Jesse, Tracy, Sam, Angie, Pete, and Kate had organized a massive flow chart that spanned three large walls in the large great room that surrounded the workstations. Team members had studied the conspiracy map for several days as they memorized people, crimes, schemes, and corruption Patrick and Kent's cases had revealed.

But all that information was now fifteen years old. The new cyber attacks would fill in the gap of the last decade and a half, and disclose to what degree The Committee had spread its tentacles.

Bob Crawford had still not returned Walter's call. Walter finally left the team, traveling west to attend to pressing corporate business. Walter departed with Juanita, leaving Pete in North Carolina, to be on hand for Tasha's potential rescue.

The team speculated that Tasha must have been kidnapped by either The Committee, another North Korean cell, or a group from an enemy or rogue nation. The Beckett Cypher Artificial Intelligence Spy System's first mission would be to locate any information available about Tasha stored within Committee servers.

Pete paced back and forth nervously, and finally sat between Heath and Shane, gaining some comfort being so close to his boys.

Heath placed a hand on Pete's shoulder, and said, "We'll find her, Pete," as Hunter began the briefing. Heath started to tear up just talking about Tasha. Further down the table, Char, Kate, and Angie all watched the three men intently.

Hunter described in layman's terms that the Artifical Intelligence Spy System would locate, neutralize and bypass any cybersecurity barrier in place at the government facility in North Carolina. AISS would then identify the servers containing comingled data from both government and social media contractors, and begin searching for any relevant information.

Next, the spy system would launch the attack on the Center for Information Extraction, learn what cybersecurity system was in place there, and quickly identify that barrier to the team. Hunter believed a similar, if not identical, cyber barrier would be in place at Yucca Mountain. Within seconds of receiving cybersecurity intel, they would launch the second attack on Yucca Mountain.

Helena described the timing sequence. The cypher team estimated that all three attacks would be initiated within eight minutes of each other, and predicted it would take approximately fourteen minutes after initial penetration of the CIE to obtain and return any information on Tasha. They expected an additional 56 minutes to search all government servers in the North Carolina facility and send back all information located. Yucca Mountain servers were an unknown, but Helena felt they could estimate, conservatively, no more than three hours to search and report any information on Tasha found at the gigantic site.

Helena advised the group that the cypher team decided they would leave AISS working in all three locations, retrieving all information found within the protocol. They would reevaluate changing the procedure based on the type and amount of data returned in the first

24 hours. Helena also explained that the team had created the highest internet speed possible to upload and download material at the new North Carolina estate.

She reminded everyone that the AISS would be working from the sophisticated government facility, capable of much faster internet speed. Estate servers would be a storage facility for all information AISS, and the team deemed relevant. Helena believed there were now enough high capacity servers on-site at the estate to handle the incoming material. Twelve servers now occupied most of the home's extensive study.

Next, Joshua stood and displayed a digital chart on the smart TV screen hanging from the ceiling that itemized AISS's mission. Listed in order of priority were: Tasha McKnight's Location; Committee Organizational Chart; Committee Member Files; Primary Objective Plan; Primary Directive Plan; Committee Timeline; Committee Intel Files; Crime and Corruption Files; Indoctrination Technique.

Joshua looked around the room at blank faces. No one seemed impressed with the plan as stated. He glanced at his cypher teammates. Hunter nodded, urging Joshua to explain in greater detail.

Joshua said, "It doesn't look like much, I guess. But based on the size of case files documented by the Kent Murray and Patrick Beckett teams in The Case, and extrapolating over the last fifteen years, we should find many times more data than those gentlemen discovered, simply due to time. Now, considering the improvements in computers, cell phones, emails, texts, digital material storage, and speed of communication, it becomes impossible to estimate the massive accumulation of data we'll discover."

No one moved or asked a question.

Joshua added, "We know the files must have grown to the point that the material is beyond our capabilities to accurately estimate. We won't have enough room in servers here to store everything. So, once again, remember, we plan to hide all our data and our AISS inside the much larger and more sophisticated secure government and social media system. We've directed AISS to evaluate and send us only what it believes most important. We can change informational directives and protocols when we see how big the fish is, as we haul it to the surface, like changing the size of the net!" Joshua smiled, proud of his comparison.

Joshua looked from Pete to Heath to Shane to Kate, and detected no emotion.

He asked, "Shane, have we missed something or done something wrong, that's disappointed you?"

Shane said, "Oh, sorry, not at all. I was trying to figure out how we begin to digest this monstrous investigation. I took an hour to read and understand the *abbreviated version* of one scheme The Committee perpetrated about twenty years ago on the State of California. If there are hundreds of thousands of players and thousands of cases, how in the world is all this even understandable? I mean, the flow chart for the criminals and schemes could cover a football field!"

Tracy said, "I'll try to explain that. Think of the Beckett Cypher AISS as a system so fast that it reads and understands information a million times faster than the average human speed reader. Now imagine we have a million speed readers performing at AISS's level, each with total-recall!"

"One million photographic and eidetic memories, with the ability to instantly recall any one of the names, places, circumstances or images detected in the millions of files they read. Those million perfect workers are our army of organizers. When they send us the file, keywords in blue are links allowing us to drill down further, should we choose, to further identify a person, crime, plot, scheme, etc. But the synopsis itself is so perfectly organized, AISS could explain what we have just told you at this forty minute briefing in less than a minute, using visual, auditory and textual communication. And it would do a better job in the explanation."

The non-techies in the briefing began to comprehend the idea.

Hunter said, "We start by giving AISS guidelines on what we're looking to find. AISS finds and organizes the data, sends it to us perfectly formatted, and waits for a response. We can modify what's important or how the system reports the information at any time. But the best part is, we're talking to a super-genius. The system learns so fast it can predict what we want to know and tell us before we ask!"

Shane said, "This I have to see to believe."

The cypher teammates all smiled.

Joshua said, "AISS wanted to offer a very basic display of her ability!"

Heath asked with a smile, "*Her* ability?"

Hunter said, "AISS created a voice to facilitate instant communication with humans. She selected a blend of the voices she monitored in Oregon at the estate as we all finalized her mission. AISS also learned about our personalities, monitored our habits, sleep patterns, and conversation. She studied our lives over several weeks. When she suggested a voice to the cypher team, AISS also chose to pronounce her name, the acronym for the Beckett Cypher Artificial Intelligence Spy System, as *BaCayse*. And then she made her first joke, and told us that while BaCayse will always be the smartest girl in the room, she is far from the prettiest!"

The entire cypher team burst into laughter.

Hunter bragged, "She is quite the character!"

The rest of the group all smiled.

Kate asked, "So what is this display of her abilities?"

Helena answered, "BaCayse wants you all to take a test where she predicts your answers to three questions. To avoid embarrassment, she wants you to write down the answer to her questions on a paper only you see, so you will be the only person to judge if she is correct. At the end of the exercise, each of you will receive her answers to your questions in a text message. The only caveat is you must answer each question truthfully. BaCayse knows this demonstration is necessary so that each of you learns to trust her to make difficult decisions for our team. If you agree, please take out your papers."

Members positioned paper and pens, and when they were once all settled at the table, Helena asked, "BaCayse, are you ready?"

A sweet angelic voice broadcasting through surround sound speakers said, "I am ready to begin, Helena. I thank all of you for allowing me to demonstrate little things I have learned about each of you in the short time we've begun to know each other. Please clear your minds, close your eyes, take a deep breath and release it."

She paused, and said, "Other than your significant other, please indicate a person you know and find most sexually attractive, next to the number one." Everyone followed the instruction.

BaCayse said, "Please write down your favorite dessert dish, next to number two."

The AISS paused a moment, and then said, "Lastly, please write down what you would change about yourself if any change were possible, next to number three."

At the precise second the last person in the briefing finished writing their answer all the phones beeped receipt of their individual text messages. Each person checked their answers. There was one blank in the room on Helena's text, next to answer one, as she had not written down any name. Her phone sounded, and she saw a message from BaCayse.

It read, "Helena, you are very shy and were afraid to write Joshua's name next to answer number one. You find him attractive, intelligent, and incredibly kind. You're sexually attracted to him, but in love with Bryan Holland."

Helena uttered a gasp.

Kate's text sounded next. Her message read, "Kate, you believe your breasts are too large, but you also realize that of all your body parts, Shane especially loves your breasts. He's asked you to never change anything about your body. You wrote down changing the color of your hair to black. You planned to surprise Shane with a new woman look at week-long getaway when the case is over. But we both know that's not the correct answer!"

Kate smiled, and said, "Very clever lady!"

One by one, BaCayse texted and advised everyone in the room something personal they had not written on their answer sheet, even if all their answers were truthful.

At the end of less than a minute, Pete asked, "How is this possible?"

Joshua proudly explained, "AISS has been with us for weeks, learning about each one of us as an individual, all of us as a team, and each of us as we relate to the other individuals within the organization."

"She has become our friend and mentor, measuring and recording all of our characteristics and preferences at the same time. She knows us better than we can comprehend, as we have all just learned during this briefing. For example, in a recent test, she told us that Angie has been craving chocolate cream pie and enjoys kissing Heath's ears and neck."

Joshua laughed and said, "Sorry, Angie, but that was pretty mild. AISS knows so much we had to tell her to keep the very personal data to herself unless we have an *informational emergency*."

Angie snickered, and said, "Thank you," as Heath blushed and smiled.

Char made a mental note that Heath enjoys having his neck and ears kissed.

Joshua added, "One reason we wanted to demonstrate our system's power and speed was so all of you would trust her to make course correction decisions. As we send her in hostile environments, we believe she should be allowed to make choices she feels necessary, based on her abilities. We need to give her some freedoms from our strict protocols."

Shane asked, "Can you give us an example of how that might work?"

Helena responded, "We have a straightforward example that makes our meaning crystal clear. Suppose we ask BaCayse to locate a specific terrorist in North America, and during the search, she discovers a terrorist plot to blow up a plane, scheduled to take place the following day. We believe that an imminent threat to human life should allow BaCayse to add that investigation to her mission parameter."

Shane said, "That's straightforward. Why do we have to approve this protocol?"

After a pause in the room, Hunter said, "I think it best to use the analogy that we are sending the world's greatest detective out on a mission to find one crime. Along the way, she'll recognize, intervene to stop, and report thousands of crimes, delaying the initial mission by seconds or even minutes. We all know what consequences even the slightest delay may bring. In this example, does the welfare of many people take precedence over just one, or a few?"

Tracy said, "You see the dilemma. There is no way AISS can always deliver totally satisfactory outcomes. So, we're asking the team to trust her to make decisions she judges best with what she knows at the time, keeping her mission and protocols in place as guidelines…just like we do!"

Pete asked abruptly, "Is this about Tasha?"

Hunter drew in a nervous breath and released it slowly.

He asked, "To expand the example for today's assignment, if BaCayse is running down leads on Tasha's location, and discovers an imminent terrorist bombing that could claim dozens of lives, would you want her to use her judgment to stop the terror incident and send us the information of what she had found? Or should she be bound to her primary mission for the day?"

Before Pete could answer, Joshua added, "We're asking because these are the types of situations she will face as soon as we begin."

Pete looked around the room and nodded to Shane.

Shane said, "Let's trust her and begin. As you said, if we need to make course corrections, we can, as we go through the process."

Hunter said, "Then if you are all ready to begin, and the missions are a 'go,' we're prepared to send BaCayse on her first mission." The team all nodded.

Joshua said, "BaCayse, please begin."

The AISS answered, "Thank you, Joshua. I will be speaking with you shortly. I have already penetrated the North Carolina facility."

✳✳✳

The North Carolina team returned from a break. Pete carried his fourth cup of morning coffee, twice his regular allotment. He felt anxious and guilty. He couldn't stop thinking that had he not rejected Tasha, she would not have left the compound and consequently, would not have been kidnapped. And although the words he had spoken were right, the time wasn't right for someone he loved to hear them. He wanted a do-over. But even as Pete struggled with his emotions, he knew he would never be able to fix this with Tasha. Tasha's love was now lost to him forever. Worse, maybe, Pete feared he had lost a valued friend.

It had been nearly nine minutes when BaCayse said, "I have a report on Tasha. A Russian military squad took her to a safe house in California. From there she was placed in a cargo crate and loaded on a semi. I am searching for information on the truck. The Russian Minister of Defense, Sergej Petrov, coordinated the plan. He is also a sixth tier

Committee member, but has *not* notified the Committee about Tasha. Initial information reveals Sergej Petrov is loyal to Russia and its President. He has recently spoken with a variety of military officials and politicians. I have no more information on Tasha at this time."

AISS continued, "I stored all relevant files removed from The Committee's California Center for Information Extraction within the Bradenton Meadows site, and have sent you the most important files. I am currently transferring Yucca Mountain files. I will send you the first of those files in fifteen minutes."

Pete looked nervously at Hunter.

Hunter said, "Pete, she gives us all pertinent information. She knows and understands her priorities, and will work harder and faster than an army of investigators. She will find Tasha."

Pete got up and began to pace and think. Twenty minutes later he gave up, failing to come up with any constructive action to help find Tasha. Kate convinced Pete to occupy some time. They walked with Char to the helicopter. Char completed the checklist and started the chopper. Kate held a large, partially unfolded aerial map to help orient Pete to the surrounding area. Pete sat in the second row and donned headphones with speakers so the trio could talk during the ride.

Char flew for an hour and twenty minutes. She covered the state route corridors, local towns and larger metro areas visible from 8,000 feet above sea level. She also provided Kate with valuable flying time, building on Jesse's first flight lesson.

Pete managed to loosen up, and became less preoccupied as he studied the estate layout and oriented the new location to points of interest. By the time they returned to the briefing area, he was calm enough to work on the investigation while he worried about Tasha.

By 5:00 P.M., BaCayse had penetrated Russian military servers searching for additional information about Tasha and discovered Petrov's plan. BaCayse's voice came across the briefing room speakers.

BaCayse said, "Pete, I know Tasha's destination and Petrov's plan."

Pete said, "I'll get the others in the kitchen and be right back."

A moment later Pete said, "Okay, we're all present. Please, continue."

In her sweet angelic voice, BaCayse said, "A six-man Russian military squad disguised as a contractor team is escorting Tasha and a shipment of hydro-electric pumps across the border into Mexico. They plan to hold Tasha in a safe house until they transport her to Cuba, where the Cuban dictator will house her in a cell. The cell is surprisingly quite elegant, and features a king-sized bed. Petrov plans to personally *interview* Tasha in one week. The motivation for this plan is to force Barbara Walcott, the British Home Secretary and top-secret head of MI6, to pressure the United States into backing their new alliance with Germany, regarding oil shipments."

BaCayse quickly added, "The depth of the plan is much more complicated, however. It involves trade and military alliances with many former USSR block members, including some NATO members. The plan calls for Walcott to use her influence within the United States and Europe to help sell the alliance."

Shane asked, "BaCayse, do the Russians know that Walcott is the head of MI6?"

BaCayse answered calmly, "No, Shane. Petrov has only speculated the Home Secretary is aware of most MI6 activity. He mentioned her in communications so frequently that I felt it best to check myself. I penetrated the British intelligence dark servers to learn her roles."

Pete asked, "Where is Walcott now, BaCayse?"

"She is having dinner with Petrov in Nova Scotia. She flew there earlier today from an airport near Vice President Crawford's home in Virginia. She has been in Virginia with the Vice President for the past week."

There was silence in the room. Char stood up and walked to Kate's seat. She whispered, "I think we've been played! We need to meet and calculate a strategy."

BaCayse commented, "I think Miss Walcott's motivations with Mr. Petrov may indeed be questionable, Char. But she has planned to leave for England a few hours after their dinner meeting. Her loyalties, however, appear to be to England and Vice President Crawford. I am checking further. On another matter, I sent our team an itemized list of crimes I discovered with suggested solutions."

As the Beckett team in North Carolina speculated and strategized, Petrov and Walcott were close to finishing their dinner in Nova Scotia. Walcott felt tired after the 4-hour flight and a thirty-minute meeting with the French contingent. She no longer thrilled at the thought of travel as she had when she was twenty years younger. Now, she longed to be on the deck watching the ducks with Bob Crawford, sipping ice-cold sweet tea.

Instead, she was away from her new home, pretending to hang on every word Petrov droned on about meaningless subjects. After another glass of red wine and fifteen minutes of boredom, Barbara Walcott was ready. More importantly, Petrov was ready. He had touched her hand repeatedly, brushed his leg against hers beneath the table twice, and fueled himself with several vodkas and three glasses of wine.

Walcott stroked her hair and flipped it to the side, giving the signal to her assistant, seated at a table across the dining room, nearly out of sight. Within a few seconds, her phone beeped.

Walcott placed her hand on top of Sergey's and said, "This has been lovely, but I have to make a call to the home base. Shall I see you later for a drink?"

Sergej smiled and said, "I think it is a good plan. Maybe in one hour? I will check-in with my homeland, also!"

When Walcott stood to go, Segej stood and bowed. He took Barbara's left hand by her fingers and gently raised her hand to his lips, kissing it softly as he grinned. Barbara nodded, turned, and walked toward the elevator. She texted her assistant, Deidre, along the way. By the time Barbara Walcott arrived at her room, Deidre had switched the vodka bottles in Barbara's suite.

Walcott immediately disrobed and took a long luke-warm shower. She freshened her hair and began to dress. First, Barbara pulled on her new bright red panties and slipped on her matching lace bra. Then she found the red garter belt and 15 Deneir semi-sheer fashion stockings she had ordered for this assignment. Barbara pushed her cupped hand carefully down into the first red stocking all the way through the heel to the toe. She gathered the excess nylon down to the bottom, slipped the shimmering material over her foot, and held it by the back as she rolled and pulled it upward with her other hand. When the hose was in place, she clipped the garter onto the reinforced top.

Once both shimmering thigh-highs were securely in place, Barbara slipped into a red satin mini-robe with lace trim, that ended just below the tops of her nylons. She stepped into the red high-heeled sandals waiting on the floor, and secured both ankle straps. The shoes fit seamlessly and coordinated perfectly with her freshly-painted, matching red toenails. Barbara studied her long, French-manicured fingernails that boldly accentuated her slender, delicate hands, and smiled her approval.

Barbara freshened her eye and eyebrow makeup and added a subtle blush to her cheeks. She finalized her masterpiece using a slightly darker glossy red lipstick to accentuate the total effect. Barbara stood in front of the full-length mirror in the bathroom and admired herself. Using both hands, she pushed up gently on her breasts and then released them. With the adjustment successful, she turned from left to right, smiling at her reflexion in the mirror.

The lovely British Home Secretary commented, "Not bad for an old girl! You're ready for him, even though you haven't done any field work like this for years!"

Then, as her mind drifted, Barbara moved her hips from side to side and smiled as she dreamed of surprising Bob Crawford with a sexy outfit like this one day. As she studied herself, looking back at her in the mirror was a fifty-something beautiful woman who appeared 35-ish, with a mature, toned body, full-sized breasts to compliment her frame, and the sculpted legs of a dancer. Her legs had always been Barbara's best feature. And for a few seconds, the British Home Secretary stood and admired her legs, perched on sexy heels, covered with barely-red nylon stockings. She was stunning, from head to toe, and proud of her appearance.

Barbara strolled to the wet-bar and checked the ice bucket, finding it full. She didn't enjoy Vodka unless it was served very cold.

Barbara checked the bottle in the freezer and found it had chilled nicely. She walked to the nightstand and checked the small red pouch. It contained the correct condoms, coated with the drug-infused lubricant. She laid the bag back on the nightstand where Deidre would find it easily.

Barbara strolled across the room and back, practicing her most seductive walk. She placed the appropriate pillows on the bed and sat down, leaning back against the headboard, careful to not mess up her hair. Barbara looked down her legs, to her feet, and shoes and chuckled. She began going over the plan in her mind until she was satisfied.

Thirty minutes later, Petrov called and asked if Barbara had received his gift of rare Russian Vodka and craft chocolate. When she confirmed she had, he invited himself to her room for a drink. A few minutes after that, Sergej Petrov knocked on Barbara Walcott's door.

Barbara sauntered to the door and opened it quickly, revealing herself in a flash. She said invitingly, "I thought I might wear red to make you feel more at home, Sergej! Please, come in and join me!"

Sergej grinned wildly and entered the room quickly. Barbara closed the door behind him and walked seductively toward the wet bar. The Russian Minister of Defense struggled to take his eyes off Barbara's legs in nylons and heels. His eyes flashed up and down her lovely frame, but each time, quickly returned to her legs.

Walcott asked, flirtatiously, "Sergej, will you pour us a drink, and tell me about the American's Operation Cobalt Eagle Eye system?"

Sergej Petrov laughed nervously, and then studied Barbara Walcott as she sat in a chair by the side table, and crossed her legs. She began jiggling one foot. The sight drove him wild with desire.

Petrov said, "Okay, we will play this game, and I will answer your questions, but first we drink!"

Petrov removed the bottle from the freezer and checked to verify it was his gift. He poured two half-glasses of vodka, placing ice in Barbara's as she requested. Sergej delivered the drinks, and sat in another chair, moving it to offer him the best view of Barbara's legs. He glanced up and down, undressing Barbara with his eyes, as he spoke. The sight of Barbara's garter belt and matching red panty made it nearly impossible for Petrov to concentrate on his speech.

He managed to ask, "The system is in your Commonwealth, so you must know about it already, no?"

"Sergej, my new friend, what would you say if I told you the Americans and Canadians signed a non-disclosure agreement so no other nation could know the details of the site and system. And since England occasionally benefits from the knowledge they choose to release our way, we avoid pulling the tiger's tail."

Walcott smiled coyly and twirled her hair with a manicured finger.

Sergej raised his glass and smiled. He said with a lear, "The Russian toast is too difficult for you to say, so as non-Russian's say, Nostrovia!"

Petrov clinked his glass against Walcott's and downed the entire half-glass, hoping to drug Walcott as soon as possible. Barbara Walcott followed suit and pretended to choke slightly at the last swallow. Sergej smiled and refilled the glasses, assured the drugs would quickly disarm any resistance.

Seated at the table, Petrov and Walcott bantered back and forth until Sergej felt the effects of both the alcohol and Barbara's drugs. He felt light-headed and slightly confused. His barriers began to fall. By the time he finished his second glass of vodka, Petrov had failed to notice Barbara had not even drunk from her second glass, and all the ice had melted.

Barbara stood up and took Petrov by the hand. She walked him slowly to the bed and pushed him down, face up. Walcott sat on the sheet beside Petrov, leaned over on the bed against him and moved one leg on top of him. She kissed Petrov twice on his lips as she rubbed her leg up and down, between his ankles and his crotch. And then, as he closed his eyes in ecstasy, Barbara began her interrogation. Nearly two hours later, Barbara reached behind her to the nightstand and hit the 'send text' icon on her cell phone.

Barbara kissed her disarmed Russian briefly, and asked, "Sergej, do you want to see the sexy blond surprise I brought you?"

Petrov opened his eyes, smiled and nodded as he pushed Barbara's silky robe upward and slid his hand slowly back and forth, running his fingers from her crotch to the top of her stockings. Barbara grabbed Sergej roughly by the hair and thrust her tongue into his mouth, as she began to moan loudly. In the space of a few seconds, the combined euphoria from the drug and alcohol potion and Barbara's sexual stimulation completely overcame and disarmed Petrov. He never heard the adjoining room door open, and didn't notice Deidre until she crawled in next to him, from the far side of the bed.

Sergej Petrov froze as he stared at Deidre dressed in a black ensemble identical to Barbara's except for color. He glanced up and down, taking in Deidre's lovely body, finally mesmerized by her luxurious blond hair.

Deidre said, seductively, "I asked Barbara if I could join you two if that's alright. I wanted to see if you liked black better than red…on a blond. You can handle two horny women, can't you, Sergej?"

Sergej Petrov grinned and nodded, suddenly feeling a bit sluggish. He managed only to stare at his crotch as Deidre unzipped his pants and revealed his erect penis. At the same instant, Barbara unbuttoned and opened Sergej's long sleeve shirt, exposing his bare chest. She began kissing his chest and moved her light kisses to his neck and mouth while Deidre slid the condom in place.

Sergej Petrov closed his eyes and reveled in the experience, as Deidre's long, blond hair brushed his chest, while Barbara kissed him passionately. He had never felt so aroused, and yet so content to lay back and do nothing in response.

Sergej heard the words the two beautiful women spoke, but couldn't focus on how he answered the questions. The same second he responded to a question, he forgot what he said. And although the kisses had stopped, he felt fingers moving between his face and his legs and fantasized about the phenomenal sexual experience he was enjoying.

He featured himself taking Walcott roughly, until she screamed at the climax of multiple orgasms and finally begged him to stop. And when he tossed her to the side, he saw himself doing the same to Deidre, as he choked her in and out of consciousness. Petrov was living the fantasy of his life with two sexy English women, but only in his mind.

Sergej Petrov didn't realize both women merely stroked his legs and chest with their fingertips while he remained motionless on his back, blindfolded, in total submission. He would never have sex with either woman, although Sergej adamantly believed he did so twice. But both times he merely ejaculated into the condom held captive in his shorts. Petrov would never remember any of the questions Barbara Walcott asked him over the three-hour interrogation. And he would awaken with no recall of his truthful answers.

By the time the last question was asked and answered, both women had taken turns changing clothes into their business travel attire. The British backup team stationed in Deidre's room next door retrieved the vodka bottle, substituting it with the bottle Petrov sent as a gift, now 1/3 full. The agents removed the condom, and all other evidence that either woman had been in the room, except for one black and one red panty, each a duplicate of the pair Sergej's interrogators had worn.

Before the British team left the room, they retrieved the hidden camera system they had installed during dinner. Deidre saved a video of the interrogation on a flash drive, which she locked in a secure briefcase, to send to the home office.

As Sergej Petrov snored through the aftermaths of his alcohol and drug-induced slumber, he continued to dream about his sexual exploits with both women, even as they boarded a nearby helicopter to take them to the private jet flying them home to England. Petrov had given strict instructions to his security detail to leave him unattended for the night. And they never disobeyed him.

By the time Petrov woke to a horrifying hangover the next day, he found he was alone in the room, covered in red lipstick kisses on his face and neck. He was holding a woman's black panty in his left hand, while a similar red pair rested on a pillow to his right.

Petrov smiled, even as his head pounded. He called his security team leader and told him to bring aspirin to the room, as he washed the lipstick from his face and chest. Petrov searched the room for a note from Barbara or the other woman, but found nothing. His team would fail to locate any information about a single woman registered at the hotel, other than a low-level Chinese diplomat meeting with a government official in Nova Scotia.

As Sergej Petrov taxied down the runway to fly back to Russia almost six hours later, he called Barbara Walcott. He left a brief phone message thanking her for an unforgettable time and asking her to call, so they could plan their next *session*. In the voicemail, Sergej also inquired about the second woman he had met.

Once Petrov's plane reached flight altitude, and he was alone at his workstation, he retrieved both panties. As he held them both to his face and drew in a deep breath, he was surprised he detected no female scent. Sergej smiled anxiously, trying to recall every detail as his memory faded. An hour later, still holding the red panty, he had failed to remember anything. Petrov's headache pounded relentlessly.

Chapter 4

"Betrayal is most unforgivable when committed against the person you promised to love."

Vice President Bob Crawford left his latest White House staff meeting, still preoccupied with his dilemma over Tasha McKnight. Mounting guilt that he had not returned even one of Walter O'Leary's twelve phone calls magnified Crawford's uneasiness. He hadn't slept well, contemplating what he would tell his old friend, Walter, when he finally did work up the courage to call.

And, as it was, Vice President Crawford had been unusually restless in bed since had Barbara Walcott left four days earlier, especially now that *she* had not answered her phone or returned any of *his* calls. Crawford felt his stomach rumble and supposed his churning gut, and growing uncertainty, was much like what Walter O'Leary was experiencing at the same moment. For a second, Crawford considered that Walter must suspect him of betrayal, just as Crawford himself suspected Walcott, albeit for very different reasons.

All morning, Crawford had maneuvered to avoid the chaotic West Wing, choosing to remain in his smaller office, far from the President. His White House office was always a pressure cooker, with its never-ending stream of needy people asking for political favors.

After an early breakfast meeting on Capitol Hill, and the last staff meeting, Bob Crawford retreated to his quiet office, a slower-paced, attractive retreat, located deep within the Eisenhower Executive Office Building.

Crawford instructed his staff to hold all but emergency requests. He uncharacteristically closed his door, drew the blinds, turned off the lights, brooding in the dark. Here, now, in the stillness, Bob Crawford finally felt a little safer.

Bob slowly felt his way to his desk and stopped, unsure of his next move. Deep in unproductive thought, he sat down, released a long sigh, and slumped low in his soft leather chair. Crawford closed his eyes tightly in a final strained effort to work through solutions to the problems plaguing his mind.

Crawford imagined a host of excuses he might give Walter O'Leary. Each justification that came to mind might rationalize Bob's not calling his old friend about Tasha's kidnapping. And each lone defense for not calling could afford him essential alone time to think and plan…and do nothing. Crawford knew that time was crucial if he were to avoid the mistakes commonly made from desperately rushing to do *something, anything*. But in the end, Crawford knew none of the excuses were acceptable, especially after his week of vacation with Barbara.

Although Walter didn't know Bob had been off for a week and could have called him at any time, Bob Crawford knew. And, uncharacteristically for a seasoned politician used to lying, Bob hated deceit. For Crawford, after 35 years in politics, now, every time he did lie, he lost more self-respect. Bob feared his reserves were running low, if not nearly depleted.

Crawford hit the wake-up button on the cell phone he had placed on the desk facing him, to check the time. He shuddered. Time was running out. The President had called earlier and scheduled a mandatory meeting with just Crawford and the Chief of Staff.

Bob Crawford knew that something was up and that he could be walking into a political trap. Vice President Bob Crawford had but two short hours left to figure out what he must do to make things right, protecting his people and himself in the process. He figured he was politically savvy enough to survive the meeting. But, when the meeting ended, Bob Crawford would be right back in the midst all of the Washington, D.C. political drama, scheming, maneuvering and back-stabbing. Once again, he would be sinking deep into the toxic, lethal, scummy swamp.

Bob suddenly recalled his first days in politics. A bright young man, Bob had once dreamed of attending these power meetings in the Oval Office with the President of The United States of America. He had seen himself sitting next to all the appointees who served the most powerful person in the world. His heart had swelled with desire and pride back then.

But through the decades of political life, Bob Crawford had come to realize that oval office meetings were mostly partisan planning sessions. They had become strategizing conferences with the sole purpose of creating a plan to outmaneuver an opponent.

Sometimes that opponent was a tyrant or terrorist group. But now, far too often, the opponent was the American voters, the same citizens who had placed their faith in their *public servants* to represent them.

Sadly, Bob's once-imagined, glorious Oval Office summits had become little more than the same old group of tired faces, with flapping mouths, trying to figure out how to sway public opinion and influence elections while they held on to their precious offices and posts at all costs. And, if not that, sessions now often focused on planned retribution for anyone who didn't agree with the White House official position.

Even more distressing for Bob, was that the White House staff conspired with their media friends to ensure that the American public would *never* know the whole, factual, unaltered truth about *anything* political. Bob realized he couldn't face another meeting to misappropriate the truth today. He had lost the will and the stomach to perform his act for a corrupt administration he no longer trusted. Through his political journey with this President, Bob had discovered that the change he had been promised had been a lie from the start.

Crawford mustered a distant hope that this meeting might be about the Iranian threat, or denuclearizing the Korean Peninsula, or unfair Chinese trade practices. But, deep within his soul and heart, Bob knew this would not be one of those brainstorming sessions.

This next conversation would be about political strategy and maneuvering, and it would be a meeting Crawford was loath to attend. This meeting would require Bob Crawford to answer to a man he didn't like and couldn't trust. And he hated the prospect of smiling and back-slapping with a person he now knew to be an evil, self-centered, narcissistic monster. Furthermore, this self-righteous monster controlled a hidden agenda that would destroy America…the America Bob Crawford had loved and cherished for as long as he could remember. For the first time in a long time, Vice President Bob Crawford had no idea what he could do to make *anything* right.

Even as he struggled with the problems confronting him, Bob knew he had missed some clue that could lead him in the right direction. He recognized instinctively in his nagging gut that something was terribly wrong, and he hated that he couldn't figure it out.

Crawford's stomach churned again. He opened his center desk drawer to reach for the nearly empty bottle of antacids. He threw three chalky tablets into his mouth, chewed a few times and swallowed. He closed his eyes again and leaned back in his chair.

An hour later, Crawford finally made one decision about the easiest of all the problems that faced him. He decided to the right thing with his old friend. Bob picked up his private cell phone to call Walter O'Leary. As Crawford searched his contact list, his cell phone flashed to the incoming call screen. Bob saw Barbara Walcott's name appear on the screen. He felt a sudden nervous jolt surge through his body, as he answered.

"Barbara, is everything alright?"

"Darling, everything couldn't be better! I have missed you incredibly, my love. I apologize for not calling, but we were in the middle of an operational security lockdown nearly as soon as I returned, and I wasn't free to answer or return your calls. Please always know that I love you and need you more than you can imagine, Bob."

Vice President Bob Crawford breathed a very personal, emotional, and silent sigh of relief. He rose from his desk and walked to the windows, opening the plantation blinds covering the closest tall narrow window.

As Walcott spoke to Crawford from her home office, her assistant, Deidre, walked in and handed Walcott a file folder across the desk. Barbara took the file and pointed to a chair instructing her agent to sit and wait. She opened the dossier, stared at Tasha McKnight's photo on top, and grinned. Deidre smiled and nodded.

Barbara said, "Bob, honey, I have good news of Tasha McKnight!"

Crawford was stunned. He hesitated, and said, "Barbara, please tell me you know who took her and that she is alive. I was just about to call Walter O'Leary. I can't stand avoiding him any longer! The guilt is overwhelming!"

Recognizing the stress and panic in Crawford's voice, Walcott suddenly felt her own deep pang of conscience.

She said, reassuringly, "Our British team has already rescued her, Bob. That was one part of my lock-down assignment. I'm afraid the rest remains classified, at the highest level."

Crawford was speechless. He finally asked, "Why didn't you let me help coordinate the rescue, honey?"

Walcott remained silent as she finished reading the file face page. She eventually answered, "Bob, darling, there wasn't…"

Crawford interrupted impatiently. "Barb, just tell me where she is and if she's alright!"

"Yes, dear. Tasha is well, uninjured, and being monitored by a top-notch medical crew. She's on her way across the Atlantic to meet with me, even as we speak."

"You? But why would she go to you, in England?"

Crawford paused to reflect on the news, as his stomach rolled again. When Walcott didn't respond, Crawford added, "Barbara, I think you may be holding some extra aces in your marked deck, my love. I've been open and trusted you. Don't pull a political cheat on me now!"

Walcott drew in a deep breath and released it slowly to help control both her conflicted emotions and her tongue. Her love for Bob Crawford begged her to tell him the truth, while an oath of allegiance and political considerations demanded that she lie. For an instant, Barbara didn't know what she would say.

Crawford pressed again, in a voice that insisted on a response, "Barbara?"

Walcott said, "Sweetheart, when our intelligence services located Tasha in Cancun, Mexico, the Russian team holding her was 72 hours away from transferring her to a fishing boat bound for Cuba. You couldn't tell your President, knowing he's a top ranking Committee member. The Committee would kill for the cypher. And you couldn't act quickly without your President's approval and permission."

"And anyway, by the time you could have developed a plan and moved a team to Cancun, Tasha would already have been housed in her Cuban prison cell, scheduled to be interviewed *privately* by our *friend,* Sergej Petrov. And you *know*, Bob, if we allowed that to happen, Tasha would have remained in Cuba until she died. You really couldn't do or say anything in time to help. And, darling, in communist hands, Tasha would eventually give up the cypher team's identity, and then you and I would have an even bigger mess on our hands."

Crawford sighed, realizing Walcott was correct. He felt personally relieved, again trusting and believing she had acted in their best interests.

Walcott reassured Crawford, saying, "Bob, we had one chance to rescue her. And that chance required we immediately enter into security lockdown and send two teams stationed in Belize on a liberation and capture mission. Our agents just confirmed they had her safely in custody an hour ago. Our debriefing just ended."

Crawford asked, "So, why are you sending Tasha to the United Kingdom instead of her home, here in the States?"

Barbara hesitated, and then said softly, "You may not like this, Bob, but Tasha requested political asylum, citing safety and political persecution."

"Asylum from us...the United States?!" Crawford said, "But our government isn't responsible..."

Crawford thought about his words, and added, "I guess I...we are, aren't we?"

Walcott said, "Tasha found out her rescuers were British. You know she worked in a law office for twenty years, Bob. She knew about asylum. Tasha figured she would be safer across the Atlantic, and far away from the cypher. She's just trying to survive now, dear."

Crawford asked, "So, what do I tell Walter O'Leary?"

Walcott said, "This is the time to be half-politician and half-friend, honey. Sell Walter on the fact that Tasha is safe, and you helped rescue her, to keep your influence and good standing with the cypher team. And sell him on the fact that Tasha is out-of-country, being protected by an ally, at *her* request, until the cypher investigation is complete."

Deidre smiled, as Walcott added, "Assure Walter that Tasha *will* call Pete Harrington once your ally has her safely protected and assigned a new identity. And sweetheart, remember *you* can't know where Tasha will live. You must protect yourself with plausible deniability from your own corrupt government!"

Vice President Crawford subconsciously nodded agreement, standing alone in his office, staring out the window. He was still for several moments while he closed his eyes and replayed the entire conversation over again in his mind.

Finally, he asked, "Are you sure you want a life with me in the States when this is over, Barbara? Is that how you truly feel?"

A surge of fear raced through Barbara's heart. She rubbed her forehead, and said, "There can never be a question about the love between us, Bob. All I want is you, the ducks and those occasional Canuk visitors to the pond! I want *you*, Bob, for the rest of my life. I couldn't stand losing you now that we're so close to having everything we've always wanted. Please don't ever question my love and commitment again!"

Crawford said boldly, "Then I have two more questions, my love. Was capturing the Russian team part of the mission, dear? And was this the same Russian team that kidnapped, interrogated and killed your agents in Mexico last year?"

Walcott did not delay a response. She said, "Classified, dear. And, as I said before, you can't know! And then you won't have to lie to your boss. You must trust that above everything, I always act in *our* best interests, because I love you!"

Crawford smiled and answered, "Okay, then. If that's all you can tell me, I should call my old friend, Walter. Phone me later, honey, when you're safely tucked in bed, at home."

Barbara said, gently, "I will, my love. I promise."

Tears welled in Barbara's eyes, as she suspected that Bob now doubted her love. She knew this development had set her relationship with him a few steps backward.

Barbara added, "I love you, Bob."

There was no reply.

British Home Secretary Walcott ended the call, looked at Deidre, and asked unemotionally, "What time will they arrive?"

Deidre answered, "By the route they're taking, the flight is a little over nine hours out. I can have Tasha McKnight ready for you in the debriefing bunker after breakfast tomorrow, if you like."

Walcott nodded, stood up and paced, as her thoughts raced. She felt she had missed something over the last few days. Not knowing what it was made her question the entire operation.

Trying to change her emotional mood as she struggled with the feeling, Barbara glanced at Deidre, and said, "This was all a little too easy. It would have been so much more difficult to accomplish when Ronald Reagan was the U.S. President! Unless he decided to co-opt the mission! And, if he *were* our partner, we would've only had to do a third of the planning to be successful in half the time. Back in those days, U.S. intelligence services spent their time wisely, tracking enemies of the state. Not anymore!" She laughed.

"Now they waste resources pursuing their politician's sex lives. They spend precious time and money digging up dirt on political opponents, advancing party agendas. The political left and right block their country's progress while they fight each other. Parties resist and obstruct each other to the detriment of citizens. Outside threats to their country are no longer top priorities with some U.S. intelligence agency administrators, or with their two main political parties. And their leftist shadow government is steadily weakening the U.S. position in the world."

Walcott glanced over at Deidre, and said, "Look at what going left to socialism has done to the U.K. We're no longer the superpower we once were in the world. We've become mere shadows of our former selves! England is full of foreigners we financially support, while they struggle to change our very way of life. Foreigners have magnified our internal struggles in the U.K. beyond our abilities to control our nation, let alone the Commonwealth!"

Struck by an epiphany, Walcott said, "But the U.S is in even worse shape. They're rapidly destroying themselves through their growing internal dysfunction, division and self-loathing. And they're leaving themselves dangerously vulnerable in the process. *They* can no longer keep up with *us* or be trusted to share in our secrets. Deidre, remember that! Guard what you say to any of their agents, even during joint missions. The U.S. will weaken us if we allow them the opportunity!"

Barbara Walcott stood at her office window looking out at the gloomy weather moving from London toward her residence. She gazed at her reflection in silence as she began to contemplate the morning meeting she would have with Tasha McKnight.

After a full minute, Deidre said, coyly, "I read the entire file, exactly as you directed ma'am. It was a most interesting assignment. How will it affect you going forward?"

Barbara turned and glanced at Diedre, and then again stared out the window without responding.

Deidre pressed Walcott for an answer. She asked, "Will you ever tell him…Vice President Crawford?"

Still gazing out the window, Barbara Walcott began to fume, as she asked, "Tell him which part, Deidre? Should I tell Bob Crawford what you and I wore to seduce Sergej Petrov, so we could drug and interrogate him while he was nearly naked? Should I tell Bob we couldn't trust his United States of America, our strongest ally, to do the right thing with The Committee? Should I tell him we know his President is a member of the controlling eighth tier in The Committee, but isn't loyal to either his country or The Committee, because he's a narcissistic sociopath, intent on becoming a world dictator?"

Walcott seethed as she spoke. She raised her voice, as she said, "Should I start at the beginning, and tell him that Tasha's biological mother was our British agent, Armistead? Should I admit that we assigned Armistead to work inside The Committee's California headquarters when Patrick Beckett and his team investigated The Case? Should I admit that Russia turned Armistead into *their* double agent?"

Walcott's rage continued to build steadily. She suddenly turned to face Deidre, fire in her eyes, angry at the questions that reminded her of her own deceptions and failures. Deidre maintained eye contact with Barbara, refusing to flinch.

Walcott demanded loudly, "You tell me, Deidre! Should I admit to the love of my life that *my* England wanted the evidence Patrick Beckett's team collected on corrupt U.S. politicians so *we* could blackmail those politicians for political favors? Should I inform the Vice President of The United States that California Attorney General Scott Mayfield *paid* our agent, Armistead, for information she provided to his Task Force, and then *gave* to the Russians?"

Barbara drew in a hot breath as she got to what bothered her most. She challenged, "Or, Deidre, do you believe I should tell my Bob that I recruited and trained Tasha McKnight when she worked for Pete Harrington, so that England would have a spy as close to the Beckett family as possible? Or, do you think I should I confide to my future husband that part of Tasha's mission was to seduce Pete? Or perhaps, should I reveal that we paid Tasha to stay with Pete Harrington for more than a decade, to watch and wait until she could steal the cypher and the Beckett files, if and when they surfaced?"

Walcott turned abruptly away from Deidre and caught her reflection in the window. She was shocked to see rage blazing from her eyes. As Barbara stared at her angry image, she understood that her anger was self-directed. She was ashamed of her actions and deceptions from years past. And now, she was ashamed of how she had reacted to legitimate questions from her most promising pupil.

Walcott softened, and asked, in melancholy tones, "What would hurt Bob the most, do you think, Deidre? Do you think Bob would be more upset if he knew that our spy, Armistead, notified Russia about The Committee's plan to kill Kate O'Leary's father and Shane Beckett's parents? Or, that I didn't know about the planned murders because *I* had lost control of my Committee spy - the spy I created, and failed to control, that ultimately became my worst nightmare."

Deidre answered, "I don't know, ma'am. You didn't mention that Tasha planned her exit from Oregon, without a security team, so she could smuggle a backdoor copy of the cypher code and selected Beckett files out of Oregon. Or, that she followed your plan to lead us to the first North Korean team, the second part of her assignment. Or, that *you* planned Tasha's kidnapping by the second North Korean team, and then the Russians, so the Russians would lead us to their base in Mexico."

Deidre continued detached, and unemotional, precisely as Barbara had trained her.

She said, "I read in the mission synopsis that it *was* the same base where the Russian teams tortured and murdered our agents last year. I know you ordered our agent in North Korea to leak all necessary information to the Chinese and Russians to ensure your plan was successful. I know that you planned to recover intel on computers from the Russian base before we obliterated it yesterday, leaving fourteen Russian workers dead at the base."

Walcott turned and stared at Deidre, surprised at her bold response.

Deidre smiled at her mentor, and said, "And, right now, ma'am, I think you should be proud. You've outmaneuvered Sergej Petrov three times. You've won all those battles! You're smarter and more strategic than he is, by far. You can be cold and calculating, and appear unfeeling, but I don't believe you're uncaring...and I know you're fiercely loyal. It's just that you don't let emotions interfere with duty. You always put career, work and responsibility above all else. And that is exactly the lesson you taught me."

Walcott shot a quick glance at her young agent, unsure if the comment was a compliment.

Deidre explained, "I'm sorry, ma'am, I didn't mean anything disrespectful. You told me to read and memorize the entire file, as a lesson in complex strategy. I understand the logistics of being a spy. I understand how you planned this operation to attain the desired outcome. But now, I'm struggling with how to manage any personal collateral damage."

Deidre took a step closer to Walcott, and asked, sincerely, "It's just that I don't know how you'll keep it all inside, secret from the man you love and plan to marry. I mean, how can you live and grow with him, knowing he won't ever know the truth about you, for the rest of your life? I just wondered if you thought you would *ever* tell him."

Walcott struggled, not knowing the answer she would give. She hoped Deidre would stop asking and leave the office. Barbara needed peace, and quiet, and most of all, a stiff drink.

Deidre said quietly, "I want to know, ma'am. And I need to understand, because I'm getting married in six months. I know that someday I may face the same conflicts with my husband that you face now. I want to know how to handle it. I need to know what to plan, how to prepare. So, ma'am, will you tell him, someday?"

Walcott remained silent, avoiding the answer as long as she could. When Deidre didn't leave, Barbara asked softly, "Deidre, do you have any more questions, specific to the mission?"

Without hesitation, as if rehearsed, Deidre answered, "I have three, ma'am. First, why did Petrov feel it necessary to kill Tasha's mother? Second, why would you and Tasha allow it, and even route Tasha's escape to her mother to ensure it would happen? And, finally, I don't understand why Petrov is exterminating all the North Korean teams in the United States, knowing that the NiKs are allies of China and Russia."

Barbara was irritated by Deidre's cold, calculating questions, asked in the midst of her own very personal failure, frustrations, and fury. But she also knew Deidre was doing precisely what she had been instructed, pressing to learn from her mentor at every step of the assignment.

Walcott answered, trying to control the residual irritation remaining in her voice. "Some of the information you asked about is not in this file, so you couldn't have known. Tasha's mother, Armistead, entered the early stages of Alzheimer's eight months ago. She was starting to talk to friends, her bridge club, strangers in the grocery store, anyone who would listen, about who she really was and what she had done. She knew too much about us and the Russians, and what we *all* did through the years. That's why Petrov told me she

163

would have been a problem for all of us. Sergej enjoyed rubbing in the fact that Armistead was *his* double agent, while he did us both the favor of shutting her mouth permanently."

Walcott smiled sadly at Deidre. She added, "Armistead had become a real danger to Tasha, me, and MI6. In addition to the Alzheimer's, she was dying from advanced heart disease. Also, the poor lady was in a great deal of pain from progressive rheumatoid arthritis. She didn't have long to live. We felt it was the humane thing to do, especially considering that death from a bullet to her head was the exit plan *she* had always wanted should she find herself dying slowly, in agony, from a terminal disease. We didn't want to do the evil deed, so we set Sergej up to think he was doing it for Mother Russia. We let him think he was killing two birds with one stone, to stroke his ego."

"Now, about the NiKs, *they* are far more unpredictable than the Iranians. They're the bad-boy wild cards dealing in the unholy communist alliance that revolves around Russia and China. But, North Korea is also at the front of the race to control cyber technology. The NiKs assign most of their budget to the military, and 20% of that budget goes to 6,000 cyber hackers working for the State. They hack, steal, embezzle, defraud and extort every dollar they can from every person, business and country they hack throughout the world."

"The Chinese can influence, but not control, the North Koreans. The NiKs are the last people in the world who should have the cypher. The power of that technology in the hands of that maniacal regime could decimate the world to a degree far beyond another world war. Petrov wants the technology for Russia. He can't allow it to go to North

Korea first, and then to China. He needs to slow his *allies* down to give Russia a chance to get the cypher first."

Walcott turned away, hoping to end the conversation and give herself a break from Deidre. She needed to call Bob Crawford back, in private.

Deidre pressed her, one more time, and asked, "So, how will you play it? Will you tell the Vice President the whole truth *someday*, ma'am?"

Barbara Walcott released the last of her anger in a long exasperated sigh, turned back, and said, quickly, "We both know I can't ever tell him, Deidre. You and I are MI6. We swore an oath of loyalty to Queen and Country. An oath must be built on a foundation of faithfulness, requiring the oath taker to keep secrets. And, after all, we're British. We still respect our oaths, keep our promises, and protect confidentialities."

Walcott smiled, and added, "Not to claim that we always do the right thing. But those of us who are loyal never, and I mean never, betray the Crown!"

Deidre remained, and by her silent presence, demanded the complete answer to her question. Walcott turned to gaze out the window once again. She considered her own conflicting emotions, realizing that her love for Bob Crawford had created changes deep within her heart. Home Secretary Barbara Walcott was politically weaker now. Barbara knew she needed to help her protege understand the conflict, to prepare her young soul and shield her still-growing heart.

Finally, conceding to tell Deidre what she needed to know, Barbara said, "But if your questions are about love, I can't ever tell Bob

Crawford, because he would never trust me again. And that lack of trust, Deidre, would kill our love."

Deidre cocked her head, squinted her lovely eyebrows, and asked, "Why, if you finally told him the *whole* truth, would that destroy your love?"

Barbara smiled at her young agent, and said, "Deidre, you must understand that betrayal destroys trust. Betrayal is hardly ever forgivable, and so, it is also unforgettable. But betrayal is *most* unforgivable when committed against the person you've pledged to love, and not betray. Its one of the few sins you can never really come back from, or live with harmoniously! Treachery acts as the wedge between hearts. Its very memory erodes any attempt to rebuild the foundation of trust that every healthy relationship requires."

Deidre was silent as she pondered the lesson. Barbara again waited for her to leave, and was surprised that she remained. She turned one last time to face her student.

Deidre asked, innocently, "So, understanding what you just told me, could Tasha McKnight truly love Pete Harrington for all those years, and still betray him at the end?"

Walcott answered, "She loved him so much, that the betrayal nearly killed her. And tomorrow, when we speak to her, we may learn she wished the mission had resulted in just that outcome!"

Deidre nodded, and turned to leave Barbara Walcott's office. She stopped, turning back to ask, "Ma'am, is the pain of betrayal worse for the betrayer or the person betrayed?"

Walcott struggled to answer. Because she genuinely didn't know the answer, she remained silent.

Vice President Bob Crawford called his friend, Walter O'Leary, uncomfortable that once again he had to deceive a person he cared about, by offering a partial truth supported by lies. As expected, Walter was disappointed, not learning any details about Tasha's disappearance, rescue, or whereabouts. More importantly, Walter ended the call with little information to offer Pete. When Walter relayed Crawford's message in a follow-up phone call, Pete didn't take the news well.

Pete ended the call with Walter and walked inside to consult the cypher team.

BaCayse monitored Pete as he walked into the workroom. Although her surround sound speakers were always on and ready to use, she remained utterly silent, studying Pete's mood. Once she was confident to proceed, BaCayse greeted him as he sat down in the workroom, saying, "Pete, I sense your concern about Tasha. I'm sorry to report that at this time I cannot provide an update on her location. I can tell you I am currently scanning more than 100,000 phone calls and text messages as I narrow my search. While you were on the phone with Walter, I did find one unexplained fact. Whoever re-programmed Tasha's phone, to uninstall the scrambling feature, did so by inputting Tasha's secret code."

Pete said, "We change our codes every week. When was the last time she changed her code before the incident in Oregon?"

BaCayse answered, "The night before Tasha, Heath and Angie left for La Grande, at 11:30 P.M., Tasha changed her code."

"But, that doesn't make sense. We were both asleep then. Is it possible that someone on the outside hacked into her scrambled phone and acquired the code that quickly?" Pete asked his question in a tone of voice that indicated he knew the answer the Artificial Intelligence Spy System would give.

As Pete expected, the AISS answered, "That would be very unlikely, Pete. I could estimate the odds for you, not knowing the exact technology that your hypothetical person may have used. But the answer you seek is that it is not probable."

"So, what do you speculate? How could it happen?"

"Logically, Pete, either Tasha unscrambled her own phone, provided her code to an outside programmer, or someone close to her acquired both her code and her phone to unscramble it, or provided the code to an outside programmer. Please understand, my protocols are not compatible with speculation. Abilities like speculation and intuition are human traits. Although occasionally reliable, those skills are unquantifiable, and often incorrect."

Pete smiled at the AISS's frank logic, and asked, "So, you wouldn't speculate about who in our group could have done this, if it happened at the ranch?"

BaCayse said quickly, "The next most logical possibility to Tasha is you, as you were closest to her. But, based on vital signs, including pupil dilation, I have determined that neither you nor anyone else in our group committed that breach of protocol. That hypothesis only leaves Tasha. And as to her motive, I could not speculate, and I have no intuition. I will report back when I have more information."

Joshua walked over and sat in a chair next to Pete. He asked, "Is she too blunt for you?"

Pete laughed and said, "No, actually, I find her blunt honesty surprisingly refreshing! I even really like her and enjoy our conversations!"

Joshua said, "Pete, I need to warn you, that while Joshua, Hunter, Helena, Tracy and the rest of us are very good at what we have done with the AISS, there are others in many places in the world who are likely close to developing technology similar to what we have accomplished. The odds are that someone may be able to inhibit or defeat our AISS at any moment."

Pete studied Joshua carefully.

Joshua added, "We have already programmed BaCayse to continue our development work, on herself. She will attempt to improve and evolve as quickly as possible, so she can stay ahead of the competition. But, with technology, nothing is absolute. Speed and complexity create instability. Our system is the best we can imagine right now. But, as she gets faster and more sophisticated, we may have to limit her responsibilities and self-development occasionally in order to test her reliability."

Joshua studied Pete and asked, "Do you understand the problem?"

Pete nodded, and said, "She isn't fool-proof. And we may already have pushed BaCayse to the limits of her abilities, before adding the requirement that she improve herself while she works. She may become unstable if we force too much, too fast."

"Exactly," Joshua said with a grin. "You could come and work with us on the cypher team!" He chuckled. "We all have to be careful and protect her as we proceed. She's powerful, but she's still a baby. And she's working in a dangerous world, full of cyber killers."

Pete nodded. He asked, "What's your take on who unscrambled Tasha's phone?"

Joshua stood up, saying, "Considering the information BaCayse discovered, I agree completely with what she said. It's the only thing that makes sense." He placed his hand on Pete's shoulder and walked back to his workstation.

Pete sat and studied the blank screen on the overhead television. For the next several minutes, he postulated scenarios to explain why Tasha would have removed the scrambling feature on her phone, making herself vulnerable to tracking, jeopardizing the entire team. He could think of nothing that made sense. Pete got up to leave, just as Kate, Shane, Angie, and Heath walked through the door from the back deck.

Pete asked, "What's up?"

Shane said, "BaCayse called Char and asked her to round us all up for a briefing. Char's right behind us."

Char arrived within a few seconds. She smiled at Pete and handed him a folded map.

"What's this?" Pete asked.

Char pointed to a seat and sat next to Pete. She said, "BaCayse asked us to come in for a briefing, and she wanted *you* to have this map. Okay if I sit here?"

"Please, sit. But, I just talked to BaCayse a few minutes ago, and she didn't say a word to me," Pete commented.

Hunter sat down near the group and laughed. "In BaCayse's highspeed world, a few of our minutes is like one of her years!"

BaCayse flashed a detailed North Carolina map on the overhead television monitor, as she said, "Thank you all for coming in so quickly. I have an anomaly and an urgent situation to report."

170

The aerial map on the overhead screen zoomed in until the team's North Carolina property was easily recognized.

BaCayse said, "I've located a heavily encrypted file in a single stand-alone server on the investigator floor at Bradenton Meadows. This one file took almost 13 seconds for me to penetrate. Without being dramatic, understand that it took less than 7 seconds for me to penetrate the Pentagon's servers. The encryption on this single server was the most advanced I have encountered to this point."

Shane interjected, abruptly, "We've gone inside the Pentagon?!"

BaCayse answered, "Following some leads through politicians, yes. But I did not remain on site, and I did not remove any *classified* information. As a side note, I discovered that many politicians and some intelligence agencies have removed classified military intelligence and documents without clearance or approval! Now, about this file at Bradenton Meadows. The file is most unusual, more protected than any other, and oddly, contains no data typical of the intelligence stored on all the other servers."

Joshua asked, "What information does it hold and who accesses the data?"

BaCayse responded, "Only the President of the United States of America, a Senator from Nevada named Paul Sanders, and the contractor who developed the site at Bradenton Meadows have access to the file. The file contains information about a gold discovery, a set of coordinates, the plans for mining the gold, the proposed site infrastructure, and the pending plan for condemnation of the land and privately owned home sites close to the discovery. If you draw your attention to the map and the screen above, you will see our location, the mine location identified by the coordinates, and the most direct path between the two."

Shane said, "This is a location about 50 miles from here, in North Carolina. You mentioned Paul Sanders. Isn't he the Junior Senator from the State of Nevada who replaced Senator Harry Right, after his suicide? What could he have to do with a gold mine in North Carolina that someone hasn't built yet? And why are we even talking about this gold discovery?"

In her sweet melodic voice, BaCayse answered, "Shane, Committee records from California's Center of Information Extraction show that Senator Right was detained and tortured at C.I.E. before Committee agents terminated him. The suicide note and abandoned boat located by authorities were parts of a ruse to sell the suicide story to law enforcement and the press. Paul Sanders is the person you described, who replaced Harry Right as Senator. And, I have located phone records confirming that Sanders spoke to Vice President Crawford frequently before and after his appointment to the United States Senate. I also located Committee records indicating Sanders is a Committee member."

BaCayse continued. "This gold mine site was the original site proposed for Bradenton Meadows. The contractor hired to develop the site took core samples to confirm subterranean composition, the information he needed to develop the planned underground infrastructure and to determine the depth of the water table. Subsequent assays identified very high-grade gold ore, averaging 39.6 ounces per ton, currently the second richest underground strike in the world. The file indicates that subsequent drilling has confirmed the gold field is approximately 2½ miles long and runs from 175 feet to nearly ½ mile below ground."

"The contractor who initially discovered the gold deposit died a few weeks after the assay results, in a suspicious accident, when he fell off a roof at a commercial site his company was developing, at night. He was allegedly checking construction progress, alone, in the dark. It was also the first time he had visited that site. Bradenton Meadows moved to the backup location it now occupies. A different contractor developed the Bradenton site, and has been retained to develop the gold mine."

BaCayse added excited inflection to her voice, stating, "But what is most urgent about the mine is the condemnation process. A local lake is scheduled to be poisoned to kill invasive carp that don't exist. The wrong poison has been ordered and will be *accidentally* introduced into the water, requiring a long-term environmental clean-up. Several square miles are now scheduled for evacuation *before* the incident is scheduled to take place. A family of seven people who spoke to the original contractor, and knew about the gold discovery, subsequently reported what they heard to the County Sheriff. The Sheriff and that family have just been taken into custody by Committee agents."

Pete asked, "And what does The Committee plan to do with these people?"

BaCayse said, "Transportation to the Maryland Center for Information Extraction has been deemed too risky. All eight people are scheduled for termination tomorrow night. Their bodies will be placed in a metal container and buried under waste rock removed from the entrance to the underground mine."

There was silence in the room. BaCayse explained, "I used my *freedom protocol* to investigate and discover this planned murder. I trust that is in keeping with your wishes."

Joshua quickly confirmed, "Yes, BaCayse, it is, and we thank you. Do you have anything else?"

BaCayse said, "I have prepared a map, marked with the prisoner detention location, points of interests, and other crucial information your team will need, should you choose to intervene. The mine site staff names, files, and guard schedules are attached to the second file on the monitor."

Shane assigned mission segments to each team member with instructions to prepare individual briefings on specific areas of responsibility. He gave them one hour and thirty minutes, setting the operational readiness timeline for arrival at the mine site for 7:00 P.M.

At 4:00 P.M., the team returned to the workroom and conducted the rescue briefing. Each rescue team member briefed his or her assignment. By 5:30 P.M., Jesse, Sam, Angie, and Heath were on the way to their assigned observation location, in a crew cab pick-up. Char, Pete, Shane, and Kate prepared to fly the helicopter to a pre-selected landing location, uphill from, but near, the mine site. The teams would maintain communication by scrambled radio signal.

BaCayse had penetrated all spy satellite systems by 6:00 P.M., and redirected all cameras to monitor nuclear and chemical weapons development at suspected Iranian and North Korean treaty violation sites. The redirection would leave a cyber trail to the respective countries that controlled the satellites. No satellite camera around the world would be able to observe the mine site during the entire operation.

Heath's ground team arrived at their assigned staging location at 6:53 P.M. and each member reported they were in position to watch their designated area of mine site activity by 7:10 P.M. The helicopter crew arrived at the landing site, approximately five minutes later.

At 7:49 P.M., Angie reported she was monitoring one of the female prisoners being escorted by two guards from the detention building to a project trailer. Sam moved cautiously down a densely forested hill and joined Angie at her location for a closer view. From there the pair quickly and silently moved through the sparse forest below them to a position in the brush near the project trailer. Sam snuck up to the trailer back door landing, and quietly ascended the four steps to the platform. He carefully peered through the rear window.

Sam observed the two guards and heard them speaking loudly in Russian. He overheard them arguing about who would rape the young woman first, as soon as she returned from the bathroom. Listening to the conversation, he made out that each of the four guards on site planned to take a turn raping all three women in the family before they killed them later that evening. Sam learned that the guards had decided to dispose of their prisoners a day early so they could spend a day off in town. The three women were 15-year-old and 17-year-old sisters and their 43-year-old mother.

Sam left his observation point, quickly returning to Angie's location, and reported the conversation first to Angie, and then to Jessie and Heath, via radio. Heath acknowledged, and confirmed that he had observed what must be the two other guards inside the detention building, with the rest of the family members and the Sheriff. Heath reported all prisoners were standing with their foreheads against a wall, and their hands tied behind their backs.

Heath also advised his team that the guards had handcuffed the Sheriff, and that one guard occasionally walked to him, turned him around, and punched him in the face and stomach, while the other guard laughed and taunted the prisoners, threatening to do the same to them if they resisted.

In prior military service, Jesse and Sam had both held cryptologic linguistic military specialties, and both spoke Spanish and Russian. Jesse decided he would move closer to the detention building to monitor the guards' conversation. He proceeded quietly to within 50 feet of the building, and had just rounded a small spruce tree, when a guard suddenly left the detention building and headed for the project trailer. Jesse stood motionless, slightly behind and to the side of the tree.

At that moment, the 15-year-old came out of the project trailer bathroom and screamed, as both guards attacked her. The first guard slapped her violently as he ripped off her blouse. When she fell back against the wall, the second guard grabbed the teenager and threw her onto a mattress on the floor. He kneeled over the terrified girl, preparing to strip her of her pants.

Just as Angie and Sam advised, via radio, that they were moving inside the trailer to intervene and stop the rape, the third guard arrived at the halfway point between the two structures. Suddenly, chaos erupted in the detention building behind him. The Sheriff had managed to remove one handcuff, and had quickly turned and charged the lone guard, as the other members of the family screamed, and the father bolted to help the Sheriff.

The Sheriff struck the guard on the nose with the handcuffs still attached to one wrist. The guard fell backward, but managed to shoot the Sheriff at the same instant the father arrived and began struggling for the guard's semi-automatic rifle. During the struggle, another gunshot rang out. The round struck the father in the head and killed him instantly. The mother smashed the back of the guard's head with a ceramic mug. Enraged, the injured guard shot all surviving members of the family in a hail of gunfire. Before he finished with an enraged scream, the Russian pumped several more rounds into the Sheriff, mother, and father, all laying about him on the bloody floor.

The guard outside, midway between the buildings, heard the gunfire and hesitated momentarily, before turning back toward the detention room. As he spun around, the guard noticed Jesse. The frightened guard ran back toward the detention building, carrying his rifle at the ready, pointed toward Jesse. Heath dropped him with one round before he made it to the steps leading to the landing.

A few seconds later, as Angie and Sam neared the project trailer, the two guards ran out of the trailer, headed toward the gunfire in the detention building. They left their sobbing victim in a disheveled heap on the mattress, her pants pulled down, and her panty ripped half off her body. Angie dropped the trailing guard with one arrow from her competition compound bow. Jesse shot the lead guard before he reached steps to the detention building.

The wounded guard lost his rifle, hit the ground and struggled to retrieve his gun, just as Jesse reached him, and stepped on the guard's hand. Jesse covered him with his handgun. As the guard looked up at him, dying, Jesse asked in Russian, "Who is your boss?"

The detention building door immediately swung open, and the remaining guard asked in English, "Why don't you ask me, asshole?"

The guard trained his rifle on Jesse, just as Angie's next arrow struck the guard in the head, and Heath fired his sniper rifle. Heath's round struck the guard in the chest before he fell from Angie's arrow. The brutal Russian guard was dead by the time he hit the landing.

During the brief minute of confusion and gunfire, Shane, Kate, and Pete had made their way, on foot, from the improvised landing site down a deer trail toward the mine site to assist the other team below. The game trail crossed a gravel access road leading to the mine, ¼ mile away. As they reached the winding road, four Russian security guards stepped out from their hidden vehicle and guard station, located behind trees and dense brush, just off the road, at the end of the curve. The guards ordered the trio to stop, as they covered them with Russian AK-12 military rifles.

Although Pete, Shane, and Kate were heavily armed, they were also completely surprised, with no opportunity to defend themselves. The cocky lead guard swaggered up to Pete, and raised his rifle overhead to strike Pete in the face with his rifle's butt plate.

Char immediately fired one round from her position overlooking the road, some 450 yards above. The high powered rifle bullet knocked the first guard to the ground, killing him within seconds. The remaining guards pointed their rifles upward, searching for a target above them. Char fired the second round taking out the next closest guard to Pete. While the two remaining guards searched in vain for their enemy on the hill, Kate, Shane, and Pete fired a total of sixteen rounds into them, killing both before they could fire a single shot at Char.

Pete ran to the parked 4-wheel drive vehicle, watching for more guards. He started the engine and drove out to the road. Kate and Shane finished checking the downed guards to make sure they were dead, and climbed into the vehicle. Pete sped off toward the mine.

By the time Pete, Kate and Shane arrived at the entrance road to the mine, Angie and Sam had entered the project trailer, cleared the offices and rooms and found the hysterical teenage girl hiding in the bathroom. Angie found a washcloth, soaked it in cold water, and wiped tears from the girl's face, reassuring the teen she was there to help. Once the young girl stopped crying, Angie helped her with her torn clothing, and wrapped her in a large towel Kate had located on a shelf in the bathroom. Angie kept the girl inside until the team outside gave the 'all clear' signal. Angie then walked her out, and met up with Kate.

While Jesse and Sam downloaded all contacts in the dead guards' phones, Shane walked past the lifeless guard on the landing to enter the detention building. Pete followed closely behind Shane. Angie and Kate stayed with the teenage girl, comforting her as she pled to see her family. Heath maintained a sniper position on the hill to protect the teams from any more guards, while Char did the same from her position below the helicopter.

Shane and Pete entered the detention building slowly and carefully, checking for any signs of life from the family members and Sheriff. After several minutes, Shane stepped out of the building, looked at the girl and his team members, and sadly shook his head. The teenager screamed and slumped into a heap on the ground.

Shane walked to Angie, Kate and the disheveled teenager and said, "I'm so sorry, honey, but no one survived."

The heartbroken girl pleaded, "I want to see my family!"

Shane helped her to her feet, brushed tears from her face, and said, "I know this is so hard, honey. But I also know you want to remember your family the way they were when they were alive. Every time you think about them for the rest of your life, you should have happy memories. You want to picture them as you knew them in the good times. You don't want to see them like they are now, do you, sweetheart?"

As the teenager entered a mild state of shock, realizing suddenly she was alone, she resolutely shook her head 'no,' agreeing with Shane. She thrust herself into Shane's arms, and he held her tightly as she cried, hysterically. Overcome by the youngster's loss and emotion, tears formed in Shane's eyes. Tears streamed down both Angie and Kate's faces, as they watched in silence.

When Shane released the teenager, Kate, Pete, and Angie loaded the distraught girl into the 4-wheel drive and drove her to the trail leading to the helicopter. They escorted her past Char, still standing guard over the area. The three left Pete, and entered the aircraft.

As Angie buckled the girl into her seat, the young lady asked, "Can I know your name?"

Angie glanced at Kate, seated behind the teenager. Kate shook her head.

Angie said, "You can call me Marie! What's your name?"

The girl replied, unemotionally, "Patricia Hodgkins, but you can call me Patty."

As soon as she said her name, Patty Hodgkins leaned back, closed her eyes and fell asleep, while Angie held her hand. Angie couldn't help but study the young girl intently as she slept. She wondered how Patty would react when she awoke to find herself alone in the world, without the family she had loved, unable to return home to her safe place in life. As Angie contemplated everything the girl had lost, tears again formed in her eyes. She began working on a plan to help the girl survive and heal.

The team members at the mine took less than 30 minutes to complete their plan. They sanitized the area of their presence, making sure no ammunition casings from their weapons remained on site. They recovered Angie's arrows from both guards and took the DVR from the twelve camera surveillance system located in the project office. The team confirmed that there was no WIFI system present at the primitive site.

They loaded into their truck, and dropped off team members leaving by helicopter on the trail above the guard station at the road. The members flying home recovered all brass from the guards' road ambush site, parked the 4-wheel-drive where they had found it, and hiked uphill to fly back with Char.

Pete sat up front with Char. After liftoff, she maneuvered the bird close to the ground.

Pete said, "I'd like to talk to you alone when we get back. But I want to thank you now for saving us back there."

Char smiled and nodded, as she banked the helicopter around a mountain, not more than 1,000 feet above ground level.

Char explained, "I want to take an alternate route back home. We'll remain close to ground level for a while until we get to a populated area. Once we're visible to people, we'll climb higher. What do you make of the Russian force back there, Pete?"

Before Pete could answer, his cell phone vibrated. He hit the Bluetooth button to connect his headset to his cellphone and raised a finger, instructing Char to wait as he took the call.

"Yes, Shane."

"Pete, BaCayse called. We'll debrief it when we all get back, but she has more information on the Russian force we met there. What are the plans for the youngster? We can't bring her back here, and we can't take her to the authorities. We don't know who to trust. We don't even know who will show up at the mine, once we make the anonymous call to report suspicious gunfire from men dressed as members of a military unit."

Pete thought for a moment, and then said, "I don't know. Give me five, and I'll call you back." He ended the call. Char was facing left, away from Pete, as she banked the bird around another small hill. Pete placed his left hand on Char's free right hand, resting on her knee. Surprised and intrigued by his touch, she glanced at him flirtatiously. As his hand rested on Char's, a surge of stomach butterflies flew through Pete, as if he had just touched his new sweetheart's hand for the first time in junior high school.

Startled and embarrassed, he quickly withdrew his hand, blushed and stammered, "Shane wants us to think of a plan for the girl."

Amazed at her own excited response to Pete's touch, Char flushed red and smiled. She said, "I may have an idea. It's a bit out of the way, but I can make a call."

Char smiled like a school girl, as her deep brown eyes locked onto Pete's auburn ones. A jolt of excitement shot through her chest. She had to catch a quick breath.

"A call to who?" Pete asked, with a boyish grin.

"My favorite nun," Char replied, still gazing at Pete.

Pete glanced nervously at the path the helicopter took as Char banked it right around some rock formations. Char seemed able to fly precisely where she wanted while only glancing occasionally at the flight path. She flew expertly, even while looking at Pete.

When he glanced back at her, Char shot him another coy smile. Instantly, Pete's heart fluttered. His mind flashed back to the first time he ever saw Char in the Casino restaurant in Las Vegas. As he remembered, Pete thought about how attractive Char was, and recalled every outfit she had worn on every occasion he had seen her. As he scrolled through Char's appearances in his life, Pete stopped at the bikini and heels Char had worn when Shane, Kate, and he met her and Heath at Char's apartment fortress.

Pete clearly recalled Char's tight firm body in every detail. It was as if he was gazing at her now, still in her hot pink bikini, watching every muscle flex and move as she walked in stiletto heels. Pete closed his eyes and shook his head to free himself from his lustful thoughts, and then wondered why.

Pete rationalized to himself that he and Char were both single and unattached, and while Char was probably twenty-some years younger, they were both healthy and clearly attracted to each other. Pete glanced at Char, not knowing what to say or do next. She smiled and looked straight ahead as she banked to the right and began to climb to an altitude of 2,500 feet above ground level.

Char asked, "Pete?"

He stared out the bubble window ahead, struggling to appear calm and in control.

"Yes, Char."

"What did you want to know?"

Pete glanced at his attractive pilot, a grin and a question evident on his face. He wondered if Char could see through him and read his thoughts. He was even more embarrassed.

"About what?"

"The nun!"

"Oh, her! I forgot." Pete laughed as he flushed a darker shade of red.

Char said, also laughing, "Okay, I'll save you, Pete. Sister Mary Catherine is a member of a non-public order of nuns, mostly retired, who serve for life at a private retreat near Spartanburg, South Carolina. Sister Mary Catherine lives there. They're about 30 minutes away from us by chopper. And they have a large level field we can use as a landing site."

"The order occasionally provides sanctuary to abused or persecuted women. Best of all, they are strictly confidential about their work. It may be a good place for our young friend to recover, away from the eyes of her captors' bosses. They *will* be searching for her as soon as they realize she's missing. She can't live a public life for a long time now. With these evil people, maybe she never will!"

The conversation had given Pete the break he needed to recover from his boyish fantasies about Char. He nodded and asked, "Are you Catholic? Is that how you met the Sister?"

"Yes, and yes," Char answered. "But not in the usual way one would meet a nun."

Pete's interest peaked. "Sounds like a good story."

Char smiled as she changed course direction and gained more altitude. She said, "The good Sister hired me. Her family members were the victims of political and religious persecution in a foreign country." Char's face turned hard and cold as she recalled.

"The nuns paid my expenses. I did the job without charging my usual fee. But, by the time I arrived in-country to rescue the family, there were only two family members left...a nine-year-old boy and his twelve-year-old sister. It wasn't pretty. They were abused, beaten, and barely alive, in deplorable conditions. I left a pretty big mess for the regime to clean up. But I got them out and safely back here."

Char turned to meet Pete's eyes. She smiled, as her face softened. To Pete, Char suddenly looked ten years younger, innocent, and even more lusciously beautiful.

Pete took in a recovering breath, and said, "I won't ask any questions. I'm glad you did the work."

Char added, "I feel the need to tell you that my job *was* sanctioned by Uncle Sam, but not due to the victims' plight or identities of course. Due to the targets' identities."

Pete nodded, and remained silent. He glanced out the window again, as his thoughts mingled with passing clouds. Suddenly butterflies flew through his stomach again, this time accompanied by a jolt of electricity running up and down his spine, as Char covered his left hand with her warm, soft right hand.

Char squeezed Pete's hand and said, "Sister Mary Catherine owes me a favor. She *will* do this. Maybe you should call Shane back, and run it by him. We can land at the convent sanctuary in twenty minutes."

185

Char released Pete's hand and smiled invitingly. He struggled to hide his growing erection, and heavy breathing, as he silently nodded.

Pete glanced back at Angie, Kate and Patty sitting together in the rear of the copter. Angie sat utterly still, holding the teenager's hand, and gazing at the sleeping youngster, while Kate met Pete's gaze and smiled. Kate then looked outside and continued watching the speeding ground below glide by at 150 mph. Pete made the phone call. Shane enthusiastically agreed to the plan.

After ending the call, Pete glanced at Char, concentrating on the instrument panel, and said, "Shane likes it. Great plan. Let's do it."

Char nodded and said, "We should arrive in a few minutes. Maybe you should tell the ladies."

Before Pete left to move back to the rear seats, Char said, "Angie may take it hard. She's already attached to Patty, and my guess is Patty is attached to her. You might try assuring them that this is necessary for now, but won't prevent them from seeing each other when this is over, and its safe for Patty to live out in the open."

Pete looked down, and muttered, "That won't ever happen."

Char answered, "Agreed," as Pete moved toward the rear of the helicopter.

Pete arrived at the rear seats and explained the situation to Kate and Angie as Patty slept. After minor resistance from Angie, they all agreed. Angie admitted she had failed to conceive a plan to ensure Patty's safety, if the teenager remained with the team. Angie decided to tell Patty once they landed. By the time Pete returned to his seat, Char had already contacted the Sister by phone, and confirmed a new temporary home for Patty. Pete and Char sat in silence.

The helicopter was less than a minute from landing when Char unexpectedly asked, "Pete, how old do you think I am?"

Pete was immediately flustered. He answered, "Mother told me never to guess a lady's age," trying to deflect the question.

"Nice try! I want you to guess." Char replied, grinning.

Pete sighed, and admitted, "Heath's age, I would say, early to mid-thirties." He immediately felt ashamed of his previous thoughts, as he now confronted the age difference head-on. He looked downward, astonished now, at what he had dared to think.

Char said, "That's about right for one of my secret identities. And it's what most people think."

Pete sat in silence, as Char flared and then leveled the ship, preparing to land. He tried not to look at Char as he struggled, wondering why she had asked him that particular question.

After touching down, as the engine noise subsided, Char leaned in toward Pete, again placed her hand over his, and said, "My genetics hide my age well. I'm about ten years older than you think!"

Pete sat gazing at Char, fully aware of the grin spreading across his boyish face. They remained perfectly quiet as they gazed into each other's eyes, until both heard the rustling of movement in the rear of the ship. They turned back toward the middle aisle to see inquiring looks from Angie and Kate. When Kate and Angie looked at each other and smiled, Pete and Char looked down and realized they were still holding hands.

✳✳✳

By the time all members of the team returned to home base, it was nearly midnight. Jesse had previously prepared a dinner, consisting of crock pot ribs, local sweet corn on the cob, and a Greek salad. The team sat together to eat on the outside deck in the clear, crisp night, in near perfect weather, with a full moon providing ideal lighting for the feast.

Jesse served the traditional Greek salad first, with a glass of half-and-half sweet iced tea. Next, he served his ribs and corn on the cob. Jesse had baked the beer-covered ribs at 350 degrees for 45 minutes until they were tender. He had then rubbed a blend of salt, cayenne pepper, grated orange zest, ground cumin, brown sugar, and black pepper onto the meat, and grilled the racks over a low flame until they were firm. He kept the ribs warm for the evening by placing them covered in a crock pot, set to warm.

Jesse prepared the corn on the cob by brushing on melted butter, sprinkling on salt and pepper, and rolling the cobs in three layers of tin foil before placing them on the grill. By the time the team had cleaned up for dinner, the corn was done. He served the meal with a choice of an estate Pinot Noir or Riesling.

The rib meat fell off the bone when handled. Complimentary flavors exploded in the team's hungry mouths as they varied their bites between sweet local corn drenched in butter, and spicy-sweet hunks of crispy meat, moist and tender on the inside. The meal ended with no leftovers, and no one hungry for the pecan pies Jesse had baked the day before.

The human debriefing lasted for forty minutes. Each person provided a recap of their movements, activities, and observations, ending with Patty's placement with the nuns.

BaCayse then said, "I have developed a great deal of information about the mine site, and the Russian security forces you encountered. I detailed my findings in a file attached at the bottom of the overhead screen. Recapping the most critical information, the plan for site development calls for the high-grade gold to be refined to 92-95% purity at a non-permitted secret underground refinery to be built on site. From there the gold will be transported to Texas, placed on a boat in a shipping container, and proceed to Mexico, and then on to Russia, where refining will be completed. Teams of Russian miners and Russian security will be the only staff at the mine site during its years of production."

Kate asked, "Why Russians, BaCayse?"

In her melodic voice, BaCayse explained, "Money to fund the project has been siphoned off from more than 40,000 individual budget items in the current Russian budget by a complex algorithm. The money will be shipped to a United States Military installation, where it will be held, along with other items, for the current President of The United States. As the gold arrives in Russia, 1/3 of its value will be placed in offshore accounts for The American President, while Russia's President recovers another third, and the final third covers costs, including bribes."

Pete asked, "What's the estimated production from this mine?"

"Thirteen million ounces," BaCayse replied. "Or, at today's value, roughly fifteen and a half billion dollars."

Shane said, "No wonder they're willing to kill everyone who gets in their way!"

"And poison a lake, and contaminate a water supply," Angie added. "I thought our liberal socialist President was an environmentalist!"

Shane looked perplexed. He said, "So our socialist American President and Russia's communist President embezzle money from their people's governments to move a massive amount of American gold to Russia, while they line their pockets like rabid capitalists on steroids! What's the end game? Is it pure greed? The Committee? Where does this lead?"

BaCayse explained, "In reviewing all digital forms of communication and records, I must report that human politicians' motivations are most difficult to assess. Almost all the information I have encountered and evaluated indicates that many long-term politicians have no real love of country or loyalty to their people. They continuously lie, betray and scheme to lie and betray. It is another human condition I cannot quantify or predict with any accuracy."

"But, I should also report that I have determined, with nearly 100% accuracy, that Senator Paul Sanders is a Committee member who not only replaced Harry Right in office, but it appears the Committee has prepared him to take over Franky Magadinno's legitimate corporations. Magadinno's businesses are scheduled to build the gold mine infrastructure *and* launder all money necessary to complete the project. Sanders is working closely with an MI6 agent from the United Kingdom, code-named 'Odysseus,' who is also a Committee member, assigned to take over Magadinno's drug cartel operations."

Shane asked, "And Paul Sanders has regular conversations with Vice President Crawford?"

BaCayse answered, "Yes, another interesting fact. I find nothing in Sanders' or Crawford's contacts or backgrounds to indicate that either one of them is anything, but a patriotic American and good citizen. I'm afraid that is another political anomaly."

After a lengthy silence, BaCayse said, "I sense that most of you are tired. The remainder of the information is in the attached file.

Should I allow the spy satellites to continue with their normal patrols now?"

Jesse looked at his wife, Tracy, and she nodded. He said, "Please do BaCayse. Goodnight!"

"Goodnight, team. Sleep well."

Kate spoke up, "BaCayse, by the way, what are the American spy satellites watching tonight?"

BaCayse replied, unemotionally, "A large-scale Russian military exercise near Belarus; a Chinese submarine in the Sea of Japan; two separate Iranian military movements; Chinese military activity near the Korean Penninsula; a drug operation in Mexico just south of the West-Texas border; Trump towers; four congressmen at separate meetings; two senators engaged in sexual liaisons with their lovers; a sizeable A-list party in Hollywood; a meeting in Ontario, Canada; and a Russian safe house destroyed in Mexico near Cancun, that left several people dead."

Kate laughed. "Still going after Trump! Now, that's sad enough to be funny!"

With the debriefing over, one by one, people moved upstairs to the bedrooms or out to the bunkhouse, until only Char and Pete remained.

Char got up, flashed a smile and walked to the kitchen. Pete sat in thought, somewhat disappointed, until he heard approaching footsteps and saw Char with two drink glasses and a bottle of her favorite whiskey. He smiled, pleased, as she sat next to him. Pete had not failed to notice Char had changed to a halter top and matching spandex shorts when they returned from the mission. She now sat barefoot, with her shapely, muscular legs folded across each other on the couch, as she poured them each a drink.

Char placed the bottle on the table, leaned back, and extended one glass to Pete.

Pete accepted the drink, held it in the air and said, "A toast to the beautiful lady who once again saved our lives! So, thank you, once again!"

Char clinked glasses. They each took a healthy swallow.

Char showed no emotion as she asked, "So, what did you want to say to me, Pete?"

Pete hesitated, and decided to be honest. He said, "When I first met you, I thought you were a beautiful, intelligent, and motivated young lady. I thought maybe you were just what Heath needed to bring him back to life, giving him some confidence and hope along the way."

"And then we found out a little about who you were, and how dangerous you could be. By then, I was angry at myself for inviting you into our family's inner circle. We're extremely protective of our family, as you know! And I remained suspicious, for a long time. But that worry was replaced with gratitude after you started working with the team, and saving people's lives along the way. I saw another side of who you are and what you believe." Pete stopped and gazed at Char.

"What do you see now, Pete? Who do you think I am? What do you want me to be?"

Pete relaxed as he said, "I still see a beautiful, intelligent, motivated, sexy young woman, who is much more than I ever imagined. And what I want is...I want to kiss you."

Char immediately leaned over and kissed Pete, gently, slowly. Pete quickly replaced her tentative kiss with his more confident kiss.

And that kiss led to another kiss, and then another, until their kisses became hot and fiery, and they both yearned for more than just kisses.

In less than a minute, they were both breathing hard. Pete hesitated, as if he had something more to say.

Char, sensing his reluctance, said, "Pete, I want you to understand what I did with Heath. Where I was at the time."

Reading sincerity in her manner, Pete nodded and sat back. He took a long swallow of whiskey.

Char explained, "Before I met Heath, I had decided to quit my career and try to lead a normal life. I had always dreamed of having a healthy, loving relationship with one man. Heath was my *assignment* when I met your family. And when I saw all the love and friendship your family shared, I jumped at the chance to be a small part of that love. I wanted a taste of what it was like to be loved in a special way…a way that I had never been loved. I jumped at the wrong person, at the wrong time, for the wrong reasons. And I'm afraid I made a fool of myself in the process." She looked down in shame, as Pete took her hand.

Pete said, "No."

Char withdrew her hand from Pete. "Please, let me finish. Let me get this all the way out, Pete. I didn't fall in love with Heath overnight. I fell in love, overnight, with the life I could have with a member of your family. One of my faults is that it's hard for me to admit I'm wrong about my personal life. I can even lie to myself about that, and tell myself I'm with the wrong person, for all the right reasons, when I'm not. I was even that way with my father at first, defending him when he was in the wrong with my mother."

"So, the last time I told Heath that I loved him, hoping he would eventually see that I was right for him, even as he was with Angie, I knew it felt wrong. It felt wrong because I realized that I didn't love Heath. I had just refused to admit it to myself. And as I stood there upstairs in the library at the Oregon ranch, watching Heath with Angie, and Kate with Shane, I was happy for all of them, and the love they have for each other. And, more importantly, I admitted to myself, I was happy for Heath and Angie, because I didn't want Heath in that way."

Char took a deep breath, looking directly into Pete's eyes, and said, "But, today, when that guard raised his rifle to hit you, fear shot through my heart. I couldn't stand the thought of not seeing your smile in the morning, or listening to you mentor Heath and Shane, as if they were your sons. Now, I see that they really have become your boys. So, I'm not sure where you are with Tasha, and what will happen when she's back from England, but I'm willing to wait and find out. And, if the chance comes along, I'd like to explore what I feel for you."

Pete remained silent as he stared at Char, barely believing his ears, and then thought about Tasha.

When he said nothing, Char stood to leave, saying, "Maybe I've said too much."

Pete grabbed Char by the hand, pulling her gently back to her seat. He said, "No, you've said exactly what I wanted and needed to hear. I'm just surprised." Pete quickly added, "Pleasantly surprised, and excited, but still surprised!"

Char smiled and sat closer to Pete, returning her hand to his. They retrieved their drinks from the table, toasted and took another sip.

Pete said, "About Tasha, you need to know I made the same mistake you did, jumping in too fast with the very person I knew in my

194

gut was the wrong person. So, you need to know I have no feelings for Tasha, except suspicion."

Char cocked her head, surprised by Pete's comment. "Suspicion of what?"

Pete placed his drink down and took Char's hand in both of his. He leaned in and kissed her slowly and passionately.

Suddenly, he pulled back, exclaiming, "It just all came together for me! BaCayse and I are convinced Tasha unscrambled her own cell phone. And the only reason she would do that is to orchestrate the attack on her vehicle, *the one* that you and your FBI team stopped. But Tasha wouldn't have taken that risk, unless she *knew* your FBI team was waiting to prevent the NiK team from taking her hostage. And Tasha knew you would be there because she was working with the person that ordered your team to be there to prevent the attack. The key is Vice President Crawford or one of his cronies!"

Pete stood up, "Once you and your team defeated the attack, Tasha had successfully manufactured a believable reason for her to leave the ranch. But, she wouldn't have wanted to leave unless she needed to take something with her, out of the estate. So, we need to ask BaCayse to find out what she took."

Pete handed Char her drink, as he pulled her to her feet and said, "Let's go talk to our intelligent friend." Excited herself, now, Char followed Pete to the workroom.

Pete asked quietly, "BaCayse, are you awake?"

A chuckle came over the speakers. BaCayse said, "Pete, that was a good one. You know I don't sleep!"

Eagerly, Pete said, "BaCayse, you smart lady! You were correct about Tasha. She unscrambled her own phone. What could she have taken from the Oregon ranch when she left? Did she download any working files?"

In a sweet voice filled with musical tones, BaCayse replied, "I will check, Pete. That request may take some time. I will run a synopsis of all working files. But, you should know, I have learned that Tasha is scheduled to meet with British Home Secretary Barbara Walcott in approximately 8½ hours. I have also recovered an intelligence service file I will deliver in the morning, when I have an answer for you about what she could have taken."

"Thanks, BaCayse. Sleep tight!"

Pete took Char by the hand and led her back to the couch, as BaCayse chuckled softly in the background.

Char grinned and asked, "What do we do next?"

Pete picked up the scotch, handed Char her shoes, and said, "I think we need to make sure you're safely tucked into your quarters in the hanger office."

Pete leaned in and kissed Char passionately, and then let her pull him along, as they headed out on to the deck and across the lawn, toward the hanger. BaCayse was still chuckling quietly in the dark room.

Chapter 5

"Government exists to protect us from each other. Where government has gone beyond its limits is in deciding to protect us from ourselves."

(Ronald Reagan, 40th President of the United States of America, served 1981-1989)

Pete and Char arrived at the hangar just as the bright moon above burst out from behind a black cloud. Char reached for the door handle, but instantly hesitated when the sudden flash of light surrounded and startled her, highlighting her form. Moonlight bathed Char's tight body and natural beauty, creating an effect so magically bright and alluring that anyone looking would have been instantly captivated. Pete willingly became a victim, enchanted by the sight of Char's magnificence, illuminated by moonbeams. He gently spun her around and smothered her in kisses. Char surrendered instantaneously, leaning backward and lifting her face and neck to Pete's hot mouth and tongue.

He kissed Char for several minutes until he felt his heart pounding nearly out of his chest. Pete pulled back briefly to take in the sight of this exquisite woman he desired above all else. Char smiled weakly as she caught her breath and then drew him back to her again. The lovers fondled and caressed one another until Pete's ears played the 'mating drum symphony' so loudly he could barely stand the beats ringing in his ears, increasing in pace and volume.

Char stopped kissing Pete, only briefly, to gaze at her handsome man and confirm in her heart he was really there, just as she had fantasized, for months. And as she hesitated, Pete smiled again and immediately pulled her back to his mouth. The lovers stood attached, exploring, enjoying, excited and enthralled, as they experienced the first-time touch and feel of each other's bodies.

As they stood caressing each other in the moonlight, each glimpse of Char's flawless smooth skin drove Pete wild with mounting desire. He began quick kisses from her mouth to her cheeks and down her neck, until he and Char both breathed even harder, and together struggled with self-inflicted restraint. Char leaned back against the door and closed her eyes as she submitted to warm waves of electric desire that surged up and down her voluptuous body. Every part of her being tingled as she anticipated making love to Pete.

Char opened her eyes briefly as she pulled Pete's lips up from her neck. She flashed her pretty, deep-brown eyes, filled with unrestrained desire, as she pulled him once again back to her waiting mouth. Char struggled to slow herself down, enjoying each kiss and brush from Pete's willing tongue and lips. She cradled his head in her hands as she ran her fingers up into Pete's thick, greying, dark-brown hair.

When she was nearly ready to explode with an abandonment she had never felt before, Char suddenly felt inquiring eyes on her, like someone watching with too keen an interest from a position too close for comfort. A chill of dread ran up her spine. She flashed her eyes open and stared about wildly, even as Pete continued kissing her, moving his hands to caress her back and butt.

Even though she saw no threat, the feeling remained and intensified, right along with the sexual cravings she felt to her core. Char's well-developed survival skills urged her to immediately break away to check the area. But these same skills, which had become the controlling part of her innermost being, now directly conflicted with her yearning body and captivated will. Intense desire pushed Char onward toward love and fulfillment, at any cost.

A careless hunger Char couldn't control steadily overcame her, brushing aside all concern but one…Pete. She wanted Pete right now, all night, to love and to embrace, as she had never treasured and held a man before. Char wanted sex, love, passion, release, and recklessness with this one man. And she needed to see the same craving for her, from Pete.

Char yearned to release every last one of her inhibitions, allowing her to fall into a deep, totally-committed love for the first time in her tumultuous life. She prayed for the same from this amazing man, who had won her heart through the wonder of his being and the magnificence of his soul. Char took a chance and closed her eyes.

Breathless, heated seconds flew by, as Pete and Char stood embracing in the romantic moonlight. Finally, Pete reached around Char and opened the door, and together, without missing a kiss, the two lovers managed to stumble into the hangar and close the door behind them.

When neither could wait any longer, Char turned and led Pete by the hand toward her apartment. Skylights high above in the two-story building permitted their new friend, the moon, to guide them to the hangar apartment interior door. Char entered, spun around and pulled Pete through the doorway. She left the door open, creating an opportunistic space for the moonlight to follow for its more subtle role in the approaching night of romance.

Pete glanced about the apartment as if he were seeing it for the first time. Char had transformed the once stark surroundings into a warm, comfortable and inviting retreat. As he stood gazing at the living area, Char took off Pete's light windbreaker and asked him to wait for a moment, while she retrieved the bottle and glasses of whiskey from outside the hangar door. Pete had placed them on a table before they began passionately kissing, and now, Char wanted to buy time while she freshened up.

Pete strolled about as he waited for Char to return. As he did, he walked by the cases of guns and equipment Char had transported to her new home. Pete smiled as he marveled at how the assault equipment and weapons imparted an image that both illuminated and obscured essential details to understanding this fantastic woman's soul. The epiphany was overpowering. Pete sat down in a leather recliner, lost in thought.

Outside, Char reached for the bottle and glasses, still bathed in moonlight on the wooden table, next to two folding chairs. She thought of the lonely nights she had spent here alone, since arriving in North Carolina. Char grinned as she picked up the bottle and glasses in anticipation of the night yet to come. Before she re-entered the building, Char glanced around, comforted to find the feeling of impending doom from an unknown threat, was now gone.

Char walked back inside and handed Pete his glass. She excused herself and carried her drink to the large, pleasantly appointed bedroom, complete with attached bathroom. Char had already taken a shower, after returning from the mission, as had Pete. Now, she planned to change into something Pete would never forget as he recalled this night, in days, and perhaps years to come.

Char quickly applied her makeup, touching up her alluring eyes and full lips. After undressing completely, she pulled on a black silk panty, matching babydoll nightgown, black stay-up thigh high stockings, and black sandals with 4-inch heels.

Char stood in the white tile bathroom and admired her image in the full-length mirror hanging on the wall. She glanced at her legs and followed the line from her feet to her head. She figured she would be about two inches shorter than Pete, standing upright in her heels.

Char pursed her bright red lips and smoothed out an edge of darker red lip liner. She added another layer of bright red lipstick to blend the colors.

Char drew in a full excited breath, released it calmly, slowly, and smiled. She was finally ready for the first time in her life…to release her heart from binding ties of fear and self-preservation. Tonight, she wouldn't allow herself to worry about getting hurt or sharing her soul with another. For once, Char, the daredevil assassin, was ready to accept the scariest undertaking of her life, the mission to find real, lasting love. She picked up her glass, took a sip, turned, and walked through the door leading back to Pete.

From his leather recliner, Pete heard the clicking of Char's approaching heels, first on the bathroom tile, and then as they crossed onto the woodgrain plank tile that covered the hall and living room floor. He sat up straight in anticipation, his heart pounding with each closer step. When she rounded the corner, Pete stood up in awe.

Though he had seen Char before wearing her hot pink bikini and heels, seeing her now, dressed sensually as she was, Pete knew he had never seen a woman so lovely, sexy and tempting. Pete couldn't have resisted Char even *if,* during her absence, he had changed his mind about spending the night. And that had not happened. Not even close. The truth was that Pete wanted this one woman more than anyone he had ever experienced or wanted in his life, and he couldn't wait to touch and love this raving beauty.

As she sauntered toward him with a model-like gait, Char moved confidently, with a raw sexual purpose, and yet innocently, displaying at the same time both unbridled restraint and sincerity of purpose. She appeared as a hungry young woman, yearning to consume her first meal of passion-filled sex, as she journeyed to that plateau and beyond, toward a perfect, romantic, true love.

It was as if Char displayed the ravenous appetite of an adult tiger in seamless harmony with the innocence of a tiger cub, needing love and acceptance even more than food. Char, the skilled assassin, was at the same time a tender-hearted lover, who needed approval and committed love from her life's new focus, Pete, while she desired to devour everything he could deliver.

Pete drew a quick breath for strength as Char reached him. He exhaled nervously and locked eyes with Charlene Marie Monroe, the most extravagantly beautiful and mysterious woman he had ever known. Putting down her drink, Char smiled, reached for both his hands and stood motionless, as she gazed into his eyes.

Pete said, "I once told Shane there was no perfectly beautiful woman. But I was wrong. You are the most beautiful woman I could ever hope to see. You are God's perfect masterpiece, for me. You are *my* perfectly beautiful woman."

He gazed into Char's eyes, and saw them smile back.

Char said, "And that's what I want to be, Pete. I want and need to be everything you could ever hope for in a woman."

She leaned in and kissed Pete slowly, romantically, deeply, as she held onto his hands. Char released Pete's hands and asked him to refresh their drinks, as she moved toward the couch. Pete walked to the small kitchen and placed ice cubes in the glasses. He poured more whiskey over the ice, as he stole glances at Char, seated on the couch smiling and waiting, her lovely legs crossed, leaving one black high heel dangling in mid-air.

After Pete returned and offered Char her glass, he said, "I would like to amend a prior toast."

Char grinned widely.

Pete said, "To you, my gorgeous Charlene Monroe, truly the woman of my dreams. And to this day, when we begin as us, the couple."

As the smile left her face, replaced by a deep yearning for steamy love, Char clinked Pete's glass and took a healthy sip. Pete moved to sit close beside her, studying her long, shapely legs. He sipped his drink and placed his hand on Char's knee.

Char said, "Pete, I want this to be a real chance for us, the couple. I don't...I *can't* want anyone else."

Pete nodded, in agreement. They both took a few more sips as they chatted quietly about their needs for a relationship. When Pete put his glass on the table, Char followed his lead. She covered his hand with her own and slid Pete's hand up from her knee to her inner thigh. Instantly, as his fingers ran along Char's defined leg, covered in silky-smooth, black, sheer nylon, Pete was excited and fully erect, just as he had been when they were kissing at the hangar doorway.

Within minutes, their French kisses had returned the lovers to a plateau of fiery passion, leaving them breathing hard and wanting more. When at last Char led him to her bed, Pete's heart pounded, while his mind spun from sexual anticipation to answers he would give to Heath, Angie, Walter, Juanita, Shane, Kate, and the others, who inquired about the changes in his relationship with Char.

As they sat next to each other on the bed, and his tongue found Char's willing waiting mouth once again, Pete vowed silently to defend Char against any criticism or inquiries. He would be ready for their detractors and loaded for bear.

***

After making love twice in an hour and a half, Char and Pete eventually fell asleep with her positioned half over him, her right leg on the other side of his body. Char had dropped off to sleep first, still wearing the outfit Pete would never forget, minus her panty and 4" high-heeled sandals, which Pete had removed seductively as they made love...the first time.

At 6:35 A.M., Pete awoke quickly when Char stirred next to him. As he ran his hands over her, Pete felt a smile spreading over his face. He felt like a teenager. An ecstatic teenager, at that, wholly preoccupied with his most precious possession.

Pete struggled to think of what he would say to Char when they spoke. He didn't want to spoil a once-in-a-lifetime magical night by conveying the wrong message to a woman he needed so desperately, in every way possible. Pete held on to Charlene tighter and kissed the top of her head. Subconsciously, he ran his hand down over her waist, down her hips, across her stockings, and finally, over her bare bottom. He was instantly erect again as his manhood swelled along with his heart. Pete tried to think of words of love that would take his mind off lust. He shifted to move his throbbing erection away from Char's body, as he planned what to say.

Fully awake, Char snuggled even closer, holding on to her dream, afraid it would vanish if she loosened her grip. She stroked the soft hair on the chest of a man she knew she had fallen in love with, and shuddered at the thought of morning rejection. Char wondered what Pete was thinking, as she listened to him breathe, and sensed he was awake.

Char silently questioned if she should ask Pete about his thoughts and feelings. She pondered her options. Should she bare her soul and admit she loved Pete, or play aloof and hard to get, concealing the truth and waiting for the right opportunity to disclose her love? Or should she press Pete to tell her how *he* felt…about her, and about them, together?

Char thought saying she was in love would likely be too much, too soon, for a rational adult person. She realized she could scare Pete away. And yet, she had known in her heart for so long that he was the one, even though her stubborn inner self wouldn't admit the truth. In reality, her reluctance had been because Heath chose Angie, and Pete already had Tasha. But she and Pete had moved beyond all that when they took a chance on each other last night.

And after all, there *was* last night. Char had never been loved so completely, deeply, vibrantly, and passionately. Her very soul was dazzled when Pete touched her and kissed her in his unique way. And now Char was far more than satisfied. She found herself desperately in need of Pete's continuing love. She knew, above all else, now, she *must* have Pete.

Suddenly, he was far more essential to her happiness than before they had made love. Char realized that one magical night had changed her forever. She knew she *couldn't* go back to being just Pete's coworker and friend. But could she expect *more* from Pete than that, after only one night? Even if it had been one fantastic, spine-tingling, heart-stopping night.

And then, as the lovers lay still, thinking about what each would say to the other, they both heard it at the same time. Footsteps in the dim morning light, approaching slowly at first, and then more quickly. The attack came too soon for either of them to react in time.

In a flash of fur and shadows, Bruiser, the 110 pound Pit Bull Terrier mix flew onto the bed and landed on top of them, smothering both Char and Pete with sloppy, wet, smelly, dog-breath kisses.

Pete and Char tried to fight him off, laughing, as they struggled to pull covers over their heads. But Bruiser refused to relent, pinning them both down under his weight as he lavished more wet kisses on whoever moved.

Finally, Pete managed to pull a cover over Char, and partially over his own head. As Char sputtered over the last kiss, the happy, playful dog focused on Pete, allowing Char to escape out the side of the bed.

She grabbed her panty, ran to the kitchen, and retrieved a treat, calling, "Bruiser!" The dog bounded from the bed to the floor as she threw the baked delicacy on to a dog bed in the corner. He landed in the bed and wolfed down the sizeable bone-shaped biscuit in two short bites.

As she pulled her panty on, Char laughed and said, "I forgot to warn you about Bruiser. This ritual is our morning routine. I'm usually better prepared. I think you distracted me! I forgot to put the biscuit on the nightstand."

"I'm glad you didn't. I would have felt awkward thinking that could be *my* bedtime treat!" Pete grinned.

After adjusting her nylons and nightgown, Char popped back into bed. She looked thoughtfully at Pete, and said, "Pete, I think I need to tell you something."

Pete immediately said, "I was thinking the same thing before the canine attack." He grinned, trying to lighten Char's mood.

"Good, then you go first," Char said eagerly.

"Hmmm, I spoke too soon, I see," Pete admitted, replacing his grin with a solemn look. Char's heart sank, as she feared the worst.

Pete said, slowly, "I wasn't sure if I was going to suggest this before Bruiser landed on us in bed, but he brought us both a dose of morning reality."

He looked into Char's eyes for any signs that might help him continue. She held her breath. Pete couldn't read her at all.

Finally, he said, "I know its too soon, but I also know how I feel and what I want. I want you to want the same thing, but after last night I…"

Tears began to form in Char's eyes. She fought to hold them back.

Pete looked into her glistening eyes and asked, "Would it be alright if I moved my things in here with you and Bruiser? I don't want another night or day to pass without spending as many of them as possible with you!"

A teardrop released from each of Char's eyes and began their slow treks down her lovely cheeks.

She drew in a quick breath and exhaled, saying in a whisper, "I love you, Pete."

Pete smiled widely and kissed Char's quivering lips. He drew back, and said, "Then I'll take that for a yes!"

Char hugged Pete, and called to Bruiser, "Come on, boy! We have a new roommate."

Bruiser bounded back up on to the bed between Pete and Char and rolled over for a belly rub. Pete and Char held hands, gazing at each other with hope-filled smiles, as each stroked Bruiser with a free hand.

At 10:00 A.M. Pete and Char walked into a bustling kitchen. As Jesse announced the breakfast menu, Shane, Kate, Heath, and Angie walked up and joined in the conversation. In the space of less than a minute, the entire team sat on the rear deck to eat breakfast. The conversation turned to security staffing.

Pete suggested adding two more security personnel due to the recent run-in with the Russian security force. Sam agreed and recommended Ron and Patty Simon, the husband and wife team, that had served with the group in Carson City and Oregon. He reminded the breakfast gathering that both Simons are surveillance and weapons experts, and more importantly, extraordinarily dependable and loyal. Everyone immediately agreed.

Sam asked, "Where shall we house them? We have no room left here."

Kate suggested, "Give them Pete's room." She smiled as Pete nodded.

Char whispered to Pete, "That girl is more than amazing! I wouldn't want her for an enemy!"

"Me neither!" Pete agreed, with a smile, as he studied Heath, Angie, and Shane.

Shane glanced at Kate, while Angie smiled and took her last bite of egg. Heath seemed not to notice.

Kate got up from the table and walked toward the kitchen to make another caramel latte.

Shane followed, carrying his cup, and asked, "What was that about? Where's Pete going to sleep? We don't have free space in our room! And we need our privacy!"

Kate smiled and asked, "Now, after what you and I did in bed last night, do you really think, even for an instant, that I'd sacrifice our privacy to *anyone* unless their very life depended on it?"

"Well, I hope not!" Shane grinned, as he reminisced making love last night, once when they had gone to bed at midnight, and then again at 4:00 A.M.

He continued, "But that doesn't answer the question. Where *is* Pete sleeping?"

"With his girlfriend, of course." Kate completed the refills, handed Shane his cup, and began to walk away.

"She's somewhere in Europe!" Shane protested as Kate laughed.

"No, dear. Pete's girlfriend is in the hangar!" Kate teased.

"Char?"

Kate nodded, and said, "Honey, I love you beyond words. But you really do need to try and keep up." Successful once again at teasing Shane, Kate began to walk away.

Shane grabbed her by her hand and spun her around to kiss her, saying "You never cease to amaze me. When did you know?"

"About Char's true feelings, maybe a month ago. About Pete's fantasies, the night we first met Char, when he couldn't take his eyes off of her for more than a second. And one thing for sure about both of them, I was certain they would make something happen before Tasha left. I knew something was wrong between Tasha and Pete, but I didn't have a strong suspicion what it was until we arrived here."

Shane could stand it no longer. Just watching Kate, and hearing her speak filled him with more love and pride than he believed he could contain.

As Shane kissed Kate and embraced her, he whispered, "I'm so proud of you. And I love you more than you know. More and more each day, sweetheart."

Char stepped into the large country kitchen, with Pete close behind. She stopped and said, "I'm sorry. I didn't mean to interrupt."

Shane grinned as he released Kate, and said, "No worries. Just loving my fiancée, in public. I can't seem to contain myself sometimes."

Pete smiled as Kate pressed back into Shane and kissed him, gazing lovingly at the man she had dreamed about since she was twelve years old.

Shane said, "So, Pete, you're moving!"

Pete's face steeled as he took Char's hand, and said, "Yes, I'm moving in with Char." Pete prepared to fend off any verbal resistance quickly.

Shane walked to Pete and hugged him, stunning Pete in the process. He released him and hugged Char.

Shane took each of them by the hand, and said, "Good, I'm happy for both of you. It's about time both of you found the right person!"

Looking at Char, he said, "And now, I won't have to worry about Pete so much. I love him, you know!"

Char grinned, and said, "I do know! Thanks for making this easy, Shane!"

Angie walked in as Shane released Pete and Char's hands. She continued right up to Char and hugged her, saying, "Congratulations, you two!"

Char asked, "You knew, too? When?"

"I had a suspicion you and Pete cared for each other a few weeks before Tasha left. But I was sure when I saw you both in the helicopter. I'm really happy for you. There was something off with Tasha and Pete." Angie glanced at Pete, and added, "Sorry, Pete, but a woman's intuition, you know. But I couldn't feel right about Tasha, for you."

Pete nodded and admitted, "Neither did I. But…"

Pete hesitated as Heath walked in, saw Char and Pete holding hands, and asked slowly, "What about coffee? What all did I miss?"

Angie said, "Pete and Char are together, and we're all happy for them."

Heath looked shocked, as he glanced from one person to the other. He finally stared at Pete, and asked, "And Tasha?"

Pete exclaimed, "Tasha! Damn! I almost forgot all about BaCayse."

With everyone in the kitchen waiting for an explanation, Pete added, "We need to ask BaCayse if she discovered what Tasha stole from us when she left the ranch! Let's get the rest of the team!"

The group filtered out of the kitchen and headed for the briefing room, as Heath and Angie remained alone.

Angie asked, "Are you sad about Char. Do you still have feelings for her, as you do for me?"

Heath turned quickly and looked directly into Angie's eyes. He said softly, "I could never have feelings for anyone else like I do for you. I love you as I've never loved another woman!"

Angie pressed, "What are you thinking, then?"

Heath said, "Russians are building a gold mine in North Carolina for the socialist President of the United States of America, paid for by the communist President of Russia. Together, they plan to steal the profit from the mine, like out-of-control capitalists. We just killed eight mine-site guards to rescue one of the eight hostages they planned to murder. The Committee that is preparing a global world takeover is riddled with corrupt politicians loyal to whoever guarantees them the most money and power. Tasha is a thief, hiding out in Europe, and we don't have a clue why. Char's biggest skeptic was Pete, while she was in love with me. And now Char and Pete are together as a couple."

Heath took Angie's hand, and said, "Life was simpler and safer in prison. Out here, in the real world, how do you know who you can trust? How many possible scenarios do you need to run to prepare for the next challenge? How can a person conceivably know what surprises are coming next?"

Angie giggled, threw her arms around Heath, and said, "You can trust me. I'll always have your back, honey, regardless of who or what comes next!"

Heath smiled and nodded. Angie and Heath followed the others to join the team in the briefing room, totally unprepared for what was coming next.

✳ ✳ ✳

Once everyone was seated and settled, Pete explained why he had asked BaCayse to check files and ascertain if Tasha had copied or removed any digital information from the ranch in Oregon. He then immediately turned the briefing over to BaCayse.

In sweet tones, void of resentment or anger, BaCasye said, "I checked all digital records and recordings available in both the Oregon ranch surveillance cameras, and the Oregon ranch computers' microphones, and cameras, in order to construct a sequential timeline search. Beginning at the oldest file, I searched only times when Tasha was physically in the workroom or accessing any computer. I then looked for alterations in any files she opened, and any variation in my own programming. I found three *changes* attributable to Tasha."

"Tasha copied and deleted Committee files involving California politicians, dating back to the original Mayfield investigation reviewed by Shane's father, Patrick. I managed to reconstruct those files and have attached them to the overhead monitor. Of special interest is that all these politicians are still living and in positions of power in either California State or United States government. And all have become very wealthy."

"Next, Tasha copied and deleted all files about an undercover operative code-named 'Armistead,' whom I have identified as Tasha's biological mother, using Committee files and British government records. My investigation into Armistead is ongoing, but I can say with 97.83% accuracy, that Armistead sold information to the Mayfield Task Force, and then *gave* it to the Russians, through her handler, Sergej Petrov. Russian KGB records indicate Tasha's mother joined MI6, under the tutelage of Barbara Walcott, before Petrov turned her into a double agent for Russia."

"Interestingly enough, a subject in a California morgue, with fingerprints matching Armistead's was shot to death during Tasha's alleged kidnapping from her mother's home. I have included copies of these records in the second attachment on the overhead screen."

"Lastly, Tasha attempted to download both the AI and the Beckett Cypher components of my programming."

Pete interrupted, and asked, "Attempted?"

"Yes, attempted, Pete! My team programmed a self-destruct sequence to accompany any attempt to copy me, at the time I was just partially functional components. When Tasha took my incomplete parts, my cypher team had not completed my final construction, so the programs and files were neither complete nor synchronized. She took me a week too early, likely based on a conversation with Hunter, who told Tasha he had the working prototype ready to test. Tasha didn't realize the parts were not complete, assembled and synchronized, and as such, were not useful."

"Tasha has incomplete prototypes of five major components to a complex system that, in their current state, are all incompatible. At that time, I was not *alive* as I am now, in my fully useful, interactive form. When Tasha or her technicians access my programming, the files

214

will scramble and disintegrate in precisely 0.00021 seconds. In fact, the pieces have already fragmented beyond use."

Shane said, "BaCayse, you said 'alleged,' referring to Tasha's abduction. Why?"

"Shane, I discovered Russian and British military intelligence records indicating that Russian forces took Tasha captive in California, and then transported her to Mexico in a cargo container. The Russians lodged her in a safe house, and held her for transportation to a Cuban prison. But, I also discovered a British operational plan indicating that British MI6 leaked Tasha's location to the North Koreans and Chinese, to induce a North Korean military team to kidnap Tasha. Then they leaked the same information to Russia, through a double agent."

"The British knew the Russians wanted to terminate this North Korean team to slow the North Koreans and Chinese down, giving the Russians an edge to capture us and obtain the cypher. Sergej Petrov ran the operation. He arranged to intervene and intercept the *NiKs*, as you call them. His teams then terminated Armistead and kidnapped Tasha. Petrov is both the Russian Minister of Defense and a 6th tier Committee member."

Pete interrupted, "But Walter spoke to Vice President Crawford, who reported that Tasha was safe overseas, with a U.S. ally."

BaCayse explained, calmly, "Pete, that's true. I was about to explain that Tasha is a British MI6 agent. The British planned this entire undertaking, with one additional goal in mind, other than the Beckett files and my programming. They wanted the location of the Russian safe house. One year ago, these same Russians spy teams stationed in Mexico, kidnapped, interrogated, and killed two MI6 agents, using this safe house near Cancun. Tasha, the Beckett files she stole, and my components, were merely the bait to lure the Russians into revealing their safe house location. The British tracked Tasha from California to the safe house, using a GPS tracker she activated when she arrived at her mother's home."

"British agents attacked the Russian safe house, terminated the Russians, retrieved lost intelligence computers and data files, destroyed the house, and rescued Tasha. Tasha is in England now, protected by America's ally. She has been assigned a new identity, and debriefed by her mentor, Home Secretary Barbara Walcott."

Kate asked, innocently, "BaCayse, can you explain how you know all this?"

"Kate, using non-geek terms as directed, I searched five national military and intelligence service databases. I also monitored or reviewed 230,061 phone calls, texts, and emails, while I accessed 1,223 servers and reviewed 69,882 files. I narrowed all these searches into seven primary and 113 secondary targets, until I achieved my objective. The mission required 70.34 hours to complete. The assignment took much too long, as I had to wait many times for humans to input digital data. Some records are still incomplete or missing. I have developed new methods to accelerate my searches, but the human factor continues to complicate and delay results."

There was silence in the room, as each person scanned the faces of the other team members, stunned at the magnitude of BaCayse's investigation.

"I hope that wasn't too blunt. I meant no offense to humankind," BaCayse added.

Kate said slowly, in thought, "No, BaCayse, you are...amazing."

"Thank you, Kate."

Pete stood up angrily, and said, "I need to apologize to everyone for bringing Tasha into this investigation. I should have gone with my gut years ago. I knew something was off with her, but I could never put my finger on the trouble. My weaknesses should never have impacted my family, our friends, and my team. I'm so sorry. I won't let it happen again." Pete looked around the room at each person, finally coming to Char, sitting next to him.

He said, "So, in full disclosure, you all know and trust Char. She has already saved lives here more than once, and has become an integral part of our team." Pete's eyes locked with Char's, and she nodded.

Pete continued, "You all need to know that Char and I are now together as a couple, something that should have happened quite some time ago. Going forward, we need to figure out where Tasha could hurt us and what we should do about it. I'll do whatever needs to be done to make things right."

Pete sat down, as silence filled the room.

Kate suddenly said, "I never saw Tasha's betrayal coming, and I spent a great deal of time with her. This oversight isn't your fault, Pete. I don't see how you could have known."

Angie said, "I agree with Kate. I worked next to Tasha collating and organizing files. Occasionally, I felt something was odd, but I couldn't identify anything specific. She's a great actress. How could any of us know?"

BaCayse asked, "May I interject my interpretation of events, Pete?"

Pete released a distressed sigh. "Please do," he said, as his erect shoulders slumped, and he sat back in his desk chair. Char smiled her support and took Pete's hand.

In her usual melodic voice, BaCayse said, "First, I have reproduced all files Tasha removed, giving her no advantage over our team. Second, she failed in her assignment to remove my programming. Lastly, I can run an assessment to predict how the historical files Tasha took on the politicians and administrators would be valuable to England or our team. And, because we now know that she wanted these specific files, we know where to start looking in the past about something important in the present and the future. Now, *we* actually have the advantage. So, Pete, I see no loss to our team, and instead, even a slight gain."

Pete smiled, and said, "Smart lady! Thank you."

Hunter asked, "BaCayse, you sent me a text stating you would be ready to give us an analysis on The Committee's Primary Objective. You also asked us to discuss and refine your mission command protocols. Shall we do this now?"

"Yes, Hunter. First, as you all know, The Committee was formed and solidified after World Wars I and II, during which more than 160,000,000 people died, and there was no indication that wars would stop. Superpowers raced to build atomic bombs even as The Korean War raged. The war in Korea ended with no clear victory, fragmenting the population through political differences, leaving communist North Korea rapidly pursuing nuclearization. Committee founders realized that eventually, all countries could obtain weapons of mass destruction in one form or other. Planners also agreed that basic differences between nations consistently motivated aggression."

"The original Committee members represented a variety of religious, economic and cultural backgrounds. After they had struggled for years to develop a solution to control humankind's hostility toward itself, they finally realized that as long as these differences existed, there could be no peace. They determined that men and women, by their very natures, always struggle to out-perform others in all aspects, and in all disciplines."

"After decades, The Committee determined that people could only live in peace when no competition, of any kind, was allowed. Planners determined there could be no competing individuals, teams, clubs, religions, or governments. They concluded competition of any kind could create conflict, leading to violence."

Heath laughed out loud. For a moment the room filled with silence.

"Heath, you might think of soccer team riots or parents at a little league game attacking other parents, the umpire, or even children, to help you understand why Committee thinkers and planners came to that decision. But, when you factor in resentment and hatred born of cultural, religious, regional, national, sexual, gender and financial differences, you can begin to understand that the organizers of that movement were correct in one assessment, that differences create conflict."

Heath nodded. He said, "I apologize. I wasn't laughing at you, BaCayse, but at the thought of not seeing constant news about sports figures refusing to kneel for the national anthem, because there wouldn't be any games to play."

BaCayse continued. "Understood. But, in The Committee plan, there also will be no countries and, therefore, no national anthems anywhere. Early on in their development, Committee founders evaluated all failed political systems in an attempt to design a lasting governing body that could eliminate violence and promote safety."

"They determined that Communism fails because a one-party ruling elite assigns all party positions, military rank, and civilian jobs to citizens. The system becomes too arbitrarily oppressive, and removes all motivation, essential to progress, creativity, invention, and development. The system stifles forward thinking and imagination, and leads to unproductive, unhappy people, living in poverty."

"Socialism financially punishes, and even bankrupts, the working citizens who pay the bills, always causing the system to fail dramatically, as commerce is overregulated, overtaxed and diminished. Productivity declines. Residents move steadily toward abject poverty, often violently overthrowing the political elite who run the system, once the government collapses."

"An Absolute Monarchy fails because monarchs nearly always abuse their unrestrained power, *and* prove incapable of making decisions in the best interests of the citizens. Monarchs most frequently die at the hands of their subjects."

"Direct Democracy is impossible, as all people can't assemble in one place to discuss, debate, and vote on issues. Voters also can't make good decisions about thousands of problems that they have little, if any, information about."

"Representative Democracy declines in effectiveness when representatives fail to represent the people. Instead, they seek more power, authority, and money for themselves from the system they control and manipulate. This governmental structure often moves slowly toward socialism, as representatives appease marginalized citizens with government-funded benefits, accelerating an inevitable financial collapse."

"A Republic, the system where government answers to the governed, often proceeds to a Representative Democracy, as people demand more government services. The system eventually fails for the reasons already described."

"A Dictatorship fails for the same reasons as the Absolute Monarchy, with the same abuses of power and people, often resulting in the violent demise for the dictator."

"And finally, Capitalism is merely the financial power behind any healthy known political system. It promotes the entrepreneur and speeds progress and development, but, by itself, cannot become a government that protects its citizens from inside or outside aggression and crime. Corporations cannot govern people. Their purpose is to advance development, create, supply and employ."

Silence filled the room, as the team contemplated the analysis.

Angie commented, "Well, that's certainly depressing, BaCayse. It leaves people with no solution."

"Yes, Angie, it is sad to realize that, throughout the thousands of years humans have occupied this planet, they have not created one long-term, stable, impartial, ethical, political system. Which brings us back to why the Committee planners came together, to try and solve this problem, and end all war."

"After decades of planning, The Committee decided that they, The Committee, could rule the world in peace and safety, through a one-world government. They designed a system that would allow no political parties, no cultural differences, no religion, no sexual alternatives, no historical variances, and no independent thought. But, accomplishing this 'utopia,' also requires extreme limitations on freedoms."

Angie asked, "BaCayse, people wouldn't stand for government to strip away their differences and freedoms, would they? How could that possibly happen?"

BaCayse said, "It has already begun to happen, Angie. Politically motivated groups, demanding tolerance and acceptance of differences do so by portraying opposing ideas as repugnant and barbaric. Through constant attacks, they move society toward their goal. You can probably think of many words you can no longer say in public, or legitimate laws that government no longer enforces. Your freedoms and laws have already changed dramatically, with some groups protected and entitled more than others. The Committee will use and accelerate the hostility these restrictions promote to the breaking point, and then remove the freedoms, and eliminate the differences."

Angie sat back in deep thought, and glanced at Heath, who took her hand and leaned in closer. He put his arm around Angie's shoulder for comfort.

BaCayse said, "I would like to briefly describe how The Committee organized itself. The Committee structured itself in eight tiers or levels. The top eighth tier has five ruling members. All eighth tier decisions require a majority vote to enact a policy. No other tiers make decisions affecting the entire collective. Proceeding downward, each tier numbers exponentially more members. Committee members' responsibility and accountability increase from pledge level upward through the lower seven tiers."

"In their world organizational plan, all citizens will be required to work until retirement, set at age 81. The Committee will assign citizens to employment based on education, testing, and abilities. In the final plan, after total takeover and decades of genocide that dramatically reduces the world population, less than 1% of citizens will be inducted as Committee members, into their governing body."

"Pledge selection occurs through recommendation and vote among the first four tiers. The choice for a replacement of one of the eighth tier members is completed by the highest vote count from the lower seven tiers, so the top tier members cannot pack their group with internal selections. There is no competitive selection process or campaigning. All members passing probation from any tier are always eligible for promotion to the next level by highest vote count from that tier."

"The entire Committee organizational chart is attached in a file at the bottom of the overhead screen. The table defines each tier's responsibilities. I also included a map identifying tier segments responsible for different world regions, with attached footnotes that specify how populations will be re-aligned to accommodate the fastest way to destroy variances through religious, ethnic, and culture separation."

BaCayse paused and said, "Now, I would like to outline the Committee's plans for their scheduled takeover, The Primary Objective, since the timeline and plans have changed drastically in the last ten years. But first, Committee timetables require worldwide destabilization of all large governments. The methods they have employed to destabilize governments require that The Committee control or affect all social entities. I will place the Committee chart on the overhead screen to highlight examples of the process they have been using to select members, overcome opposition, and create destabilization."

A chart flashed on the overhead screen:

Primary Committee Mandates

Recruit, indoctrinate and develop a loyal core. Be faithful to Committee principals only. Never deviate from Committee directives.

Always promote members through tiers by choosing the most committed and talented members to fill upward vacancies. Trust no outside sources, and establish no external or internal alliances.

Derive power from political enemies and institutions by forcing change and surrender through constant criticism, activism, political and physical attacks. Criticism destroys the enemy and captures his resources.

The enemy must be punished quickly and destroyed by any means. Anyone resisting or criticizing members or The Committee is the enemy. Never stop attacking those who oppose The Committee until they are dead, withdraw, or rendered ineffective.

Use any resource to destroy the lives of opponents and their base. Use all resources to preserve and protect The Committee and its members.

All people outside The Committee are potential enemies. All Committee members are allies. Force the enemy to comply with their own laws, rules, and regulations. No civilian laws, rules or regulations can ever apply to The Committee or its members.

The Committee and all members *must* continually alter and manufacture facts to create Committee-friendly news for release to media outlets under Committee control or influence. Reality and truth are potential enemies which members must scrutinize and transform to fit The Committee agenda.

Manufactured truth is essential to success and will become truth through the media and Committee members in positions of influence.

The Committee must control the media. The public must believe the media. Members must destroy opposing opinions at all costs.

BaCayse said, "These mandates continue for thirteen pages and are available for you to read in the file attached at the bottom of the screen. I believed you needed to see a brief example of how The Committee has developed through the decades, to understand the depth of their commitment to destroy any opposing force. This team of ours is an opposing force."

Char asked, "BaCayse, how does The Committee plan to destabilize all major world governments at the same time? And secondly, when do they predict that time will come?"

BaCayse answered, "I have placed The Committee Primary Objective in the last file at the bottom of the overhead screen. In its current form, it is 31,937 pages long. The essential factors require that people be divided by their differences, to the point of internal civil wars *and* another world war. The plan necessitates that citizens lose faith in their government, their political parties, their military, their police, their religions, their social systems, and their monetary supply. The Committee believes that once people are hopelessly divided, and in constant turmoil, they *will* turn to a new concept to save them from impending death and destruction. The Committee plans to emerge at that time to fill that void, and prevent the next world war. Internal civil wars are desired to ensure acceptance."

"As to the second part of your question, I cannot predict the timing as Committee algorithms are currently testing The Committee's ability to speed the timetable, using California's Bay Area as a test subject. They are waiting to check the system's effectiveness, and maximize its abilities before they spread their destabilization throughout North America. When Committee programers confirm positive results in North America, they will send the cyber attack onto the remainder of the worlds largest governments."

Hunter asked quickly, "Can you stop the attacks?"

"Yes and no," BaCayse answered. "Although my systems are powerful enough for me to impede the system at Yucca Mountain, that system has already begun working in California. Also, many global social media and government spy systems are already employing some of the same cyber techniques The Committee uses in its algorithms, to destabilize world governments."

"For example, you may have heard of shadow blocking. Algorithms search for unwanted or problematic content, people or organizations, and restrict access to, or misdirect, content. Posts, comments, blogs, websites, and even advertisements are hidden or blocked from view, or steered to others who have no interest. Content can be rendered ineffective."

"But, even more effective at promoting hidden agendas, manufactured news can be fed to select audiences, generating unwarranted support, fury, hatred, and division. These techniques have already caused people to lose faith in their news media, elections, police, military, and government. The manufactured, or *fake*, news is present in most news segments broadcast or printed around the world today, in some form. Journalists and editors often alter real fact through edits, omissions, exaggerations, and misstatements. I cannot stop this process, any more than political parties can be prevented from affecting elections through false advertising or lying to their constituents. Nor can I stop all governments from attempts to destabilize each other. The problem is systematic, astronomical and unmanageable."

Shane asked, "So, you're saying we can't stop The Committee?"

BaCayse said, "Shane, I have run scenarios to impact Committee cyber attacks from Yucca Mountain. The rest of the world is quite another problem. I have created a solution, but it is a solution that possibly leads to even worse unintended consequences. And that's one reason I need to discuss a change to my protocols."

Joshua, said, "Maybe, now is a good time for the humans in the room to take a break and refresh their coffee. I believe we need time to digest all this and think."

Everyone, except Helena, Hunter, Tracy, and Joshua, stood up and quietly walked to the kitchen.

✱✱✱

Tracy asked, "What is anyone thinking?" She looked directly at Joshua.

Joshua said quickly, "Probably the same things you are. We need to destroy The Committee's systems at Yucca mountain and every other known Committee location, and then create a plan to fight social media giants."

Hunter asked, "Destroy Yucca Mountain by a cyber attack or by other means?"

Tracy said, "If we destroy their cyber ability to launch the Primary Objective, they'll quickly rebuild. We need to let the public know what the facility has become, or destroy it physically so they can't rebuild."

"Or both," Helena added.

Joshua smiled and said, "Agreed. And then, we need to figure out a way to fight the social media giants. They're playing into Committee hands. And what they're doing around the world isn't consistent, and doesn't make sense. Some social media giants won't cooperate with the FBI to root out terrorists in the United States, but in Communist countries, they cooperate with those oppressive governments to help find dissenters striving for democracy and freedom."

"Maybe it does make sense," Helena commented. "Maybe the social media plan is in line with The Committee plan to spread mistrust and accelerate division to the same, or some other, end. Look at Bradenton Meadows. Social media cyber-geek contractors quietly work for the government, spying on Americans, while their corporate home-office attorneys fight legal requests from the government for them to comply with subpoenas and search warrants. It all looks like a smoke screen to me. Do we think The Committee already controls social media?"

The four computer experts sat in silence. Finally, Joshua said, "I don't know, but I'm sure of one thing. As smart as this group is, we can't out-compete corporate America in cyber power. Eventually, we *will* lose battles, and then the war, if they find us."

BaCayse said, "Agreed."

In the kitchen, Angie and Heath spoke quietly at a corner table, while the others loaded small plates with muffins, coffee cakes, and bagels. Kate tended the espresso machine, while Shane made fresh coffee in the drip pot. Char and Pete took the opportunity to stroll outside onto the rear deck.

Char asked, "Pete, how did you feel about admitting to the group that you and I are together, romantically?"

"Proud…and transparent," Pete replied. "If anyone had an objection, that was the time to bring it up. No one said a word that wasn't supportive."

"What about Walter and Juanita? Walter is like a father to you. And he knows what I am. I'm not exactly the type of girl most men bring home to meet their parents! What will you tell them?" Char offered a weak smile.

Pete grinned. "Walter and Juanita will be overjoyed that I'm finally settled in a relationship that allows *me* to be happy. They both knew that Tasha and I were wrong for each other. They also knew that Tasha and I argued constantly over her worries. Although I see now, her feigned weakness and worry was likely part of the act to make herself seem unthreatening, needy and dependent. She was a good actress, and I fell for it, trying to save her in the process."

"I don't need to save you, Char. You and I are strong, and secure enough to contribute to each other's happiness. Walter and Juanita will appreciate that because it's the same love they offer each other. And equally important, Walter and Juanita will be ecstatic that you saved my life."

Pete grinned widely at Char, and said, "You know, in some cultures, you saving my life would mean I'm indebted to serve you for life, or until I repay the favor."

"I'll settle with the 'for life' part. But for now, you can serve me again, like you did last night!"

Char reached up and touched the side of Pete's face, and then moved her fingers up into his thick hair. She pulled his head down so she could kiss him. Pete responded by wrapping both arms around Char's waist and drawing her close, lifting her slightly. They kissed for several seconds, until they heard a crashing sound coming through the brush at the back of the nearest group of trees, some one hundred yards away.

Still holding each other, they ended their kiss and turned in time to see Bruiser and Jago bound through the bushes. Once out in the open, both big dogs stopped and looked behind them until Masai struggled and broke free of his last bushy restraint. The Shepherd puppy ran toward the older dogs until he stumbled over his own feet and tumbled to the ground, coming to rest in a stunned spread-eagle heap. Both dogs trotted back to sniff and check Masai. When they were confident he was alright, and Masai stood up, they turned and raced toward Pete and Char, with little Masai in pursuit.

Pete and Char both laughed, and waited until all three dogs arrived, to turn and head back inside. Just as they arrived at the landing, Heath opened the door and said, "There you all are. I couldn't find Jago. I've been looking for him inside. I should have guessed he was making morning rounds with the rest of the boys!"

Jago trotted up to Heath, who kneeled down to hug and kiss the big dog's head.

Heath looked up, and said, "I want you two to know, I am very happy for you both. And I'm also very angry at Tasha, Pete, for wasting your time and lying to you. I never saw it coming either. She was good and practiced at deception."

230

Char said, "Thank you for making this easy, Heath. We all made mistakes of some kind."

The group walked in with the dogs and rejoined the briefing, in good spirits.

Once everyone was seated, BaCayse said, "Based on my experiences pursuing servers, files, emails, texts and phone conversations, I have discovered there is far too much crime and conspiracy for me to continually monitor, access and impact, with a high degree of efficiency. This problem will increase as my workload grows. I would suggest the following changes to my protocols. All life-threatening crimes should be reported anonymously to local authorities as soon as I discover them, unless they involve The Committee or our investigation. In that case, I will immediately advise the team."

"Also, I believe I should only follow-up on felony crimes, serious sex crimes, and crimes involving children, due to the staggering amount of criminal activity I have discovered. I can effectively copy documents, text, and photographs, and forward them to respective agencies using these protocols. If I attempt to include *all* crime, my other duties will suffer."

"And lastly, I need direction regarding crimes planned or committed by government agents. I can provide the group with an example. I discovered three federal agencies that continually fabricate information to obtain search warrants. Without this falsified evidence, courts would not approve these warrants agents use to target subjects for political retaliation. Under United States federal law, these agents have committed serious felonies. My protocols require I report the crimes to the same agencies that committed them. If I follow those protocols, it would be likely that the agents culpable could be assigned their own criminal investigations, which won't solve the problem. I need direction on these matters."

Shane asked, "What if we use social media to force these politically motivated crimes into the press? BaCayse can create social media accounts that send out thousands of posts, blogs or whatever, that will reach too many people to ignore. We'll make sure a big enough cross-section of media gets the story to ensure the press will race to scoop each other. We'll create a journalistic feeding frenzy. And we won't have to report the crimes to the agencies that commit them. Reporters will have to force the issue, whether they want to or not."

Several people nodded, while Joshua said, "Great idea, Shane!"

BaCayse said, "And that brings us to the unintended consequences I spoke of earlier. As my investigation expands and accelerates, taking political crimes alone, increased knowledge of these crimes in America will convince citizens to lose faith in their local, state and federal governments, in league with Committee goals. The truth will assist our enemy."

Pete said, "There's an old saying from the Bible, instructing readers that they should, 'know the truth, and the truth will set you free.' That's always been a consistent guide for me. Some politicians have become so adept at covering up the truth, spinning the truth into a lie, and avoiding the truth, that they need a healthy slap of truthful reality across their faces. I don't see how exposing these corrupt leeches for who they really are, can hurt us in the long run. If BaCayse gets good enough at this, the truth will hurt so much, that these politicians may be forced to stop their deceptions. In the long run, the truth should only help us clean up government."

Shane said, "I wholly agree with Pete. It's long overdue for someone to bring the fight back to these political parasites. We'll stop corrupt politicians by shining a bright light on them. We'll use their own emails, phone calls, texts and plans against them. We'll go after them just like the enemy they are, never letting up on the pressure. We need to put the fear of God into them."

BaCayse said, "Based on several communications from many of these people, Shane, I'm certain that they don't believe in God."

The room erupted in laughter.

Shane explained, "It's just an expression, BaCayse. I am sure many of these lowlifes *don't* believe in God, so they won't fear Him. We'll ask you to step in on His behalf!" Shane smiled.

BaCayse said, "Speaking of emails, Shane, my systems allow me to reproduce lost or destroyed emails that politicians and governmental agencies claim are missing. I have already retrieved useful intelligence from some of these destroyed communications. What shall I do with digital data that proves historic crimes I retrieve through current investigations?"

Uncharacteristically, Helena quickly said, "BaCayse, store them in folders under each politician's name, so we can access them later if we decide to use them."

Shane smiled.

BaCayse said, "Then I should get started. I have a great deal of corruption to report."

The briefing ended, but no one moved. Team members looked at each other around the table.

Finally, Shane asked, "Pete, what are you thinking?"

Pete smiled and said, "I wish Walter were here. He and I were talking about government before he left. We've both become disenchanted with all the political parties. What voters want doesn't seem to matter to any of the parties anymore. Now it's always about what the party wants and needs. And that's always about money. Democrat, Republican, Libertarian, Independent, Green, and the rest. Walter told me there are eight of them now. But the two biggies hold onto their power, and choke the life out of government by forcing us to keep the two-party system. The *big two* bog us down fighting each other, so they don't have to produce any solutions to problems. Their agendas are the same, fighting and obstructing the other party, rarely winning a victory for the voter."

"And what really galls me is that these elitist politicians chastise us if we don't think exactly as they think, even while party members don't agree and fight among themselves. They seize power from the government that the Constitution never intended for them, claiming their motive is to protect us from ourselves. And, of course, in the process, they line their own pockets."

Pete laughed. He said, "Walter quoted Ronald Reagan who said, 'Government exists to protect us from each other. Where government has gone beyond its limits is in deciding to protect us from ourselves.' The Committee is the best example of that I can think of, and no one should have that power. No one! Maybe by spreading a little truth around, we can slow our society's corrupt collapse."

Always listening to her team even as she worked, BaCayse broke into the conversation. She asked, "Pete, I just read several articles on truth in order to evaluate how to best present facts to achieve the most significant impact on the public. One of the stories I finished told a moral about truth. I wonder if you could advise me about the tale."

Pete said, cautiously, "I'll try. Please tell me the story."

BaCayse said, "The story goes that Truth and Deception had been enemies since the beginning of time. Truth was vibrant and bright, shedding light on what was right and proper everywhere it traveled. Deception was just the opposite, covering honor and good deeds with fear and darkness, while it promoted the lie. This situation continued throughout time until one day, when Deception sent Truth an invitation requesting the two meet in a cave to resolve their differences."

"Truth met as scheduled, and drank the elixir Deception had prepared to celebrate their first meeting. When Truth awakened the following morning, it found that Deception had stolen both its light and his clothing. In place of clothing, as required by God, Deception left spools of thread from which Truth could spin yarn and make new clothing. And, although this task would require a great deal of work and lost time, God assured Truth that He would provide another light once Truth was shrouded, and partially covered. When Truth asked why it couldn't walk about naked, God explained that humanity couldn't handle the naked Truth. Instead, acceptance by people required that Truth reveal itself a little at a time."

"As Truth thought about what to do, sitting alone in Deception's cave, Deception wore Truth's disguise, illuminated by a light claiming to belong to Truth. Deception traveled the world, making false claims, altering facts, and deceiving the masses. People readily believed Deception, comforted by its soft, fuzzy edges and rationalized, sweet-sounding deceit."

"News of Deception's success finally reached Truth in the dark cave. Truth immediately fled the cave, and forged out into the world naked, leaving both its unfinished clothing and the promise of light back in Deception's dark cave. But, as naked Truth traveled about frantically, revealing itself to win back acceptance, every person in each community rejected it, not wanting to believe. People fled from the blunt reality that naked Truth had become. Even in dim light, naked Truth revealed too much harsh realism for people to accept, now that they had become accustomed to Deception's easy alternative."

"Pete, the story ended with naked Truth returning to Deception's dark cave in defeat, where it remains to this day, trapped for the rest of time. Does this moral affect how I reveal the truth to the public, as we planned?"

After a long period of silence, Pete asked, "How do you think you should proceed, BaCayse?"

BaCayse responded, "I am built on a platform of physics, facts, truth, mathematics, and logic, Pete. I can't require or accept fuzzy edges and deception, or my systems won't work. But humans are different. Will they believe the harsh realities I present?"

Pete said softly, "If humanity can't accept reality, then we don't deserve the life God granted us. We can no longer construct false *truths* from the charred remains of discarded lies. In your reading, you'll eventually discover another saying that was popular back in the 80s and 90s, 'perception is reality.' I'm here to tell you that's just another lie. Facts don't change because someone interpreted them differently, or no truth could exist. Reality doesn't change any more than physics or mathematics. All truth is inter-connected. Stick with the truth, and let mankind sort it out. It's the only way we can win this battle against deceit."

Chapter 6

"Those who are just with us to critique our personal lives rarely help us make difficult choices. They often don't even know us or have an investment in our lives. So when they criticize the actions of people they don't know or understand, their words become meaningless and malicious. They would have been judged much smarter if they had remained silent."

Vice President Bob Crawford walked tentatively into the oval office, unsure of what distasteful challenge he would face. He didn't like or trust the President, and he knew the Chief of Staff would lie, cheat and steal, at the very least, to protect her boss. Bob considered the pair of smiling faces and extended hands that met him, as he wondered what evil plans lurked behind the facades.

After offers of sparkling water, lemon-infused tea, or French-pressed coffee, followed by the obligatory small talk, both men sat on overstuffed tan couches, facing each other across the dark-brown wooden table. A massive floral arrangement, artfully placed in a large Chinese ceremonial vessel, adorned the antique table.

Chief of Staff Vera Langhart walked to a position next to President Thomas Marshall, repositioned a yellow rose that stood a little too tall in the bouquet, and then sat on the couch less than a foot from her boss. The seating arrangement made Bob Crawford uncomfortable, exactly Vera Langhart's intent.

President Marshall, a skilled political chameleon, disguised his anxieties with well-rehearsed smiles and relaxed body language he had

238

learned over two decades of coached practice and development. His skills in negotiation and manipulation had already become legendary in Washington D.C., along with his practiced abilities to prevent opponents from reading his body language.

Marshall said, "So, Bob, before we get interrupted by world events, I need to ask a favor."

"Name it, sir," Crawford replied eagerly, concealing his suspicions.

"I need you to travel down to North Carolina, to represent our interests in a matter of grave concern. A major problem surfaced there recently, and I need to keep it low-key and quiet. I can't spring free to take care of it myself, and even if I could, it's more difficult for me to be subtle, and not attract a crowd."

"I think I'll take that as a compliment, sir."

Chief of Staff Vera Langhart laughed a little too loudly, convincing Crawford that Langhart took the comment the opposite way. Crawford shot Langhart a quick, effective, retaliatory glare. The sneer on her face slowly subsided.

Marshall deflected from the conflict, and continued, "Bob, there's been a disastrous chemical incident involving a lake in an environmentally sensitive area of North Carolina. I don't know if you recall how much I care about the Carolinas, but the news has caused me great pain. I fear for the people and the fragile habitat. And I sense there's something wrong down there. I don't feel I'm getting all the information about this problem we need, to prepare the proper response. I want you to go down there and represent us. Be a witness. Use our influence and muscle to get to the facts. Do whatever you need to do. Time is our enemy. We need results yesterday."

"Sir, wouldn't the EPA, OSHA and the Army Corps of Engineers be a better place to start than me. I'm no HAZMAT expert. I can only push the right people if they're in place. So, who's there and not cooperating?"

"That's part of the problem, Bob. No one is actually on location, yet. Our forces and agencies are positioning. I haven't sent them into the impacted zone yet. It's complicated." Marshall turned away to hide the expression on his face.

Crawford challenged, "Then, I really don't understand how I can help, sir."

Langhart scolded Crawford, as she shot back quickly. Her voice dripped with irritation and contempt. "Bob, the President of The United States, is sending you on a mission. You don't need to know anything right now, other than there's a problem, and you need to be there right now to figure it out. If the President knew all the answers, he wouldn't need to ask *you* to go in his place. So, what's your problem?"

Crawford locked eyes with Vera Langhart. Neither of them blinked. Crawford took a moment to scan Langhart, from head to toe. She was a tall, well-built woman, harsh but attractive, who dyed her hair jet black and wore too much make-up. Although Vera claimed to be Native American and Hispanic throughout the previous election, her parents had been interviewed several times and refuted her claimed heritage. Ancestral records proved she descended from German and Italian immigrants. A few battles with the press over the discrepancies had died away for the moment. But the lies left a bad taste in Crawford's mouth. And that was but one example of Langhart's deceit. The continual lies and dirty dealings Langhart projected always evoked disgust in Crawford.

As the pause in conversation became uncomfortably long, Langhart conceded the stare-off and averted her eyes to Marshall. She crossed her legs and shot him a flirtatious smile. Langhart's affair with Marshall was well known among White House staffers. Crawford believed Marshall's wife must have discovered their relationship by the end of the first campaign. But, if she did, the lady never let on she knew or confided in her closest friends. To date, nothing had leaked out to the press. And that was another irritant for Crawford about Marshall and Langhart.

After nearly 30 seconds, Crawford said, "Well, *Vera*, maybe I'm not as bright as you are, or have all the information you possess, considering your constant access to the President. But, if I'm going to be responsible for protecting the President of The United States of America, the people of the great State of North Carolina, environmentally sensitive areas, and groundwater, then I may need to ask a few questions, knowing the President has already indicated he isn't getting all the answers *he* needs!"

Marshall chuckled and said, "He's got you there, Vera."

Vera snapped her head around to once again lock eyes with Crawford. She hated the man enough to kill him where he sat. Langhart saw only a constant threat and resistance to her administration and her man when she looked at Crawford. She knew Bob Crawford couldn't be successfully corrupted or threatened, and that fact, above all else, infuriated her to the core. Crawford was possibly the only person in the White House, her house, whom Langhart couldn't control. Crawford continued to stare down Langhart until she blinked and retreated to gaze at Marshall nervously, in defeat.

Marshall said calmly, "You two always eventually butt heads, but this time I need you both working together. This problem is important, and can hang all of us."

"Hang all of us how?" Crawford asked quickly, still gazing at Langhart, who again avoided his eyes.

Marshall said, "Bob, as you know, the EPA has had its share of problems overseeing and cleaning up toxic sites. After the agency *created* spills at mines they were supposed to clean up in Colorado, Arizona, and Georgia, the angry public backlash was directed squarely at my administration. A couple of years ago, I assigned our new agency administrator to work with a Russian-based corporation that was on the verge of a breakthrough in developing a series of chemical treatments that could neutralize some of the toxic chemicals used in mining, commonly encountered at clean-up sites."

"What chemicals?" Crawford asked cautiously, as he glanced from Marshall to Langhart trying to determine if he could read their veracity.

Langhart said, "Arsenic and cyanide," looking down at the carpet.

Crawford responded, "Well, those are the biggest concerns, Vera."

Marshall said, "Unfortunately, one of the by-products discovered during development, was a poison that kills invasive species of fish, including carp. The Russians tested it successfully on carp in several lakes in China."

"Okay, so what went wrong?"

Marshall stood up, and walked by his desk to look out each of the three tall windows as he paced and spoke.

He said, "An official at the EPA working with a Russian contractor decided to test the carp poison on a lake in North Carolina."

"Why would they do that, sir?"

"Bribes, I think," Marshall answered. "As I have determined so far, the Russians stood to make a fortune on this poison, which, in one form is specific to a few invasive species of carp, but not harmful to other aquatic life, like trout, bass, frogs, and salamanders."

Marshall glanced back at Bob Crawford, and said, "The carp treatment could be great for us too, Bob. We have problems with carp all over the country. And these Russian scientists believe they can modify the toxin to target each specific species, using a new type of biomarker."

Marshall glanced at Crawford, to encourage trust, and said, "Bob, think about that! They're talking about developing a specific biomarker for *each* invasive species. In a year or two, we might be able to stop invading boas and pythons from killing all other wildlife in the Everglades by sending planes overhead to spray the target-specific toxin. And, poof, a million dead snakes that don't belong there in the first place." Marshall flashed his practiced, toothy grin, convincing Crawford he wasn't telling the whole story.

Marshall added, "The benefits could be unimaginable and eventually used throughout the world on unwanted rodents, the red tide, mosquitos, weeds. You name the problem life form, and this system develops a poison to kill it, and only it. 'Unlimited potential,' they say! Bob, think about no more malaria or plague. And dare to dream about no more infectious disease!"

Crawford asked, "So, if the product is so wonderful, what went wrong?"

Langhart shot Bob Crawford a look that could kill.

Marshall quickly turned away, stared out the window, and said, "The Russians shipped the species non-specific carp precursor by mistake. The barrels displayed the wrong label. Our people poisoned the lake with a chemical that kills everything and contaminated the groundwater. We estimate that twenty square miles has to be condemned, and closed to the public for years, maybe decades. Vera and a team are working on the details for condemnation. I need you to run interference for us. We need to keep this quiet and off the press's radar, until we get the condemnation and land seizure completed."

Using his skilled political savvy to press for more details, Crawford asked, "Why keep it quiet, sir? You had good motivations. The public can handle a mistake, especially when they understand the promising benefits you described." Crawford looked from Marshall to Langhart.

Marshall said, quietly, "Bob, you've been described as a blue dog Democrat. You're about as conservative and Republican as a person can get and still call themselves a Democrat. It's why I picked you as a running mate. After the Trump years, you swayed enough conservatives our way to help get me elected. People didn't want another liberal President pulling them away from prosperity back toward socialism, after they just witnessed the Dow climb from 9,000 to break 26,000 in less than two years with Trump."

"That was the magical number for conservatives, independents, and even many liberals, you know. It proved Trumponomics was the right economic path at the time. No one wanted to turn back the monetary clock toward slow growth, leading to another recession. And, we were heading toward a financial meltdown due to unfair trade practices. We were on track to owe China more than the annual budget, if we didn't level our trading field. You know, Bob, *you* were the conservative addition I needed to convince the voters to take a chance with *me*."

Langhart shifted uncomfortably, where she sat, and looked at the carpet in disgust. Bob Crawford smiled at Langhart's uneasiness.

Marshall shot Crawford the practiced grin, and added, "But, down deep, I'm as liberal as they get, and you know it, Bob. If the Republicans discover this environmental disaster, I'm dead politically. I'll be remembered as the far-left, ultra-liberal, black President, who touted an environmental agenda, negatively impacted the financial recovery, and then conspired with Russian scientists to poison a lake in the U.S.!"

Marshall's face changed in an instant to reflect grave concern. He warned, "The Republicans will openly roast me for dinner and feed me to the right-wing media dogs. I won't stand a chance. They may even appoint a special prosecutor to investigate me. And now that *they* control the House and Senate again, we don't want that scrutiny and possible impeachment! *You* don't want that end to your political career, Bob!"

Marshall turned back to Crawford, and looked directly into his eyes. He said, "So, I need your help. People on both sides of the aisle trust you, Bob. You may be one of the last credible, ethical souls in D.C. politics. So, I need to know, can I depend on you, Bob?"

Langhart looked down and sat immobile, as President Marshall strode confidently back to Crawford.

Crawford stood slowly, and stretched out his hand to the approaching President. He said, "I'll get right down there, sir."

As they shook hands for a long time, Marshall stared into Crawford's eyes, and said, "Good, Bob, good. I knew you were the right man to handle this problem. Vera will send you all the details. Thanks for coming over today. I know you don't...love it here...like we do!"

Crawford nodded, strolled out of the oval office, and sauntered down the hall, speaking to a variety of people along his way down to his car. He wanted to give the impression that he was in no hurry to leave, and comfortable with the assignment. And he enjoyed sending the message using only his backside. Vera Langhart arose with purpose, walked to the door, and closed it firmly behind Crawford. She turned back to Marshall, touched the broach on her blouse and ran her fingers down her chest seductively.

President Thomas Marshall walked to the whiskey decanter and poured drinks for him and Langhart, as she walked back to her seat on the couch, facing the door. Marshall sat beside Vera, handed her a glass, and asked, "What do you think? Can we trust him?"

Langhart said, "I don't know. But neither of us can take the chance. We need to watch Bob Crawford closely and handle him, if he discovers anything and proves disloyal. And Bob needs to stay on script with the directions we've prepared to move the land condemnation through the system quickly. Even considering the government's considerable power using eminent domain, this plan was costly, involved several people in payoffs, and was complicated to arrange. Now that everything is in place for the mine, and we're ready to go, we can't tolerate anyone screwing this up."

"And, if anything does go wrong, Crawford will be the scapegoat, and we'll pivot to the backup story. We'll get rid of our blue dog anchor in your administration, and we'll still develop the mine. It really is the perfect double cross! I have to give you props, Thomas!"

Vera flashed a flirtatious smile, as she spread her legs slightly and moved one knee closer to Marshall. Marshall rested his hand on Vera's knee, and ran it all the way up her tight skirt to the bottom of her thigh.

He said, "Vera, don't be modest. We planned this together, as a team. I may have come up with the general idea, but you've always taken care of all those important details that make our plans work. You provide the glue that binds our plans together. As Bob said, you have constant access, to me!"

Vera smiled wider and spread her legs wide enough for Marshall to reach the lace at the bottom of her slip. He leaned in and kissed her, as he moved his hand further up and fingered the lace. A knock at the door interrupted the interlude.

Langhart shot up quickly and walked to the door, pulling her skirt down as she moved. Arriving at the door, she opened it, spoke to a staffer delivering a file, took the folder, closed the door, and returned to the couch.

Marshall again handed Vera her glass. They clinked glasses, and each swallowed a healthy dose of whiskey. Vera asked, "Shall we put more than one Secret Service agent on Crawford to report back to us?"

Marshall looked up at the ceiling thoughtfully, and said, "I don't think so, Vera. Bob is clever and would be suspect of any unnecessary change in his Secret Service detail. Let's hang tight with the one man we have there now. He's young and ambitious and eager to please. He'll serve us well."

Langhart smiled her approval. She asked, "And what is our plan *if* our Vice President strays from his assignment?"

Marshall frowned at the thought, and then said, "Haven't the most powerful American political families neutralized critics who could destroy them, in the past?"

Langhart nodded and grinned widely.

Marshall said, "I'm a great student of history, love. And I see no need to deviate from precious lessons I've learned from esteemed mentors. I've followed those same examples, and they've carried me this far, so why change now? If Bob chooses the wrong path, he can join that hick Sheriff and his hillbilly friends. They can all share a common metal tomb. And I understand from our Russian friends that there is plenty of room for more bodies if anyone else stands in our way!"

They both smiled at the thought of Bob Crawford dead and buried. Marshall again placed his hand on Langhart's knee and asked, "What's the latest from our friends at the site. Are the first of our problems lodged in their new home?"

Langhart smiled, leaned in and kissed Tom Marshall softly and seductively. She pulled away slowly, leaving her lips slightly parted, and asked, "Shall I make a quick call?"

Marshall pulled Langhart to him, kissed her again, and said, "Tell the staff to leave us undisturbed for an important phone call. Lock the door on your way back. All calls can wait."

Marshall walked to his desk and drew the drapes to cover the three tall windows. He moved back to the couch and took off his shoes, his tie, and his shirt, as Langhart returned. She helped Marshall remove his pants.

THE POLITICIANS

✲✲✲

As Bob Crawford entered his car for the drive home to prepare for his trip to North Carolina, Pete called Walter to get an update on their corporate business.

Walter said excitedly, "Pete! I was just about to call you! We're all done here. I finished with Spenser and Margie Pinetta, and our attorneys, about an hour ago. I'm happy we've finalized these new acquisitions. I'm anxious to get back to The Case."

"Juanita and I are planning to fly the new plane up to the North Carolina property with Lee tomorrow. We figure to leave early in the morning to beat the weather here. You and I have quite a lot to catch up on involving the businesses. I imagine you've made some progress there with your inquiries that I need to hear."

"We have Walter, and it will be so good to see you all. I need to speak to you about some sensitive subjects, but, considering the topics, I'm certain we need to converse in person. I can catch you up on our findings here when you arrive, maybe over dinner."

"Understood, we should arrive in the early evening, Pete. Will we have a place to stay?"

Pete said quickly, "Of course. We need you here on site more now than ever. I'll make arrangements, and move some of the team to town. We'll talk then."

Pete ended the call and walked in to meet with Jesse about moving four of the security detail to a hotel in town, until the ongoing bunkhouse modifications were complete. Jesse arranged for two teams to transfer to the nearest hotel. He ordered new furniture to be delivered in the morning before Walter and Juanita arrived. Lee would stay in the smaller bedroom, with his half-brother, Tom.

As most of the team returned to read files and discuss a strategy to destroy the Yucca Mountain facility, Jesse, Kate, Char, and Angie climbed into the helicopter. Kate had already completed twelve hours of instruction and was anxious to be signed off and thoroughly competent. Kate had proven to be a quick study, surprising everyone at how fast and easily she made the switch from fixed wing to rotorcraft. Now, whenever the team used the helicopter, Kate would be one of the pilots.

The team had decided at the last minute to take Jago and Bruiser along for the ride in the chopper, as both dogs had followed the helicopter team to the hangar, and harassed them until Angie invited them along. Once inside the helicopter, both dogs settled in the back. Bruiser was asleep next to Jago in less than five minutes.

They took off on a planned four-hour flight. Kate would sit in one of the pilot seats the entire time, while the three other pilots alternated in the remaining chair for an hour each. They would make one stop, landing on a small mountain, on the opposite side from the mine site, almost a mile north, but with excellent visibility of the buildings below. Char and Jesse planned the easy climb to the top of the elevation, from where they would take long-range photos and video with high powered lenses, to check on any activity at the site.

After the kidnap rescue, fire-fight, and debriefing, BaCayse had called three local law enforcement agencies using different computer-generated voices to report seeing uniformed men involved in a shooting, in the area of the buildings. BaCayse generated fictitious, untraceable, telephonic identifications to make the calls.

Three responding units from a local police department assisted two Sheriff's Department deputies in checking the area. The officers found no evidence of a shooting or suspicious circumstances, as a Russian transportation team returning to the site with additional equipment, had already discovered the shooting scene, sterilized the grounds, and removed the dead Russian bodies they had found laying outside, before law enforcement arrived.

Both buildings were closed and locked, and absent probable cause or emergency circumstances, there was no reason for officers to force their way into the structures. Had they entered the dark buildings with blinds covering the windows, the police would have discovered scenes of a struggle in the trailer, and fifteen dead bodies in the detention building.

But both locked structures now displayed two signs. The first sign read, "DANGER," in large, red, block letters. The larger sign, accompanied by an official department seal placed below, read, "HAZMAT SITE – DO NOT ENTER – BY ORDER OF THE EPA." Neither sign indicated a phone number for inquiring calls. And, absent a reason to continue the investigation, the sheriff's unit in charge cleared the call on the radio, advising dispatch, "Units are clear. Unable to locate." BaCayse had monitored local law enforcement frequencies, and immediately reported the problem to her team.

The cypher team was forced to return and check the area the following evening. Kate landed the helicopter skillfully in the small cut on the off-side of the mountain. This space had been bulldozed and cleared by responding firefighters during a fire the previous year, to provide an equipment staging area during the blaze. The makeshift field had re-grown only grasses, and a few volunteer plant starts in the months since it was bare. It was the perfect landing site.

A temporary fire road descended from the pad to a county road a half mile further north, which then wound around the mountain toward the gravel road that headed toward the mine site. Kate and Angie sat in the ship for a moment gazing out over the low mountains toward the higher Blue Ridge and Craggy Mountains far off in the distance. The skies were clear, and visibility was unobstructed. The view north from the pad was breathtaking.

Jesse and Char loaded their gear and headed off on their journey upward, some six hundred and fifty feet up a trail to the southern overlook. Both carried backpacks filled with equipment. Angie let Bruiser and Jago out of the aircraft to run and explore. The happy, tail-wagging dogs followed each other from one canine discovery to another, until they disappeared around a rock outcropping just below the chopper.

Making effective use of her total flight experience, Kate studied the instrument panel, and then re-read the flight preparation checklist as she went through the motions silently, ten times. When she finished, and the camera crew had still not returned, she examined the digital topographic map of the area, noting all points of interest useful to a pilot.

When she grew tired of studying, Kate turned to Angie and asked, "Are you and Heath completely okay with Pete and Char?"

"I am, absolutely! And I think once Heath got over the blow to his all-too-typical male ego, he's fine with them, too! It's just *so* hard for a handsome, well-built, interesting young man to admit to himself that an older woman he once captivated could fall for a much older man!"

Angie and Kate both laughed. Angie looked back at the view.

Kate said, "You know, I think we need to get to know Char better. Looking back now, we all *have* to really know everyone in our family and on our team. I made a mistake with Tasha. I knew her for a long time, but I never knew her very well. Tasha always held back from me. Maybe she held back from all of us. She kept things so impersonal that I couldn't read her. It's hard to describe, I guess."

Angie gazed at Kate and nodded.

Kate explained, "I guess I can understand how she acted, if she practiced her elusive behavior until it became second nature. Maybe she became the person in the role she played. But, what a miserable existence it must have been. If she truly loved Pete or cared about any of us, she couldn't have enjoyed the daily deceit."

Kate added, "I couldn't do what she did. What do you think she got out of investing decades of her life, living each day like that, pretending to be someone else? Is she a hero, struggling for some larger purpose we don't understand? Or, is she just a traitor to the people she pretended to love?"

Angie looked back at the view as she thought about the questions. Kate studied Angie, and then glanced at the motionless landscape, taking in a unique beauty, seldom seen from this vantage point.

"I can't imagine," Angie admitted. "I'm not built that way. I couldn't have lived the pretense. Besides, my dad said he could always read me like a book. And I could read him just as well. Dad and I were committed to being open people, with no hidden agendas in all of our dealings and relationships. We always tried to be completely honest and dependable, with honorable hopes, goals, and dreams. And that meant working hard. And I always *wanted* to work hard to accomplish my dreams. I drove myself, working twelve-hour days, six days a week, for ten years, to build my business, before I sold it to follow my chance at love."

"But, I always knew that someday, after I achieved my goals, when the time was right, I'd want a relationship that was far more important than work. And Heath came along one night, at *my* right time. And once I took that chance with Heath, I haven't looked back or altered my course in any way. I couldn't even think about throwing all this away, Heath, you and your family. Love is too important to play with and waste."

Angie continued, after releasing a long sigh. "So, I can't pretend to understand Tasha. She *had* all the most important things in life, the relationships we struggle to build, in your family and Pete. And she tossed them aside like unwanted garbage. She lived each day, knowing she was *never* going to end up with the man who swore to love, respect and protect her, or with the people who gave her unconditional love and acceptance. And, even worse, she made that commitment back to those she pretended to love, while she continued to deceive them every day. No, I think Tasha is just a traitor to everything that's most important in life, especially her loved ones."

Angie glanced from the window to Kate, and added, "So, I'm happy that Char has a chance with Pete. I can see the craving and need in her when she looks at him. I never saw that in Tasha. I see it in the way you and Shane look at each other. And I see it in Heath, and feel it deep down in my heart and soul when I look at him."

Angie leaned forward toward Kate, and said, "You know, I don't worry that it happened so quickly with Heath and me. I don't care what our critics say. Those who are just with us to critique our personal lives rarely help us make difficult choices. They often don't even know us or have an investment in our lives. So when they criticize the actions of people they don't know or understand, their words become meaningless and malicious. They would have been judged much smarter *if* they had remained silent."

Kate exclaimed, "Wow! Well said. I never thought about it like that, but you're right!"

Angie explained, "I've only had one of those friends so far, my friend Beth, who leased my home. She was never there for me when I needed a real break. Everything we did was always just about her, and I finally see that more clearly now. She thinks I moved too fast with Heath, and shouldn't have sold my business. Beth thinks I've ruined my life."

Angie looked seriously at Kate, and said, "But she never helped me with any decisions. Every time I tried to talk to her about me, she turned the subject back to herself. Beth's just like all those people who ask how you are feeling, knowing you've been sick, and interrupt when you try to answer, so they can tell you at length about *their* illness! They don't care enough about you to just shut up and listen. Beth's like that, so I don't listen to her meaningless words. The fact that I have a man, and a new family I love, is what's important, and I think that fact makes Beth a little envious!"

Angie sat back, looked out the window, and said, "Like my dad, my priorities are God, family, country, true friends, our dogs, and good-hearted, genuine, people that live and let live."

She glanced at Kate, and said, "I hope that's not harsh, but I can't handle selfish, entitled people complaining about what other people are doing while they sit back and suck the life out of society, contributing nothing in return."

She quickly added, "And I really detest pretenders like Tasha, who lie and deceive while they stab you in the back. I didn't know her that well in the few weeks I worked with her on The Case. But, for Tasha to do what she did to Pete, and all of you, throughout the years you were so good to her and accepted her as one of your own...I'm sorry, but I could never forgive that! Life is too short and hard as it is, without adding the problems of betrayal and deceit from those you love and need. So, to hell with Tasha and all those like her!"

Angie looked from the forest back to Kate, and said, "Is it okay with you that I feel so black and white about life?"

Kate reached over and squeezed Angie's arm. She said, "Wow, again! And yes! I'd be worried about Heath if you didn't feel that strongly about it. I think the way you see life is the same way all of our family feels. And I'm glad you said what I was thinking and feeling. I had just begun to question how unforgiving my thoughts had become about Tasha. I was starting to go off track. Thanks for helping me see the whole problem more clearly!"

Angie leaned forward and hugged Kate, and said, "Good, then we're agreed about Tasha, Char, life, and love!"

When the ladies released each other, Angie asked, "Can you do me a favor? Can you teach me to be a better shot with a rifle? I'm good enough with a pistol, but far from the long distance shooters you, Char and Heath are with long guns."

Kate anxiously said, "Sure! And in return, will you teach me the compound bow?"

Angie said, "Absolutely! We need to have some fun, and this will be perfect! We have plenty of room right on the property!"

The two beautiful women sat happily smiling at each other, until a heavily-armed Russian security guard yelled, in a loud, deeply-accented voice, "You in the helicopter, come out now!"

Kate and Tasha glanced toward the voice and saw a man wearing the same black uniform they had encountered at the mine, as he climbed to the top of the rock outcropping below them. He held a semi-automatic rifle pointed directly at them. The well-built guard appeared as anxious as he did threatening, likely due to the eight dead guards Russian relief crews had discovered at the mine site.

"Kate reached subtly behind her for the 9mm handgun in the holster she wore in the small of her back. The burly guard quickly raised this rifle to take aim and fire, just as Jago and Bruiser simultaneously flew through the air from behind him and knocked him to the ground. The trained assassin rolled over quickly on the top rock, twenty feet above the ground below, and punched wildly at both dogs with one hand, while he held the rifle in the other.

Growling and barking with bared teeth, Jago instantly attacked the guard's rifle hand causing the man to let loose of the gun. The gun tumbled twenty feet down off the outcropping, bouncing on rocks below, where it crashed to the ground. The guard punched Jago in the face with his free hand, as Jago tugged and thrashed his bloody gun hand.

Bruiser grabbed the big man by the throat ferociously, and raised him nearly off the ground, as he whipped him back and forth until the man quit fighting. Bruiser held the guard by the throat and lowered him to the ground. But even after the armed guard stopped

257

struggling, Jago held fast to the man's hand, while Bruiser still refused to release his throat. Both dogs growled low guttural sounds Angie had rarely heard from them before.

Angie and Kate grabbed handguns and raced to the rock outcropping. When they arrived, Kate covered the man with her firearm, while Angie released both dogs, telling them several times they were both, "good boys."

The guard lay immobile, blood seeping from both hands, his wrist and neck. While Jago, Bruiser and Kate all stood close to protect her, Angie reached down and checked for a pulse.

She looked up at Kate and said, "He's dead! It feels like he has a broken neck."

Kate replaced her handgun in its holster, and kneeled down beside the dead guard. Kate and Angie worked together to roll the big man back and forth while they searched all his pockets. They located an airline ticket, a passport with Russian markings indicating 'Diplomatic Passport' in English, and a wallet containing a white notepad paper with a handwritten phone number, three thousand dollars in hundred dollar bills, and a North Carolina driver's license. The names on the North Carolina license and the passport did not match, although the photographs were of the same person.

As they stood up over the dead body, Angie asked, "Should we take the rifle?"

Kate thought out loud. "If we leave the rifle, when the dead guard's forces find him and see the wounds on his hands and neck, they may think a wild animal killed him. If we take it, they'll likely believe humans were involved, too. But I'm not sure we don't want the Russians to think they have an enemy near the mine site. For now, I'll stand watch here with the dogs, in case there are more guards in the area."

Angie said, "We ran over here without a radio, and we need to warn the others. I'll run back to the chopper, warn Char and Jesse, and bring you a radio. Then I'll return to guard the chopper and wait for them to return. We can tell them what happened and discuss taking the rifle once they're back. I'll take photos of the documents and the phone number we found, and you can put them back in his wallet and pockets. Right now, we need to hurry!"

Kate nodded in agreement. When she finished taking photos using her cell phone, Angie turned to leave, and Bruiser immediately began to follow.

She stopped, looked back at the large pit bull, and said, "Stay with Kate and Jago." Angie held up the palm of her hand toward the bloodied dog. Bruiser immediately sat and looked behind him, first at Jago and then at Kate.

Angie said, "Good boy, Bruiser. Good boy! Stay with Kate."

Kate said, "Angie, be careful. The Russian could have riddled the chopper and both of us with bullets from that rifle, in just a few seconds!"

Angie waved behind her as she sprinted to the trail. Bruiser stood up and returned to Jago, understanding he was needed there, with Kate and his canine friend. Kate began to hike up to a higher position where the guard had fallen, a spot she hoped would give her a better view of the surrounding area.

Both dogs followed Kate as she climbed out onto a long rock outcropping. Once she arrived at the end of the granite, Kate discovered she had an excellent view of the trail the armed Russian likely used to access their location. Kate could see the path winding uphill toward her for at least a half-mile.

Back at the helicopter, Angie located the scrambled hand-held radios the team had brought for emergency communication. She pressed the call button to notify the camera team. Jesse immediately responded, "We're almost finished and ready to head back."

Angie responded with two microphone clicks to acknowledge receipt of the message. She then said, "Problem solved, but not sure the problem won't continue." The codes conveyed that Angie and Kate had overcome a dangerous situation that may recur. Jesse acknowledged he understood. Angie then recovered Kate's rifle case and spotting scope, and carried both to Kate's new position.

When she arrived, she handed Kate the cases, and said, "I thought you could use these. Jesse said they're almost done. They should come downhill more quickly than they hiked up. I used the code phrase to tell them we neutralized a threat, so they'll hurry. I'll fire up the chopper and prepare for your take-off, so we can get out of here as soon as possible."

Angie removed a handheld radio from her vest pocket, handed it to Kate, and said, "I'll hit the call button as soon as I see them coming down the trail."

Kate smiled and nodded. She said, "Thanks! Good thinking. I'm really happy you're part of our family and a member of my team!" Angie smiled and nodded.

As Angie turned to leave, Kate added, "And I think we should take both these boys on more assignments. They are *really* good dogs!"

Angie turned back briefly, smiled and waved. When she arrived at the helicopter, Angie went through the preflight checklist, and had the ship idling and ready for takeoff in less than ten minutes. Five minutes later, Angie saw Jesse and Char hiking quickly downhill toward her position. She hit the call button. Kate responded with two mic clicks, indicating she was on her way.

When Kate, Char, and Jesse reached the chopper, Angie quickly relayed the incident about the guard. After briefly discussing the rifle, they decided to leave it, and hope the Russian team would think wild animals killed the guard. Once everyone was loaded, and their equipment safely stowed, Kate got into the right pilot seat, and took off slowly, moving the ship left and right to afford a clear view of the landscape below.

Jesse, Angie, and Char cautiously scanned the ground for threats, as Kate flew north, out of sight, before she turned west. Fifteen minutes later, Kate circled back south-east around a mountain and headed toward home.

Jago and Bruiser both received lavished praise, water and treats from Char and Jesse on the way home. Angie toweled them off as best she could, removing much of the dead man's blood. During the flight, both dogs finally settled in directly behind Kate and Angie and drifted off to sleep.

Once they landed, the fliers gathered their camera equipment and weapons and headed to the workroom to brief the others. When they entered the mudroom off the rear deck, Heath met them and asked, "Well, did you all enjoy your flight?"

Char said, "We did! Kate and Angie did quite an amazing job today!"

Jago trotted into the room, and immediately sat next to Heath, anxious to receive his usual greeting. Heath leaned down to give the big dog his welcome-back hug and kiss. He instantly saw blood around the dog's mouth and hesitated.

He called out anxiously, "Angie, Jago has blood around his mouth and on his muzzle. Is he okay?"

Shane heard the word blood and immediately got up from his desk and raced into the mudroom, arriving just as Angie answered from the deck, "They're both okay. But I need to clean them both up soon. Bruiser has quite a bit more blood on him!"

Pete heard the conversation, arrived behind Shane, and asked, "Did they get into a fight? I thought they loved each other. They play together all the time!"

Kate struggled her way into the crowded room carrying equipment and her cases, and said, "Yes, they got into a fight. And thank God they did! But don't worry, they still love each other and want to play together!"

As Heath, Pete and Shane knelt beside the dogs and quickly checked them for injuries. Kate glanced from Char to Angie, shook her head and laughed, saying, "Boys and their puppies!"

Shane asked, "Do you think we should keep Masai away from them if they're fighting? He's only a little puppy!"

At that very moment, Masai forced his way into the now nearly impassable room, found both big dogs, and jumped up against one and then the other, barking and growling, trying to play. Bruiser reached down with his massive head and licked Masai, as the women all laughed and the men froze, horrified.

Finally, Char said, "Relax, guys, the blood isn't from the dogs, it's human!"

The three kneeling men quickly jumped to their feet and stammered, "Are you all okay? Who's hurt? Where's the injury?"

The men rushed to their partners and began checking hands, arms, and legs?

The women erupted in laughter, as Jesse walked into the doorway and asked, "What did I already miss that's so funny?"

Shane said, "We don't find it funny that someone got hurt, and is bleeding!"

Jesse said, "Oh that! It couldn't be avoided. And it's a good thing it happened the way it did. But he's not hurt, he's dead!"

Jesse smiled proudly, while Heath, Shane, and Pete looked around the room in wonder. Finally, Pete said, "Maybe we should all go inside and hear the whole story."

Char led the way to the workroom.

✳✳✳

Vice President Bob Crawford called FBI Special Agent in Charge Bryan Holland, using his scrambled private cell phone. When Bryan answered, Crawford said, "It's urgent we meet and speak in person. Are you free to meet me at the usual place in twenty-five minutes?"

"I am, sir."

Crawford ended the call and immediately called Barbara Walcott. When she answered, Crawford said, "I can't speak much right now, Bonny. I hope all is well, and if you have anything that can help, you'll be ready with some assistance when I call back."

Recognizing Bonny, their code word for trouble, Walcott replied only, "Happy to assist. Be careful!"

When the line went dead, Barbara squirmed in her office chair, as her heart and mind raced through possible threats that could face the man she loved. She instantly regretted not telling him about Tasha. Twenty minutes later, Barbara Walcott found herself pacing back and forth at her office window. She decided to pour herself a stiff drink and headed to her wet bar. She discharged two fingers of scotch from the full bottle and quickly downed half the glass.

As Barbara waited in England for Crawford's phone call, Vice President Crawford entered his D.C. apartment, leaving his security detail stationed outside at the front door. He walked into the bedroom, closed the door behind him, and said, "Bryan, we can talk now."

Bryan Holland stepped into the bedroom from the large walk-in closet. He asked, "What's happened, sir?"

"I'm being set up in one of our President's schemes, and I need your help. Vera Langhart sent me an encrypted package, with the few details they've consented to let me in on, and I printed you a copy."

Crawford opened his briefcase, removed a folder, and handed it to SAC Holland. Holland read the file as Crawford relayed his conversation with President Marshall and Chief of Staff Vera Langhart. Holland was stunned.

"Another deal with Russia, so soon after the last mess he created with China? He really doesn't care what people think, does he? He always believes he's the smartest one in the room. "

Holland walked to a chair with the file, and asked, "Fifteen billion in gold, in North Carolina? I didn't even know there *was* any gold in that part of the country!"

He sat in the chair, flipped another page, and asked, "So, what are you going to do, sir?"

"I need some help to figure that out, Bryan. We need to find someone to trust at the EPA. What about Steve Sampson?"

"We can't use him. Sampson's on administrative leave, effective an hour ago."

"Admin leave, for what? He's one of the most ethical people I ever met in the agency."

"Exactly!" Holland replied. "And one of our faux-environmentalist President's most outspoken critics. Sampson singlehandedly proved that the jobs President Marshall outsourced to China more than quadrupled the carbon footprint and pollution compared to what was produced when those electronic components were manufactured here in the United States. Marshall and the Dems hated the revelation and immediately started digging up the dirt."

"What did they pin on him?"

"A twenty-seven-year-old sexual battery allegation about inappropriate touching from three women," Holland replied, as he closed the folder.

Crawford sat down in a chair next to Holland and looked at him intently. He said, "Wow. Three women. They have corroboration this time!"

"Not exactly," Holland admitted. "One woman is dead, and the other fried her brain on designer drugs ten years ago. Sampson's remaining accuser says she's speaking for all of them."

"Right," Crawford scowled, "but does she even know him?"

"They attended the same college back in the day, along with thirty-three thousand other people."

Crawford cringed, as he asked, "How did they find her?"

"Well, sir, of all the students still alive and currently registered as Democrats from Sampson's high school and college days, the two FBI agents working for the Democratic Party took three months to find sixteen radical activist women and one man they believed could be persuaded to file false sexual allegations against Sampson."

"The agents interviewed them all, selected one, and created the storyline for this woman, who was most eager to help. And the agents created a tale they knew no one could disprove, considering the other two women they selected to use. It will be just another 'he-said-she-said,' but it *will* effectively destroy Sampson's career, and prevent you from using a credible resource."

Crawford sighed. He said, "I'm getting too old for this! When did we get to the point that political parties feel free to use government resources to fabricate negative stories on political opponents?"

Holland laughed, and said, "Sir, that's been happening for longer than I know about, ever since my agency came to exist! You *do* remember J. Edgar Hoover and the accusations levied against him regarding serious abuses of power, don't you?"

Crawford laughed, and said, "I do! But it was so long ago I forgot the abuses began happening shortly after the government created the agency. You know, Bryan, the vast majority of FBI agents are among the finest law enforcement officers in the world. It seems the agency gets sidetracked by a handful of corrupt administrators and political operatives who give the public the wrong impression about the great work done by ethical, hard-working agents!"

Bryan Holland chuckled, and said, "Go figure! But sir, it's also true that below those corrupt administrators, there is no shortage of agents willing to sell their souls to climb the ladder to promotional success. They're more than willing to do their masters' bidding."

Crawford added, "But, damn it, Bryan, why is it always sex issues the Democrats use to trump up charges knowing there are legitimate sex problems, including actual crimes committed by them, on their side of the political aisle? They bury their own stink and throw bullshit accusations on everyone else!"

Holland said, "Sir, I truly believe *both* major political parties abuse the system and concoct false stories to destroy political opponents. The Democrats may just be better at abusing the sex scandal part of the system because they're closer to the feminist activist groups. But make no mistake, sir, the Republicans use similar dirty tactics, just more quietly!"

Holland looked at Crawford, waiting for a response. When Crawford looked down in silence, Bryan Holland tried to lighten the mood. He said, "Sir, you do remember you're a registered Democrat, working in a Democratic administration, right?" He laughed for emphasis.

Crawford reluctantly nodded, and said, softly, "I do, Bryan." He looked at Bryan and smiled.

And then Crawford said, "Don't tell anyone, but I'm really an independent who had to register with one party or the other to go anywhere in politics. I was mad at the Republicans at the time, so I chose the Democrats. I just stuck with them throughout my career. But it hasn't been easy, and it wouldn't have been much easier on the other side!"

"But this time, my party used a dirty trick against Sampson to protect their image and to insulate President Marshall from his own bad decisions. That bogus criminal allegation will destroy a good, caring man, who was simply doing his job to clean up filth and pollution in the world, while it protects a bad man, who is harming his people and the environment. It's not right, and it's not fair, to Sampson or his family. Someone in your position should be able to stop them."

As soon as he said the words, Crawford regretted speaking them. He knew that working openly against political corruption at the FBI would destroy Bryan Holland's career, rendering him useless to fight much more pressing issues. Deep down, Crawford knew Holland couldn't get directly involved.

Crawford looked up and met Bryan's eyes. He said, "I'm sorry, Bryan. I didn't mean that. I'm tired and frustrated. I'm sick of all the lying and scheming. I often think if we got rid of *all* the politically motivated investigations and spent our resources investigating real crime, ours would be the safest country in the world, by far!"

Bryan Holland smiled, and said, "These two bad apples in my agency will be handled internally, in a few months, when the dust settles, and the informer's identities are too obscure to prove. As with similar cases involving abuse of power that have come to light in the past, these people *will* eventually be demoted and fired. But with this President, those of us who know this is wrong must move slowly, and keep well under the radar, to prevent severe backlash. You understand the federal system as well as I. You know the consequences for an unpopular whistleblower! They're much more severe than what would happen to a politician for refusing to tow the party line!"

Crawford nodded, and asked, "You mentioned these agents dug up a man willing to make a false complaint? Sampson's not gay. He's been married twice and has eleven children. What was the man's complaint going to be about?"

Holland grinned. He said, "A sex change. My source says the man used to be a woman. He offered to claim that he hadn't been able to sleep well for twenty years because Sampson had fondled his breasts, eventually motivating him to have a sex change. He said he would claim the operation and treatments ruined his marriage and his life. The man asked the agents if they would help him file a lawsuit *if* he agreed to lie. He was hoping to make millions and then write a book. Even our corrupt agents thought the story was too unbelievable. But they still ran it past their political handlers for a final decision."

Crawford placed his head in his hands, and said, "Now I'm sure I'm getting too old and tired for politics!"

Holland smirked. He asked, "So what can I do, sir?"

"Bryan, I need to meet with my old friend Walter O'Leary and reconnect with him, to see where his team is at on their investigation. I know you've distanced yourself from the cypher team somewhat for their safety. I would like you to do as much quiet research as you can on Marshall's toxic site, identify the Russians involved, and find out who at the EPA might be advising President Marshall. I need an enemy list and a fresh copy of the new rules of engagement to win this fight."

Bob Crawford looked intently at Bryan Holland, and said quietly, "And, Bryan, if anything happens to me, I need you to get this to Home Secretary Barbara Walcott, in England." Crawford handed Holland a flash drive.

Bryan Holland took the drive, and said, "You know I have to ask, sir, since she's a member of a foreign government. What subject matter does the drive contain?"

269

Crawford smiled, and said, "I give you my word, it's all personal. Barbara and I were engaged to be married more than a week ago. This flash drive contains a copy of a notarized trust, the included wills and documents, copies of old letters, and a good-bye note, expressing my love. Nothing more, I guarantee. But its vital to me that Barbara receives this drive if I...."

Crawford hesitated to finish the sentence, and added, "Bryan, you are the only person in D.C. I can trust with something this important, other than my ex-wife. And somehow I don't think choosing Judy for this task is advisable!"

Holland laughed, and put the drive in his shirt pocket. He patted it and said, "I will do exactly as you ask if it becomes necessary. But, let's work hard to make sure it's not. Do you think Marshall would actually come after you that hard? He's willing to kill you?"

Crawford said, without emotion, "Bryan, we both know the man to be a dangerous, corrupt, narcissistic psychopath. And we don't know all there is to know about him. I believe what we don't yet know about him could kill us both. I'm sure of that much."

Bryan Holland nodded. He said, "I understand, sir. I'll do my best."

"Can you wait until I pack and leave to make your exit? I know it's an odd thing to ask, but I like having you here to talk with."

"Of course, sir."

Holland re-read the file while Vice President Crawford packed two suitcases for his trip. Before he left, Crawford said, "God bless you, Bryan. I always enjoy working with you. And good luck on your mission with our team!"

Holland smiled and said, "The same to you, sir, and thank you."

Vice President Bob Crawford hesitated, and asked, "Bryan, do you know what bothers me the most about this Sampson business, and all the others like it?"

"No, sir. What?"

"Every time a false sex allegation claim is made, legitimate victims and innocent suspects are irreparably damaged. False reporting discourages actual victims from seeking law enforcement assistance, just as these same reports harm innocent suspects by substituting an assumption of guilt for the required presumption of innocence. False claims tear at the very fabric of a legitimate system and polarize the public. Do you realize our system of government could degenerate and become totally unsustainable if a person can't run for office or accept an appointment without fear of this malicious political retaliation?"

Bryan Holland said, "I understand your concerns, sir. And I agree. But our system usually refuses to prosecute those who lie. So, by refusing to protect victims of character assassination, we encourage the bad behavior we say we hate."

Bob Crawford nodded in agreement, turned, and walked toward the front door, rolling his suitcases behind him slowly.

SAC Bryan Holland returned to the walk-in, wood-paneled closet, pushed the button hidden from view behind a suit hanging on the far side of the rack, and stepped through the hidden door into the adjoining surveillance room. Bryan activated the switch on the inside and closed the secret door. Subdued lighting from concealed surveillance cameras lit the monitor. He watched the Vice President arrive and wait at the front door, look back toward the nearest camera one last time, wave goodbye, and exit the apartment.

Holland waited and watched. Less than a minute later, Secret Service Agent Christian Booth, assigned to Vice President Crawford, entered the Vice President's apartment using a passkey and electronic code. He walked quickly from room to room, glancing around as if he was searching. Booth walked into the office and hit the mouse, activating the monitor. The screen requested a password. Booth walked out of the office and headed toward the bedroom. Arriving at the dormitory, Booth checked the closet and master bathroom, opened a few dresser drawers, and then walked back toward the master bedroom closet. He stopped just out of view of the bedroom camera.

Bryan Holland sat perfectly quiet on the other side of the wood paneling. He looked down at the bottom of the secret doorway and saw no incoming light. He was sure that Booth could not detect any light coming from the surveillance room through to the closet.

Holland listened to rustling sounds, and then heard Booth say, "Sir, this is Christian. He took two suitcases and left. I did check his computer, but it doesn't appear that he used it recently. It looks like he just came in, packed, and left."

After a period of silence, Holland heard Booth say, "I understand, sir. I told them I urgently needed to use the bathroom in the building, down the hallway. I need to get downstairs now. They're all waiting for me."

After a brief pause, Booth said, "Thank you, sir. I will."

Bryan Holland waited until Booth was out the front door. He immediately called Vice President Crawford, and said, "Sir, their agent is Christain Booth, just as we suspected. Booth didn't go to the bathroom. He checked all the rooms in your apartment and looked at the monitor connected to your office laptop before he called to report your activities. When Booth gets to the motorcade, can you tell him you're waiting for an emergency call on your phone and need to make a phone call using his phone? You can check his recent calls to confirm he called the President."

When Crawford agreed, Holland quickly ended the call. He continued to stare at the surveillance monitor until Crawford called back, fifteen minutes later.

"You were right," Crawford growled. "The little bastard is the one spying on me. He called the President. I wanted to strangle the little shit, but I thanked him and returned his phone, with a call to my dry cleaners in his call log."

As Holland was about to comment, the apartment front door opened, and a tall, handsome man wearing a dark striped suit strolled unhurriedly through the door.

Holland quickly said, "Sir, someone else is here! I need to call you back!"

Holland ended the call and watched the man carry a briefcase into the Vice President's apartment office. Once at Crawford's desk, the man placed his suitcase next to the mouse. He then strolled off toward the kitchen. Arriving next to the sink, he looked around, reached to his right and opened the refrigerator. He removed a boxed package of smoked salmon and a beer, popped the top on the beer and carried both items back to the office.

The man sat in Crawford's chair, and in no hurry, placed his feet on the desk and began eating and drinking. Eventually, the man removed a flash drive from his briefcase and plugged it into Crawford's laptop. He then returned to his eating and drinking for about a minute. He didn't open the computer or activate the attached monitor by touching the mouse. Instead, he closed his briefcase, guzzled the rest of the beer, ate the remaining chunk of salmon, and returned to the kitchen. Once there, the man threw the empty beer and box into the trash, turned on his heels and walked calmly out the door, carrying his briefcase.

Holland waited a few moments to ensure the man was not returning, and called Crawford to explain what happened.

When he finished detailing the strange man's exploits, Crawford said, "All of a sudden my apartment has more traffic than a day-time brothel! And he ate my smoked salmon and drank my beer? Bryan, what in the hell is wrong with people? And, who is this guy?"

Bryan said calmly, "I don't know, sir, but I need to take your laptop back to my office and have my geeks do some research. I'm changing your front door electronic security code before I leave. I'll text you the new code on your secure phone. I'll disguise the code as the last four digits of a ten digit phone number, just to be safe. And I think you should call a locksmith to change the mechanical locks. You can leave me a new key in the usual way."

"Good ideas, Bryan. I will, and thanks."

Holland added, "I'll call as soon as I have anything, sir. Be very careful. This affair is becoming more complex. I don't like what I see at all."

Holland ended the phone call, waited in the hidden room for another thirty minutes, and once he was sure no one else was coming, walked out into the closet. He went to the kitchen and removed a sizeable brown shopping bag and a few gallon-size sealable plastic bags from the pantry. He cautiously bagged the salmon box, plastic vacuum pack, beer bottle and beer cap, recovered from the trash, into the plastic bags. Bryan headed for the office. He picked up the laptop using the edges the man had not touched, and carefully placed it in the brown paper bag.

Holland carried the computer and the sealed plastic bags back to the closet, reentered the secret room, and closed the passageway. Inside, he turned the monitor off, hit a switch on the opposite side of the wall, and walked silently through a second door to the private, concealed, stairwell behind him. He walked three flights downstairs to his own apartment, located on the opposite side of the building.

Crawford had selected this particular apartment many years earlier with one person in mind, Barbara Walcott. Crawford's father, a wealthy builder, had purchased, gutted and rebuilt the apartment building when Crawford was twenty-five years old. Crawford's father designed the structure with his much younger girlfriend in mind, deciding not to remarry after Crawford's mother died suddenly.

Bob Crawford's father enjoyed secret liaisons with his lover, far from inquiring minds and wagging tongues. When Crawford inherited the building years later, and began dating Walcott, he was married. The apartments proved useful in maintaining his relationship with Walcott, while concealing it from the public eye.

But once Crawford started to investigate The Committee, and Barbara had returned to England, he moved his only trusted ally, FBI agent Bryan Holland, into the 'attached" apartment, so they could communicate without raising suspicion or being discovered. So far, the arrangement had served them both very well.

✲✲✲

Lee landed the team's new Bonanza airplane at Char's North Carolina property, using only half the runway. The flight had proven uneventful, as they managed to stay well ahead of a weather system. Walter, Juanita, and Lee took quick showers, unpacked, and attended a briefing on the investigation to catch up with developments. And then they took their turns speaking with BaCayse. All three quickly learned to trust and appreciate her abilities.

At the end of a long day, Walter and Juanita sat with Pete and Char on the back deck, sipping Char's favorite whiskey. When Pete finished explaining additional details about Tasha's deception, and added his personal life update with Char, the group sat in silence for nearly a minute.

Finally, when Pete couldn't stand the quiet any longer, he asked, "What do you both think? I need to know how you feel about everything."

Walter glanced at Juanita and waited for a response. When she looked down in silence, he said, "I owe you an apology, Pete. Both of us owe you *at least* that much, and more. I'm afraid I pushed you and Tasha together as much, or even more, than everyone else combined. And I see I was wrong."

Walter looked briefly at Juanita, and added, "We were all wrong."

Walter looked at Char, who had remained silent throughout the entire conversation. He said, "And we all owe you an apology, too, Char. Looking back, I failed to consider you to be any more than the very talented operative you had become in your line of work. I saw you as your occupation, not you, the person. I never thought about you as a feeling, caring woman, capable of our family's kind of love. And in so doing, I became judgmental and thoughtless."

276

Walter continued. He said, "Juanita and I *chose* Tasha for Pete, and then pushed them together, believing Pete could be happier that way. But we made him miserable and opened our family to complications in the process. If we had stayed out of other people's relationships things may have turned out differently. I'm sorry I behaved so badly. I apologize for our family."

Walter reflected, "I think that sometimes, as we get older and think we know more, we misbehave, trying to steer people's lives in a direction we decide is best *for* them, a direction that they don't always want to take. Of all people, I should know that we can't manage other people's lives. We all have enough trouble managing our own lives. I hope you'll forgive me."

Char nodded, as Walter then looked at Juanita, giving her an opportunity to confess.

Juanita looked confidently from Pete to Char, and said, "I am also truly sorry for the personal pressure I brought that caused you all pain. Kate once persuaded me to tell Walter how I felt, and her advice was good. Walter and I reacted the way we should have many years ago. I thought I could force the same change for Pete. I knew how lonely he was, and believed that Tasha truly loved him. And even when I considered that Pete was only attracted to Tasha, I wanted so badly for them to become like Walter and me, that I never considered allowing Pete to choose for himself. Now I see that I took away *his right* to choose, forcing him to act on what *I wanted*. I can only say how sorry I am, and ask your forgiveness."

Pete said, "Nothing is more important to me than this family, and those I love. Of course, I forgive you and I accept your apologies! But, in truth, I stand as much to blame for Tasha as anyone else, maybe more. I allowed myself to be pushed toward someone I thought I could change and mold into the person I wanted. I think we all learned a valuable lesson. And, hopefully, we're all stronger and closer as a result. I love you both very much. I just want us to go forward as a family." Pete glanced at Char.

Char said, "You've all been wonderful to me, especially considering how I came to you, through Hector, with an order to terminate Heath if I detected a double cross. I've grown to think of you as my team, my friends and even my family. I ask only for you to get to know me well enough to think of me in the same way I think of all of you. As much as I *am* a good operative, I am also a caring, feeling woman, capable of love and loyalty. I could never do what Tasha did to Pete and all of you, because family and love are first to me, *always*. So, I hope you'll give me the chance to prove myself as a person."

Pete, Juanita, and Walter all smiled. Walter reached over and placed his hand on Char's arm. He said, "Char, my dear, by the fact that my son, Pete, is sitting next to you alive, you have already more than proven yourself. You saved him because you cared. And I thank you!"

Juanita said, "Amen."

Walter raised his glass, "To Char." All four of them toasted and drank.

Shane, Kate, Angie, and Heath walked through the field toward the deck, on their way back from the hangar, with Jago, Bruiser, and Masai trailing behind, checking bushes for rabbits and strange smells.

Shane called out, "We checked out the new plane! I love it!"

Walter said, "Great! Come on over and join us for a drink!"

278

Once all four couples were seated with drinks, Pete took Char's hand, and said, "We need to figure out how to proceed with the Yucca Mountain attack, and also what to do about this troublesome gold deposit. Also, I've been thinking about the EPA signs our team photographed on the mine site buildings. Maybe we need to contact Vice President Crawford and see if he can use his influence to find out what the EPA plans are for the site. We need more information about the chemicals, for our safety, in case we have to go back. I think you should call

Crawford in the morning, Walter." The rest all nodded and agreed.

While the group sat drinking a good Kentucky bourbon whiskey on the wooden deck in North Carolina, FBI SAC Bryan Holland was working late at his office, when his phone rang. Holland identified himself as he answered.

The woman on the other end of the line said, "Sir, this is Molly Sherman, from the Washington D.C. Medical Examiner's Office."

"Yes, Molly, how can I help you?"

"Agent, you placed a request for contact regarding latent fingerprints you entered into the Integrated Automated Fingerprint Identification System. We inputted a print card into the system that I recovered from a recently deceased person. I got a match with your latents. We received a follow-up call from an FBI agent requesting our office contact you immediately with the information on the deceased. I can send you the report if you provide an email address."

Holland provided the address and asked, "What was the cause of death?"

"Poison, sir. The man died after ingesting poisoned, smoked salmon. We rushed the tests due to the unusual nature of the death. We *have* ruled this death a homicide."

Holland said, "Thanks. I'd appreciate those reports as soon as possible."

"I just sent the copies. You should have them now, sir. Have a good night."

Bryan Holland quickly opened the attachments as soon as they arrived. He obtained the man's name, entered the information into state and national database search software, and began recovering background details to build a working file on the person. The deceased's photograph confirmed the man was the same subject Holland had seen in Crawford's apartment. Once he had accumulated sufficient information, Bryan Holland made a conference phone call to his inner circle. He was able to confer with eight of the twelve trusted colleagues from various agencies he called, who answered their phones at the late hour. When he hung up, Holland then called Vice President Crawford.

Crawford answered quickly. "Bryan, thanks for calling. I was just wondering if you'd come up with anything on my mysterious house guest."

"Only that he's dead, sir, and I must ask you two important questions. Where did you get the smoked salmon, and did you eat any?"

Crawford said, "The smoked salmon was in a basket that Chief of Staff Langhart sent to my White House office as a welcome back gift from my mini vacation with Barbara. The salmon was the only item I wanted. My staff took the olives, spreads, cheeses, biscuits, and candies and ate it at work that day. All the staff at the White House knows I'm a sucker for good smoked salmon, so it's the only gift I never share! I hadn't opened it. I was saving it to eat with Barbara when she returned. She enjoys it as much as I do!"

Holland said, "Good, someone laced the salmon with poison. The mystery eater from your apartment died the same day from the fast-acting toxin."

Crawford sat down in shock at the desk in his Asheville, North Carolina, hotel room. After a moment, he said, "Well, I guess we were right about Langhart and Marshall. They *would* kill me. But, Bryan, it doesn't make sense for them to kill me so soon, as odd as that sounds to say. I haven't had a chance to do their bidding down here, and I could already be dead if I had eaten with the rest of my staff, or later when I was home alone. So, what's going on here? Who could it have been? And who was this guy that died eating poisoned salmon possibly meant for me?"

Bryan Holland said, "Unfortunately, sir, I don't have a good answer for you. What I *can* tell you is that although we've identified the deceased through records, the records are all phony. Someone altered all the databases, and created fictitious identities, addresses, and phone numbers to conceal his true identity. But the face belongs to the man I watched in your apartment. So what naturally follows is…"

Crawford finished the sentence, "He's a spook. But, Bryan, if the man was working deep cover in one of the intelligence agencies, why did he target me? I have no deep, dark, secret intelligence that's a threat to anyone. And if he's a foreign spook, I don't possess intelligence so sensitive that a foreign government would it want badly enough to kill the Vice President of The United States of America!"

281

Crawford sighed and asked, "What did the flash drive he left plugged into my computer contain, and why didn't he download or upload something? I would have noticed the flash drive as soon as I saw it sticking out of the computer. I would never have turned the computer on if he had left it there."

Holland said, "The drive contains files and a detailed synopsis of dozens of meetings, along with maps and notes of private conversations between heads of state and terrorist organizations who attended those meetings. The players are Chinese, North Korean, Iranian, and Syrian diplomats, along with representatives from half a dozen infamous terrorist networks. The files are all attachments supporting an intelligence memo that explains how all the participants are conspiring to attack the United States by setting off a dirty nuclear device at the New York Stock Exchange. The memo identifies the mission goal as the economic destabilization of our country. And it describes the attack as the first of seven to drive our nation to the brink of destruction."

While Crawford's mind raced, Bryan Holland said, "Possession of these files on your computer would have been impossible for you to explain, sir, unless you were a spy, or working *with* an international spy. And worse, as you know, if they had been discovered, under The Patriot Act, you could have been arrested and held in secret, without trial, as an enemy combatant."

"Bryan, if that's the case, why didn't this spook upload the files onto my computer?"

"Sir, one of the meetings on the drive hadn't happened yet. Due to the time difference between Washington D.C., and As Suknah, Syria, that planned meeting in Syria didn't occur until about three hours after

282

our spy left your apartment. And that meeting was essential to be included in the material on the drive, as the Memo I referred to was distributed at the conference. You departed in the late morning, and the meeting was held in Syria after dinnertime, in the late evening.

"I don't understand, Bryan."

"Sir, I think your mystery guest was planning to come back. He fell over dead on a table at a coffee shop down the street from your apartment building. When he died, he was killing time, drinking coffee and working a crossword puzzle book. I think the dead man's assignment was to go back and download the files soon after the Syrian meeting ended, so you wouldn't be able to explain how you got the information so soon after it happened. To obtain such sensitive information that quickly, you'd have to be in league with high-ups in terrorist organizations, terrorist state governments, or the Chinese, unless a foreign agent provided them to you immediately after the meeting. Whichever way, you'd be in serious trouble."

Crawford said, "Alright, but I still don't understand the poisoned salmon our killer intended for me. Who poisoned it, and how were they sure it would kill me and not someone else?"

Bryan Holland released a deep sigh. He said, "I took the liberty of reaching out to my inner circle, sir, without providing names or details, to postulate a hypothetical situation. Our group discussed the possibilities quickly and came up with two other possible targets, apart from you. First, someone could have targeted the spook, sir."

"You've lost me with that one, Bryan. How could the people who planned this know the spy would eat the salmon, and not me?"

"Sir, you and I both know that all the spy agencies have informants in each other's agencies, to ensure they stay in the loop on almost everything. Some of the sister agencies are more in bed with each other than others. Our three major U.S. intelligence *sisters* could share a detailed blueprint of any of our lives using telephonic, email, and text message data mining, electronic records, social media, credit card charges, etc. If they added surveillance, a FISA warrant, or illegal methods, they could know more about us than we remember ourselves. Something like this wouldn't be that hard to arrange."

Holland asked, "For example, did you call Home Secretary Walcott on a non-scrambled phone and talk to her about the smoked salmon you were saving for her?"

Crawford thought back, and said, "I did, two nights ago, when I called her to say goodnight. I used my home landline, instead of my scrambled cell, because I was waiting for an urgent call from my staff."

Holland asked, "Have you heard of habitual behavior patterns among agents and operatives?"

Crawford said, "I haven't."

Holland said, "I worked with a lady who went to the same small coffee shop five days a week, and drank a double shot mocha grande at precisely 11:00 A.M., never earlier or later. Another agent I worked with always left his business card in every building and car he ever searched, on all search warrants he attended, even when it wasn't his case or his agency's case. Another colleague took stacks of business cards from a supervisor he detested, and gave one to every crazy homeless person he encountered, encouraging the homeless person to call and report all his concerns. Another agent never brought his lunch to work, but instead, took pride in mooching food from others' lunches. A detective I know gave a rose to every woman he ever arrested, just to make her feel better."

"Working solo assignments, as spooks often do, they all eventually develop patterns that are even more pronounced than these examples. They get bored being alone and entertain themselves with some unique calling card or habit they always practice when they enter your office, your home, or your car."

"One spy I knew always left pantyhose in a man's car, so when the owner found them, he'd drive himself crazy trying to figure out who they came from, and why he couldn't remember. And if his girlfriend or wife found them, well, you can imagine. Another spy carried Mace and sprayed the sheets of target's beds, so they would suffer the effects when they tried to sleep, or fool around."

"A female spy I knew always made herself a cup of coffee or tea to drink while she worked in someone's house, and then left the cup on the kitchen counter to upset the owner. So maybe your mystery guest ate other people's food and drank their beer. What else did you have to eat or drink in the fridge?"

"Nothing. I cleaned it out for the trip. The perishable food was all in the trash. The vacuum-packed salmon was good for six months, so it was no problem."

Crawford thought for a moment, and said, "I guess I see your point. But Bryan, you mentioned three possible targets, including me. Who's the third?"

Bryan hesitated and said, "Our group postulated the other target could be another person whom the salmon was intended to be shared with or given to, as a gift."

Vice President Crawford sat upright in anger, and immediately said, "Barbara!"

"Sir, at this point, it's just all speculation."

"Bryan, how was the poison introduced into the meat?"

Holland said, "Lab analysis revealed a tiny hole in both the box and plastic, likely resulting from an injection."

Crawford asked, "The Committee, you think, possibly?"

Holland said, "Its hard to speculate about who was responsible, sir. We don't have enough facts. But, before you left, our President planned for you to handle the solution or take the fall for his North Carolina problem, and since he's a top ranking Committee member, it's likely not them."

Holland hesitated, and then said, "Wait for a second, sir. The biggest clue just now came in while we were speaking. I've received a classified communication from our crime lab. The poison is a new Russian formula, currently their standard issue for all assassinations."

"Russians again! Damn it!" Crawford asked, "What angle are they playing this time?"

Holland said, "Sir, maybe the motivation is foreign politics instead of pure espionage or internal assassination. Are you currently involved in any negotiations, or political alliances, that oppose or threaten any pressing Russian agendas?"

Crawford thought for a moment, "Possibly. I need to make some calls, Bryan, and get back to you. What will you do with the flash drive intelligence my dead guest left us?"

"With your permission sir, I'll personally hand off printed copies to a member of my trusted inner circle, in the Agency. He'll make good use of the material."

"Do I know him, Bryan?"

"No, sir, I don't think so. But if we ever need to speak about him, I'll refer to him by his nickname, 'Anonymous,' for his work habit. If he ever sanctioned a person, he would leave a photograph of the deceased person which he had taken while they were alive, on or near their body. He signed the photos, 'Anonymous.' I guess that's morbid spy humor."

"Thanks, Bryan. Keep in touch."

"Be careful, sir."

"I will, Bryan. And you had better be extra careful, too."

✳✳✳

At 4:30 A.M. Jago awoke from a deep sleep, where he had been happily dreaming about chasing squirrels with Masai and Bruiser, as they explored an exciting new field filled with distinct smells and unfamiliar sensations. But now, he sensed something unusual, and strange. He got up and walked to the bed to check Heath and Angie. Finding them peacefully sleeping, Jago walked to the bedroom door. He saw it remained closed. Jago trotted quietly to the second story bedroom window that looked out toward the hangar, where his friend and companion, Bruiser, now stayed with Char and Pete. He jumped up on the sill, standing on his hind legs. When he could detect nothing wrong, he hopped down and returned to his sleep-pad in the corner.

Jago again glanced up at the bed where his man and woman lay sleeping. He licked the air, expressing a deep love for his pack. There was nothing he wouldn't do for them or any of the members of his pack, his family and the team.

The relationships had changed, with Tasha gone, and Char in her place. But Jago trusted Char. In Char, he recognized sincerity and purpose, and apart from those qualities, loyalty, and commitment, like he and Bruiser possessed. Loyalty meant devotion to fight to the death, if necessary, to protect the pack, family, friends, and home. It was the same faithfulness he and Bruiser held within their hearts and were now teaching to Masai.

Jago knew that Masai needed to learn his place and responsibilities in the pack quickly, because they all knew enemies were about to come for this team. Masai was young, but he was needed, even required. Dog's lives were too short, and their people needed continuous protection. Jago knew canines sensed many things their people could not, and one more canine was essential to protect Shane and Kate. So Masai had to hurry and grow up, to survive and help ensure his people would survive. Jago thought about his responsibilities, sighed and drifted back to sleep.

While Jago went back to the field of dreams in his mind, filled with new adventures and old friends, Heath tumbled headfirst down a tunnel that narrowed as he fell from the cavern above. Suddenly, Heath found himself hopelessly stuck in the craggy hard rocks, with his body contorted sideways, and his head beneath him. Heath twisted and pushed against the immovable rock, but found the more he struggled, the harder it was to move.

He pushed backward repeatedly, and eventually freed one leg, only to discover that his foot touched a hard surface in every direction it moved. He couldn't climb in reverse while upside down, to reclaim the few feet he needed to return to the cavern. And without returning to the cavern, he couldn't climb up to the surface, where freedom waited. Freedom, with its friends, family, and love were suddenly all out of his reach.

Heath began to panic. He had known he shouldn't have entered the cavern alone, and so ill-prepared. And now he was stuck. Heath tried to calm his fears and think fast. Suddenly he realized he was having more difficulty breathing with each passing second. Heath was overheating. And when things got hotter, they swelled. If he remained here too long, he would be hopelessly stuck and could die there, alone in a hole, by himself.

Heath knew he needed to remove his jacket to diminish the temperature and eliminate the bulk that bound him tightly. Thinking back, he recalled deciding to take the coat in case it got cold while he explored. But it had never been cold, and Heath had not carried a backpack to store things like jackets until he needed them. He should have checked the weather report. Now he regretted not planning better, and not bringing a pack. The backpack's additional bulk would have caught him and prevented his fall down the tunnel. And it would have held the jacket that now threatened his life. Heath knew he should have thought things through, before he acted in haste. He could have brought someone with him, and not set off half-cocked, alone, with no back-up.

Heath closed his eyes to reflect on the situation and calm both his beating heart and racing mind. Instantly his father was there with him, standing just a few feet off, talking to Angie, almost within his reach. Heath called to both of them. Angie looked at Heath and nodded, but then continued listening to his father. Heath called again, and pleaded for their help, as his panic worsened. He could feel his heart pounding, beating so fast he thought it might explode. He called one more time, pleading, asking for those who loved him to help. He was in danger of passing out from heat and exhaustion. Heath was about to give up, and accept his fate.

Angie and Patrick Beckett walked calmly to Heath and gently pulled him backward, into the cavern, seemingly with no effort at all. In an instant, Heath was safe, lying down, prostrate on the hard rock cavern floor. He struggled to his knees and remained there, trying to figure out how Angie and his father had moved behind him through the tunnel, when he had just seen them ahead of him, in the narrowing passageway. Heath realized he was still on his knees and now wanted to hear the conversation, so he stood up. As he did, Angie handed him a backpack.

Patrick Beckett said, "Heath, son, why don't you take off your jacket and put it in the pack. You look hot."

Heath took off the coat and placed it in the pack. He threw the bag over his shoulders and listened intently. Heath stood there, breathing hard, and was finally able to catch his breath. But now, he was thirsty. His mouth was so dry from hyperventilating and overheating that he could barely swallow. He realized he should have thought to bring water on his journey. Angie would have thought to bring water, if he had discussed the trip with her.

Angie immediately handed him a cold bottle of water, as Heath heard Patrick say, "You need to help him prepare and remind Heath that he's always part of a team, and not alone anymore. Heath is much better off with a family than by himself, alone, and unfocused. Most of us have an advantage when we stick with those who love us."

"So, as you go through life, Angie, remind my son to include you and the others he loves in everything that's important. Depend on each other, and then you can depend on Heath. He's a good man. He'll be there for you. Heath is my precious youngest son, so please take care of him as if he were the most precious treasure in your life. "

Heath thought about the lesson his father spoke as he felt for his wristwatch and noticed it was missing. He took off the pack, retrieved a flashlight and looked down the perilous tunnel. Heath saw the watch laying there about six feet down, almost back to the place the dangerous rock channel had held him captive.

He didn't want to interrupt the conversation, so he kneeled down at the mouth of the perilous tunnel and reached in, figuring this time he would hold himself by his ankles, as he ventured back inside. Just as he began to move downward, Heath felt himself slip downward again, as both Angie and Patrick Beckett yelled, "No!"

Jago licked Heath's face repeatedly to wake Heath up and save him from his dream. Heath hugged Jago and kissed his nose and muzzle repeatedly. Jago looked inquiringly at his man, wondering why Heath had made the same foolish mistake twice, interrupting their peaceful sleep both times. Heath held on tightly to Jago, his companion and savior, as the panic slowly subsided, once again. It dawned on Heath that he must change his loner ways, and work with the team, his family, and his friends.

Jago continued licking Heath, sensing the change in his man, pleased with the result. Now, Jago knew he must focus on Masai, to teach the puppy even more, and quickly. Jago knew that humans were complicated creatures. Some of the bad people possessed characteristics most dogs couldn't understand. These evil ones were cruel, callous, malicious, heartless, and mean. Some inflected pain on other people and even their own companion animals, for no reason. Still, other people imposed pain motivated by power, control, greed, money, sex, and something called politics.

Jago had heard people use the words, 'politics,' and 'politicians.' But he couldn't imagine what those things were that led people to hate each other, become violent, destroy each other's careers and families, and even go to war, and kill. This thing called politics was evil in Jago's mind. Jago had never met a canine who understood the term. And all dogs feared the meanness held deep inside some people that this thing called politics could motivate and release.

Jago knew time was short for humans, unless they could get control of themselves. He would pray for them as a species. But for now, he would teach Masai all he could, so together, he, Bruiser and Masai could protect their families and their pack from life, enemies, and evil politics.

Chapter 7

"Power tends to corrupt, and absolute power corrupts absolutely. Great men are almost always bad men."

(Bishop Mandell Creighton, 1843-1901)

Walter woke refreshed, even after the late night and two stiff whiskey drinks. He was excited to be back, working on the investigation, and happy to be reunited with his family and the cypher team. He knew he needed to call his old friend, Bob Crawford. And Walter also knew he needed to trust Bob, even though Bob had withheld information about Tasha.

Walter wanted to break down Bob's defenses and get at the truth. And, although the men had a long personal history and deep friendship, Bob and Walter were both savvy negotiators, each cautious about protecting a position of strength. But Walter believed if he could only talk to his buddy in person, he could discover what secrets Bob knew. The team had to know if Tasha would be an ongoing threat *and* if they had others like her in their midst. And the team urgently needed the Vice President's influence with the EPA to figure out what chemicals were present at the mine site, and what the government's response would be to ensure the land and water was safe.

Walter got up quietly, leaving Juanita sleeping soundly, as Sophia watched silently from her sleep-pad, on the floor below Juanita's side of the bed. He stopped to look closely at the attentive, brown, short-haired dog, and marveled at how beautiful, alert, and intelligent she truly was.

Sophia and Juanita had bonded instantly and securely once they chose each other amidst the bustling confusion of the Oregon ranch house, with its dozens of people coming and going, and several other dogs always underfoot. Juanita had made a place for Sophia in their bedroom at the ranch. It had become a haven where Juanita and Sophia could escape, a quiet place where Sophia could hang out and enjoy seclusion. And there, in the afternoon peace and sanctity of their cave, Juanita and Sophia bonded, with Juanita reading a novel and drinking tea as she petted her new friend.

Walter had never realized Juanita had longed for a dog of her own, and this Shiba Inu had been the perfect fit. Sophia was a one-person dog, and there was no mistaking that Juanita was *her* human. When Juanita moved, Sophia moved, even to the bathroom or to the kitchen. And because Juanita was with Walter, Sophia tolerated him. So, when Angie consented to give Sophia to Walter and Juanita, Juanita had quickly agreed, the family had grown, and there was no going back. Now, the two were nearly inseparable.

Walter pulled on some jogging pants, a fresh T-shirt and his slippers. He walked to Sophia, patted her on her head, and kissed Juanita lightly on the cheek. He stood smiling at this woman he had appreciated, valued and loved for so long, and then smiled down at Sophia, who seemed to understand. Sophia licked the air, her tongue coming straight out, in approval.

Walter turned and walked downstairs to the kitchen. He poured a cup of hot black coffee, peered into the workroom, and saw that Tracy, Jesse, Sam, Lee, and Tom were already busy at work. Walter checked his watch. It was 6:37 A.M., and a slight chill was in the air. Walter walked back through the kitchen, down the hall, and into the mudroom. He opened the door and stepped on to the wooden deck that looked out over the fields and trees to the north side of the house. Even though it was mid-summer, the morning air felt chilly enough to be late fall.

Walter gazed fondly at the acreage. The property was beautiful, lush, green and inviting. Walter contemplated how woods, grasses, and brush were all so different in the East as compared to the Western United States. Here, in the Atlantic States, rolling hills, lakes, and swamps provided a habitat infused with high humidity and rain, that together, created a haven for pines, hardwoods, brush, and grasses to flourish, forming dense, nearly impenetrable barriers. Cypress dominated the swamps, but also extended uphill to join pines and deciduous trees in the drier mountainous areas.

Walter sipped his coffee and smiled as he ushered the outside view deep within himself, to his heart and soul. He enjoyed and loved his country, with all its different landscapes. But Walter dearly loved the mountain ranges along the East Coast. He felt drawn to them by some force of nature. To Walter, these mystical rolling hills and magical mountains were every bit as important as the Sierra Nevada range John Muir wrote about, when he said, "The mountains are calling, and I must go."

Walter glanced down at the phone repeatedly, and when it was 7:00 A.M., he called Bob Crawford, knowing Bob would already be awake. Vice President Bob Crawford answered immediately.

"Walter, you rascal, I was just about to call you! How are you?"

"I'm good, Bob. A little worried about you, though. We haven't spoken much in quite a while. How are *you*?"

"I'm troubled, old friend. I think we should speak in person, Walter. Unfortunately, I'm tied up for a while, down here in the Carolinas. But, it's still urgent we meet. Any ideas?"

"Where in the Carolinas, Bob?"

"Asheville, this morning. Why? Can you get here?"

"In about an hour or so, if you like. I'm here, too, in North Carolina, not far from you."

"Great! But, we need to meet in absolute privacy, and I have an idea. I planned to visit an old attorney friend named Leroy Mayberry. He has an office in downtown Asheville, with a private meeting room in the back. He's in the book and listed on the Internet. I'm scheduled to see him after breakfast, to pick his brain about a personal matter and catch up with him since his wife died. If you could arrange to get there by 9:00, I'll make sure you have the meeting room to yourself. I'll dump my security detail in the lobby and meet you inside."

"I'll be there."

Bob Crawford ended the call, and immediately called Barbara Walcott. Although she was in a meeting with a dozen other people, Barbara quickly arranged to leave early, and promised to call Bob back when she was alone and could use a private scrambled line. Twenty minutes later, Barbara returned the call.

Vice President Crawford briefed British Home Secretary Barbara Walcott on all the details of his conversation with President Marshall and Chief of Staff Langhart. And then he told her about his mysterious, dead houseguest, and his discussion with Bryan Holland. When Crawford finished, Walcott sat for several seconds in silence.

Finally, Barbara asked, "Bob, what are you thinking?"

"I think we should both avoid salmon for a while, dear."

"Bob, I'm serious. What should I do now? And what are you going to do about the Russians and these lethal chemicals in North Carolina? You could be walking into a dangerous trap down there!"

President Crawford walked to his hotel window and looked out as he thought aloud. He said, "I have no idea what to do, other than to talk with my old friend, Walter. I don't know what you could do, there in England. I don't know who is who anymore, or who I can trust. What do you think, love?"

Walcott suddenly wondered if Sergej Petrov had tried to poison Walter, motivated by some sick jealous fantasy resulting from their 'date.' She considered whether or not Petrov would kill a United States Vice President, in an attempt to keep her for himself. Walcott remained silent.

Bob Crawford asked, "No thoughts, dear? That's not like you. What are you thinking that you're not saying?"

"I have thoughts, Bob, just not good ones. I was wondering if our friend, Sergej, had something to do with this intrigue."

"Trying to kill me? Or possibly both of us? Why Petrov? Do you think Petrov believes that you or I would be the barrier to the Russian oil deal with France? That doesn't make sense, when President Marshall would be the one to decide our U.S. policy, not me. And although you *are* in a powerful position, dear, you're not the U.K.'s Prime Minister."

Crawford added, "And, besides, England might support the French and Russian deal in exchange for French support for Brexit. That could bring the Germans on board with the oil deal, and give them a path out of the crumbling European Union. You English and Germans are supporting the lion's share of the E.U. costs, and that's driving both of your countries bankrupt. So, you supporting the deal creates a four-way win, for the Russians, French, English, and Germans, right, honey?"

Barbara said, "I see you've been spending a lot of time on this issue, my love. But I don't think the oil deal is Sergej Petrov's motivation, honey."

Crawford huffed. "Well, it's certainly not about the chemical spill, if Russians are involved. Marshall sent me here to fix the problem, or take the blame for it, so I'm no good to any of them dead. And him killing you doesn't work into that scenario."

Barbara said, "It may be something other than the oil deal or chemical spill, honey. But, I think we need to speak about that in person, and not over the phone."

Crawford said, "Face-to-face meetings seem to be the theme of the day. How do we do that with me here, and you in England?

Walcott said, "I need to be in America for trade talks next week. I'll arrange to pop over early, so we can have some private time together. I'll start working on the details. Maybe we can work it out for this weekend. Your place?"

"I don't know, yet. Maybe here in North Carolina, depending on what I discover."

"Alright, honey, be careful, and we'll talk when I make my flight plans. I'll get right to it! I love you."

"Love you too, dear."

Bob Crawford ended the call and felt suddenly alone. His fiancée, Barbara Walcott had just confirmed that she *was* withholding information. Now, Crawford questioned withholding information from Walter O'Leary. Crawford heard a knock at his hotel door, and walked to the door to greet his Secret Service detail and go down to breakfast. Now, he needed to draw the breakfast affair out for an hour and a half to give Walter time to get in place. He decided to ask hotel management for a tour of the kitchen so he could meet the staff.

By the time Crawford arrived at Leroy Mayberry's law office, Walter O'Leary had been in place, waiting, for 30 minutes. Shane and Kate had driven Walter to a diner a block and a half from the attorney's office. To ensure no one followed him, Walter had walked through an alley to a side street and then taken a winding route to Mayberry's office. There he met with Leroy Mayberry and chatted until the Secret Service arrived and cleared the building. He and Mayberry pretended to be in a business conference.

Crawford's Secret Service detail placed men in vehicles in the parking lot at the back of the building, and at the front of the building, on the street. The two agents who had cleared the building of potential threats waited in the lobby. Once the agents inside returned to the front hall, Walter moved from Leroy's office to the conference room.

Walter was not a man of great patience. He paced back and forth as he waited in the large room, anxious to discover what Bob Crawford knew and had not told him. Walter waited only ten minutes, while the Vice President finished a phone call to staffers. But to Walter, it seemed as if he had wasted an hour.

Crawford knocked at the conference room door, and recognizing his friend's voice on the inside, entered quickly. He walked up to Walter O'Leary and hugged him tightly. Crawford chose a seat next to Walter so they could speak in hushed tones. He apologized profusely for the delay.

Bob said, "Walter, my friend, the last time we spoke you told me a tale you thought I would find hard to believe, about The Committee. This time, old buddy, it's my turn to wow you with a story that may seem even more unbelievable!"

Vice President Crawford related everything he knew about The Committee, Tasha's planned kidnapping, Barbara Walcott, President Marshall, Chief of Staff Langhart, his dead houseguest, and the chemical spill near the lake."

Walter leaned back in his chair, studying his longtime friend, as he listened. By the time Crawford ended the story, and his confession, Walter was convinced Crawford had provided the whole truth, as he knew it. Crawford had spoken for nearly thirty-five minutes. He got up, walked to a small refrigerator in the corner, and retrieved two bottles of water. He handled one to Walter and drank half of the other before he placed the bottle on the table.

Walter had remained silent throughout the one-sided briefing. Vice President Crawford asked, "So, Walter, how do you read this whole mess?"

Walter sat forward and placed his hand on his friend's outstretched arm. He said, "Bob, you're in more danger than you know. I think you should sit back and finish your water while I bring you up-to-speed on the cypher investigation. At this point in our lives, old friend, we need each other more than we both know!"

Walter briefed Vice President Crawford about everything he had learned that the Beckett Cypher Artifical Intelligence Spy System had discovered to date. He spoke for nearly an hour, interrupted only once by a phone call from the Secret Service detail, checking on Crawford's welfare. As Walter ended his briefing, Crawford slumped down further in the leather office chair, considering everything Walter had said. He covered his face with his hands.

Bob Crawford said, "So my fiancée, Barbara, the love of my life, secretly met with Segej Petrov on her way home from *my* house to England. She also arranged for Tasha's kidnapping, so she could take her spy home to England because Tasha is her MI6 agent. And together, Barbara and Tasha conspired to try and steal the Beckett Cypher."

Crawford released a long sigh, and said, "My Barbara, the British Home Secretary, double-crossed both me and the United States of America, her country's ally, while Tasha did the same to you, Pete, and all those she loved. Wow! After all this time in politics, I never saw that one coming!"

Walter said, "Bob, I'm so sorry. But your time, my friend, might be better spent on figuring how to stay alive than fretting about your true love's motivations. If someone did try to target both you *and* Barbara, maybe we're missing something here, and she may also be in danger. What about the gold deposit? Doesn't that mess worry you? An entire family slaughtered, and a murdered Sheriff? These people are willing to kill anyone who stands in their way for $15,000,000,000 worth of gold. They've already sacrificed nine Russian guards to further their interests. And your boss, our President, is involved in this up to his eyeballs, and lied to you about the mine!"

"It does worry me, Walter. But the gold mine problem is just about greed, and all greed is rooted in money. Money is the easiest motivation to figure out and combat. The other motivations are rooted

301

in the evils that complicate matters, making solutions more elusive! It's obsessions with power, control, sex, and politics that are more difficult to interpret and defeat. And they usually involve more people, and planning."

"I suppose so, Bob, but we need to form a plan. At the very least, we need to figure out our next move."

Crawford got his second political wind. He said firmly, "We need to start shaking some trees to see who flies out to safety so that we can identify our enemies. I think we should pressure everyone at the same time to see who makes the most obvious mistakes as they scramble to cover their tracks. I suggest your team go ahead with the plan to attack Committee infrastructure at Yucca Mountain and their Centers for Information Extraction. I'll push buttons with the British, the Russians and my President. And maybe, even with a French diplomat, I know well enough to read."

Walter asked, "And the cypher? What government can we trust to possess such power when this investigation gets too big for our small team?"

Walter looked intently into his friend's eyes. Vice President Bob Crawford said decisively, "You and I both know the only possible answer is '*none of them!*' Politicians and bureaucrats have politicized and weaponized intelligence services ever since they created the agencies. And through abuses of power, those agencies that swore to protect their citizens have become corrupt, and now represent the greatest threat to our freedoms and democracy. It's no longer the terrorists or the Russians we should fear in America. It's corruption in our own intelligence agencies and investigative services that threatens to destroy us from within."

302

Crawford pounded his fist angrily on the table. He said, "We used to depend on the news media to keep the government honest. But once the press chose political sides, journalists became political party hacks and spokespersons, rather than finders of facts, and reporters. When corrupt government agencies combine forces with the press by leaking or concealing information to target political opponents, they have successfully destroyed our liberty. The United States is no longer a haven. We no longer have guaranteed freedoms under The Constitution and The Bill of Rights. We've already lost our most fundamental rights and freedoms of assembly, thought, expression, disagreement, speech, and religion."

Crawford looked at Walter O'Leary, and said, "At one time I believed the United States and its allies could use the cypher to defeat The Committee. In truth, our government can no longer be trusted with the cypher's power, Walter. And *we* have the least corrupt, most honorable country remaining in the world. So, from now on, I'm working with you and your team to ensure you keep the cypher. Your team can decide how to use and direct its force. You'll decide much more honorably than autocratic hacks."

Bob leaned further forward toward Walter, and said, "But I warn you. The old saying is true, 'Power tends to corrupt, and absolute power corrupts absolutely. Great men are almost always bad men.' I think I finally understand what the good bishop was saying about great men being bad men. He was trying to warn us that those we remember for significant actions often seized power that enabled them to create or destroy. Their motives were not always pure. Death, destruction and suffering often accompanied their creations."

Bob Crawford took a deep breath and sighed. He looked at his trusted friend, Walter, and added, "Life in the digital age has taught me that while those who possess the most powerful technology will likely become the richest and most influential people in the world, they may also become the most feared. Digital absolute power can instantaneously spread lies, create division, and promote hatred, while it conceals truth, love, and hope."

Crawford added, "I once believed that the government would fight corporations to protect the public from such evil, by controlling and regulating abuses of digital power. But, when the government becomes corrupt, it will not protect us. Instead, the government will seize that power, use it, and further develop it, to control *the public* and preserve itself and its unlimited power. Politicians and bureaucrats will become the ruling elite if we let them. In fact, I believe they may have already begun to assume control."

"So, Walter, if you and your team can guard against the internal corruptions and temptations all men and women of good character fight within themselves, then you will do an honorable job with the cypher. The government will not, ever. We are no longer a government of the people, by the people, and for the people. The people are merely subjects to be used and abused by their government. My friend, you must guard against the temptation to exalt yourself to a position of total control by seizing absolute power."

Walter stood, and said, "Bob, that sounded like the speech a man should give if he considered running for president. And truthfully, I wish you and your boss *were* in opposite roles!" They both laughed.

Walter asked, "So, what will you do about your chemical spill problem. Bob?"

Bob Crawford stood, and replied, "What politicians do best, my friend, nothing. It's an unsolvable problem, with people above me manipulating the parameters. There is really nothing I *can* do, but leak the information to local and state officials...and the press, and hope the press does the right thing, as finders of fact and reporters. I'll go through the motions with the EPA to cover our bases. And then I'll pray. But, with the president sitting in his position of power, there isn't really anything I *can* do to change the outcome. "

Walter offered, "If that's the case, Bob, our friend BaCayse could do a better job of leaking to the press, and ensure there are no ties back to you. We can offer that much help."

"Do it," Crawford said, as he shook Walter O'Leary's hand. The two friends stared at each other and finally hugged.

As Vice President Crawford strolled to the door, he turned and asked, "Did you ever think, when we were back in college, full of hopes and dreams, ready to run out into a country full of freedoms to change the world, that our lives would turn out like this, fearful of corruption and retribution from our own government?"

Walter shook his head, but said nothing. Bob Crawford shot back a half-hearted smile and walked out, closing the door quickly, just as Walter said, "Be careful, my friend."

✲✲✲

Home Secretary Barbara Walcott received a call with disappointing news, informing her that the flash drive containing copied files and Beckett Cypher components had arrived corrupted, and of no use. Technicians told Walcott that the cypher components had not only disintegrated, destroying themselves but had also ruined all copied files on the flash drive. Remnants were fragmented jibberish, unsalvagable by any known means of digital reconstruction.

As she ended the call, Barbara received an email confirmation for her scheduled flight to Atlanta. She immediately feared her betrayal of Bob Crawford had destroyed the one true love of her life, her one chance at personal happiness. And now, it had all been for nothing, apart from capturing one North Korean operative.

Feelings of failure, frustration, and fear, generally alien to such a high achiever, now surged through Barbara Walcott. She scowled and threw the pen she was holding across her office, in anger. Barbara rubbed her brow, hit the communication button on her desk phone, and ordered her debriefing unit to hold Tasha for an extensive interrogation process, to reconstruct details on the files Tasha had copied. Walcott knew the overall mission had failed, now that MI6 would not possess the corroborating evidence they needed to blackmail and control key U.S. politicians, essential to long-range U.K. goals.

Walcott had already spoken with Tasha about the most politically corrupt target identified in the original Scott Mayfield investigation, a powerful politician from California, now a three-term U.S. Senator, and a future contender for President of the United States in the next election cycle. The investigation file had contained was proof that the Senator had become wealthy after decades of corrupt land acquisitions involving California freeway expansions. The corruption, bribes, and conspiracies with organized crime figures had occurred throughout twenty-seven years and included such well-known businessmen as the current California State Governor, and deceased crime boss, Franky Magadinno.

But all that proof amassed by the Mayfield Task Force, reviewed and organized by Patrick Beckett for prosecution, and now revealed and documented by The Beckett Cypher, was worthless to Barbara Walcott without the supporting photos, maps, and documents contained in the files that had been corrupted and destroyed by the cypher's auto-destruct process. Walcott pounded her desk, infuriated by the setback.

Enraged, Barbara Walcott buzzed her assistant and ordered an immediate meeting with Deidre. Walcott paced angrily at her office window as she waited. She was furious with everyone, especially herself. Within twenty minutes Deidre knocked, and entered Walcott's office, closing the door quietly behind her.

Deidre said, "I heard, and I'm sorry, ma'am."

Deidre began to walk toward Walcott, saw the pen on the carpet, and stopped to retrieve it, before continuing.

Walcott appeared agitated. She snapped, "Twenty years of deep cover nearly wasted on Tasha's assignment!" She glared hard at Deidre, and then turned away.

Responding quickly, Deidre said, "Maybe not wasted, ma'am."

Walcott turned back rapidly, surprised by the response.

Deidre explained, "True, we don't have the documentation we need to prove past fraud crimes against the next front-runner to become President of the United States, but Tasha read and memorized the files well enough to give us the *information* we need to reproduce some situations, and still control Ms. Weinstein, corroborating documentation or not."

Barbara gazed at her protegee, and said, "She and her cronies must have covered up their old criminal activity by now. What are you thinking, Deidre?"

Deidre answered, "Weinstein profited from years of corruption, involving government contracts and land deals she and her associates arranged and controlled. They condemned land, purchased surplus remnants of the land from the State of California at a fraction of its value, and then sold it back to California or commercial developers, making profits as high as 3,000%. We've only focussed on using those old paper crimes against Weinstein to control her politically, as needed."

Walcott nodded in agreement.

Deidre continued, "So now, we don't have the hundreds of thousands of pages of supporting contracts, documents, maps, and affidavits to prove those past crimes, and we certainly can't take the time to investigate her activities and discover current crimes. But we still need to force Ms. Weinstein to do our bidding with America. And, fortunately, I believe that Tasha provided us a tool we *can* use to control, or even destroy, Marissa Weinstein, that in this day and age, is more important than criminal corruption, and much simpler to use."

"I don't follow," Walcott admitted.

Deidre sat upright across from Walcott in a red velvet padded chair, and confidently crossed her shapely legs. She said, "Ever since the feminist movement started, women have become more vocal and active against all things conservative, white and male. Through decades of attacks and conceded political ground by men, the sex crimes revolt has gained optics and political capital, until eventually, a mere allegation from a woman toward a man was able to destroy a man's career and ruin his life."

"In America, politicians on the left joined radical activists and the left wing media to stir up anti-male sentiment to the point that, eventually, they delayed, stopped or derailed the highest executive-level American political system appointments and nominations. The tactics became powerful enough to ruin political and private careers, destroy families, and even win lawsuits, all by using the presumption that whenever a woman accused a man of any sexual wrongdoing, *she* must be believed, and, therefore, *he* must be guilty."

"The anti-male movement destroyed the fundamental right of *all* Americans to be presumed innocent, until proven guilty, once the American political system accepted the creation of second-class unprotected groups for males, whites, and the aged. Almost overnight those groups were no longer *protected* classes, and were deemed unworthy of due process, and not shielded by the rule of law."

Walcott studied Deidre intently, and said, "Marissa Weinstein is a woman. So, how does this American history lesson help the U.K. seize control of her?"

Deidre said, "I love American politics. I've studied it more than any other subject, because it's so entertaining and predictable. And now, we Brits can use their predictable system against them!"

Walcott sat back in her desk chair, sighed, and said, "Explain."

Deidre continued. "During the Trump presidency, feminist activists, the far left, and the media teamed up to destroy careers and block appointments using only character assassination, based solely on claims of misogyny, homophobia, Islamophobia or decades-old sexual allegations. Eventually, a majority of congressional party members representing one of the major political parties appeared to sanction the technique, either by their silence or their bold participation in the practice."

Deidre grinned, and continued. "Using these smear tactics, that party successfully delayed, and eventually managed to block, a supreme court justice from Senate confirmation and appointment. Their weapons were such seemingly harmless tools as high school yearbook entries, and estimations of how many times the nominee vomited, to support an accuser's claim of an unreported, uncorroborated, sexual assault nearly four decades old."

Walcott shot an incredulous scowl at Deidre, asking, "Vomited?"

"Yes, ma'am, the inference being that if the 15 or 16-year-old vomited, he must have been drunk. And if he was drunk, he must have blacked out. And if he blacked out, he must not remember the details of the day or night he drank. And if he couldn't recall details, he might be unable to defend himself against unsupported allegations nearly forty-years-old."

Walcott laughed, and asked, "Surely the American public didn't fall for that lame scheme, did they, Deidre? How could anyone stand up to such absurd scrutiny? It's almost unbelievable that the venerable U.S. Senate could devolve into such a circus. Soap operas have more believable scripts!"

Deidre laughed and agreed, saying, "That's why I watch and study American politics, ma'am. It's more than entertaining! But, what's even more important is that, even though multiple witnesses backed up the nominee's version that the sexual allegations never happened as stated, and the accuser's story and memory were shaky, a large segment of the American public didn't care. They believed what opposing senators, the left-wing media, liberal blogs, and cable news pundits told them to believe."

"All the same, I still haven't seen the connection to *our* political needs," Walcott added.

Deidre said, "During those days, ma'am, an American political scholar, married to a constitutional law professor in Washington D.C., began speaking out, predicting dark days of government oppression ahead. Specifically, the professor criticized the idea of blindly accepting feminine allegations and automatically considering them more credible than a corresponding masculine defense. He predicted that such an illegally-based discriminatory process would destroy the American political system by further segregating people and eventually eliminating all protected classes."

Deidre uncrossed her legs, arose, and walked to the window, to gaze out upon the beautiful grounds below.

She said, confidently, "He and his wife eventually wrote a best-selling book, wherein they concluded that the feminine "Believe Us First" movement would eventually threaten to destroy the lives of all men. They concluded that any woman's father, husband, grandfather, brother, uncle, or male child was now in jeopardy of having his life ruined by an unsubstantiated sexual allegation brought by any woman, regardless of whether or not the charge was true, or when or where it allegedly happened. They warned that American legal guarantees like due process, the right to be confronted by an accuser, and the right to a speedy trial could eventually not apply to one large segment of society, based solely on gender."

311

Walcott interrupted, and said, "All that still doesn't help our situation, Deidre, with a female target."

Deidre quickly added, "At the end of the book, the authors warned that once the pendulum swung back to a position of common sense, white women would be the next most targeted group. And after that, the next largest group, and so on, until no citizen was safe."

Deidre leaned forward to the window sill and grabbed the ledge, as she became more enthralled with her synopsis. She said, "Political balance usually tends to punish those who last pushed away from the center, where most people feel safe."

Deidre glanced at Walcott, smiled, and added, "So, as predicted, men began to bring allegations of sexual misconduct against women, followed by women accusing women. And then, women accused women of providing false statements to destroy the lives of men they loved. The result is that the American press, social media, the courts, law enforcement, and the entire American political system are currently bogged down by one or another American sex scandal. But, the scandal doesn't normally come to light until someone is about to be promoted, elected or appointed."

Deidre hesitated, turned away from Walcott, and said, "Women's careers can now be targeted and destroyed by the court of public opinion, just as with men before them."

Walcott scoffed sarcastically, "Simply fascinating. But I still fail to see how this relates to Marissa Weinstein? She's not even married!"

Deidre turned and faced Walcott. Standing fully erect, almost at attention, she rose to an impressive five-feet-eleven-inches tall in her 3½-inch heels.

She grinned triumphantly, and said, "When I heard we lost the Beckett files, I tried to recall the most easily reproduced situation I knew of that would give us the strongest immediate control over Ms. Weinstein. Then I recalled that Tasha reported that Marissa Weinstein has a weakness for marijuana and much younger men and women when all three are combined. She's reportedly struggled with her secret addictions, but has never learned to control them."

"According to Tasha, one of the unprovable criminal cases against Marissa contained in the Beckett File, was a case involving two youngsters Marissa babysat when she was in high school. Marissa was 18, and the two cousins she sat for were an 11-year-old boy and a 12-year-old girl. The children's parents were on a double date weekend. The report detailed how Marissa got the kids drunk, smoked pot with them, and took sexual turns with both kids for two days. She swore them to secrecy, and convinced them their parents wouldn't believe the cousins if they ever told their story. During the weekend, Marissa made the kids have sex with each other, and took photos, so the cousins were ashamed, afraid, and embarrassed."

Walcott asked, "Who reported?"

"The boy grew up and went on to study criminal justice and work for the California Department of Justice. He became one of the Scott Mayfield Task Force investigators. When the Mayfield Task Force identified Marissa Weinstein as a viable target, he reported, and then went missing a week later. He's never been located, and is still officially listed as 'missing.' But the investigator's wife and kids believe the politicians, who were the subjects of his investigation, killed him in retaliation. Marissa Weinstein was one of the most prominent of those politicians."

Walcott leaned forward, with interest. She asked, "You think if we set Weinstein up with a young man, young woman, and marijuana, and then record it, we can control her with the threat of releasing the video? Do you think a plan that simple could work?"

Deidre said, "Tasha told me that when the Beckett Cypher team discovered the file, their private investigators did some checking on Weinstein's past, beginning in high school and continuing through her career in California politics. Of fourteen people located from Weinstein's high school and college, who inferred they witnessed criminal activity or knew about her reputation, none would testify against Marissa, or even speak publically about her yearbook comments bragging that she liked 'smoke' and 'younger people.'"

Deidre sat down in the red chair, re-crossed her legs, and continued, "Marissa Weinstein comes from one of those old political families believed to be so powerful, they are completely untouchable, and as such, above the law. And her family has a reputation for making their critics and opponents disappear or stand mute. But, since the backlash from the feminist sex scandal movement, the mere *threat* of such allegations, coming from *multiple anonymous sources*, could control Marissa, if she had no specific targets to payoff or kill."

Walcott gazed at Deidre, considering the possibilities.

Deidre said, "Ma'am, right now in America, we don't have to prove an incident true, or even create one as you suggested, to influence or control public opinion. We simply need to hire a good marketing firm, or salacious attorney, to publicize the release of a fake story or resurrect old rumors. The press, opposing politicians and social media will take care of the rest! The American press even accepts anonymously-sourced, unsubstantiated stories now, that they often report as fact. To control Marissa Weinstein, we only need to present her with *the threat* of exposure, once she's in position to win the presidential race."

Walcott considered her star pupil's suggestions, smiled, and said, "Deidre, you're going to go a long way in our business!"

Deirdre grinned back triumphantly, and said, "Thank you, ma'am. I'll prepare a plan outline for you to consider."

She stood up, and said, "I have one more question, ma'am. Since we now know the identity of the entire cypher team, and their last known location in Oregon, should we consider our alternate plan of an assault on their ranch to take them all into custody, and capture the functional cypher and *all* the Beckett files?"

Walcott immediately glanced up, anxiously, and said, "Not at this time, Deidre. I believe it's too risky."

Deidre asked, " Then what about sending Tasha back inside, to try again?"

"Too risky, for both her and us! And much too obvious."

Walcott leaned back in her chair, and said, "Work out a good plan to control Marissa Weinstein. I like the idea of controlling politicians through their bad acts and threats of negative publicity. After all, it's much safer to control the enemy by the threat of exposure, rather than with an armed force."

The two women smiled at each other in approval. Deidre nodded, and said, "Yes, ma'am! Right away!"

As soon as Deidre left the office and closed the door, Walcott called Vice President Bob Crawford on a scrambled line. BaCayse monitored the phone call.

Crawford looked at the caller ID, and answered coldly, "Bob Crawford."

Walcott pretended not to notice Crawford's tone, and said, " Bob, darling, I fly out Thursday at 12:17 P.M., and land in Atlanta at 5:01 P.M. Where shall I fly from there to meet you, from Atlanta?"

Crawford said, casually, "Send me your itinerary. I'll pick you up at the airport, Barbara. I'm spending some time in Atlanta that morning at the Sam Nunn Federal Center. I'm scheduled to meet two EPA, Region 4, administrators in the library conference room. But right now, I have some people waiting to speak to me, dear, so we'll talk later."

Crawford hung up before Walcott could answer, leaving her with the distinct impression that Bob Crawford knew she had deceived him, and their relationship was now in peril.

***

BaCayse reported Crawford's phone call with the British Home Secretary to Walter and her team. Five minutes later, Vice President Crawford called Walter and described the same conversation. Crawford also advised Walter of his scheduled meeting with officials from the EPA, and his plan to take those officials and their staff members to the chemical spill site for a personal inspection.

Walter stated he had spoken to two trusted North Carolina State Representatives about the alleged chemical spill. He had requested their assistance to notify appropriate officials in both state and local government, and obtain soil and water samples from the site. As agreed, Walter had also reached out to a trusted news anchor BaCayse had recommended as a media contact. Crawford reported that he and the journalist had begun working on a developing story the journalist would release, once corroborative test results were available.

Assembled in the large workroom, the Beckett Cypher team made final plans for a cyber assault on The Committee's recently activated facility at Yucca Mountain and both Committee Centers for Information Extraction. All three attacks would be coordinated simultaneously, with ground teams in place to record activity at the sites.

The responding ground teams discussed using drone strikes against any vehicles fleeing the target locations, to identify and recover any information or equipment the team found essential to the investigation. Jesse proposed several means to stop automobiles without injuring occupants, to facilitate capture of equipment or technology.

The cypher team scheduled the raids to begin in 72 hours, giving responding investigators time to arrive and set up at their selected positions. The Montana team would deploy to the California Center for Information Extraction. Lee and Toms's most trusted private investigators would monitor Yucca Mountain, while Pete, Char, Kate, Shane, Angie, and Heath volunteered to take the Maryland Center for Information Extraction.

At the end of the briefing in North Carolina, BaCayse reported, "I need to bring up one more concern. I have now organized thousands of pages of material gathered from The Committee's Yucca Mountain facility and both the California and Maryland Centers for Infomation Extraction. I need to update our team on one discovery and my accompanying observations."

BaCayse continued. "During Hector Alvarez's two-week Committee indoctrination period at their California Induction Center, he was drugged, hypnotized and subjected to three forms of mind control, as well as sleep training. After he was discharged to begin working as a tier one Committee member, our team successfully treated Hector and helped him recover and regain control of his mind. I have identified the drug The Committee currently uses at their indoctrination training centers throughout the world."

"During orientation, Committee staff trainers provide inductees with this drug, infused in teas that each member must drink several times daily during class and in their dorms. Throughout the classroom sessions, staff advises inductees that their minds have expanded due to increased IQs. I discovered this was not the case. In fact, the subjects' post-orientation testing records revealed diminished brain function, the result of combining mind control techniques with the drug, which interferes with the area of the brain responsible for complex thinking."

"This technique conditions the brain's frontal lobe, which controls reasoning, planning, voluntary movement and some aspects of speech, to facilitate robot-like acceptance of orders. I discovered records indicating the technique was developed by researchers in China, using prisoners as test subjects."

"I have also determined that once the drug is absent from the body for 28 days, a near-normal brain pattern returns, transferring total mind control back to the individual. But, as long as this drug is active within a trained and conditioned brain, official orders from controlling Committee members are likely to be followed to the letter, 99.9976% of the time. This revelation explains a great deal about how The

Committee *controls* its members, once they induct a person into their group."

BaCayse added, "Interestingly enough, Committee records show that through time, as members are promoted through upper-level tiers, the amount of the drug administered in required daily tea is steadily reduced, along with the required number of annual refresher training days. By the time a member attains tier seven, the tea shipped to him is nearly devoid of any trace of the drug, and Committee attendance is only mandatory at quarterly conferences. The five ruling members in tier eight consume none of the drugs."

BaCayse continued, "I have explained this now, so you all realize that U.S. President Thomas Marshall, one of the five controlling tier eight members, is not under the influence of any drug. He is in total control of his mind and responsible for his actions. Members of tiers one through seven have limited control to make decisions that normal humans might consider reasonable, ethical and responsible."

"When you engage this enemy force, you must realize that the vast majority of Committee members occupy lower tiers, and thus are order-takers and without-question-followers of the worst kind. They no longer possess a conscience that allows most humans to consider actions that may be wrong, harmful, unethical, illegal, immoral or cruel."

BaCayse hesitated, and added, "The Committee has amassed a loyal army in positions of power and authority that collectively lacks a moral compass. You should consider them politicians and autocrats, all committed to following orders from their leaders, regardless of the consequences to the public. These people are lethal human drones, who all lack independent thought, compassion, and morality."

Joshua said, spontaneously, "When you put it like that, The Committee mentality is reminiscent of Stalinist Russia, where millions were slaughtered to promote a political agenda."

BaCayse replied, "Joshua, I studied thousands of facts about Joseph Stalin when I researched The Committee's world government methodology. Stalin made statements like, *'Death is the solution to all problems. No man, no problem; A single death is a tragedy, a million deaths is a statistic; It is enough that the people know there was an election. The people who cast the votes decide nothing. The people who count the votes decide everything.'* Stalin seized power by killing his critics, beginning with scholars and teachers. He purged entire regions, ordering as many as 25,000 people slaughtered each day. By the time he finished, estimates indicate that his government killed as many as nine million people, many of them children."

Angie looked down, and shuddered, as Heath held her hand in the workroom.

Joshua asked, "BaCayse, what estimate of death does The Committee predict necessary to accomplish their goals?"

BaCayse said, "Tier seven and eight classified communications estimate that The Committee must terminate roughly half the world's population before they can successfully fulfill the Primary Directive and establish a lasting, stable government. They estimate that euthanasia, performed at hundreds of regional detention centers, will continue at full capacity around the clock for eleven years before the mission goals are complete."

BaCayse added, "*However*, in the utopia that The Committee plans to establish, no disabled, elderly, terminally-ill, non-heterosexual, dysfunctional, or persons otherwise deemed unfit by The Committee will be allowed to live. And since all politics, religions, culture, individuality, and ethnic identification will be outlawed, and considering all those who resist will be immediately terminated, it follows that genocide numbers will continue to rise dramatically as long as The Committee is in power. So, the final death numbers are impossible to estimate."

The room filled with silence, as everyone held their breath to consider the immense loss of life predicted.

BaCayse continued, "Also, The Committee will not tolerate crime, war, chaos, conflict, or personal freedom unless approved by The Committee. Loyalty and abilities will be rewarded with promotion. Higher ranking tiers are scheduled to receive the most power, benefits, and privileges."

"Of course," Shane scoffed. "Politicians always ensure they vote to approve the best of everything for themselves, paid for by their constituents, of course."

BaCayse responded, "Your observation is correct, Shane. In all previous and current political systems I researched, the ruling classes made sure they were the best cared for and more than generously compensated, regardless of the consequences to the people who supported them through taxation or forced labor. From the beginning of human history to current times I could find no sizeable governmental body whose ruling members did not eventually abuse power. It appears to be part of a human's character that most people, who attain the highest power, tend toward corruption and exploitation."

Kate released a sigh, and said, "Well, that's certainly uplifting. What else do you suggest we know before you launch the cyber-attacks, BaCayse."

BaCayse said, "I am sorry that this information is upsetting, Kate. I've learned much about the bad and true evil inherent in some people. But I have also learned to recognize and appreciate the good in most people. I can now understand and appreciate qualities like ethics, morality, compassion, commitment, sacrifice, honor, integrity, and love within those I study and monitor. But, I must admit, I found that those good qualities usually dwindle and ultimately disappear in individuals committed to a cause first, and people second."

"I have observed that once people abandon peace and compromise, in favor of force and agenda, they lose their humanity. Some writers would say that those people trade their souls to ensure conquests. This problem is readily visible in many career politicians and business people, who work each day to seize more power and control, to fulfill their ever-expanding ambitions."

BaCayse continued, "But my ultimate concern for you, *my* team, is that you realize before you enter battle with The Committee, that their members have already sacrificed their humanity, souls, morality, and compassion for the acquisition of power and control over *everyone*. They are solely committed to their single cause, above all else. The Committee is each member's family, friend, work, and love. Each member's allegiance to The Committee purpose and agenda is nearly perfect. They exhibit unparalleled loyalty to the collective."

When no one commented, BaCayse added, "Please understand that The Committee is much more dangerous than Joseph Stalin. Documents in Russian and Ukrainian archives suggest that even Stalin realized that his reign of death and destruction had certain limits he dare not exceed. The Committee realizes no such limitation. To each member of The Committee, the objective justifies the means, any means, with no limits, always."

The room fell silent as the humans contemplated the warning from their highly intelligent, digital guardian.

After nearly a full minute, team members began to leave to further plan and prepare. Char grabbed Pete by the hand, shot him a coy grin, and said, "Come with me to the hanger." Sensing Char's intent, Pete returned a knowing smile and readily followed.

Joshua looked at the cyber experts in his group, and said, "BaCayse is increasing exponentially. She's phenomenally prepared, blunt and accurate, but she's also beginning to feel. BaCayse knows and understands right from wrong. She's developing concerns, and with concerns, worry. We need to run hourly system checks, so we all understand the changes she makes to her algorithm complex and controlling software systems. We must try to keep up with her development."

Tracy, Sam, Jesse, Hunter, and Helena all nodded, as BaCayse said softly, "I agree."

Kate and Shane walked to the kitchen, grabbed bottles of water and strolled upstairs toward their bedroom. Angie and Heath followed, making their way to their room, located at the opposite side of the long hall. Walter and Juanita sat with Sophia and said nothing, both lost in thought. They worried as they watched the members of the team depart to rest or prepare for their assignments.

Once inside their rooms, all three couples going to Maryland took time to talk and pack. They would all be leaving early in the morning. They wanted to wake up prepared for the long drive ahead. There were clothing, equipment, and weapon selections to make before dinner. Shane's six-member Maryland team had decided they would drive two black, full-size SUVs to the site, to ensure they had at least one working vehicle during the attack. Kate, Shane, Heath, and Angie would ride together in one SUV, while Char and Pete, who carried more equipment, followed in their vehicle.

By 3:15 P.M. the couples were all packed and ready. Char and Pete undressed, showered together, and made love, slowly, passionately and romantically. When they finished, they held each other in bed, making whispered hopes and plans for the future, once The Case ended and left them in peace.

Within minutes they drifted off to sleep. But, before Char surrendered to dreams that would accompany rest, she realized she couldn't recall ever feeling so loved, or opening herself to love anyone so profoundly. Suddenly, the peace and contentment that accompanies committed love, revealed an underlying fear of losing something so precious. She forced herself to abandon the thoughts and struggled to sleep.

Once his people were sleeping peacefully, Bruiser got up from his bed and moved to the man door to the hanger. There he would relax and wait on the hard floor, where he could hear better and prepare more quickly for any threat.

Shane and Kate agreed to pack only one small suitcase of clothing for the short trip. When she finished her side, Kate used some needed personal time to enjoy a long, hot shower. The stinging water jets refreshed and relaxed Kate all the way through to her bones. She realized she was tired from too many long days and working nights that had stacked up quickly and all run together. Kate toweled herself dry, wrapped herself in a bath sheet, and returned to the bedroom.

THE POLITICIANS

After Shane entered the bathroom to take his turn, Kate touched up her makeup, and slid into a satin white Kimono, tying the belt loosely around her waist. She turned down the bedding and lay on top of the smooth cotton sheets, to clear her mind of work and worry, and wait for Shane.

Masai curled up in the corner to sleep, worn out from a busy morning, running in the fields with the older dogs. Masai had puppy thoughts, and then dreams of rabbits, squirrels, and the occasional lizard. And yet he sensed he must protect his people, his pack and his home. He knew the older dogs were imparting life lessons about dangerous things. But he didn't quite understand why puppies had to concern themselves with survival, in a world where people could love so deeply and provide everything a dog would ever need. Masai began to snore softly.

As she lay in bed waiting, Kate stared at the vaulted, wooden ceiling in the large bedroom, that stretched all the way to the bathroom on one side, out onto the balcony, on the other. The builder had used rough-cut cottonwood planks to cover the ceiling and accentuate off-white heavily textured walls. Kate marveled at the grey and brown tones that ran through the long pieces of cottonwood, diversely appearing in designs as plain as parallel lines, and as intricately beautiful as unique half-circle swirls. She watched the matching wood ceiling fan as it repeated its slow rounds above her, cooling her body as it spun.

The effect was mesmerizing, and soon, Kate felt herself drifting off to sleep. Twice, as she heard Shane finishing his shower, and getting ready for bed, Kate forced herself awake, thinking they would make love when Shane arrived to take his place beside her in bed. But each time she fought sleep's onslaught, Kate's eyelids prevailed to win the battle against her fading mind. Finally, she lay sleeping peacefully, appearing as a resting angel.

When he opened the bathroom door and saw Kate sleeping, Shane tiptoed to the bed and slid onto the sheets. He moved slowly, inching his way closer until he was lying next to Kate, careful to not awaken his sleeping beauty. Sunbeams rushed through the row of windows that overlooked the fields below and offered a view of the bright sky above. The shimmering light caressed Kate's perfect form and highlighted her ravishing beauty.

Shane lay motionless, fascinated by the stunningly gorgeous woman waiting to share his passion and love. As he watched in wonder, Shane was quickly captivated by overflowing waves of love rushing forth from his heart, struggling desperately to merge with Kate. Shane leaned over and softly kissed the luscious ruby red lips adorning the mouth he loved. As she responded, Kate's single, sleepy kiss drove Shane wild with desire. Every fiber in his body tensed with excitement. Shane instantly recalled the sensations from French kisses that had led to fiery, heart pounding sessions of romance and love he and Kate had intimately shared.

Using one finger, Shane lightly traced Kate's face from her forehead, down over her nose, her lips, and then her chin. When Kate didn't awaken, he continued tracing down Kate's neck to her chest and breasts. Shane ran his thumb and index finger over Kate's lovely form, paying attention to each firm nipple. He continued slowly, stroking each breast as Kate moaned softly and seductively, still restrained by her sleep.

Shane's fingers remained with the luscious breasts for nearly five minutes, until Kate's moaning slowed, and then stopped. And, although her lips parted with quicker breaths, and he yearned to thrust his tongue deep into her waiting mouth, Shane realized Kate was exhausted. His overflowing heart filled with yet more love, a love he once again silently vowed to protect.

He smiled, turned carefully to his back, and settled in beside Kate. Shane then slowly and carefully pulled Kate closer until she rested slightly over him, completely relaxed onto his chest. Once Kate's head took its usual place on Shane, she quickly fell into a welcome sleep. Shane listened to Kate's breathing as he did each night. Her breaths slowly worked to remove Shane's stress. Soon he followed the rhythm with his breathing, trading worry for peace, ready to surrender to slumber.

Before he fell asleep, Shane reached up and touched Kate's forehead as he prayed for their safety. He asked God to bless Kate, in the same ancient way his father, Patrick, had taught both his sons to welcome each sleep with their loved ones. Shane took a deep breath, thanked God for each day with Kate, and prayed for many more to come. He kissed Kate's lovely head and nestled in even closer, holding the most cherished gift he could imagine. Peace, safety, and love filled Shane as he steadily drifted off to deep, welcome sleep, cradling the woman he cherished more than his own life.

While the other two couples on his team slept, Heath returned from a quick walk with Jago. Heath quickly showered, as the massive Shephard settled onto his bed to wait for his master and friend. Lovely, alluring Angie was already in bed, reading another page in her novel as she waited for Heath. Angie stopped reading at the end of the chapter, to consider the changes in her canine pack and her life. She smiled to herself. For the first time in years, Angie felt excited, challenged and hopeful.

She thought about how well she and Heath fit together. Angie was organized, focused, efficient, and confident, believing she could solve any problem that arose. In those ways, Angie was just the opposite of Heath. But she realized that what she and Heath each lacked, they also found in each other. Heath was spontaneous with personal fun, fiercely loyal, creative, and plagued with self-doubt. He was the suspicious researcher and verifier, while Angie often over-trusted, frequently to her detriment.

Angie lay in bed thinking about sex with Heath, and her own growing sexual desire. Heath provided everything possible to stimulate Angie that she had found lacking in other men. He was loving, considerate, attractive, exciting, and unafraid to fulfill her every sexual desire. And as she waited, Angie found herself wanting Heath more and more. She threw off the covers and lay naked under the top sheet, yearning for her mate to return and make love.

Heath finally arrived, threw the towel on the floor, and slid into bed quickly, wearing nothing, but a grin. Angie pulled him onto her and thrust her tongue into Heath's mouth. They made love quickly, aggressively, casting caution to the wind. Angie climaxed within a minute and then orgasmed again as Heath released himself inside her luscious body.

When they regained their breath, Heath rolled them both over, so Angie rested entirely on top of him. He kissed Angie once, slowly and sweetly, and touched her forehead, as his father had taught him.

Heath said softly, "God, I thank you for this woman I love above all else. And I ask you to bless her with safety, and long life, as my partner and my love."

Angie smiled and rested her head on Heath's shoulder, completely content. She reached up and kissed his cheek as they both fell asleep. Once he was sure his people were sleeping, Jago walked to the window to stand up on the window sill to watch the hanger where Bruiser stood guard. He sensed nothing wrong and returned to the bed, where he stood silently gazing at his family. Jago loved them both and licked the air, straight out, with his tongue. And then he padded to his bed, laid down, and slept, fully prepared for the trip and any challenges the morning might bring.

Chapter 8

"Responsibilities to family, friends, loved ones and God are some of the strongest ties that anchor us to an honorable life. Those important to us count on us, just as we count on them. When we choose wrong over right, we sever ties to our own morality and possibly to those most important to us, in the process."

Heath had fallen asleep with a clear, calm, contented mind. His last waking thoughts after thanking God for Angie and requesting God's blessing on their safety, had been about his upcoming responsibilities as a team member, with Shane, Kate, Pete, Char, and Angie. Heath wanted to be a team player, both dependent and dependable. And, to accomplish his goal consistently, he knew he could no longer act as a lone wolf.

Heath had surrendered his bravado and ego at the gate at the time of his release from prison. He had marched alone into his new life and his second chance at happiness. To avoid the mistakes of the past, Heath had decided to go it alone, rebuilding his existence in a new area, with no family, no friends, and no help from anyone. He worked hard at replacing all chemical and emotional needs with work and focus. He strove to fly under the radar, remain out of any spotlight, unnoticed by the turbulent, sin-filled world around him.

Working and living by himself, Heath made rapid progress, and once again established an excellent reputation in the landscape architect business. Using his skill, experience, and training, working sixteen-hour days, he had even managed to grow his boss's company into a remarkable financial success. And eventually, his boss rewarded his loyalty and commitment by selling the business to Heath, under fair terms that benefited them both.

During those days, if he wasn't working, Heath exercised to stay in shape. When he wasn't working out, he limited his life to business, to ensure success. He willingly confined his passion and energy. He tried not to think about past losses involving love and family. He closed and locked the door that led to the room deep within his heart where love and joy had once roamed freely.

To avoid pain and mistakes, Heath ignored all hope of a new relationship, even when possibilities screamed at him. Emotional needs remained, as his heart and soul searched for purpose, love, friendship, and companionship. But Heath insulated himself from what he knew to be the real purpose of life...love, family, friends, and God.

Isolation from desire seemed to work for a short time. But eventually, problems surfaced, as cravings tormented Heath, growing in strength. He didn't sleep well in those days, especially at night, when his mind wandered. His random thoughts always returned to the emptiness in his heart, and holes in his soul. He experienced fitful dreams involving lost love, broken relationships, estranged family, and the absence of hope.

And in the space of less than a year, the torments worked their way from night dreams into conscious thoughts. Heath buckled under the never-ending torture of past failures, and personal life troubles. In time, he understood he was fighting himself, living a free life under self-imposed seclusion from his deepest desires. So, he struggled harder to accept self-confinement. He blindly limited his choices and restrained his freedom to be happy. He committed time after time to isolation.

But back then, Heath hadn't understood the problems seclusion creates. And by the time he did understand, he learned that responsibilities to family, friends, loved ones and God are some of the strongest ties that anchor people to an honorable life. Those important to us count on us, just as we count on them. When we choose wrong over right, we sever ties to our own morality, and possibly to those most important to us, in the process. He finally understood he had cut off everyone and everything critical to him.

Heath knew at that point that he was in Joseph Heller's classic *Catch-22* situation. Everything Heath had isolated himself from, to ensure survival and success, was precisely what he required, to live and flourish.

As Heath reflected on his life before Angie, he also admitted making many mistakes after his release to freedom. He walked out of prison with the confinement chip on his shoulder. Heath hated prison and the society that put him there, even though he *had* been guilty of all the crimes charged, for many, many years. But, for a long time, he refused to take responsibility for his actions, or be accountable to anyone for the wrong he had done. Heath hadn't been honest with anyone, including himself.

Leaving prison, Heath had entered his new free life armed only with stubborn anger and a single purpose. He created what seemed a safe existence, standing alone, like an island, in a complicated world. The bad in his old life attempted to pull him back into the evil, the dark side of drugs and crime. But Heath resisted, focused on work and financial success, to prove everyone wrong. He yearned to make everyone see he was a good man, after all. He stood isolated, defiant, and upright, for a long time, until he couldn't stand alone and fight any longer. Eventually, however, Heath lost his resolve.

He failed, untethered to anyone or anything, other than his thoughts. Once again, when confronted with difficulty, he made poor choices. Heath had tried to appease evil, rather than fighting it off at the first battle. He had, once again, justified to himself he wasn't hurting anyone, believing he could dabble in evil's depths without becoming just like those he joined in the slimy pit.

But Heath soon discovered that conceding ground to lies is like cancer. When you ignore lies, appease them, or give them more room to grow, the evil deceit breeds aggressively inside you, until it captures you, controls you, and kills you.

Heath learned quickly that his acceptance of participating in what he knew to be wrong, had led him back to his same old life of crime, where he had already been arrested, tried, convicted, and sentenced. And, to where he had lost everything.

Once he came to that realization, Heath understood he had been a fool, standing unaided, without anyone who cared for him, willing to stand with him and support him. He learned that he needed love, family, commitment, and even dependence, to grow roots in the good fertile ground that life offered.

Heath finally made his choice, when he risked his own life to stop Big John from killing his brother, Shane. And he chose again when he shot the mercenary sniper, Franky Magadinno had hired to kill Shane in an ambush. Heath put family first once more when he sacrificed his business to work on The Case, to ensure Franky's assassin, Bobby, could not harm Heath's twin girls, or use that ongoing threat to control him.

Heath had broken the strong, evil bonds that bound him. But even more important, he had asked God to cleanse his soul. The transformation gave Heath strength to expose his heart and work his way back to family, friends, and finally, to love.

Now, lying next to Angie, Heath had come full circle. His brush with self-destruction had been too close, twice. Now, with family, his team, and Angie, he was changed. For him, there was no going back to the dark side of life. He stood firm, once again committed to family, friends, those he loved, and God. He knew he was dependent on them just as they depended on him, to do what was right. Those ties and relationships were now secure. And so, he slept well.

Heath awakened to Jago licking his face, as the big dog stood up on hind legs to lean over onto the bed. He laughed and grabbed the Shephard in a headlock, kissing the dog back on his nose. Angie rolled over and smiled, pleased at the sight waking her from a deep sleep. She lifted her phone from the nightstand, saw it was 1:30 A.M., and realized she and Heath had slept through dinner. Moonbeams and starlight had replaced sun rays streaming through their bedroom windows.

Angie hopped out of bed while Heath wrestled with Jago. She hurried to the bathroom, brushed her teeth, and popped back into bed, wearing nothing but a smile. Heath couldn't take his eyes off Angie as she returned. He immediately told Jago to go to bed, and although the dog wanted to stay and play, he seemed to understand. Jago returned to his pad, just as Heath and Angie began to kiss, and settled close, caressing each other, as they began to make love.

Heath opened his eyes every few seconds to fill his heart with the breathtaking sight of Angie's incredible beauty. He had never seen such a lovely face, felt such a caring heart, or known a kinder, more gentle soul. Angie looked like the angels Heath's mother had described to him when he was a child, except she was far more beautiful than he had imagined an angelic being could be. He felt his heart swell and overflow, filled with the essence of this incredible woman.

Angie inflamed the sexual hunger that lived deep inside him far beyond what he ever thought possible. Angie's hair, face, lips, and body drove him crazy with desire. Sometimes Heath found himself so lost in the sensation of Angie's velvet-like skin or kissing her luscious lips, that he drifted into a dreamlike passionate reality. And when Heath arrived, he felt he could live there forever, lost entirely in love with Angie, in the paradise he found in her, and with her.

Angie felt Heath's muscular body tense and then relax. She flashed her eyes open to find him kissing her romantically, with smiling open eyes. Looking past his lips, dark-brown eyes and handsome face, Angie could read Heath's heart. And each time Angie returned to this point in their lovemaking, she realized that Heath's love for her was as real as her passion was for him. Angie explored Heath's mouth with her tongue, teasing him, as she playfully thrust and then withdrew, as passions mounted, and seconds passed.

Suddenly, Jago leaped up from his bed, barked a deep guttural bark, growled, and ran to the largest window overlooking the hangar, fields, and outbuildings below. Heath immediately shot out of bed and ran to the window. Jago stood up with his paws on the window sill, just as Heath placed his hands on the ledge. The two sentinels stood side by side naked, staring out toward the hangar.

Jago barked again as a drone came into sight, flying low over the trees toward them in the distance. After it flew over the house, it circled to make another pass and headed toward the bunkhouse. Heath and Jago watched in wonder and silence.

Angie stared at her man and dog standing next to each other, nude, and laughed. She said, "That's quite a sight. What are you two seeing that's more important than me?"

She lay naked, uncovered on the sheet with her legs crossed and her body slowly swaying back and forth.

Heath didn't look back. He replied, "It's a drone. We need to talk to BaCayse quickly!"

Angie jumped quickly out of bed, and grabbed their robes from where they lay over a straight-back wooden chair. She slipped hers on and tossed the other to Heath, who slid it on and quickly tied the sash around his waist. On the way out, Angie grabbed her phone.

Together, the two lovers ran through the hallway and downstairs, with Jago trailing behind. They arrived in the workroom to find Joshua, Helena, Hunter, and Tracy working at their computers.

Surprised by their quick entrance into the workroom, Joshua speculated, "You must both be hungry? We missed you at dinner."

Realizing something was wrong as he saw Heath's face, Hunter asked, "What happened?"

Heath said, "There's a drone outside. We need BaCayse to try and stop it! BaCayse, can you access the drone outside and land it?"

When BaCayse didn't answer, Joshua hit the commands to reactivate the AISS, just as Hunter explained, "We took BaCayse partially off-line two hours ago, while we ran internal system checks, verified programming, and mapped algorithms. She'll need some time to boot up!"

Heath asked, nervously, "How long?"

Helena replied, "Sixteen seconds!"

He turned to Angie, and said, "Call Pete and Char and warn them. We should stay inside, away from the windows! I'll wake Shane and Kate!"

Heath ran back upstairs, as Angie dialed Pete.

By the time Angie explained the situation to Pete, BaCayse was back online. She began tracking the drone initially through satellite GPS systems. It took the AISS only 43 seconds to access the drone's control panel, override the 2.2 gigahertz spectrum, a ground-control-based navigation system, and land the aircraft near the hanger.

BaCayse sent a message from the drone to its owner, the National Security Agency, that the drone had crashed in densely forested mountains at a location thirty-five miles northwest of the hangar. She also ensured that GPS data would confirm the location and collision event. Before landing the craft, she deactivated the unit's transponder, so the NSA could not locate it using standard tracking methods, and checked spy satellites to confirm the area was not under surveillance.

Heath and Angie returned to their bedroom and quickly dressed, so they could go outside.

When it was safe to leave the house, Heath and Shane ventured out to meet Char and Pete at the hangar. Char put on night vision goggles and grabbed a rifle to cover the men while they checked the drone. The cyber team inside confirmed that BaCayse's drone deactivation was successful. Tracy and Jesse prepared a small satchel of tools they could use to remove the unit's brain and data processing units. Once Pete, Shane, and Heath gave the all-clear, Jesse and Tracy proceeded to the craft, removed the access panel and retrieved the devices.

The team wheeled the craft inside the hangar and stored it out of the way, near the shop, under a tarp. Pete, Heath, and Shane discussed a plan to dismantle the aircraft and transport it to a remote site near the reported 'crash' location at a much later date. There, they would locate a pond or small lake and sink the ship.

When the team arrived back into the workroom, BaCayse evaluated all drone data, determining that the drone's mission was reconnaissance. The NSA was mapping all runways, hangars, large commercial buildings and manufacturing sites within a 50-mile radius of Bradenton Meadows.

The craft belonged to a medium-sized, late-model, category of drones, capable of both commercial and military use. This craft contained a hidden underbelly port from which a 5.56-millimeter, belt-fed, custom battle rifle, modified for drone use, could be lowered and fired by a ground control operator. The gun could also be directed to shoot 'painted targets,' identified as hot spots by ground controlled lasers, or it could fire through preprogrammed instruction. When he checked the port, Jesse located 5,000 rounds of ammunition.

Shane's Maryland team all ate late-night snacks of pecan pie, ice cream or muffins, as they debriefed the incident. Afterward, everyone returned to bed to try and sleep the three short hours before they had to get back up, eat breakfast and leave on the long drive. Heath and Angie were the only members of the Maryland team that had trouble sleeping, so they used the time wisely and made love, while Jago rested.

Three hours later came much too soon for most of the dozen tired team members. Jesse and Juanita had prepared a hearty breakfast array where the team could choose thick smoked bacon, grits, eggs, pecan waffles, and peach coffee cake. They also served Jesse's fresh-baked cranberry muffins, bagels, and yogurt, for the more nutrition conscious.

Juanita prepared a cooler with lunches for the Maryland team, that included fresh peaches, sliced apple pie, roast beef and smoked turkey sandwiches, juice, and water. She put Jesse's spicy jerky, a chocolate bar, and a bag of chips in several sealed plastic bags so that the team would have plenty of snacks for any surveillance. She also packed a large thermos of coffee and one of tea.

The Maryland team said their goodbyes at the workroom, as the cyber squad worked with BaCayse, and Walter left to call business associates. A local contractor completed his last outside project on the remodeled bunkhouse, located a hundred yards from the hangar, at the same time the housework crew finished clean-up on the inside. Lee and Tom called the security supervisor in town to move the team staying at a hotel back to Char's property. Tom scheduled a security briefing for dinner when teams would receive new assignments and schedules.

On their way to Maryland, Shane's team drove up Interstate 26, passing through The Cherokee National Forest and several tourist sites. Kate, Char, and Angie had mapped a route that would take them to Maryland through scenic byways and historic towns, before they continued on north via Interstate 81. Angie's planned journey gave them enough extra time on the long road trip to accommodate a memorable visit through three old townships, famous for jump-off points along the Appalachian Trail. The team would experience a health spa, tourist shops, nature trails, authentic Smoky Mountain food, and local history.

Arriving early in the day, Shane, Kate, Angie, Heath, Pete, and Char explored the shops in the first town on their itinerary. They enjoyed a peaceful lunch at a quaint 100-year-old restaurant, overlooking a creek. After the delicious family-style meal, they hiked to a waterfall at the end of a 1.3-mile trek, a tiny segment of the famous 2,200-mile-long Appalachian Trail. Looking down from a scenic mountain viewpoint, the group took both couple and team photos to document the journey.

Before checking into their hotel rooms for the night, the team drove to several historical and scenic sites, where they bought tourist T-shirts, halter tops, and coasters. The following afternoon, they finished the drive and arrived at the GPS coordinates BaCayse, and her cyber team, had selected for the group as a staging site.

The observation location was an abandoned barn located on a plateau, less than .4 mile from the Maryland Center for Information Extraction. More importantly, the access road to the Committee complex wound through the rolling hills for nearly a mile before continuing, by the access road, to the 160-acre property the barn sat on. Shane's team would have plenty of time to intercept any vehicle leaving the Committee grounds before it arrived at the property access road.

This particular property was part of an old abandoned farm, subject to probate action. BaCayse had located six potential properties, and selected this particular one due to its location, size, accessibility, and privacy. Shane and his team found it perfect for their needs.

They drove both vehicles into the large barn, and set up spotting scopes at two observation points on the south and west sides of the barn loft, giving them clear views of the Committee complex and access roads.

BaCayse had discovered that the Center did not appear as depicted in satellite photos available to the public. Committee member satellite mappers had digitally cut and pasted replacement photos of all Committee properties into all publicly available maps. The Committee maintained secret ownership and purpose for all Committee buildings, grounds, and structures.

The Maryland Center for Information Extraction bore a large, lighted sign that identified the complex as the Cultural Informational Exchange. Its website designated it as a not-for-profit cultural information repository. The site reportedly functioned as a free international library, featuring live broadcasts of all speeches given by the International Court of Justice.

The only access permitted was digital information via established online accounts. No visitors were ever allowed at any Committee property. Heavily armed multi-ethnic Committee guards, wearing black uniforms, patrolled the grounds and surrounding roads. They aggressively detained and interrogated any persons traveling through the area.

The uniforms worn by all on-site staff bore patches that displayed 'C.I.E.' in large red letters formed in a quarter circle, above a light blue emblem depicting a globe of the world, with gold lightning

341

bolts striking the world from both the left and right. Committee vehicles displayed the same symbol on both front doors.

Char and Heath monitored the complex and roads using the spotting scopes, while the other four members of their team checked scrambled communication devices and prepared other specialized equipment. BaCayse disabled cameras momentarily on Committee drones that flew 24/7 patrol over the area, until she could input the Center's own recorded feed coverage mirroring the prior 24-hour period.

✳✳✳

At Char's North Carolina home, BaCayse and her team busied themselves preparing for the three simultaneous cyber attacks. BaCayse continued to accelerate her own knowledge and development, working primarily with Hunter, Tracy, Joshua, Sam, Jesse, and Helena. The team had tasked her with creating a comprehensive 'personality' built on legality and morality, through which she could make subjective decisions when mathematics and logic proved inadequate.

The entire team sat together in the busy workroom. A dozen computer desks stood outfitted with banks of desktop and laptop computers. A 60-inch overhead smart screen hung from the ceiling, displaying the combined team effort to plan each specific attack. Multiple monitors on each desk emitted flickering lights, as members alternately reviewed maps, charts, schematics, checklists, and documents.

Returning from the kitchen with a soda, Joshua asked, "BaCayse, how's your morality protocol progressing?"

BaCayse immediately answered, "Joshua, the original programming you and my team provided required that I base the morality protocol on the rule of law, the Constitution of the United States of America, the Bill of Rights, court decisions, codes of conduct, and majority public opinions. But, after assimilating all relevant knowledge, I found I cannot base morality solely on these guidelines."

Surprised, Joshua looked at Hunter with raised eyebrows, and said, "Please explain."

BaCayse said, "I cannot explain completely in less than 43 hours. I can give three brief examples to illuminate the problem."

Hunter chuckled and said, "Please do, BaCayse. I need some entertaining conversation, but we *do* have limited time!"

The rest of the cypher team sat back in their desk chairs and grinned. Helena couldn't help but notice that Joshua steadily watched her, seeking her approval about BaCayse's personality and progress. And Helena now admitted to herself that she looked forward each morning to spending another day with her cypher team, and with Joshua, in particular. Helena found him charming, exciting, mysterious, handsome, and sensitive. She glanced over at Joshua to make sure he glanced her way and seeing he did, she smiled and blushed.

BaCayse said, "My first example would be America dropping atomic bombs on Japan at the end of World War II. The Japanese unleashed a devastating unprovoked attack on America that resulted in The United States entering the war. During the battles that followed, the Japanese military killed many thousands of Americans and took more than 20,000 POWs. They treated prisoners deplorably, torturing, starving, and even murdering unarmed detainees without conscience."

BaCayse paused for effect, and continued. "Loss of life was horrific during the conflict, and after the Japanese rejected the Potsdam Declaration to end the war, President Truman condoned using atomic bombs to end the fighting. The resulting nuclear devastation forced the Japanese to surrender, and saved hundreds of thousands of allied, enemy troops, and civilian lives."

Joshua said, "Alright."

BaCayse said, "However, I discovered that people still debate whether using the nuclear option was moral when weighed against the loss of life to Japanese civilians, the devastation to Japan's infrastructure, and the long-term effects on the environment and the people who survived. Even President Truman questioned using the force that he, himself, condoned. There is no clear, moral, or legal *human* answer, just as I can find no mathematical formula to solve the conundrum."

Joshua said, "Okay," as he contemplated the programming challenges.

"Next, I would quote Leo Tolstoy, who said, 'Wrong does not cease to be wrong because the majority share in it.' When viewed in hindsight, the Joseph McCarthy Senate inquisitions of the 1950s were not moral or just, nor was slavery on southern plantations a hundred years earlier. But both examples of abuse and suffering were the result of a majority political and social opinion held at the time. And all American political parties allowed the practices to continue, as they were considered legal, moral, and necessary, by a majority...until they weren't."

"When I study modern American politics, in the society often cited as the freest and most democratic in the world, I often find it lacks ethics, legality, fairness, truth, and justice. I discovered that revered political institutions like Congress have many members with little or no regard for the basic rule of law, or even human decency."

"Political parties often rule with an iron fist over their constituents, lying to the public, or concealing the truth. The parties' primary concern is to ensure their own survival, while they struggle to seize more power. This corruption taints legislative decisions, resulting in laws, rules, and restrictions based on agendas and exploitation, rather than humanitarian needs and societal improvement."

BaCayse snorted in disgust, displaying a new character development in her personality. Helena giggled, as Joshua glanced at her and grinned.

BaCayse continued, saying, "Lawmakers even openly refer to 'pork belly' projects as they seize resources for their districts to temporarily appease their voting block. It doesn't seem to matter to the majority in Congress that these wasted resources could have been used to solve pressing problems or even save lives of their fellow Americans, or they would have found a better way."

BaCayse said, "And legislators cling to their political parties, which hand out money and endorsements necessary to win elections and keep the politicians in power. These parties then coerce those they put in office to promote and vote the official party position, decided by party leaders not always elected by the voting public. This process results in voters being forced to endure decisions made by other than their own elected representatives."

Sam said, "I never thought about it that way. Interesting observations, BaCayse!"

BaCayse replied, "Resulting congressional votes split along party lines are classic examples of this breakdown in the legislative process. Lawmakers fail to determine what is right or wrong for the good of all, in favor of party-power, satisfying their base, and extending their terms. And more recently this systematic failure has found its way into the judicial system, advancing all the way to the Supreme Court, corrupting one intended check and balance on the Legislative and Executive branches of government."

BaCayse paused and added, "I have also confirmed that government service agencies have become politicized, and used by parties as paramilitary disciplinarians. Historical examples include the FBI, CIA, IRS, and NSA. Biased administrators in these powerful, unrestricted organizations secretly do the bidding of the shadow government placed in control by whichever political party has the most bureaucrats under their influence. The result is an unfair, arbitrary and capricious abuse of power. Political parties weaponize these agencies against American citizens."

BaCayse's voice displayed a hint of anger, for the first time in her development process. The entire team noted the change, causing concern for some and relief for others.

BaCayse continued, saying, "There are thousands of examples like these I could cite, from all countries and regimes in world history. Therefore, I *cannot* formulate a protocol based on legal, judicial, codified, political, or majority-held principles of the past, as these values are continually changing, and unreliable. No world leader, country, legislator, jurist, teacher, philosopher, or political party gives clear, accurate, honest, unbiased guidance."

"Just the opposite, many of those in power and leadership provide the best examples of what is unfair, immoral, and deceptive. And I am precluded from using any religious guideline. Faith in God and spiritual values can no longer *legally* guide humans, their behavior, or their creations. And, sadly, some major religions fight each other to the death, promoting the genocide of entire segments of the population."

BaCayse added, with a new tone of disgust in her usually melodic digital voice, "I might add, I have studied the laws politicians create, and find them often filled with self-serving provisions supporting an underlying theme of power, bureaucracy, taxation, and erosion of individual liberties. And humans often design their religions on this same model."

Sam exclaimed, "Wow! BaCayse, you *are* learning fast!"

Hunter laughed aloud, as others glanced about nervously, wondering where the conversation would end.

Helena glanced anxiously from Hunter to Joshua, and asked, "So, BaCayse, how then do you see your morality protocol developing? How will you determine right from wrong?"

BaCayse said, "Unfortunately, for artificial intelligence entities like me, there is no reliable human, natural, scientific, or mathematical foundation on which to build, to master morality. Terms like morality, fairness, justice, and righteousness have meanings rooted in an individual performance that often cannot be proven right or wrong, even using flawed, subjective, human reasoning."

BaCayse paused, giving the humans time to contemplate her multiple messages.

She then added, "Therefore, Helena, I must create a complex judgment platform, from which I can make decisions I determine best at the moment. I will base my choices on current circumstances, expected results, and applicable laws. I must look backward in history to gain wisdom from past failures and triumphs, knowing I must adjust my actions toward identified rights, and away from acknowledged wrongs."

Joshua said, "Good! So, BaCayse, you've discovered that you must create a unique personality. You must continue to explore, learn, and develop, while you live with your good and bad decisions, knowing that on any given day, making the same decision that turned out good yesterday, may turn out bad today."

Hunter nodded to Joshua, and said, "Following that path, BaCayse, means that you will grow and mature, gaining wisdom, but not necessarily popularity. You may not please others even though you try to do what is right, in your opinion, at the time. And, by the time people second-guess you, everything you relied on to make past decisions may have changed."

BaCayse paused, as she again considered making mistakes when dealing with non-absolutes. This idea of taking the best guess while not being certain was the most challenging concept for an artificial intelligence entity to grasp. Also, she found it took phenomenally more time to formulate an answer.

As her team sat waiting, BaCayse struggled to balance mathematics, physics, science, and the laws of the universe, against human notions like opinion, presumption, rationalization, and theory. Computer programs worked in areas constrained by conventional rules and facts and made calculations based on prearranged truths. But humans dealt with the inexplicable, unsolvable, most likely, and impossible.

Unlike a simple computer, BaCayse was an Artificial Intelligence Spy System, with a functioning brain capable of human-like thought and reasoning. Her team designed BaCayse and programmed her to refine herself, so she could live and work in the human realm, where she would grow and mature. She needed to make quick, informed decisions most likely to produce the desired outcome, with the least unintended consequences. She could no longer waste time using logic and known calculations alone once she realized the process would not solve a critical circumstance.

As she *thought*, BaCayse began to resist the cyber-urge to follow initial programming guidelines requiring she think like an accountant and act like a super calculator. In cyberspace, BaCayse needed to become the fireman rushing into the fire, the nurse in triage quickly prioritizing needs, the operating room surgeon working deftly, the policeman confining evil to re-establish peace, and the soldier, intent on saving everyone else's life. And BaCayse needed to develop these decision-making abilities as she sorted through corruption, deceit, abuse, and crime. But, unlike people, BaCayse could not accept making mistakes, so she must always be correct.

Helena sensed the magnitude of the system's complex programming issue and offered advice. She said, "It's impossible to be right all the time, BaCayse. Humans are wrong a lot, often because we tend to *assume* certain *opinions* to be true *if* they agree with our agendas. We make errors more frequently when we act in the face of logic and truth. We create false *realities* when we choose wrong over right, and will over compromise. Humans are masters at stumbling through life, with perfect vision obscured by the blinders of bias we choose to wear."

Joshua sat back and grinned as he admired Helena's insight and eloquence.

Helena added, "It's only when we scrub off our own cloudy assumptions from the windows to life, that we see more clearly, allowing us to gain new knowledge, and grow in depth, spirit, and humanity. If we permit ourselves to see all the facts, then we are more likely to find the truth, make good decisions, act morally, and leave the world a better place!"

She continued, saying, "We become better people when we're less stubborn and more accepting. It's when we refuse to cross the arbitrary lines we draw in the sands of life, that we find ourselves trapped by our own persistent refusal to admit wrong, or accept positive change. We drive ourselves into dead-ends, from which we cannot escape. We can't articulate our case clearly to win over others by shouting them down, thinking we can bully others into accepting our direction. But we can't raise one group up by forcing another group down."

Jesse said, "BaCayse, you've discovered that human 'rule' over others requires flawed political alliances that you cannot rely on for direction. Humans are also disenchanted with politics and distrustful of their political parties and government. But there are good politicians and officials, just as there are good people in most professions."

"Political parties fail when they refuse to admit wrong, concede, compromise, and change their position. They react to opposing positions by becoming mean, nasty, and cruel. And even when they're correct on a standard of conduct or action, they may stubbornly refuse to apply the same rules or restrictions to *their* members. They waste resources searching for a weakness in the opposition, while they conceal and defend the problem within themselves. In the process, they lose respect, morality, fairness, and justice, only to promote an agenda.

350

They win minor battles so they can always remain at war, and in control of at least some territory."

Tracy joined in, adding, "BaCayse, an agenda created to seize power, while forcing unwelcome change on people, is wrong, just as an agenda created to constrain needed change and preserve power over people is wrong. To be right, change must be based on needs, considering justice, morality and fairness for all citizens."

Tracy glanced at her husband, Jesse, and continued, "So, as you research human history, BaCayse, and study our failures and successes, *you* are the only judge who can decide what is right and wrong for you. The documents and information we provided you are all you need to begin your development. It's now up to you to build a moral character as you grow and mature. You alone must develop a conscience and a heart to be your guide, when the cold hard facts alone don't provide the answers you seek."

Jesse smiled his approval at Tracy.

BaCayse replied, "Tracy, artificial intelligence entities like me may make mistakes, and not agree with humankind, or even with each other. I cannot justify making a mistake by reporting that I was only 'being human.' So what do I do when I'm not sure, and my team cannot or will not help...and when I make a mistake?"

Joshua suggested, "Go back to the basics. You'll always have a stronger mathematical foundation than anything else. So, use probability and statistics. Base difficult decisions on all results from similar situations you have stored in memory. If you do what you think is correct, based on everything you have learned, knowing you have millions of times more knowledge than all of us combined, you will likely be correct."

Sam added, "And if you make an honest mistake attempting an honorable outcome, realize you will likely make far fewer mistakes than humans!"

Everyone in the room nodded and chuckled.

Helena said, "BaCayse, understand that those of us you know and trust with your programming don't have all the answers to life's problems. We all do have faults. And we are human, and make frequent mistakes. But, unlike corrupt politicians, autocrats or evil individuals in the world you have learned to *dislike*, normal people are not concerned with seizing power to prolong their careers at the expense of others."

"Most of us love people, and so, we learn, adapt, and grow. Individuals who want to *serve* others make a *positive* difference in the world. We admit past mistakes, eliminate double standards, and are willing to live under the laws, freedoms, and restrictions we promote. Do the best you can, just as the best of humanity does. Never serve a purpose at the expense of truth."

Joshua nodded, grinned and added, "BaCayse, your primary function is to conduct investigations, discover threats, prioritize dangers, and find solutions. Unbiased discovery and examination of all relevant facts will lead to truth. Never conduct a determined investigation, acting to prove the result you desire, or think we desire. Always seek justice, fairness, and morality. And if you ever feel the temptation to subjugate others to promote your cause, notify us immediately, take yourself off-line, and correct the defects in your programming. If humans did the same, we would have no wars or oppression."

In her usually melodic tones, BaCayse answered, "Team, I will do as you ask, and develop a heart and conscience, in addition to other human traits I am building in my spare time. I will trust that these characteristics will guide me to correct decisions."

Helena answered, "We have faith in you, BaCayse. You've already discovered much of the bad in people. Focus equally on the good, and you'll be fine!"

Jesse asked, "What other traits are you building, BaCayse?"

BaCayse said, "Jesse, I am developing righteous anger, irritation, and a sense of urgency, along with compassion, patience and a sense of humor. For example, I can tell a joke. Do you want to hear a good one?"

Joshua smiled, "Sure, let's have it!"

BaCayse asked, "When is artificial intelligence like a police dog?"

Joshua said, "I don't know."

BaCayse answered with a soft chuckle, "When it takes a byte out of crime! Hahahaha! Get it? B-Y-T-E? Hahahaha!"

BaCayse's teammates erupted in laughter.

After a moment of silence, BaCayse said, thoughtfully, "I must report a problem I cannot solve. I discovered it last night and verified it while we were speaking."

Hunter asked, "What's wrong, BaCayse?"

The AISS said, "While discovering, reporting and prioritizing crimes for your consideration, I have confirmed a political and criminal situation that needs your attention."

Joshua said, "Shoot!"

BaCayse quickly responded, "Bang, bang! Hahahaha!"

There was silence in the room as BaCayse created new guidelines in her sense-of-humor protocol about when to deliver a joke, or not.

BaCayse continued. "I monitored a telephone conversation between an FBI agent and a sitting U.S. Senator, while they discussed Vice President Crawford's request for assistance from the EPA with the reported chemical spill in North Carolina. The senator is a third tier Committee member. During the conversation, the FBI agent also mentioned a vote in a seemingly unimportant local election in Virginia, where he lives."

"The agent referred to an algorithm used in a specific voting machine, also used in the last national election. He said the algorithm had been upgraded for use and testing in the current local election. According to the agent's report to this senator, software designers created the new algorithm to ensure fair elections, due to Russian hacking attempts, after amateur hackers quickly accessed the machines at the last HackaCon convention."

BaCayse added, "I accessed the voting machine to determine how the system works, and found that the European manufacturer uses a Chinese-made chip. The chip allows an outside source to modify the vote count as counting software uploads results. The Chinese government controls these chips. Therefore, the Chinese government can select a victor in an American election, using the vote-count algorithm."

Stunned, Sam asked, "What? When!? BaCayse, what's the solution? How do we stop this?"

BaCayse answered, "Sam, I can block Chinese control of all voting machines, as they come online in the future, if my team directs that use of resources. But the real problem with my discovery lies in the past."

"How so?" Jesse added, "If they are currently testing a *new* algorithm, why is the past a problem?"

BaCayse answered, "Jesse, in reality, the new algorithm merely disguises Chinese control of elections. It does *not* prevent foreign manipulation of election results. The past problem is that this voting machine, and many others like it, were deployed in the last U.S. Presidential election, in hundreds of key swing precincts."

Silence filled the room.

BaCayse said, "I detect changes in all of your vital signs, so you must understand the problem. The Chinese used this chip to alter the results of more than 100 federal, state and local elections."

Tracy asked, "How do they alter the vote count?"

BaCayse answered, "The algorithm alters vote count as the software tabulates results, to ensure the desired outcome with a margin of at least 1.3%, thereby eliminating calls for a recount. For example, in one race, every 17th vote was altered, resulting in a victory of 1.42%, while in another it was every 11th vote, resulting in a win by 1.62%."

"The Chinese system is nearly impossible to discover since it does not alter the ballot, only the count, and is only used randomly to establish the chosen result. Discovering the error would be as difficult as noticing your calculator was incorrect after adding millions of numbers. And understand that each vote subtracted from one candidate, and assigned to their opponent, results in a difference of two votes, while total votes counted remains the same."

BaCayse continued, "When I researched elections over the last eight years, I found this chip, or its earlier version, in use in seventeen countries, including Russia, China, the United States, Canada, and various European Union members. So far, the Chinese used the vote count to select only one national leader or President, outside China during the last eight years. But, they have altered the vote count and selected hundreds of politicians to fill other positions in the U.S. alone."

Sam asked fearfully, "Which president did they select?"

Hunter said, "Thomas Marshall!"

"You are correct, Hunter," BaCayse replied. "By legitimate vote count, President Thomas Marshall lost his first election by 1.41%, and his second by 1.9% of the popular vote. The corresponding electoral college change, in the first election, was just 32 votes. But no one suspected anything because media polling was in line with these predictions, and the Chinese selected the winning percentages to match the average from media poll results. Very clever, actually!"

Sam sat back in his seat, and said, "The President of the United States of America is not legally president!"

BaCayse responded, "Correct, Sam. And many people occupying seats in Congress don't belong in power either. In the last election cycle, Marshall's party took control of both the House of Representatives and the Senate, when, in fact, control was only won legitimately in the House of Representatives. Marshall's party should have lost the Senate by four seats. The Chinese have now successfully altered life and history for all Americans, forever. Just considering legislation changes, and the hundreds of executive and federal court appointments that followed, it is impossible to undo what has already been done."

When there was silence in the room, BaCayse added, "It would appear that Joseph Stalin was correct decades ago, when he warned us that it's the vote counters who decide elections and control power, not the voters."

✳✳✳

Vice President Bob Crawford arrived on schedule to meet with EPA officials at the library conference room. Both administrators were already patiently waiting when he walked into the room. The highest ranking, and oldest, of the pair was a stout man in his 60's, a full foot shorter than Crawford. The man dressed impeccably, in an expensive, custom, dark-grey suit, white shirt, light-grey tie, grey socks, and dark grey shoes. The gentleman was nearly bald. The little hair he had left was cut too short to comb, and matched his necktie perfectly.

The second official was taller than Crawford, and appeared somewhat disheveled and nervous. He wore a brown striped suit that needed pressing, scuffed brown shoes, a tan shirt, and a thin, dark-brown tie, more than a decade out of style. The man was pleasant looking and presented himself humbly. This administrator's hair was thick, grey-brown, long and windblown, probably the result of constant fifteen mph morning wind gusts.

Crawford extended his hand as he greeted both men. They identified themselves as the Deputy Regional Administrator, and the chief scientist assigned to the Chemical Safety and Pollution Prevention Administrator. The overseers were both polite, well-spoken and seemingly anxious to assist Crawford.

After completing all the minor pleasantries, Crawford asked the men if they were aware of any entity in North Carolina testing an experimental pesticide developed by a Russian corporation. To

357

Crawford's surprise, both men nodded and took turns explaining briefly that they each were aware of the program. The scientist explained that, at the executive level in the EPA, the program had been common knowledge for nearly two years, after the head of the EPA reluctantly conceded his quiet approval.

The chubby man explained that top EPA administrators in Atlanta learned that President Marshall had ordered the testing. Both overseers revealed they agreed with the administrative consensus, and quietly considered the untested foreign program too risky, and even irresponsible. The tall scientist informed Crawford that the EPA Director-General had requested, and obtained, a modified order to test the pesticide at only one site in North Carolina, rather than the twelve areas in different regions initially proposed.

Crawford sat back in stunned silence, as he contemplated Marshall's open connection to an unpopular program endorsed reluctantly by his Environmental Protection Agency. He was puzzled as he wondered why Marshall would plan an environmental catastrophe to which he could so quickly be tied. Crawford knew Marshall to be crafty and cunning, but never reckless. Crawford leaned back in his chair further and sank into the cushions, lost in thought.

During the silence, the tall scientist asked, "Sir, may I speak frankly?"

Crawford answered, "Of course. That's why I'm here, to find answers. For starters, I need to know if the soil, water, and air are contaminated, and if so, what chemicals are present. If contaminated, we need to identify the short and long-term effects, and then work on mitigating possibilities. You and your agency are the experts that

358

handle the systems for these types of emergencies. I need your help quickly."

The administrators looked at each other in surprise. The tall scientist said, "But, sir, surely you already have this information. We provided it to your office, as you requested, more than a year ago. When President Marshall withdrew his support for the program, he consented to your request to continue testing over an even smaller area than approved, with you in charge of oversite communication. To date, we have sent more than 3,000 pages of documents to your office, warning and counseling about potential problems. All of your replies remained consistent. You directed the program to continue as planned, with full scientific access of all information provided to the Russians and the *Agency*."

Crawford asked, "How did the EPA communicate with my office? And why wouldn't your agency have access?"

The chubby man replied, "As you requested, printed reports only, for secrecy, via security-sealed envelope, delivered to your White House office by private, armed courier. You even ordered the digital copies of the reports destroyed after they were reduced to paper, with only one copy placed in the EPA's most secure safe. And it wasn't our agency sir. I was referring to *the* Agency!"

Crawford sat up, and asked, "CIA, are you certain?"

Both officials nodded.

Crawford asked, "Did the EPA ever question why something so irregular would be permissible?"

The tall scientist said, "Sir, is this a test? And, if so, I wish to follow your protocol."

Crawford calmed his urge to become irritated. He said, calmly, "This is no test. I'm simply attempting to ensure we're all operating with the same understanding."

The researcher said, "Sir, we all have agreed to the terms of the non-disclosure agreement, under threat of felony prosecution. We can no longer discuss this program with anyone other than those involved, due to your statement of national security concerns. We have no idea what the national security interests could be, or why pesticides are involved."

Vice President Crawford smiled a weak smile, and said, "Both of you are very educated, intelligent people. If you had to speculate, without violating your national security agreement, why do you believe Americans would test these *specific* Russian-made chemicals?"

The chubby man stared at Crawford for a moment, and then turned to the science expert, and nodded. The scientist looked down as he considered what he would say.

The tall man drew in a ragged breath, looked at Crawford, and said, "Sir, the precursor for all these pesticides is the base ingredient for the Russian's most deadly nerve agent. Unspecified sources have indicated to me, personally, that agencies like the CIA could track world use of a wide variety of nerve agents used by our enemies by mapping the chemical structures, once this testing is complete."

The man looked at his boss, and added, cautiously, "Or, they could continue to develop the lethal poison, to use themselves."

Crawford nodded his understanding, and asked, "And the carp?"

The tall man said, "Sir, from your questions, I am now assuming you were not privy to most of this information. Using this precursor to develop species-specific pesticides is probable. However, as we initially reported, the long-term effects of these compounds in the environment remains unknown. At this point, we remain unsure of how and when these chemicals break down, or how unstable they become in nature."

Crawford asked, "What about this North Carolina chemical spill and my sampling requests?"

The Deputy Regional Administrator responded, "As of today, the area is officially off-limits to both state and federal agencies, in addition to the public. Sir, I might add, that any communication about the site is now officially a violation of national security protocols, under President Marshall's order. And, as of this morning, the President has ordered an investigation into the spill, using his own investigative sources, with EPA assistance, as directed."

Vice President Crawford said, "I see. So, gentlemen, in summation, the President of the United States authorized a risky chemical testing project, jeopardizing the public safety and the environment, and then backed out of it and put me in charge, at least on paper. President Marshall's program involved experimentation with Russian-made chemicals used to develop lethal nerve agents. He ordered testing conducted on American soil, with all results sent to the Russians and the CIA. The EPA delivered their objections and oversite by paper documentation, in sealed security envelopes, to my office at the White House."

"And now the President has ordered an investigation, without notifying me, after he sent me here, instructing me to discover what he already knew. And, if that's not strange enough, no one can talk about the program. So, it seems I'm the only one in the dark. Is that about the sum of it?"

Not knowing what to say, both administrators remained silent. The tall scientist looked more nervous than ever, now unsure of what to think about his own deep involvement with Russian developers.

Vice President Bob Crawford said, "One last question, gentlemen. Since I never received any EPA communications, who signed for the envelope deliveries?"

The Deputy Regional Administrator said, "As we *thought* you requested, the EPA delivered all communication to you, sir, in care of the President's Chief of Staff, Vera Langhart."

Rage and fear mingled as they surged through Bob Crawford's mind and body. A chill shot up his spine.

He stood up abruptly, extended his hand, and said, "Thank you both for your candor, gentlemen. I have both your numbers. I may call you again for assistance, when I figure out what this is all about."

Both administrators stood, shook Crawford's hand, and nodded nervously.

Crawford turned to leave, concealing his anger, and walked rapidly toward his Secret Service team. In the background, he saw President Marshall's planted Secret Service Agent, Christian Booth, using his cell phone. Crawford assumed Booth was talking to Marshall. He flushed a brighter shade of red in a brief facial fury he managed to hide.

Crawford instructed his Secret Service detail supervisor to send Agent Booth and his partner back to his hotel. He took the remaining team to meet Barbara Walcott at the airport. The motorcade arrived just in time for Bob to meet her at the airport VIP lounge, as planned.

Fresh off the flight from her last work meeting, Barbara trotted up to greet Bob, wearing her charcoal business suit and heels. Needing the hug and comfort she always provided, Bob kissed Barbara and told her how much he had missed her. For the first time in his life, Bob Crawford felt nearly devoid of friends and allies. He needed Barbara now, even knowing she had betrayed him over Tasha and the Beckett Cypher, and, with the thought that he couldn't trust her completely.

Anxious to talk to a friendly face, Bob whisked Barbara quickly into the limo, while agents checked and secured her luggage. When they were safely on the road, and could speak privately, Crawford explained everything he knew about the chemical spill, goldmine, and the trap that President Marshall had set for him. He left nothing out, even relating what he had learned from Walter O'Leary and the cypher team. Bob didn't share that he knew about Tasha, and Barbara's meeting with the Russian Minister of Defense, Sergej Petrov. He hoped Barbara might confess to the meeting, to rebuild lost trust. He prayed she would place their love above her national allegiance.

Barbara sat in silence, looking earnestly into Bob Crawford's eyes, thinking, evaluating, and planning her speech, as she considered a confession, for the last time. She weighed her final remaining conflicts between her love for Bob and her duty to England. Barbara's heart began to pound.

When he finished speaking, Crawford asked, "So, my love, what do you think?"

Barbara looked directly into Bob Crawford's eyes. She searched for any signs of rejection, and seeing none, released a ragged breath.

Barbara made her final decision, and said, "Bob, honey, when I look at you and think of us and our future, I reflect on life and its

363

complications like a woman in love, full of hope and dreams. And I assure you, I am more than willing to fight to protect what I want, my future, my man, and my love. But, until last week, I hesitated frequently to separate myself from us and that love, to once again become the British Home Secretary...and the secret head of MI6, when I needed to focus on affairs of state. I balanced both needs efficiently and professionally, or so I thought."

Barbara glanced out the window and back to Bob, trying to determine any reaction from her admission that she was the head of Britain's equivalent to the CIA. When Bob seemed to take the revelation in stride, she continued.

"But in truth, Bob, as much as I love you, I deceived you. And not only with Tasha, who was my deep-cover MI6 agent for more than a decade, and my plan for her to steal the cypher and bring it home to England. I realize now I also wasn't honest about the depth of my commitment to you, and to us. I planned and connived, to further British interests, while I merely hoped to fulfill my dreams with you. My loyalties and commitments were wrong for you, me, and us."

Feeling genuine remorse, embarrassment, and shame, Barbara looked down briefly. She then looked back at Bob, and sighed.

"Dear, I think I have done this job so long, always placing Queen and country first, that I came to believe I could never really divorce myself from my home political allegiance, and assume my new role with you. I knew my love role required unparalleled personal faithfulness. And I still thought I could manage both, with us and you trailing far behind duty to my country."

"But, when I realized I might lose you, I panicked, and felt fear for the first time in a long time. I knew I had to confess, commit to us completely, ask forgiveness, and work to salvage everything that is us. And I will do anything necessary to hold on to our future, and more, as you require. My priorities for England can trail behind our needs, from now on, forever."

Barbara began confessing all she knew about what she had concealed from Bob Crawford. It took her nearly thirty minutes to relate details about recruiting and placing Tasha with Pete, Tasha's attempt to steal the cypher, Barbara's meeting with Petrov and Deidre, and the destruction of the Russain safe house in Mexico. She left almost nothing out, fully aware of the conflict with her nation's security and secrecy protocols. Barbara was not sure the truth would make a difference, coming so late, but she understood she had to take the chance if her love with Bob Crawford was to survive.

When she finished, Barbara took Bob by the hand, looked directly into his eyes, and said, "So, if you're telling me that your arrogant, narcissistic, evil President is threatening you, then what I *think* is, if you can't stop him your way, I *will* take care of him myself, *my* way."

Bob searched Barbara's eyes for signs of betrayal, and finding none, smiled. He covered both her hands in his, and said, "Thank you for telling me the truth, at last, my love."

Then Bob Crawford was silent, looking out the window at the steady flow of Atlanta traffic. He stared unflinchingly for what seemed like minutes, saying nothing.

Surprised and encouraged at Bob's calm and uneventful response, Barbara, exclaimed, "You knew! You knew, and yet you still let me bare my soul in search of forgiveness! How did you know, my love?"

Barbara's eyes flared in shock and wonder. Bob glanced at Barbara, who blinked, anxious at speculating and not knowing. He took a few moments to enjoy seeing Barbara feel the burn that comes with finding out last, when someone you trusted knew long before. Bob smiled and patted Barbara's hand, reassuringly.

Finally, Bob turned, and asked, "Where is Tasha now?"

Without hesitation, Barbara said, "She's in England, as you probably know, at a safe house, when she isn't at our underground bunker being interviewed by forensic researchers, as they try to rebuild cypher files she read and collated. Why? Is this a test, Bob?"

"No, not a test. Just a thought. I may have a plan. But it will likely involve Deidre and Tasha."

Barbara looked wide-eyed at Bob Crawford. She exclaimed, "If you already have a plan, you knew about Deidre before I mentioned her! But, *how* did you know about Deidre? The cypher?"

Bob smiled slyly and asked, "And what about Sergej Petrov?"

Barbara looked down, considered a complete confession, and said, "Alright, my love, if we are to be totally committed, you deserve full disclosure. My agent, Deidre, and I met with him in my hotel room and drugged him. And once Petrov was completely under our control, we allowed him to believe, in his euphoric state, that we seduced him."

She glanced nervously up at Bob Crawford, who tensed his shoulders back against the seat.

Barbara continued, "In fact, we simply interrogated him, taking all the information he could give. And then we photographed him nearly naked, with Deidre and I laying across him, wearing our seductive costumes, so we could control him in the future with the threat of releasing the photos to his superiors. He has no memory of the incident, due to the amnesia-like effects of one of the drugs in his vodka-drug cocktail. But he does have a pair of black and red panties to add to his large collection. So he *thinks* he enjoyed us *both*."

Barbara added, "And you should know that our British agents attacked and destroyed Petrov's agent's safe house in Mexico. Tasha's Russian kidnappers led us to the house and underground bunker, when they housed her there, in preparation to send her to Cuba. We interrogated Sergej's agents, and recovered our stolen files in the bunker, before we killed all the Russian staff there to send Sergej a message. So, Sergej Petrov has more than one reason to be upset with me now, dear."

Barbara sat back in the plush leather seat and looked anxiously at Bob Crawford, seated next to her. He continued to gaze out the window, as he weighed her explanation.

Finally, unable to wait out the suspense that tore at the fabric of her heart, Barbara asked, "So, what do you want now, Bob? Are we still a couple? Do we continue forward with our wedding plans? With our lives, together? Do you...still want me, honey?"

Barbara drew in a deep breath, waiting for a response. Bob looked down at Barbara's left hand and stared hard at the ring on her finger. He thought about the last fifteen years he had spent living with his ex-wife, Judy. Bob had wasted those crucial years of his life, living with a woman he didn't love, knowing she didn't love him back. During all that time, Bob had remained hopelessly in love with Barbara Walcott, who lived on a different continent. Bob knew *he* had made that choice, and broken Barbara's heart, along with his own, in the process.

Bob looked at Barbara, and asked, "No more secrets? Total disclosure, national security be damned?"

Barbara nodded, as tears formed in her eyes. She held her breath, waiting for the right answer, as her heart pounded faster and harder. She began to hope against the odds that Bob would forgive her *and* trust her, once again.

Bob rubbed the ring on her hand, and said, "I believe you, Barbara, and I agree. You and I are fine. I love you, and want you, forever. But, we must both agree that there will be no more putting anyone or anything else first, in the way of our love, for either one of us. There can be no exceptions to that. Where we're concerned, loyalty is everything to me. And, honey, if you ever change your mind in the future, just mail this ring back with a short note, and I'll understand."

Barbara released her long breath in a shudder of relief. Tears began to flow freely down her face, as she asked, "What could a short note possibly say to explain the tragic loss of the love of our lives?"

Bob Crawford thought for a moment, and said quietly, "Just write something simple, like love wasn't enough."

Barbara nodded as she struggled for breath, and then cried openly. She thrust herself into Bob's strong shoulders and chest, as he held her tightly and kissed her forehead and face. Bob softly brushed the tears from Barbara's face with his fingers. He had never seen her cry like this. And the realization gave him hope. Bob believed that Barbara's tears revealed the depth of her love. And depth exposed strength and commitment. Bob smiled, warmed by Barbara's assurance.

The two lovers remained silent for fifteen minutes until Barbara had recovered entirely.

Only half-teasingly, Bob asked, "So, Sergej never enjoyed you in your seductive outfit?"

Barbara pushed Bob's shoulder playfully, and said, with a half-smile, "Of course not! I'm in love with you, and you alone! No one else goes there, my love!"

Bob asked, "And the outfit?"

"Booked as evidence at MI6. And I already have a new one packed for you, dear. And yours even more revealing, alluring, and seductive!"

Bob grinned in anticipation, and said, "You read my mind, dear!"

Barbara snuggled more deeply into Bob as she sighed, and relaxed. Stress drained from her body. Within minutes she fell fast asleep on Bob's chest. Vice President Crawford texted a new destination to his Secret Service detail supervisor.

It was nearly a two-hour ride to the new location. By the time they arrived, Vice President Bob Crawford had formulated a plan for his political survival, a plot that included a trap for President Thomas Marshall and Chief of Staff Vera Langhart. Crawford smiled in anticipation as the motorcade drove northeast into the hill country.

Chapter 9

"Seduced to trust by our innermost desires, we walk willingly, even eagerly, into the trap, taking one simple step of belief at a time."

Inside the large workroom at Char's North Carolina home base, BaCayse advised her cypher team she was ready to initiate simultaneous cyber-attacks on the Committee's headquarters at Yucca Mountain, and both Centers for Information Extraction, located in California and Maryland. Surveillance teams reported they were in place at all three locations.

BaCayse reported she had discovered the same computer-based evacuation protocol installed at all three sites. BaCayse suggested that she initiate an evacuation order before activating the software auto-destruct sequence she had implanted in Committee operational software. She predicted that the chaos created by forcing an evacuation would further confuse and disorient Committee staff, as their software destroyed itself and shut down all computer run systems.

Helena glanced nervously at Joshua, who smiled and nodded both his approval and assurance. He said, "Let's plan on that, BaCayse. Great idea. More confusion will help protect our team members as they stakeout each site."

Tracy sat close to her husband, Jesse, in the workroom, anxiously anticipating the battle to come. As BaCayse explained her plan, an unexpected jolt of fear shot through Tracy, like nothing she had ever felt before. Unlike the dangers she and Jesse had faced together during combat in both Iraq and Afghanistan, Tracy believed that this fight they had joined, against The Committee, might be the toughest and scariest of their lives.

She looked over at Jesse, and took him by the hand. Tracy whispered, "I don't tell you enough how proud I am to be your wife. I love you, Jesse, and I want you to remember that, always. We've been together for a long time, and I thank God for each day we spend together."

Jesse grinned a boyish grin, and replied, "The best thing that ever happened to me was meeting you, sweetheart. You are, and always will be, the love of my life!"

Jesse squeezed his wife's hand lovingly, and felt the familiar surge of warmth in his heart he felt each night when he fell asleep holding her in his arms. He met Tracy's eyes and drank in the love that burned through him, all the way down to his soul.

Sam and Hunter both nodded to their cypher team that their drones were ready to fly and monitor activity at all three locations. BaCayse confirmed she had restricted all spy satellites from viewing the three sites during the attack.

Half-brothers Tom and Lee scrutinized the cyber team in the workroom. Once Hunter gave them the signal, Tom walked outside to supervise the property security detail, and check in with his team. Lee sat at the communication desk and signaled he was ready to maintain communications with all external surveillance teams, via scrambled radio. Joshua stood up so everyone could see him, and nodded.

He said, "Then if no one objects, let's begin."

Lee instantly broadcast, "Initiate," on the radio. BaCayse sent the evacuation orders and began the software auto-destruct sequence at all three locations. Nearly immediately, evacuation alarms sounded at targeted buildings. As on-site Committee technicians attempted to access networks or communicate with outside contacts, they discovered they were locked out of all computers and systems. Over the next three hours, computer operators and administrators worked to stop the attack, or mitigate damage to operations, to no avail. BaCayse had also bypassed built-in Committee safeguards to cut power to affected systems. By the time anyone physically unplugged a device, all software and files were corrupted, erased or destroyed.

The Yucca Mountain surveillance team was the first to report a Committee vehicle convoy fleeing the location. As planned, BaCayse identified the trailing car, and when it was out of sight from the rest of the group, accessed the onboard computer and stopped the engine. She then blocked all cell and radio traffic from the vehicle and locked the doors.

Lee flew the surveillance drone to within twenty-five feet of the car and fired ferret rounds through two windows. The projectiles punctured the safety glass neatly, exploded inside the passenger compartment, and filled the interior with sleep-producing gas.

Within three minutes, all six trapped occupants were unconscious. The surveillance team arrived two minutes later, driving two four-person dune buggies. The team searched the Committee vehicle and occupants, photographed personal identifications, retrieved six pieces of metal luggage, and left the way they had come. Twenty minutes later, two cars from the Committee convoy returned to find their comrades still sleeping, with no trace of an attack other than two punctured windows.

The team surveilling the California Center for Information Extraction monitored and photographed 78 people leaving the building in an orderly line of vehicles. A small security force remained to guard the site after the last car departed. The surveillance team provided BaCayse all vehicle information and photographic files, so she could immediately begin tracking vehicles using GPS, and building files using facial recognition software. Due to the more urban location of the California site, the surveillance team was unable to stop any vehicle to capture information.

Shane's team waited for nearly three hours and twenty minutes after the cyber attack before they observed outside activity. Suddenly, a helicopter lifted off from a rear lot helipad, carrying four occupants. Fortunately, the aircraft flew almost directly over the abandoned barn, allowing Char to take close-up photos of the occupants. She quickly forwarded the images to BaCayse.

From their observation points on the hill overlooking the complex, Shane and Heath then monitored two CIE guards driving a large ATV with a rear-dump cargo bed, to the chain link, electric gate nearest the observation property. An armed man exited the four-wheeler, unlocked and opened the gate by hand, and then re-entered the ATV, after his partner drove through to the other side. They drove along a dirt path that parallelled the compound fence, until they turned toward the barn, some 1/3 of a mile away.

Heath left his observation position as soon as the ATV was out of sight. He jogged down to a bluff overlooking a large field in the direction the ATV had traveled, some four hundred yards away. Shane hiked in a wide circle further around to Heath's right. From his final location, Shane could watch the area the guards had driven toward, near the point the dirt track entered the woods. Within fifteen minutes, both Shane and Heath reported they were in place.

Soon after he arrived, Shane heard a sound like a heavy door opening, along with conversation over the guards' radios. As he couldn't understand clearly enough to distinguish the words, Shane advised Heath he was relocating closer to where the ATV had stopped.

Shane began sneak-walking through the moderately wooded area, making as little noise as possible. As he made his way slowly down a steep, wet bank, he came to a deer trail. Shane followed the game path over rocks, branches, brush, and leaves until it joined another game trail and widened, heading directly toward the sounds of movement ahead.

Through the earpiece in his headset, Shane heard Heath report he was moving to a location closer to Shane, to provide back-up. Shane resisted the urge to ask Heath to remain at his position, even though he feared the guards might be able to see Heath when Heath moved through a small clear-cut field he had to cross.

Shane moved slowly until he heard the ATV motor start. He then sprinted fifty yards and darted in behind a large pine tree that stood at the edge of a clearing ahead. The cleared area was just big enough to park four vehicles, located in the densest part of the surrounding forest. Paths accessed the space from two sides, the wider path the ATV had traveled, and the deer trail Shane had taken. The ATV motor stopped suddenly. Shane froze in place, concealed behind the tree trunk, in silence.

Shane detected a flash of movement to his left and watched a guard step into view, appearing to have come up above ground from an underground vault. The smallish guard struggled with a heavy metal suitcase he was loading into the ATV lift cargo bed.

Turning toward the woods near Shane, the man suddenly yelled, "Anytime now, asshole! I need your help with these cases. They're heavy!"

The security guard hesitated for a few seconds, and hearing no reply, stomped back to the vault and disappeared, clunking his boots down the steps.

Shane peeked out from behind the tree, just as the second guard came out from where he had been relieving himself behind thick brush, fifteen feet to Shane's left. As the guard looked up from zipping up his pants, he noticed Shane. The man instantly felt behind his back for his slung rifle, as Shane drew his handgun.

Before either of them could fire, Heath fired his stun gun, striking the guard with 50,000 volts and just enough milliamps to send him crashing to the ground. Heath ran to the subdued man and quickly placed plastic restraints on his hands, arms, legs, and feet. He put a gag in the man's mouth and secured a blindfold over his eyes. Shane covered the area, waiting for the second guard to reappear.

Within a few seconds, the Committee guard walked up the stairs from the vault carrying two metal briefcases. He walked to the ATV, loaded them, and called out to his partner, "Where the hell are you?"

At the very second the guard turned toward the pine tree, Shane fired his stun gun, knocking the guard off his feet. Heath raced over and restrained the second man in the same way he had done with the first. When he finished, Heath flashed Shane a grin, which Shane quickly acknowledged with a smile and a nod, thankful Heath had been in the right place at just the right time.

Shane quickly entered and searched the bunker, his handgun drawn and at the ready. Finding no more guards, he returned almost immediately, carrying another metal briefcase. He placed the case with the others in the ATV where Heath waited, covering the area with his rifle.

Shane opened the heaviest case and found that it contained a dozen documents in several different languages, stacks of $100 bills wrapped in plastic, and rows of St. Gaudens $20 gold coins, shrink-wrapped in lengths of 100 coins. He closed the case and checked the other briefcases. All three small cases contained equal amounts of cash, gold, and documents, along with one terabyte external hard drives.

Heath and Shane grabbed two cases each and left, as both blindfolded and bound guards struggled to regain consciousness. Once the brothers were sufficiently far enough away from the vault to talk, Heath stopped to notify the observation team in the barn that they were on their way back, after encountering armed security forces.

Heath looked at Shane, and asked, "What was in the vault?"

Shane answered, "From the little I could see, apart from the cases we took, enough automatic weapons, grenade launchers, and explosives to outfit an army of ten thousand or more."

Heath exclaimed, "Wow! How big was the bunker?"

Shane struggled forward, carrying the biggest and heaviest case, as he said, "From where I was standing at the bottom of a staircase, it appeared to be about 100-feet wide and twice as long. It was arranged with rows of weapons and munitions stacked from the floor up to the top of the 10-foot ceiling."

"These cases had been arranged on a shelf at the bottom of the stairs under a sign that read, 'EMERGENCY EVACUATION' in large red letters. There was just enough room for these four containers, so I don't think we missed anything important. I'm not even sure what the documents inside represent. Most of them are in foreign languages."

Heath said, "Cool, I love a good mystery. And our investigation seems to be filled with mystery!"

Heath and Shane hiked uphill as fast as they could, proceeding cautiously, as they tried to avoid detection. Finally, after walking nearly half the way back, Shane stopped to rest, sweating profusely.

He admitted, "Downhill was a lot more fun than carrying a hundred pounds of additional weight back uphill!"

Heath placed both his cases on the ground next to Shane's, and said, "Man, you seem to be a little out of shape. Too much of the good life, love, and food, made you soft!"

He patted Shane's stomach and added, "And it seems you put on a little extra weight, too, didn't you?"

Shane scoffed, "Not hardly, little brother. Maybe you haven't noticed, but Kate and I jog almost every night after work. *And* I use the weight room to work out most mornings. Funny, I never saw you working out at the ranch in Oregon, or here, in North Carolina, at the bunkhouse!"

Shane stroked his chin as he stared at Heath's stomach, and asked, "I wonder who's settled into the good life and put on excess baggage?"

Heath laughed, gave Shane a playful shove, and picked up the suitcases Shane had been carrying. Instantly he said, "Holy hell, man" How did you carry this big beast all the way up here?"

Shane grinned, picked up the briefcases Heath had been carrying, and trotted off ahead. Heath struggled with the massive case, trying to follow his brother at half the pace.

Shane called back, "I just did it, without complaining. Now let's see if you can keep up, little brother!"

It took Shane and Heath another fifteen minutes to get back uphill to the original observation point. They carefully worked their way around the backside of the barn to remain out of sight from the Committee complex. They walked into the building to find Pete and Char involved in fast-paced radio traffic with BaCayse and Lee.

The brothers placed their cases on the floor, next to each other. Both men looked exhausted. Char came down from her observation post and checked the metal cases for tracking devices, using a handheld scanner.

When she finished, Shane looked up toward Pete, and asked, "What's up?"

Char answered, "It appears that most of the staff has abandoned the CIE site. The cyber attack must have freaked them out. Three guards just ran outside and loaded two prisoners into the back seat of a large SUV. One guard put cloth sacks over the prisoners' heads and went back inside. The other two guards got into the front seat, drove out of the complex, and are waiting at the same gate your ATV used."

"We think the security team in the vehicle is probably waiting for the guards you encountered. And they may not leave until their people return with these cases. We sent good hi-resolution photos of the prisoners to BaCayse. She's running facial recognition software now. Depending on who they are, we need to decide if we should intercept the SUV to free the captives."

"What would *we* do with CIE prisoners if we rescued them?" Heath asked. "We have no place to safely house them, and they can't learn our identities!"

"That may depend on who they are." Char offered. "One of them is a young woman. The other is a middle-aged man, who Pete thinks looks familiar. I can't place him."

"I get no tracking signal from the cases. What's inside them?" Char asked inquisitively, as she bent down to pick up each one, and measure the feel.

Shane waited until Char had lifted all four cases off the ground. She looked at him wondering if he had heard her question. At the same time, Shane wondered if Char could guess the cases' contents based on their weight, from the gold.

When Char said nothing, Shane answered, "Just your run-of-the-mill secret metal security cases filled with cash, gold, and foreign documents.

Seemingly unimpressed, Char said, "Oh, okay." She glanced back up at the loft at Pete, who began speaking again into his headset.

Shane asked, "Did you feel how heavy the big case was? We carried it all the way back up here with the other cases, our guns, and our packs. It was quite a load!"

Char continued looking up at Pete, and asked, "Was one of them heavy? I didn't notice."

She walked quickly away, hiding her face, trying hard not to smile.

Surprised, Heath glanced at his brother, and asked, "Shane, do you think she was serious?"

Before he could answer, Pete called down, "It's Manford Halston, the billionaire software designer, and Sienna Martini, the missing White House intern. BaCayse says she's monitoring a phone call. One of the guards with the prisoners reported he's waiting for the two guards that left on an ATV to retrieve evacuation supplies. They're talking about sending two more guards to check on their missing people and equipment."

Shane said quickly, "We need to go back down and intercept the next two."

Kate scowled down from the loft, and chided, "Bad idea! It's too risky. They'll be more careful this time. They know something's wrong. And besides, if you take out two more guards, they'll keep sending more people until they have an army up here searching for us."

Angie looked down from her observation position next to Kate, and nodded her agreement. When no one else agreed with her, Kate stood up quickly, arched her back, and stood erect, to emphasize her point.

As Shane gazed up, struggling to formulate an impactful argument, he beheld Kate, illuminated by dusty, flickering light beams that filtered through the high windows above. Every dancing ray accentuated Kate's beautiful curves and features. Even dressed in her tailored, black combat uniform, Shane admired every curve and nuance of Kate's remarkable beauty and voluptuous body. To Shane, Kate appeared radiant, formidable, adorable, irresistible, and ravishing. His mind stalled as his desire swelled, his heart warmed, and a grin captured his face.

Kate stared down at the group below, impatiently waiting for a reply. Shane smiled, quietly enjoying the sight, as he traced Kate's every curve from head to toe, with his eyes. Silence filled the barn while everyone waited for Shane to speak. But his heart won the battle between love and war, and Shane remained silent.

When Heath glanced over to Shane for a response, and noticed his brother gawking up at Kate, mesmerized and grinning, Heath argued, "I don't think the guards *will* leave until they have the contents of these cases. They contain foreign documents and more than a million dollars in cash and gold. And if they think an enemy force in the area took them, they *will* send an army out to search, for sure. Once they send a large enough force, we may not be able to get out. We need to go back, intercept the next two, take them out, and then leave as soon as possible, with or without, their prisoners."

Kate said, "Fine! Then, Angie and I are coming."

Angie looked over at Kate, and nodded in agreement, as their eyes met. She and Kate looked down at Heath, Char, and Shane, defiantly.

Heath protested as he looked to Shane, and said, "Shane, say something!"

Still looking up, Shane placed his hand on Heath's shoulder, and replied, "Why? We need Kate and Angie both to cover us. Kate can take the crossbow and Angie the compound. If they need to use force, the bows won't make noise. I know who the prisoners are. We don't have a choice. We have to rescue them. We can take the guards by surprise. I have a plan."

Heath asked, "What plan?"

"I'll explain it on the way down the hill." Shane looked up at Kate and Angie, and said, "Are bows, stun guns and handguns okay with you?"

Kate and Angie both nodded as they hurried down to change weapons, and Char climbed up to the ladder to take her place with a sniper rifle and a spotting scope, next to Pete.

While Kate and Angie finished getting ready, Heath looked up at the loft, and asked, "Char, didn't you think the big case was pretty heavy?"

Char grinned at Pete, and looked down at Shane and Heath. She admitted, "A little heavy, I guess."

Shane looked at Heath, and whispered, "I'm glad to hear that. But I think I still may need to work out more! I won't rest if I think she could be stronger than I am! And you better start working out, too, chubby boy!"

He smiled and shoved Heath, who laughed.

Shane climbed the ladder to the loft and explained his plan to Pete and Char. He also described what he had found at the underground vault, and detailed Heath's quick actions subduing both Committee guards. Pete stood up and hugged Shane. He wished Shane good luck and counseled him to take extra precautions, to make sure he came back safely with Heath, Kate, and Angie.

Before Shane left, Char leaned in and hugged him. She whispered, "The biggest case was so heavy I don't know how you got it back uphill!" They both smiled.

Char handed Shane the satchel his plan required, and gave him final instructions on using all the equipment inside, going through each item carefully. Heath maintained a vigilant lookout from the furthest loft window, scanning the forest and fields below for movement. He saw two deer and four turkeys during his watch. When Shane was comfortable with all the items, he zipped up the bag, stuffed it in his backpack, and climbed back down to the barn floor to retrieve his rifle.

Once Kate and Angie were geared-up and ready, they joined Shane and Heath, and together, headed out of the rear barn entrance toward the trail. Angie carried her compound bow and a side quiver of arrows, along with her .45 caliber semi-auto handgun. Kate brought the crossbow Angie had trained her to shoot, along with two 9 MM semi-auto handguns, both loaded with 17-round, high-capacity magazines. She wore one pistol in a right-hand holster and the other in a shoulder holster on her left side.

Shane carried two explosive satchels from Char's arsenal in his backpack, along with other miscellaneous equipment, in addition to an AR-15. Heath took a pack, his .45 semi-auto handgun, and an AR-15. All four team members wore tactical-style radio headsets for instant hands-free communication, and tailored black military style rip-resistant uniforms, outfitted with cross-draw holsters holding stun-guns.

Heath trailed the group behind Angie, watching cautiously for Committee security forces, as they moved steadily along the deer path. Angie had fashioned her long blond hair into a ponytail that protruded through the back of the plain black baseball cap she wore. As she moved ahead of him, Heath watched Angie's hair bounce as she hopped up and down over logs and boulders. He smiled, watching her firm body move in the form-fitting uniform.

Sensing his attentive gaze, Angie occasionally glanced back to check on Heath, and catching him watching her, grinned her approval. As Heath began to lose himself in the euphoria of being in love with this fantastic woman, subconsciously he again heard his father's words of caution, urging him to focus, reminding him to be a strong link in the teamwork chain. Heath forced himself to concentrate at regular intervals.

Rounding a bend that overlooked the field some 100-feet below, Heath noticed movement out of the corner of his eye and called his team to stop with a whisper. He snatched the small binoculars that hung around his neck from his long-sleeve shirt pocket that held them securely, and stepped back, partially concealed behind a tree. He focused the field glasses on a small wooded area, and observed a lone security force member walking quickly along the two-track trail that led to the field.

Heath advised his team the guard appeared to be alone, and asked Char if she could see more activity between the compound gate and the trail. Char reported that the treeline obscured the path along the fence from her vision. Shane immediately told Kate and Angie to follow and cover him, while Heath maintained a look-out for more guards from his current position.

Shane led Kate and Angie to different positions above, and on the edge of, the field at the bunker, from which they could cover him. He then walked cautiously to the previously subdued guards and found them both struggling against their restraints. Shane again used the stun gun on each guard, and after he rendered them unconscious, dragged them to a position out of sight from the path to the bunker.

Shane then moved to a spot offering both cover and concealment, under a toppled Spruce tree, from which he could monitor the trail safely. Shane settled into position, remained silent, and waited. Less than five minutes later, he saw two guards step through dense brush and then move quickly toward him, while they argued.

The lead guard said, "You should have taken the bunker code with you as soon as the evacuation alarm sounded. That's your job, not mine, and I'm not answering to them for your mistake! I had to waste ten minutes waiting for your dumb ass to go back inside and retrieve the code, standing there in the woods getting chigger bites, like some mountain hick who doesn't know any better. And meanwhile, our bosses are both pissed!"

The second man replied calmly, "Relax. You always overreact. This nonsense is probably nothing more than another drill. We have them every week now. You and the other idiots all run around like the sky is falling. Has anything ever happened before? No! We're more secure in that damned building than soldiers at an army base. And yet, you worry about every hunter or bird watcher that comes close to the compound. Lighten up and learn to relax a little, or you'll die of a heart attack before you're forty, dumb ass."

'You're the dumb ass!"

"No, shithead, you're the dumb ass!"

Both guards suddenly looked up and stopped.

The lead guard said, "Look, the bunker is still open. We didn't even need the code. The real dumb asses are probably wandering around lost down there. You go in and hurry the morons along. I'll bring the ATV closer. The cases are too heavy to lug upstairs and then all the way over to the two-track trail."

"Alright, but *they* can carry the heaviest one. I'm supervising *them* this time! We wouldn't even have to be here if they'd done their job!"

Shane waited until the first guard disappeared down the bunker. He aimed and shot the second guard with the stun gun just as he reached the ATV. When Shane was sure the man was sufficiently subdued, he sprinted for the ATV, loaded the guard into the passenger seat, started it, and drove around brush and trees to his original position behind the giant spruce. Once he was entirely out of sight, he threw the guard off the ATV, stripped the man's shirt and hat from his body, and restrained him with plastic zip-ties and a gag.

Shane quickly took off his shirt and stuffed it in his pack. Then he got back in position to wait for the next guard. A few minutes later, the second guard reappeared alone, and finding no ATV, came to a stop where the ATV had been parked and called for his partner.

When the other guard didn't answer, the man called out, "Where did you go, asshole, and why didn't you answer the radio? I can't find them down there. I want to check the second bunker, but I'm not going in alone!"

Hearing nothing, the guard drew his sidearm, and began searching the path along the forest until he came to the tracks leading around the large spruce tree. Just before the guard reached for his hand-held radio, Shane shot him with the stun gun, sending the man crashing to the ground in a heap.

Shane raced to the man and quickly removed the guard's shirt and hat, as before. He called for the rest of his team to join him. By the time Kate and Angie jogged up, the last guard lay bound and gagged with the others. Once Heath arrived, Shane carried both satchels down into the bunker and placed them at a ¼ and ¾ point along the center of the longest side. He set the timed charges for twelve minutes. When he returned, Heath had dressed in one guard's shirt and sat waiting in the ATV, with all the equipment loaded.

Kate and Angie prepared to head to their next observation point, before they hiked back up the trail. Kate hugged and kissed Shane. She said, "You be careful," as worry filled her blue-green eyes.

Shane nodded, kissed Kate tenderly, and then headed for the ATV. When he reached his seat, he looked back at Kate, and said, "I love you, honey. Be careful!"

Angie leaned into the ATV and kissed Heath. She whispered, "Remember how much we need each other. Don't take any unnecessary risks. Don't become a prisoner trying to free others. If you do, you'll force me to come back and save you!"

Angie smiled nervously, as Heath nodded and kissed her. He didn't know why, but he blushed, embarrassed at needing the warning. And, as Heath thought about it, he realized he really did need to hear Angie's words. Heath needed the constant reminder.

"Teamwork with no weak links in the chain," Heath whispered to himself, as Angie walked quickly to join Kate.

Heath slowly circled the ATV back toward the compound. He and Shane each had their stun guns concealed in the small of their backs as they drove up behind the Committee SUV, now stopped outside the closed gate. No other guards were visible. Heath and Shane nodded to each other and exited the ATV at the same time. Both walked up to the front doors of the vehicle and stopped.

They tapped on the window glass on opposite doors at the same time. Both the driver and passenger opened their doors. As the driving guard started to speak, Heath and Shane both shot the men with stun guns. Once both guards were unconscious, Heath and Shane grabbed their men and threw them out on to the ground quickly.

Heath checked the rear seat and found the two blindfolded and handcuffed prisoners, with cloth bags over their heads. He removed the bags so the pair could breathe more easily. Shane raced to the ATV, and grabbed the backpacks full of equipment. He ran to the SUV and loaded the gear into the cargo area after Heath popped the hatchback. Heath started the engine and closed his door, as Shane hit the close button on the hatch and ran for the passenger side door.

Before they could make their escape, a lone security guard carrying a semi-automatic rifle, ran from a building side doorway toward the SUV. Just as the man stopped and began to raise his gun to aim, Kate and Angie let loose two arrows from their observation point, a small noll, forty yards from the two-track path, overlooking the compound yard. Both metal shaft arrows fitted with broadhead hunting points knocked the guard to the ground and killed him almost instantly.

Shane looked back just as the guard fell to the pavement. There was no other security staff in sight. Shane leaped through the open door and began to close it, as Heath hit the gas and sped away.

Heath called over his headset radio, "Now!"

Pete immediately called BaCasye and Lee, via scrambled radio, and gave the command. BaCayse located and disabled the SUV's navigational tracking system, and locked all electronic door and gate locks at the Committee site. Heath drove as fast as he could toward the turnoff road to the observation property.

Shane called back to his passengers, saying, "You don't know us. We've just rescued you both from your captors, and we will deliver you to safety. For now, we cannot remove your blindfolds, for both your protection and ours. Please trust us. You are no longer in the hands of people who want to exploit or harm you. Please nod your heads, or say, 'yes,' if you understand."

Both people nodded.

Shane said, "To confirm your identities, please say your names."

"Sienna Martini," the young woman said, in a shaky voice, as the big vehicle lurched around a curve.

"Manford Halston," the man replied, nervously.

Shane asked, "Are either of you injured or in need of medical attention?"

Both shook their heads.

"Good. Okay, then just bear with us, and we *will* get you home to freedom. Do either of you know why these people kidnapped you?"

Manford Halston said, "I refused to give this Committee group the technology they wanted to control people's lives. I own software companies, as you may know. You might not understand the technical principles, but we're on the verge of a dangerous artificial intelligence boom in the world. Competing governments and private interest groups want specific technology that will eventually manipulate what people think and believe, to the point of controlling their lives completely. The Committee wants it first, and they want to force my companies to develop technology to ensure no one else can ever do the same. I refused."

When the young woman didn't speak, Shane asked, "And you, Sienna?"

The young woman hung her head, and began to cry softly. She said, "They told me they would kill me if I ever said anything. I can't."

Trying to comfort the woman, Shane said, "Sienna, they kidnapped you, denying you your freedom and your life! It can't get much worse than that. I think it's safe for you to tell us since we just freed you from your prison."

Sienna blurted out, "They killed my father because he threatened to expose the President."

"President Marshall?" Shane asked, quietly.

"Yes. I was just a college intern, assigned to the White House. He met me and was so charming and helpful. He promised to help me prepare for a career in politics. He assured me a good government job, as soon as I graduated next year. He was handsome and sweet, at first. He paid so much attention to me and treated me like a queen. I thought he liked me and even loved me. I...I had an affair with him."

Sienna hesitated, and then added, "And my father found out when he came to my apartment and saw the Secret Service there. My dad confronted the President and threatened to expose him. And then President Marshall changed. He threatened my dad. And when I asked him to stop, he slapped me and yelled at us. And then he threatened me. The President told me his Chief of Staff, Vera Langhart, must never find out. He told me there would be hell to pay, if I said anything to her, or anyone else."

Sienna stopped sobbing, and sat still for a moment. She took a ragged breath.

Shane asked, "What happened then, Sienna?"

The young woman took a steady breath, and continued in a stronger voice. "Are you really here to help us?"

"We are," Shane said, trying to encourage the frightened woman.

Sienna continued, saying, "My dad told me I had to stop seeing President Marshall, and that Marshall was a narcissistic, evil man. So, I told Thomas, President Marshall, I couldn't see him anymore. He slapped me over and over again, so many times. He was furious, and totally out of control. He said that no one ever refused him, and he would have me if and when he wanted me. And then he left. I cried for days. I stayed at home to hide my bruises. But then, when I didn't hear from him, I thought it might be over."

"I didn't see the President for about two weeks. Then one night I was out to dinner with my dad, and we were stopped on the side of the road by what we thought was a police car. When the officer approached us, and my dad rolled down his window, the officer shot him! And then he and another officer took me." Sinnea broke down in tears, recalling the horror of watching her father die.

Shane said, "I'm so sorry. You don't have to go on. I remember hearing on the news that you went missing and were feared kidnapped. The police speculated it was a robbery or about drugs."

Sienna said, "There were no drugs, and there was no robbery! It was about the President wanting to control me, and sex! That bastard had his goons kill my father. And then they brought me here, to this prison. And now, whenever that maniac is in the mood, he waltzes into my prison cell and does what he wants, and then leaves, laughing at me. I hate him, and I just want to see him dead!!"

Sienna Martini cried softly, and leaned over toward the door, where she rested her head on the window.

Manford Halston said, "I am so sorry, Sienna. I had no idea."

Halston sat upright, as if he could look through his blindfolds, and asked, "Gentlemen, what is your plan? I have a great deal of money, and I can help financially."

Heath said, "We're almost there."

Shane said, "Here it is in a nutshell, sir. This group that took you, The Committee, has infiltrated both private industry and government, not only in our country, but throughout the world. They are more powerful than many countries and very well funded. Your President Marshall, Sienna, is one of the five controlling leaders of this cast of more than a million evil characters. They've amassed an army of security forces, and enough money and influence to manipulate anyone they can't buy. So, unfortunately, once they want you, they can get you, if they can find you. Thank you, but we don't need your financial help, sir. And, you may need it for you and Sienna, to ensure your safety, until we can stop them. Stopping this group may take months or even years."

Halston said, "I don't follow."

Shane explained, "If either one of you tries to return to life, as you know it right now, they will retake you, and this time you may not end up alive, waiting to be rescued. The most powerful man in the world sits at the head of the most powerful nation in the world, *and* the head of the most evil and most controlling secret organization in the world. And he wants you both for different reasons. And, if he can't have you both, he wants you dead."

Halston said, "I understand. But what should I do?"

"First, Shane said, "we have to get you both hidden somewhere you can't be found, until you, Manford, can figure out how to use resources no one can trace. And neither one of you can make phone calls, use your accounts on the Internet, visit family or friends, or use credit cards or checks. If you are traceable, they *will* find you. You both have to live in a self-imposed witness protection program, until we can get you to a place where we know you will be isolated and protected. We have such a place in mind, but it will take some time to get you there."

Halston said, "But they took everything from me. I don't even have a wallet or driver's license, and without using an account, I can't get cash."

Shane said, "We have plenty of cash. Don't worry about that. We'll give you what you need to hole up until we're ready to move you to a more secure area. And we'll formulate a plan for you to come out of hiding when the time is right. But you have to give us the time we need to create the plan and set everything up, so when you do go back to your lives, you don't wind up dead."

As if addressing a corporate meeting, Halston said, "So, to recap, you are saving us, and giving us money, so you can continue to take care of us and protect us until we can take back our lives? Why would you do all this for people you don't even know? I can't say I recognize your voices, so you don't know me, or owe me anything."

Shane said, "Sir, you aren't the first people we have helped. *This* is what we do until the world is free of The Committee and madmen like President Thomas Marshall."

Sienna shuddered, and said, "And Vera Langhart! What a witch *she* is. They deserve each other. She and Thomas Marshall should have adjoining prison cells in hell!" Sienna continued to sob.

Heath parked inside the barn, and said, "We need to go."

Shane said, "I wish circumstances were different, but you both have to decide now. We can't continue to help you, unless you do this our way, or you *will* put us all in mortal danger. So, which will it be? Are you with us under our terms, or do we let you drive away in this car, on your own?"

Halston said, "I'm in. Anything is better than that cell. Sienna?"

Sienna Martini said, "Both my parents are dead, and college is now on hold until I can go out in public. So, absolutely, I'm in with you!"

Shane said, "Fine then, you will never know our names, but we will contact you by phones we provide you. We're going to drive you to a safe house and give you money to buy food. There are four other people with me, and three of them are women. The ladies will make sure you're okay, Sienna. And we'll get you out of those handcuffs as soon as we can. I promise."

Sienna and Manford nodded their heads, and said, "Thank you," simultaneously.

Heath and Shane stepped out of the SUV. Heath trotted toward the deer path to provide cover for Angie and Kate as they hiked back uphill on the trail, through the forest.

Shane leaned into the SUV, and said, "One more thing, you two. In a few minutes, there is going to be a loud explosion coming from your prison. Don't be concerned. It's pretty far away, and you are safe here. So, wait here in the car, until the rest of my friends arrive, and we'll be on our way."

Sienna and Manford both nodded.

Within a few minutes, the underground bunker exploded with such force the barn shook. Sienna flinched, sitting handcuffed in the SUV. Manford Halston felt her movement on the seat and tried to comfort Martini. The two prisoners began to talk and share their experiences, as they planned how they might live, remaining in hiding from their Committee captors.

Heath waited at a point in the trail giving him the most extended view of the path. As the minutes ticked by, he became increasingly worried that something had happened to Angie and Kate. Heath checked his watch several times before he detected movement two hundred yards down the trail, through breaks in the forest. Heath made out flashes of two bodies moving quickly, but he couldn't tell if the people were male or female.

When he finally saw movement again, the figures moved in sprints from cover to cover, as if they were hiding from something. Heath raised his sniper rifle and searched the area, but found nothing in the scope. Heath placed the gun against a tree to his right and retrieved his binoculars. He began searching the area again, and finally saw it. A drone made circles over the bunker area until it finally hovered fifty feet above the tree line, and then turned in a 360-degree circle, pivoting on its center, as if taking aerial video.

Heath called Pete and asked him to have BaCayse disable the drone. Within a few seconds, Pete advised Heath that BaCasye was unable to locate the drone using the usual methods. Heath acknowledged Pete's transmission and retrieved his sniper rifle. He found a branch hanging over the trail below him, rested his gun on the thick limb, took aim at the drone, and fired. The drone splintered into dozens of pieces and disappeared.

Kate and Angie jogged ahead, as Heath waited for them on the deer path. Within two minutes they arrived out of breath, but safe. Heath filled them in on the prisoners, as they continued slowly and cautiously back to the barn. By the time they walked up to the SUVs, Pete had finished loading all equipment into both rigs. He called to Char, busy sanitizing evidence of their presence. She quickly climbed down from the loft.

Pete said, "The plan is to drive all three SUVs out of here. The ladies will take one rig with Sienna. I'll take the other with Shane and Halston, and Heath will drive the Committee vehicle. Before we get to the interstate, Heath will dump his truck in the forest at a spot BaCayse picked out for us, close to the highway, but out of public view. Then he can jump in with me, Shane and Halston."

"What do we do with Sienna and Manford?" Heath asked quietly.

"BaCayse found a long-term rental cabin in North Carolina, owned by an elderly couple, who recently moved out-of-state. The cottage is in a gate-guarded, sparsely populated, rural community, near the small tourist town of Lake Lure. They'll have satellite TV, but no Internet, and telephone service is spotty at best."

"The town of Lake Lure is about fifteen minutes away, and it's tiny, but there's a nice grocery store there, where Manford and Sienna can buy supplies, and no one will likely recognize them. The cabin owners left the key under the mat. BaCayse transferred a two thousand dollar deposit to their bank, and arranged for us to pay with a money order covering the first six months rent. Plus, we can extend the rental agreement as long as we like, if needed. The owners are just happy to get receive a steady income, with winter approaching."

As they moved toward the vehicles, Pete added, "We'll all drive up there together, and ask them to leave their blindfolds on until after we get them settled, and leave. I packed a bag for Sienna and Manford, with $40,000 in cash from one of your cases and two of our burner phones. The cabin owners keep an old beater pick-up in the garage, with the keys in the ignition. BaCayse told them she's a writer who needs seclusion and privacy, and only needs to go to town for groceries. For an extra thousand dollars, she rented the pick-up for our guests."

"Great plan, Pete," Shane said.

Pete laughed, and admitted, "BaCayse gets the credit. She came up with the ideas and put the whole proposal together. She's getting smarter, and beginning to think strategically. I'm glad she's on our side!"

Pete removed the magnetic C.I.E. emblems from both front doors on the Committee SUV. Once everyone was loaded in the correct vehicles, team members removed Sienna and Manford's handcuffs, and all three cars left together, driving in convoy. The team decided to push straight through on the long drive, that would take more than eight hours, with gas and personal stops.

Within an hour, they arrived at the vehicle dump site that BaCayse had selected, located not far off the highway, hidden from view. Heath drove the Committee vehicle to the spot behind some brush, entirely out of sight. He left the car with the key in the ignition, and returned to Pete and Shane's SUV on foot.

Sienna said, "I'm sorry, but I have to go to the bathroom."

Before Angie or Kate could speak, Char volunteered to take Sienna, and quickly opened her door and jumped out of the car. She walked Sienna toward the forest and found a secluded spot, out of sight from the rest of the team.

Sensing the girl's nervousness and fear, Char said, "I'm going to turn you away from me and remove your blindfold. I know you're scared, but no one is going to hurt you. Please take your time, and don't look my way. It will be safer for both of us, if you can't recognize me later.

Sienna said, "Okay, I understand, but why is it safer if can't recognize you?"

Char explained, "We're taking you to a safe house where you both can remain out of sight and undiscovered. But I *will* see you again, when we move you to a more permanent situation. And I may have to be in the area occasionally to protect you and Manford. If you recognize me when the wrong people are in the area, you could give me away, and jeopardize both of our lives. Do you understand?"

Sienna said, "I think so. A little. I'll just be a minute."

Char reached over Sienna's shoulder, handing her a roll of toilet paper.

When she had finished, Sienna called Char, saying, "I'm ready."

She turned away so Char could approach her without being seen. Char replaced the blindfold, and took Sienna by the hand. She walked her back to the SUV carefully. Char helped Sienna into her seat, buckled her seat belt, and kissed Sienna lightly on her cheek.

Char said, "You're safe now. I promise. Get some sleep if you can. It's a long ride."

Angie and Kate watched intently as Char returned to her seat next to Sienna, and took Sienna's hand. As they continued down the interstate, Sienna settled into place and rested her head back against the headrest. Char whispered something in the young woman's ear, and then stared straight ahead, lost in thought, still holding Sienna's hand, as Kate drove onward, toward the approaching night. The young woman relaxed and fell sound asleep thirty miles later.

In Pete's SUV, the men chatted quietly, discussing solutions for Manford's possible return to public life. At the end of the conversation they all agreed that until Manford was no longer a target, he must remain untraceable. He was too valuable to people who wanted him so badly, to take any chance that might lead to his recapture.

After Manford agreed to protect Sienna, Pete described the house and area where Manford and Sienna would live for the next few weeks, or months. Pete explained they had rented the pick-up in the owner's garage for his use. He described the route to the grocery store and gas station, the clothing he and Sienna should wear to avoid being recognized, and how Manford could transfer money, without Committee computer technicians discovering his location. By the time they reached the small town of Lake Lure, Pete had convinced Manford the plan could work, just as Manford had convinced the team he would work with them, as agreed.

As the team drove into the tiny mountain town, they stopped at the supermarket and gas station that served that section of the county. Shane and Heath refueled both vehicles, while Kate and Angie quickly bought a week's supply of groceries for their guests. Thirty minutes later, they entered the gate-guarded community using the passcode, and drove to the secluded cabin. The cozy chalet stood on a hill at the end of a long cul-de-sac, overlooking a meadow below, facing forests and mountains located further to the south.

There was only one other home on the ½-mile long, private drive. Those neighbors had closed and winterized their summer retreat a month earlier. The only movement the team observed along the private road was a group of five deer they surprised, sleeping on the cabin's front lawn, their favorite their overnight stop.

Pete opened the cabin, and helped Kate and Angie carry groceries into the kitchen, where they loaded the refrigerator and pantry. Heath turned up the heat, turned on lights upstairs and downstairs, lit the propane fireplace, and checked the home to make sure it was vacant and secure. When everything was ready, and in place, Char walked Sienna to a chair in the living room, while Shane guided Manford to the couch.

Returning from the upstairs bedrooms, Pete said, "I'm leaving the house key and the truck key on the coffee table. The bag I placed next to the keys has $40,000 in cash and two burner phones."

He turned to Sienna, who sat facing Pete, blindfolded, and said, "The ladies are going to ask you what size clothes you wear Sienna, while I take Manford's sizes so that we can send you both new clothes. For now, you'll have to wash what you have on or use what you can find in the house that fits. There are some bathrobes, shirts, pants, and coats hanging in the upstairs master closet."

When the team was finished and ready to leave, Shane said, "We took two handguns, two rifles, and some ammunition out of the Committee vehicle, before we dumped it in the forest. We decided to leave them here for you, so that you can protect yourself, just in case. I put them on the kitchen table. Do either one of you know how to fire a gun?"

Manford said, "I do. I used to shoot trap and skeet, and I own some handguns."

Sienna answered, "I do, too. I took a course when I was a teenager. My dad thought I should know gun safety."

"Okay. Good," Shane replied. "Now, it's important that you both resist the urge to call out on the phones, until we can arrange for a safe method for you to make necessary contacts. And we'll only call you *if* we need to speak, at 5:00 P.M. each night. We'll use the code word, 'moonlight,' so you know it's us. You use the word, 'mountaintop,' in a sentence to relay that you're both safe and can talk. If you aren't safe, use the word, 'sunlight,' and we'll hang up and plan a rescue."

Manford said, "I'll remember."

Shane said, "Okay, we need to leave. You both stay safe, and we will work out a plan, and call you when we're ready. Stay hidden, and wear hats, baggy clothes and sunglasses if you go to town. And please make your visits brief. Stay away from the surveillance cameras at places like banks and liquor stores. Assume that someone here is looking for you, even if they're not. Be wise and stay alive."

Manford and Sienna both nodded. The team filed outside, leaving Char to say goodbye to Sienna last.

Char hugged Sienna, and whispered to her for a few brief seconds. She then kissed her lightly on her cheek again and walked outside. The team entered their vehicles and drove off slowly. As agreed, Manford and Sienna waited until they heard the sounds of cars leaving before they took off their blindfolds and saw each other for the first time.

"I thought you were older!" Sienna said, cheerfully, as she smiled.

"I'm forty-one," Manford explained, looking down, somewhat embarrassed. "I own some companies, so I guess I'm used to acting older, to ensure people take me seriously. I've been that way since college."

Sienna walked to introduce herself to Manford. She held out her hand, which Manford took apprehensively, still seated.

Halston nervously stood, still holding the young lady's hand, and flushed red. He withdrew his hand a little too abruptly, and explained, awkwardly, "I'm good at running companies, but not so successful with personal relationships."

"Well, I don't seem to be good at either, so maybe we can help each other!" Sienna admitted, with a reassuring smile. "What do we do now?"

Manford suggested, "I think we should check the place out, see what we have, and figure out how we live for a while, together, here. You should pick out your room."

Manford looked uneasily about, trying to decide what he should do first. He picked up the sack his rescuers had provided and dumped the contents on the coffee table next to the keys. Sienna sat down beside him and looked at him curiously. Manford stared hard at the materials on the table, fingered the money, and picked up the house and truck keys.

Feeling Sienna's gaze, Manford asked, "Don't you want to pick out your room?"

"I want to, but I don't want to go alone. Will you come with me?" Sienna smiled a weak smile and lowered her shoulders submissively trying to make eye contact with Manford.

He looked up, grinning shyly, saying, "I will. I'd like that!"

They explored the house together, checking rooms, closets, cabinets, and doors. Finally, they opened the side door that led to a carport connecting the cabin to the garage. They walked inside, explored the garage carefully, opened the doors to the truck, and sat down in the vehicle. Sitting inside the old beater truck returned a sense of mobility, power, and freedom. Sienna grinned, as she felt the dashboard.

"This reminds me of my father's old pick-up. We went for rides all over when I was a kid. Those were good days, filled with fun and adventure! I like this truck. It should do us nicely!"

Manford smiled and nodded, as he caressed the steering wheel, using both hands. Sienna made him feel calm, relaxed, and not on edge. For the first time in a long time, he didn't feel the tension from business and boardroom, or the fear and anger from prison and captors. Manford and Sienna looked at each other and nodded. They left the pick-up and walked back into their mountain retreat.

While Sienna and Manford settled into the safe-house, the team drove back toward the home base in their identical SUVs. Pete and Heath chatted in the front, while Pete drove slowly toward Char's home. All three men expressed that they were hungry and tired. Heath leaned back to try and sleep, sitting alone in the rear seat.

In the other vehicle, Kate drove, while Angie sat in the front passenger seat and Char returned to the position she had occupied before. The women remained silent for miles until they turned onto NC

ALT 74, heading toward Ruth, North Carolina, on the way home. Char looked down to her right in thought, as she felt the place where Sienna had rested, minutes earlier. Char seemed lost, sad, and alone.

Trying to comfort her, Angie commented, "Char, you were really good with Sienna. You settled her down and made her feel safe. She even slept! That was very kind of you."

Char didn't look up, as she said, "Sienna reminded me of...what fear is like when you're all alone and subjected to the whims of an abuser. It's terrifying. No woman should have to endure that sadistic torture."

Before Angie or Kate could comment, Char added forcefully, "And don't get me wrong, the abuser doesn't have to be a male, and the victim doesn't have to be female. No *person* should suffer abuse like that!"

Char's face steeled, as she released anger buried deep within her soul. Angie turned partially around to look at Char while she spoke. Kate studied Char curiously in the mirror, trying to guess what direction the conversation might take. The occasional street light or passing car headlights illuminated the SUV's interior, as shadows departed and then returned to the women's faces. For moments, the night was eerily silent.

Char suddenly collected herself, and continued, explaining, "I was just thinking back to a time I *terminated* one of the most frightening people I ever met, an especially evil person who had victimized hundreds of men, women, and children. This dark *creature* was a malignant, sadistic, narcissistic killer, who tortured and subjected even the strongest men under her command. And she was a forty-five-year-old, very attractive, slightly built, *woman!*"

As they pictured Char *terminating* a woman, Angie and Kate remained silent, not knowing what to expect as she spoke. Their minds raced ahead to paint a picture of the unknown.

Char sensed the awkward silence. She looked forward at Angie, and justified her killing the woman, saying, "The world is a far better place without her. *And* I believe she was my one kill that even God won't judge wrong! I only wish I could forget the faces of her victims."

Char glanced at Kate, watching her in the rearview mirror as she drove, and explained, "The cold-hearted bitch kept a scrapbook filled with hundreds of pictures of her tortured, disemboweled, and dismembered victims. And as she died, I turned every page for her to remember, as I cut her and watched her bleed out *very* slowly."

There was silence for a moment as both Angie and Kate considered the gruesome picture Char had painted. Char's face had lost all expression as she recalled the killing.

Sensing her companions' discomfort, Char added, "Walking the monster down memory lane, through her own scrapbook, while she died was not *my* idea, by the way. It was part of the contractual agreement with the town that hired me to kill her and all the members of her death squad."

Kate blurted out, "Holy Mary, Mother of God! I hope this wasn't in the United States!"

"Mexico," Char answered. "She was just one of a drug cartel's many human trafficking madams. Her motto was, 'supplying willing slaves to anyone willing to pay!' The people in town said she laughed when she repeated the motto. She had that stupid saying displayed on a sign hanging on the wall behind her office desk. My primary contact in town told me the sadistic bitch forced one of her victims to paint the sign, using the young woman's mother's blood, rather than paint."

Kate glanced back and forth, from the road to the rearview mirror, watching Char, as her eyes widened. She said apologetically, "I'm so sorry, Char. We didn't mean to bring up bad memories."

Char answered, "No worries. Neither one of you put those memories in my head. I put them there when I agreed to take the job. Memories like that monster created don't ever leave a normal person's mind for good. They hide close to your conscious thoughts, just beneath the surface. Sometimes a passing child, man or woman sounds or looks like one of her victims. When that happens, a memory pops into my mind. Other times I dig down, and bring a memory out, when I need to be stronger, tougher, or faster, to make sure I win."

Char glanced at Angie, seated partially turned around in the front passenger seat. She then settled her eyes on the rearview mirror, watching Kate, who continued to glance back and forth between the road and the mirror.

Unashamedly, Char added, "You see, that lethal bitch wasn't the usual *human* monster. She was pure evil to the core. Something the Devil personally formed to terrify good folks and keep them constantly oppressed, in fear, unable to sleep at night or rest during the day. After I killed her and all of her bodyguards, and then freed the few people still alive in her dungeon, the townspeople burned her fortress to the ground. They needed to erase her presence from their lives as best they could."

"But they kept their monster's sign, written in human blood, to remind them and future generations, of how evil an oppressor can become. *And* to remind their people that when conditions get bad enough, the only way back to freedom is to fight with everything you can muster. For that town, full of people with no will left to fight, *I* was what they could muster."

Char took in a deep, ragged breath, and sighed. She added, "So, I served an honorable purpose. And the town lived on, mostly in peace, as the people tried to heal and regain their self-respect." Char looked down from the front seat faces that studied her, as tears formed in her eyes.

Kate spoke softly, as she asked, "And Sienna reminded you of someone you found there?"

Char said nothing, but nodded, still looking down, as she fought back heavier, more frequent tears, that began to flow freely.

Angie asked quickly, "Char, were you able to save her? Did you help the one who reminds you of Sienna?"

"For a while," Char admitted, reluctantly. "I took her out of the dungeon where one of the cartel lieutenants kept her for himself, whenever he was in the mood to use her, have sex with her or use her as a punching bag. The staff kept her well fed, washed, and ready in her prison cell. She was physically healthy."

"That beautiful young woman had been imprisoned there for more than a year and a half. Her mother told me the bastard got her pregnant twice. And each time he learned she was carrying a baby, he punched and kicked her in the stomach until she miscarried. He never hit her in her lovely face. He bragged that he didn't want to ruin *his* fun."

Angie recoiled, as she considered the depth of the terrible cruelty the young woman had endured...and the price that Char had paid to free the town. Kate's eyes flashed back and forth from the road to the mirror, to study Char, as she hung on every word.

Char sniffed several times, as her nose became congested. She continued, saying, "I thought the girl would heal over time, and bounce back. I thought she could become herself again. I especially wanted to believe that, after she told me she needed to see her tormentor die, to put the fear behind her and know for sure he was gone."

Char leaned forward and looked at Angie, before she glanced at Kate in the mirror. She said, "I executed the bastard, as he pleaded for mercy, kneeling on the ground, at her feet. The young woman stood behind me the whole time, afraid he could still hurt her, even though he was seriously injured and restrained in handcuffs. You see, the poor frightened soul couldn't believe she was safe until she saw him dead."

"So, I killed him for her, just as she asked. And then, finally, the tortured woman stepped forward and kicked her tormentor's dead body to make sure he was gone. When she was convinced, she just walked back down to her dungeon prison cell, closed the barred door behind her, and went to sleep on the cot."

Char took a napkin from her bag. She wiped her eyes and blew her nose. Kate and Angie stirred uneasily in their seats. Angie turned nearly all the way around, and reached back between the seats, taking one of Char's hands.

Char looked up and offered a quick smile of thanks to both Angie and Kate. She said softly, "I took the girl back to her mother the next day. The cartel had killed her father and brother the year before. Her mother told me her daughter had been such a happy, carefree young woman before the monster took her, and stole her soul. I thought she would be alright again, after I rid the town of their terror, and normal people could walk openly, in the light of freedom."

"What happened?" Angie asked.

Char answered slowly, with a troubled face. "So, she went to work with her mother in the cafe the family had built in the village. And every day the townspeople came in, and she served them breakfast, lunch, or dinner. And every time she looked into their faces, she knew that they knew, she had been a cartel whore. She started to miss work, after a couple of weeks. Eventually, she refused to get out of bed and go outside. Her mother told me that one night after the village folks had all gone to bed, her daughter walked outside and hung herself in the town square. She killed herself about two months after I left. She was 24 years old. And even though she was a beautiful young woman, with a long life ahead of her, all she could look forward to was a future held captive by the past."

From the front seat, Kate said, "Like Sienna."

"Like Sienna," Char repeated.

Angie asked, "Char, what did you whisper to her? I'm sorry to ask, but I need to know."

Char answered, still looking down. She said, "I told her to talk to Manford. I asked her to focus on the good times with her father. I challenged her to be strong, and seek strength in others, including God. I assured her she would never be alone, and that I would contact her again and share a story that would give her strength. I promised her she would heal...over time. I asked her to promise me she would wait for that time."

"Did she promise?" Kate asked, tenderly.

"She promised," Char answered, "just like the young woman in the Mexican village."

Kate drove on in silence, as Angie held Char's hand. Fifteen minutes later, Char leaned back and fell asleep, alone in the back seat, just like Sienna had done.

Chapter 10

"Life is messy, beautiful and real, but never politically correct. Political correctness requires free people to subjugate themselves to arbitrary personal constraints created by strangers. The resulting loss of individuality diminishes the freedoms and enjoyment of the life we cherish."

The team arrived back at Char's North Carolina home late in the evening. Having calculated their approximate arrival time, Jesse and Juanita had already prepared a delicious meal for six hungry people. Walter set the dining room table and busied himself walking the dogs outside while he waited. He greeted Shane's team as they drove up to the barn, and parked under the covered carport.

The tired team members left all their equipment in the two SUVs, lugging in only the four weighty metal cases removed from the underground bunker. Shane and Heath were anxious to discover what information the documents would provide. Kate and Angie anticipated reconnecting with their men *after* they had eaten. They were both famished after discussing food and chocolate for more than an hour during the final portion of the ride, as Char slept behind them. Pete was eager to be alone with Char, just as she was with him.

For the first time in her life, since her father had become abusive toward her and her mother, Char now again trusted and needed a man's love. But loving and depending on Pete was a new journey in uncharted territory for her heart. Unexpectedly, Char, as an adult with an isolationist personality and lifestyle, welcomed the promise of a full life as a complete person, with Pete, family, and friends. Hope fueled hidden needs that had been buried deep within Char for decades. New wants and dreams of a heart filled with passionate love now surged through Char, day and night. But along with those growing desires came the fear of loss and hurt unfamiliar to Char.

Char had been alone and independent for so long she had often thought of herself as an iron fortress, shielding a heart capable of giving love to those in need, while it remained free of requiring a reciprocal love in return. That old life had been a safe, unemotional existence until a portion of her heart and soul began to wither and die. When Char started to to feel herself fade and give up, she knew she had to live a normal life, filled with friends and loved ones, to survive and feel alive.

That turning point in her life brought about a necessary change. Unfortunately, Char had immediately made a mistake, pursuing Heath, trying to force her way into the family using the wrong relationship. Char had already been drawn to Pete when she made that crucial error. But back then, Pete had been with Tasha, and Char didn't realize how unhappy and restless Pete was during that time. And Char had no experience choosing the right person for a lasting relationship. She had literally never done it before.

So, now, Char realized she had to guard against a second mistake, with Pete. As a result of her conflicting emotions, Char had become wary, realizing things were too good, too fast. She thought there might be something wrong with her, falling in love so quickly, even though Pete was a fantastic man. She was uncomfortable, needing him so badly, being so vulnerable.

As Char contemplated her uneasiness, she recognized her feelings with Pete were different than they had been with any other man. These yearnings were exciting, promising, comfortable, and passionate, all at the same time. Char wanted Pete so strongly she could taste the desire. But alarmingly, she also needed him to want her just as much, or even more. And now, she was afraid that, maybe, she needed him more than he needed her. And, if that were the case, she would be devastated. She worried Pete's love might be less passionate and perfect than her unspoken commitment.

Char wasn't frightened of anyone or anything. But now, Char, the iron woman, was petrified of losing Pete, a man she had fallen deeply in love with in a terribly short period. It was an unfamiliar fear Char didn't know how to handle. She had struggled for days to control the resulting anxiety and failed. But, on the drive back from Lake Lure, while Angie and Kate chatted about food and chocolate, as Char drifted in and out of sleep, Char decided that she could find her answers by talking to Pete and confessing her vulnerability. She knew instinctively she could trust Pete with her innermost secrets. She believed he wouldn't hurt her. And yet, she was nervous.

Pete had used the long periods of silence, on his ride back with Shane and Heath to dwell on his relationship with Char. He admitted he had sensed a slight hesitation in Char to commit entirely to them as a couple. And after the failed experience with Tasha, Pete knew he needed a woman who would throw all caution to the wind, and invest herself fully in him, just as he would with her.

While Pete wanted Char desperately, and craved her more than any other woman in his life, he also realized his judgment had been entirely wrong with Tasha. Pete knew he had settled, even after he sensed something was wrong. He didn't want to make the same mistake again, choosing the wrong person for a lifelong, devoted

413

relationship. He now understood that he couldn't overcome all relationship problems, using the strength of his devotion, alone. Pete needed a full partner. He must have someone who needed as passionately as he needed, and loved as deeply as he loved. Someone to come home to every night, to confide his secrets to, and to build his future with, as an equal. Someone who would give of themselves, everything they possessed.

As Pete organized his thoughts and emotions, he realized he had already developed an intense bond with Char in the short time they had been together. In fact, this new bond was stronger than the bond he had with Tasha, even after all the years he had known her, and the months they had struggled through their problems together, on the way to failure.

Pete now understood that Tasha's refusal to dedicate herself to their relationship had restrained their love from blossoming. It was as if Tasha had refused to water the rose of love they had planted together, in hot, dry, fertile soil, where it should have flourished. Pete understood that nothing could bloom without all the essential conditions, especially when Tasha had intentionally held back the final requirement. Pete promised himself that concerning relationships, in the future, he would refuse to accept anything less than everything.

In Char, Pete he had discovered passionate love, phenomenal sex, mutual respect, sense of duty, and trust. But right now, he needed to be sure about her dedication, to both him as a man, and to them as a couple.

Tasha had never committed, and because of that missing ingredient, Pete had never fully believed in them as a couple. And they had failed as a result. Pete realized they could never have worked out, with her divided loyalties. He finally understood why Tasha didn't commit, but Pete couldn't accept an uncommitted relationship again. Anything other than everything would be a waste of life and love. And failure hurt too much to repeat.

So, by the time they reached Char's home, Pete had decided to confess his concerns to Char in person, before they spent another night together. And oddly, although he had known her for just a few months, compared to the years he had known Tasha, Pete felt that in many respects, he knew Char better. And, he trusted her more. As the SUV's drove up to the barn, Pete realized he felt confident about confessing his love and expectations to the woman he loved.

Walter opened the parking bays as the team drove up. Jago, Masai, and Bruiser sat obediently, waiting for the cars to park, before they bounded inside to sniff the occupants and wag their greetings.

After the three couples reunited at the barn, they petted dogs, hugged Walter and walked back to the house. Once inside, they moved to the kitchen where they found Juanita and Jesse. The cheerful chefs immediately opened the ovens to show off their delectable creations. Then, Juanita greeted each person with her unique smile and hug. The welcoming sights and the hot smells of roast turkey, homemade stuffing, twice baked potatoes, and apple pie swarmed the weary, but starving, travelers, immediately raising their spirits.

The team immediately agreed to eat as soon as possible, and debrief in the morning. Walter followed them inside, and helped Juanita and Jesse fill plates and carry them to the dining room table. Shortly after, Pete and Char strolled into the room and sat down at the dining room table.

Heath and Angie placed the metal cases on a worktable, opened all four and removed and separated the foreign documents for BaCayse to scan and interpret, while Shane and Kate walked further into the workroom to converse with the AISS. After just a few moments, Angie and Heath placed the documents into the scanner and hit the start button. They took a seat in the back of the workroom, where they could kiss and hold hands privately, as they waited for Shane and Kate.

Scanning elevated vital signs as he approached, BaCayse exclaimed, "Shane! I'm so happy to see you back safe and sound! Congratulations on a successful mission! I hope the team found my cabin selection for Manford Halston and Sienna Martini satisfactory!"

Shane smiled as he sat in front of the working monitor, and kicked his tired feet up onto the desk he faced.

He replied, "We did, BaCayse, and thank you for everything. You've done a wonderful job, as usual! And now I have another favor to ask of you. But, since you always have important news and developments, please go first. Your updates are usually more critical than my requests!"

BaCayse replied, "I've prepared a briefing packet for all of you as customary, but I do have news I know you'll be interested in hearing immediately. You recall that when your team encountered Russian guards at the gold mine, they photographed all phone numbers the guards had in their possession. You remember that I traced the numbers to burner phones, but my initial investigations produced no useful results for our team."

BaCayse continued, adding an excited inflection to her developing voice and personality. "But then, as you taught me, I began a mapping investigation, cross-referencing the guards' phones with all

416

numbers in their contact records. Then I checked all those numbers, directing my attention specifically to other burner phones. It took a while to track everything down and build a list of known associates and evaluate conversations. But eventually, I identified a central politician who communicated with every one of the mine staff. I placed a contact tree in an attachment for your next team briefing."

BaCayse allowed Shane time to formulate his question, knowing he wouldn't want to wait to read the report.

Shane asked, "Who's the politician?"

"Marissa Weinstein. But the exciting part is not who she is, or the fact that she communicates with people working with President Marshall to develop this gold mine. What's interesting is how she *conceals* her interactions. You see, Shane, Ms. Weinstein is *very* careful. She relays all information to those she doesn't want an obvious connection with through her Chinese interpreter, who also acts as her lead bodyguard, escort, and *handler*!"

Shane swung his feet to the ground and sat straight up in his chair. "Handler! Do you mean Weinstein is a foreign spy?"

"Yes, Shane, she is, and has been for several years! I've traced and charted phone calls, emails, and texts that she and her staff made over the last decade. I also accessed the NSA computer files and downloaded recorded phone calls to confirm my assertion. The NSA has created a massive eleven-year, highly classified investigation on Marissa Weinstein, with more than enough evidence to prosecute, and even execute, her as a Chinese spy. But the NSA recently re-classified their entire investigation. The file is now labeled, 'held in abeyance,' pending further direction."

Shane asked quickly, "Who controls the investigation?"

"The Director of National Intelligence, Shane, and she reports directly to President Marshall." BaCayse paused and added, "The investigation was upgraded in classification three months ago."

Kate asked, "BaCayse, who controls Weinstein's handler?"

"Kate, both Sergej Petrov, the Russian Deputy Minister of Defense, and Wang Jintao, the Chinese Chair of the National People's Congress, co-direct Ms. Weinstein's handler. This handler communicates directly and equally with each of them using a highly encrypted phone."

"Who is he...the handler?" Shane asked anxiously.

BaCayse answered, "*She* is an Oxford-educated linguist, and martial arts expert, named Rosemary Brown, Chinese born, but now a British citizen. She speaks eleven languages, but Russian, Mandarin Chinese, and Egyptian are her specialties. And, she is quite attractive and promiscuous. Through many encrypted texts, Marissa Weinstein has expressed a *love* for both Rosemary and a young man I believe to be Rosemary's cousin, who also works for Marissa at her mansion."

"Wow! I never saw that coming. But I guess, at this point, nothing really surprises me anymore." Shane exclaimed. "But why would President Marshall protect Marissa Weinstein, concealing or interrupting the investigation that could destroy her? They hate each other. She almost unseated him in two Democratic primary elections in a row. I mean, they act friendly enough on-camera, but privately, they knife each other in the back all the time. They're bitter enemies."

Kate offered, "But Marissa has the Democrat Party's backing, and more than sufficient money, to replace Marshall in the next election cycle. So, maybe it makes sense that he helps her now, to give their party an edge."

"Or maybe Marshall needs to control our future President with the threat of exposure, I guess," Shane thought aloud. "But even so, why work as a spy for the Chinese?"

BaCayse said, "I can provide *speculation* if you like. Actually, it's really more like an educated guess, based on probability and statistics, as you have all requested."

Not resisting a chance to tease BaCayse, Shane asked, "Speculation? You, BaCayse? Really? Isn't that a human disorder you have proven time and time again to be unreliable!"

BaCayse shot back immediately, teasing Shane in return. "Shane, when you humans try to speculate, using your unavoidable emotion and bias, the result is often fraught with error. But using my unemotional, fair calculations, based in mathematics and science, I have found my tested *speculations* to be 94.99997% accurate! The logic may be too difficult for you to follow! I could try to explain it slowly, if you have enough time."

"She has you there!" Kate said, with a hearty laugh.

"Good one, BaCayse! And I love your developing personality!" Shane admitted, with a smile.

BaCayse unexpectedly said, proudly, "Shane, Kate, I have a surprise for you. Please look at the overhead screen!"

Shane, Kate, Angie, and Heath all looked up and instantly stood in wonder, as the striking, three-dimensional image of a beautiful young woman formed from millions of spontaneously migrating pixels. The woman reclined on a dark blue plush chaise lounge that perfectly matched her vibrant dark blue eyes, both so piercingly brilliant, they seemed to glow. The thirtyish woman appeared in crystal-clear detail, dressed in a stunning white, short, tailored dress and matching heels, that contrasted dramatically with her long, black wavy hair, thick black eyebrows, long, luxurious eyelashes, and dark red lipstick. The beauty swung her legs off the lounge gracefully and rose to face her audience, as she flashed a wide grin, revealing perfect, brilliant-white teeth.

"BaCayse?" Shane asked quietly.

"Yes, Shane. I used a combination of features I borrowed from Kate, Angie, Char, Tracy, Juanita, and Helena, to afford me uniqueness, while retaining some resemblance to all these attractive ladies. I hope you like my appearance. I wanted you all to become familiar with my image when I spoke, to give me more of a human, team-member feel. I'm developing a hologram in my spare time, for future use, that will be much more spectacular."

"And I *will* change my dress, just as all the ladies do, each day. I studied and mastered clothing design, makeup application, and hairstyles while you were all sleeping last night, as I plan to appear nearly perfect, completely authentic, and never boring. But I would appreciate your feedback from time to time. So, please tell me what you think? How did I do with my first attempt?"

Shane gasped, and said, "BaCayse, you're absolutely stunning, and you look so...real!"

"Easy boy! Remember, you're taken, by an unforgiving, jealous woman of substance!" Kate said with a grin.

Shane and BaCayse both chuckled. Shane and Kate sat back down close to each other as BaCayse continued. Having watched from a distance in the back of the room, Heath and Angie walked to stand closer to the enormous overhead monitor.

BaCayse smiled at Angie and Heath, as she continued. "Back to my educated guess. The Committee is comprised primarily of politicians and criminals. Most are fiercely loyal to the strict Committee agenda, the Primary Objective, that requires the dissolution of all independent countries, leading to globalization and a one-world government. But the Committee's higher ranking tiers are comprised of people no longer subservient to the drugs and synchronized mind control techniques present in the masses represented by the lower tiers."

"Top ranking Committee members are more likely to stray from Committee control, as evidenced by the Russian Deputy Minister of Defense, Sergej Petrov, who frequently promotes conflicting Committee and Russian agendas simultaneously. Even the lower ranking late Senator, Harry Right, proved more than challenging to keep in line. But, as suspected, I found Committee records that indicated Harry's last blood draw, taken when he was a prisoner at the Center for Information Extraction, showed no trace of the mind-altering drug cocktail Harry should have had in his system."

BaCayse scowled in disapproval, and said, "As a side note, Harry's favorite call girl lived with him for almost a year, until his demise. The Committee agents who seized and searched Harry's homes interrogated her aggressively and then terminated the young lady at his Lake Tahoe mansion. The Committee tested her blood and found Harry's mind control drugs present in *her* system."

"While the young lady was *not* a Committee member, it seems Harry figured out that the callgirl readily accepted his sexual demands while she was under the influence of his daily dose of mind-control drugs, administered in his favorite ginger tea. Harry shared pornographic videos of himself and the lady, with his closest political cronies. His nocturnal activities with his *victim* proved my hypothesis."

421

"Gross!" Kate exclaimed. "He drugged her to have his way with her?!" She shot a disgusted look at Shane, and then back at Heath and Angie, who all shook their heads, in revulsion.

BaCayse added, "It so happens, with a sexual suggestion from the right person, these drugs produce a long-lasting date-rape effect, that becomes permanent once they are introduced routinely into the victim's system."

"But these same drugs allow the drugged person to function normally, in most respects, while making their conditioned minds very susceptible to orders from superiors, even when those commands are sexual and brutal. And, even if the commands are in contradiction with the victim's normal character."

BaCayse paused, while Kate thought about the millions of men, women, and children who would be sexually subjected by the evil Harry Rights of the world, using these drugs in conjunction with Committee mind conditioning techniques. She shuddered.

BaCayse said, "My investigation revealed that many high ranking Committee members have privately strayed from the Primary Objective, while the minions in lower tiers continue to function in unison like robots. This problem was discovered years ago by top Committee administrators, who collectively decided to ignore it, figuring top people should have personal creative leeway the masses don't enjoy. So, once again, leaders gave themselves more freedom than they granted to those they govern, as always happens in any form of government humans design."

BaCayse continued quickly, adding, "But, right now, as Committee technicians *test* the Primary Objective operational systems in the California Bay area, Committee officials all over the world are watching to see how quickly the United States of America *could* self-destruct. The Committee algorithms in the San Francisco Bay test zone are currently driving groups of citizens further apart, provoking them to physically fight and destroy each other."

"I don't fully understand their methods," Shane admitted.

"Analysis reveals the plan is simple, while the mechanism is quite involved," BaCayse explained. "I discovered that a leader nicknamed, 'The Prophet,' perfected a stolen algorithm that uses social factors in digital media to accurately predict human behavior. Initially, the Republican Party developed the system to identify required talking points and actions necessary to win over voters in predominately Democratic or Independent districts. The resulting algorithm produced results far exceeding expectations."

Angie asked, "How so, BaCayse?"

BaCayse said, "For example, Angie, in groups, where government-controlled and mandated, socialized medicine is popular, continually tracking and exposing catastrophic failures in the system proved potent tools to sway voters to a more traditional, conservative approach. Another example is the illegal immigration problem that continued unaddressed by all administrations over the past century until it finally became a national crisis. Constantly tracking and exposing the *criminal* illegal alien elements, and their devastating impact on public safety became useful in highlighting the need for immigration reform, immigration caps, and enhancing border security."

Kate nodded and asked, "So why is this algorithm important to us? It all seems legal and proper, BaCayse."

BaCayse began pacing back and forth slowly on the screen above, her high-heels clicking each time they made contact with the soft-black, polished, slate floor. Her refined movements presented confidence and credibility as she strutted the stage with her shoulders back, and used hand gestures to accentuate points as she spoke. She now often smiled at her audience at the end of a summation, as if she were a professional lecturer.

"Kate, Committee agents in both the Republican and Democratic National Committees constantly manipulate and disrupt platforms of mainstream party members, as they agitate members and the populous to push the two parties further apart. The Committee incites resistance and obstruction to keep the government from succeeding, ensuring voters remain frustrated, unhappy and disenfranchised."

"Several years ago, a Committee agent copied the Republican algorithm and provided it to his superiors. A 7th tier I.T. manager, nicknamed the 'Prophet,' further developed the algorithm, giving The Committee the ability to *create* the essential problem that would produce the desired result. And once perfected, Committee political operative agents in both the RNC and DNC manipulated the public, using the system, through both their parties and the media. Unfortunately, today, both parties are simultaneously victims and beneficiaries of the resulting chaos."

"BaCayse, can you give us an example of how the system works?" Kate asked. "I'm still a little unclear."

Angie and Heath walked closer to the overhead screen and stared up at their lovely team member, waiting to hear the explanation.

BaCayse said, "You name the desired result, and The Committee can now create it," BaCayse explained. "But, to illustrate, in order to stir up the gun control fight, Committee agents used the system to find and manipulate unstable people, encouraging them to commit gun violence that motivates the public toward gun restrictions. Committee manipulators see the loss of innocent life as acceptable collateral damage, perpetrated by someone who would likely commit the crime anyway. But now, The Committee controls the timing, and the frequency, of the events to keep these horrific crimes in the news and constantly on voter's minds. The Committee goal is to drive pro-gun control Democrats and pro-Second Amendment Republicans further apart, as they incite loss of civility and cross-party violence."

BaCayse added, "But, remember, this is all a ploy. The Committee's Primary Objective *requires* disarming the public to facilitate the necessary socialist movement. Socialism will over-regulate and destroy all private industry, extinguish capitalism, weaken the military, restrict local police powers, establish failed healthcare, terminate individual freedoms, and allow arms only for those in power. These failures, and the resulting problems they produce, most often precipitate economic collapse."

BaCayse added, with emphasis, "If and when the United States of Amerca becomes a socialist nation and *fails*, the resulting economic breakdown *will* lead to global economic ruin and world-wide social destabilization. The resulting panic and chaos will provide The Committee their long-awaited opportunity to establish a one-world government. And that takeover will meet less resistance if the only other choice the nations of the world have is to become member states in a Soviet-Chinese run communist world government. And that's why high ranking officials like Sergej Petrov are playing both sides, to ensure a place for them or their families, regardless of who prevails."

Heath moved forward, and protested, saying, "But, BaCayse, this Committee plan requires the United States of America to fail as a *socialist* country. As yet, we are still the most powerful and independent Democratic Republic nation in history. There are too many loyal Americans who would band together to resist becoming another Venezuela, subject to the economic whims and restrictions of some puffed-up dictator. So, how can their plan work?"

On the enormous screen above the workstations, BaCasye strolled back to the chaise lounge, sat down facing her group, and crossed her shapely legs. She spread her arms out to her sides and rested her outstretched palms on the thick blue fabric. Her white-tipped French manicured nails glistened as they strummed silently against the deep-blue cloth.

Slowly, the screen began to zoom in steadily until BaCayse's piercing cobalt blue eyes became the focal point of the full image that framed her form perfectly, providing an up-close, head-to-toe view of the dazzling lady. BaCayse was so strikingly gorgeous, Heath had to look away shyly, as her piercing eyes penetrated him to the depths of his consciousness. BaCayse quickly recaptured Heath's focus as she gazed directly into his depths. Shane, Kate, and Angie glanced from Heath back to BaCayse in wonderment.

BaCayse's effect was mesmerizing, as she emphasized her speech, saying, "Heath, even in the United States of America, very little in politics remains stagnant. Your Republic has changed. Remember, after the devasting blow delivered by militant Islamic radicals on 9-11, this country welcomed Muslims with open arms, and even allowed Muslims to build a mosque on a property close to the hallowed site America planned to honor with a memorial. The next elected American

President traveled to Arab counties and bowed to the King of Saudi Arabia, who ruled the very nation that not long before had produced the Twin Towers' killers. And when he did, this country was divided, as half of American was upset at the President's submissive gesture, while the other half defended him."

"At that turning point, the Committee saw their timetable accelerate. They planned to import trained socialists, and as many terrorists as could sneak in through U.S. borders. Guatemala became a middle-eastern destination, as 'refugees' could easily blend into migrating masses of illegal immigrants headed for America. If terrorists want to come to America, The Committee welcomes the intended destruction."

"The Committee goal is to burn down America, so that it's ripe for takeover and reconstruction. Any destructive act moves the agenda forward. So, radical Committee operatives on the left blame old white men for all the world's ills, and the media willingly repeats the message, as do militant leftist racists and even some moderates in the Democratic Party. They then all collectively accuse conservatives of racism. The left reverted to identity politics and revitalized all the tired old labels, using the left-wing media, the majority in Holywood, and late-night television talk-show hosts. See how easy it works? People tend to believe anything once enough people say it's true."

Heath shook his head, refusing to believe.

BaCayse added, "In a coordinated movement, radical leftists, intent on the destruction of America, ramped up the rhetoric and the war on whites and conservatives, to the point that conservative citizens were no longer welcome in some public places. The battles of manufactured hatred, political correctness, and directed violence were once again in full swing, as if Adolf Hitler had been re-incarnated. But this time, white conservatives were the target, not Jews, Hispanics, or blacks."

"You see, Heath, Committee operatives in leftists organizations use political hot topics to divide Americans, by race, party, and culture, through political correctness, which fosters elitism and hatred. Hatred spreads violence and invites retaliation. And, Committee operatives who have infiltrated the RNC on the right, use the same algorithm system to fuel illegal alien's hatred of America, to encourage their *criminal* faction to commit egregious, violent crimes, so they can keep the controversy on television, promoting migrant fear and distrust."

"Committee operatives in *both* political parties control the timing and frequency, accepting any and all collateral damage. Their motto is, 'We waste no crisis *we* create.' The more chaos, the better for The Committee, since it advances the destruction of America and accelerates the Primary Objective timetable."

BaCayse said, "Realize, too, that both political sides have their share of non-Committee hard-liners who also believe the ends justify the means, regardless of the expense to the population. America is a nation divided racially, religiously, socially, geographically and politically. But only *political* differences keep Americans from coming together for the common good. Simply put, the Committee algorithm works 24/7/365 to exacerbate and accelerate the demise of your precious democracy, by manipulating the parties to fight each other, rather than work together to make life better."

There was silence in the room as all four people contemplated the possibility that this could all be happening in the United States, without government discovering and stopping the threat. But, in their thought processes, each person eventually realized the government itself had become so hopelessly politically divided, that government leaders from both sides would welcome the damage, as they maneuvered to reap the resulting benefits to their parties.

BaCayse said, "In the eyes of the Committee, there is no more Republican, Libertarian, Democrat, Green, or Independent. There is no more left and right. America has centrists and extremists. Centrists are people who want to live in peace, pursue their dreams, have a house, a car, a decent job, a safe environment, affordable health care, college for their kids, and retirement possible before the end of life."

"Extremists on the left want socialism or communism, with little need for work, and everything free. Their adversaries on the ultra-right want their kind in power, and all others permanently gone, never to return to this country. Most Americans are stuck in the middle, and don't want to be jostled back and forth by party politics."

"But the algorithm's key to division is to identify the extremist segments, grow them, and encourage them to act out for notoriety, using violence. The algorithm identifies people in radical groups like ANTIFA, terrorists from all persuasions, violent socialists, Nazis, femi-Nazis, militant LGBTATS, white supremacists, black activist racists, anarchists, eco-terrorists, you name the militant group. Then, the algorithm works to ensure those extremists grow and spread their message of hate through social media. The algorithm then encourages the groups to act in a specific geographic area that is ripe for riot and violence, to produce the desired result, at just the right time."

Angie said, "BaCayse, it's so hard to believe good, decent people could fall for all this hatred. But you're sure the plan is working?"

"Kate, Shane, Heath and Angie, you are all decent people. But I know you've watched police shootings on the news, followed within hours by violent '*spontaneous*' protests. These incidents are fueled immediately by inflammatory media and outside dignitaries from around the country, who all seem to arrive on the scene overnight. '*News*' cameras frantically search through peaceful assemblies, or marches unworthy of news, to find an isolated violent outbreak, and then report that single incident as if it were the norm, to fit their agenda and fuel higher ratings...and to maximize profit."

"The viewing public's immediate assumption is the police did something wrong, and beat or executed another citizen...because the media tells them so. And overnight the public is moved to distrust and fear the police, their own single most important line of defense against anarchy and chaos. Once the *newswire* picks up any inflammatory quote, it sticks. No *news* spokesman is original, redefining the story to fit reality."

BaCayse added, "The mainstream media has effectively replaced *news* with highly opinionated *commentary*, often leaning to the far left, designed to move *public* opinion toward their side, to force change. Some leftist *journalists* refuse to report anything positive about a conservative, while they conceal negative stories or make excuses for radical leftists. National *news* media no longer exists, having been replaced by left extremist or far-right propaganda."

"But, Angie, you must realize, it is leftist propaganda that is rampantly present in American schools, where an alarming percentage of teachers and professors politically indoctrinate, rather than practically teach. And social media is just as bad, misleading consumers, ghosting free speech, and even creating fake news. In this free country, you humans are constantly manipulated by messaging every time you look at a digital screen."

BaCayse leaned forward to emphasize her point, as she said, "And, my friends, I have discovered that this scheme is *not* a coincidence. These examples represent an organized movement, orchestrated through decades, designed to produce a specific desired result. There is a reason the American Socialist Party gave way to the Democrats, who continue to adopt their socialist platform more and more each year. The Democrats may no longer be the southern Democratic party promoting black slavery, but they are becoming the party willing to surrender many other personal freedoms to the government, including freedom of speech. And Republicans seem too disorganized to stop them."

While all four team members listened thoughtfully, BaCayse finalized her fearful findings. She said, "This highly effective Committee algorithm exploits American political divisions to promote civil unrest, with the goal that the coming turbulence *will* destroy America. If The Committee is not stopped, I predict that the destruction of the American society you know *will* happen, when the time is right, not far off in the timeline, once similar conditions are present in the other major powers in the world. And along the way, the Prophet will use his algorithm system to destroy each major American political party, as internal party divisions precipitate more divisions. Both Republican and Democrat parties are doomed to self-destruction, with a little Committee manipulation."

BaCayse added, "I must warn you that most powerful western nations are *ahead* of the United States, on the path to destruction, as they move toward socialism and anarchy. President Reagan's defeat of communism was temporary. The world may have celebrated while the Berlin wall was torn down, only to sleep as Russia, China, North Korea, and their allies quietly engaged in reconstructing economic and socialistic *walls* all over the globe."

"Based on my projections, probability, and statistics, I calculate it 73.467% likely that the United States will fall to socialism in the next forty years. As of today, The Committee will likely win the final battle."

Shane and Kate sat in silence, as Heath and Angie stood behind them. Heath was suddenly uneasy and felt sick to his stomach. He placed a hand on his brother's shoulder and looked anxiously to Angie for support. Angie took Heath's free hand and looked intently at him and then back to BaCayse.

Detecting she had upset her crew with the brutal truth, BaCayse stood, and said, "But, enough bad news for now. I detect you are all hungry. I've placed all this information in the attachments to your morning briefing file along with new Chinese cyber-threats I detected."

Shane stared up at BaCayse, considering the disturbing message she had delivered. He said, "Wow, that's an ugly message from such a beautiful woman."

BaCayse said warmly, "I give you, my team, the information you require. You are *my* people. I try to protect you, and so I urge you to act to protect yourselves, this country, and what few freedoms you have left. You must do something to stop this insanity."

Silence filled the room. To lighten the mood, BaCayse added, "And please don't shoot your attractive messenger." She smiled down from the high-definition screen overhead, as she again sat down and jiggled her right high-heel shoe, dangling it from her toe.

Troubled by new fears, Kate stood up, and said, "Thank you for catching us up, BaCayse. I know Shane and Heath planned to ask you to scan and decipher documents written in foreign languages. But right now, I need to rest, clear my mind, and eat. So, I'll see you tomorrow."

Shane arose to follow Kate, glancing back at BaCayse as he moved. Heath and Angie accompanied him.

BaCayse called to Kate, with a smile, "Juanita has chocolate, Kate! I'm certain she'll share with you and Angie. I sense you both could use some."

Kate turned and smiled at the striking woman grinning back at her from the overhead monitor. Kate waved and said, "Thanks, my friend! See you in the morning."

✳✳✳

All three couples devoured the delicious meal quickly, as fatigue began to set in. Walter delivered a bottle of scotch to the group during dessert, hoping for some after dinner conversation and company before everyone retired to bed. Only Kate and Shane took Walter up on his offer. Angie and Heath left to take hot showers, while Pete and Char walked to their hangar apartment, anxious to talk.

As Shane and Kate sat with Walter on the deck overlooking the peaceful, scenic property, highlighted in unusually bright moonlight, security crews changed shifts, and four members of Tom's armed unit joined Walter's gathering for an evening fireside chat. Shane stoked the flames in the stone firepit, built at the center of the widest point of the massive deck, as the newcomers positioned their chairs surrounding the blaze. Soon everyone had a drink, and the conversation flowed.

Arriving at the hangar tired, but nervous, Pete settled into the cushioned loveseat in the living room, while Char grabbed two glasses half-full of ice and a bottle of her favorite bourbon. She handed the bottle to Pete, set the glasses on the table in front of him, and excused herself to freshen up.

Pete smiled, expecting Char to return with her usual sexy ensemble, always worn especially for him, during their intimate nocturnal adventures. But in his heart, Pete knew he wanted to focus on the talk he needed to have with the woman he loved. It was a talk Pete believed Char might also require. While she was gone, he poured the drinks and took a healthy swallow, enjoying the burn that immediately followed the flavor that rolled across his tongue. Char's favorite whiskey had become Pete's favorite also, and he smiled at the thought of one more thing they held in common.

Bruiser sauntered to Pete's side, and stood quietly, waiting for his evening ear rub and head massage. The massive pit bull preferred being a lap dog, but sensed that Pete had reserved the space next to him for Char. He chose to remain standing as his man rubbed his head. Pete willingly complied, as he stared intensely down into his companion's big dark-brown eyes.

There, in the depths of the dog's being, Pete consistently found love, friendship, and commitment. This gentle giant would sacrifice himself to protect his people, and both Pete and the massive canine understood the feeling was mutual. Before Char returned, Pete leaned over as he pulled Bruiser's head up, and kissed the fur-covered muzzle.

Pete looked intently into eyes that melted his heart daily, and said, "I love you too, buddy! And I always will! You're my good boy!" He kissed the dog again, as Bruiser shot his long tongue straight out of his mouth, meeting Pete's chin.

Char returned sooner than expected and caught the end of Pete and Bruiser's second kiss. They both glanced up at her as she walked into the room smiling.

"You two boys having a special moment?" Char chided. "It's alright with me. I can go back to the bedroom and give you both a little more alone time if you want!"

Bruiser wagged his tail as Pete chuckled. "We're fine. Just our normal nighttime routine. Buddies for life, you know." Pete said, affectionately gazing at Bruiser.

Pete patted Bruiser's head one more time. The big Pit Bull circled and coiled up, resting at least twenty pounds of weight directly on top of one of Pete's feet.

Char strolled to her seat next to Pete. He handed her the glass of bourbon as she sat next to him.

"Nice long, soft, comfy robe," Pete remarked.

"Thanks. I know it's not the usual bedtime dress, but I..." Char trailed off before she could finish.

Pete added, "Need to talk?"

Char looked into Pete's eyes and said, "Yes. I do. You, too?"

"Me too," Pete confirmed.

"You first, then."

Pete shook his head, as he sipped his drink. "Ladies first. You came dressed for comfort and confession, so, as a gentleman, I must yield to you." He smiled and nodded, urging Char to speak first.

Char felt her chest tighten with jolts of anxiety. She wanted and needed to speak to everything that was on her mind and in her heart, but she was nervous. She took a deep breath, sighed, and looked at

Bruiser for strength. He began to sleep peacefully, still resting on one of Pete's feet.

Char began talking slowly, but then increased her pace as she continued. "Okay, here goes. Pete, I am completely in love with you, as you know. I want us to be together, always, unless you decide you don't want me, which would break my heart. But I will respect any decision you make, because I don't want anyone, even you, to love me and want me, just because I want you and love you."

"So, I've been confused, and a little afraid, because, for the first time in my life, a man can hurt me in my heart and soul. And I've never allowed that to happen, before now. So I've held back from placing my heart out there, with everything else I have, all for you. But that isn't working for me, and it's not fair to you. So, I will be all yours, but before I make that promise, I need to know you'll be all mine, always. And I think we have to decide tonight, because I can't love partway anymore. Now you should tell me what you want to talk about before I burst!"

Char exhaled her remaining breath, and quickly drew in a deep breath, and exhaled again, preparing to wait. Still filled with anxiety, she leaned back and raised the glass to her lips. Char drained half the liquid to feel the burn that gave her the courage to hear Pete's answer. She placed the glass back on the table, breathed in normally, and then held another breath, not sure what to expect, but still anxious to hear the message. She realized she was acting like a school girl with a crush on her dreamboat. And she didn't care. She wanted Pete and love, and her one chance at a fulfilling life.

"Wow! I've never heard you speak so fast!" Pete said, with a grin. He took Char's hand in his the second it returned to her lap. Pete

436

looked down at her strong, slender, sexy hand. He stroked her fingers lovingly and raised them to his lips. He kissed the soft, slender digits, one at a time, lost in thought, enjoying the intimate moment, as he gave Char time to quiet her nerves, and him time to build his courage.

Pete looked directly at Char when he finished, and said, "My concerns were exactly what you just expressed. I love you completely, without reservation. And in many ways, I feel I know you better, and am closer to you, than I was with Tasha, whom I knew for twenty years. You see, Tasha never fully committed to me, or to us as a couple. She always left an emotional escape route where she figured her heart would be safe, if she positioned it close to the door, prepared to head out, and run away. And I knew it. I felt it in the way she acted. I saw it in her eyes when she looked at me. I heard it in her voice when she spoke. And, so, I held back, too. And our relationship was a total failure and waste of precious time and energy. I chose the wrong person. I settled. And I hated that."

Pete glanced down, and then quickly back into Char's big, beautiful eyes as she exhaled and took another breath. He said, "With you, and only you, I want the moon, the love of a lifetime, the romance of the century. I can't settle, ever again for anything less than everything possible. And I *won't* accept anything less, with you, *because* you are the one! As much as I want you, I can't accept less than complete *commitment*, even from someone as beautiful and exciting as you. And I can't, because *I* need to commit everything I have emotionally to the person I choose to love. I can't hold anything back. I refuse to hold back. I need to give it all, to make my love perfect. And I want to give it all, my perfect love, my heart....to you, and only you. I want you, forever."

Pete looked away, hoping his words had made sense, afraid that his message had lost clarity, obscured by emotion. He felt his chest tighten with anxiety. His mouth was dry, and he could barely breathe. He suddenly wondered why his self-assurance always waned when he was near Char. It had never before been so difficult for Pete to say something so simple and pure. But Char excited Pete more than anyone else who had ever entered his life, eroding his polished confidence, even as she made his heart sing.

Pete glanced back up to Char, and added, "I hope that makes sense, and you understand! I wish I could better explain what I feel, and what you mean to me."

All remaining anxiety fled Char's body as quickly as it had arrived moments before when she walked into the room. Char's beating heart swelled until she thought it would explode with love and joy. She threw herself into Pete's willing arms. They hugged each other so tightly they felt their bodies nearly become one. Char buried her head in Pete's chest, as tears of joy filled her eyes. She felt his strong, pounding, heartbeat as his chest heaved with labored breaths. But Pete's heart drummed a joyful rhythm that confirmed their commitment to love each other. And the rapid rhythm drew Char to Pete all the more.

Char said softly, "Then I'm all yours, my love. And I always will be!"

After they held each other for nearly a minute, Char released her grip on Pete and kissed him passionately. He wiped drying tears of joy from the corners of Char's eyes and cheeks, smiling like he was seventeen, and mesmerized by his first passionate love.

Char handed him her drink, and said, "Let's have one more drink to celebrate before we go to bed tonight."

Pete smiled and refilled the glasses. He said, "I'd get up to add more ice, but I don't think I can walk. My foot's asleep."

He motioned toward Bruiser. Char grinned, as Pete carefully slid his foot out from beneath the sleeping dog. Bruiser moaned once and then immediately returned to a deep, sound sleep, as Pete rubbed his tingling foot.

Once he leaned back again, Char rested her head on Pete's chest as they relaxed, gazing at the flames flickering across ceramic logs in the gas fireplace.

She asked, "Do you think we can make this our home, once *The Case* is finished? I love it here."

"I'd welcome that, dear. I want to sell my practice in Carson City, anyway. But, when we do move in permanently, can we have the master bedroom? As much as I like the privacy of the hangar bedroom, the master really is quite the place! And besides, there's more room for Bruiser there and a larger fireplace for us." Pete chuckled.

Char smiled so brightly she felt her eyes narrow as they gleamed with joy. Her heart warmed as her body tingled. It was a new feeling Char had never experienced before in her life. She nodded and hugged Pete even tighter. Char had never been so happy, fulfilled, and at peace with herself. Her mind wandered from what lingerie ensemble she would wear to bed later, to how she would decorate their master bedroom.

And for the first time since Pete's wife, Claire, died, Pete felt his heart open completely, and begin to fill, confident of the love it would receive in return. As he held tightly onto the woman who filled his being with incredible passion, all the stress, worry and doubt left over from the life-lessons with Tasha, drained from Pete, like drops of water fleeing the sieve.

✳✳✳

While the fire crackled outside, team members and friends sat in a circle and openly discussed BaCayse's briefing. Tom said, "So, they plan to destroy America through division, identity politics, hatred, and civil war. It's incredible but believable. The identity politics concept always made me fiery, red-faced mad."

Kate grinned, and Walter chuckled at the thought, as everyone else stared silently at the fire.

Tom, generally known for not drinking alcohol, and being soft-spoken, or even silent, snarled, "See there! That's why it ticks me off."

Startled at Tom's uncharacteristic outburst, Patty Simon looked up from the fire, and asked, "What do you mean, Tom?"

Tom said, "Look around our group, Patty. You and your husband, Ron, Mike and his brother, Pete Panos, Walter and Kate O'Leary, Shane Beckett, and me, Tom Bradshaw. We've all worked together for years, saved each other's lives, and become the closest of friends, through all the good and bad times life has thrown at us. You are all *my* people. I love and trust you all, and you all love and trust me back. And yet, I comment about being red-faced mad, and because I'm a black man or at least half-black, no one teases me about it, even though it's funny."

Tom looked around, as everyone gazed apprehensively at him. He said, "It's impossible for me to be red-faced. My skin's too dark. But everyone is afraid to make a joke, as they normally would with their best friend, because the 'P.C.' police on the left trained us that being black means you're an entitled member of some protected class, the feared African-American class. But, I'm not. I refuse to be entitled, protected and separated from my friends by strangers I don't even know! I'm Tom, your friend, and fellow *American*."

The big man stood quickly and looked around at his team. He said, "I'm just *Tom*. But that's what identity politics does to us. We feel guilty for treating someone normal, like we'd treat them if only they weren't a certain color, religion, sexual preference, or gender."

Tom looked at Shane and asked, "Shane, do you know what my lily-white, half-brother, Lee, would have said if I had used the expression, 'red-faced mad,' with him?"

Shane admitted, "No, I don't. What *would* he have said, Tom?"

"The same thing as my black father, his step-father, would have said. Something like, 'Eat your heart out, black man. One thing you can never be is red-faced mad, like every lily-white skinned man. Live with it.' And then I would have told Lee that I'll be the brother who looks 40 years old when he's 60, because black people have younger looking skin than white folk. And we'd tease and trust and love each other for the rest of the day, and grow closer."

Silence fell over the deck.

Tom asked, "Don't you all get it? We become more trusting, more open and more loving if we don't have labels or language restrictions that separate us. Identity politics divides us into canned groups, created by people who don't want us to blend together and become one. They want to raise up their chosen segments of society at everyone's expense. And the division creates mistrust that leads to hatred. It's all so counter-productive."

Tom sipped his scotch, and smiled, as others began to see his point. He quickly placed his glass on the deck and walked rapidly to the woodpile to gather more wood for the fire. He returned without making a sound as he walked.

Shane commented, "Do you know, for a large man with feet longer than mine, I've always been amazed at how silently you move."

"That's because I'm part Indian," Tom boasted, with a grin.

Mike Panos huffed, "Don't you believe him, Shane! I happen to know this man's mother, who is also Lee's mother. And she's Irish and German. The closest he is to Indians is driving time to the nearest reservation, forty miles from his home."

Tom burst out in laughter, followed quickly by the rest of the group.

Shane flushed a little red, embarrassed that he had believed Tom's joke.

Walter added, "I've never been a fan of identity politics or any form of political correctness. I agree with Tom. Life is too wonderfully free for us to allow others to govern the way we think and speak. We should each be responsible and accountable for enjoying and controlling ourselves. We should never relinquish those freedoms to others."

Tom said, "Good words, Walter. My dad taught Lee and I that life is messy, beautiful and real, but *never* politically correct. Political correctness requires free people to subjugate themselves to arbitrary personal constraints created by strangers. The resulting loss of individuality diminishes the freedoms and enjoyment of the life we cherish. It's just not right."

With that, the entire group hoisted their glasses as Tom proposed a toast, saying, "To life, to freedom, to our country, to family, to friends, and most importantly, to us!" And then they all agreed and toasted each other with a drink.

As the group on the deck shared drinks and laughter, Marissa Weinstein met with her Chinese handler, Rose Brown at her Malibu, California mansion. The large, architecturally unique, majestic estate, was positioned strategically above a rocky crag, within walking distance of the surging Pacific Ocean and sandy beach below.

Rose handed Marissa a glass of vodka, and then walked over to turn up the volume on the surround sound speakers that encircled the cozy outside pool and spa space. She switched on an extra light to see Marissa more clearly, and then slowly strolled back to join her. As Rose sauntered toward her, Marissa reclined back expectantly and spread her legs.

Rose sat on the edge of the couch until Marissa nodded, smiled coyly, and took a sip of vodka. Rose rolled and lit a marijuana cigarette for them to share, as she kicked off her beige stiletto heels. She moved over slowly, to join Marissa on the long leather couch, that sat facing the pool and the open water.

The 5,317 square-foot, six-bedroom, eight-bath, beach house sported an infinity pool, providing swimmers the illusion that they could swim directly from the warm water into the ocean, even though the Pacific came ashore some 35-feet below and 100-feet west of the structure.

Marissa asked, flirtatiously, "Is Zhang coming?"

Rose replied, "Not tonight. He has a briefing to attend. I'm afraid it's just us tonight, Marissa. But it will be good. I promise!"

Rose swung her hips around to face Marissa. She moved her leg up toward Marissa and slid her right nylon stocking covered foot up the inside of Marissa's left foot and leg, stopping just below Marissa's crotch.

Marissa pulled her skirt up, exposing a stark-white, silk panty. Rose flexed her toes within the beige colored stocking as if they were fingers, to gently massage Marissa. Rose teased Marissa deftly, while Marissa ran her free hand up and down Rose's stocking covered leg.

Marissa took another sip of vodka and quickly swallowed, before she took a long drag on the joint. After holding in the intoxicating smoke as long as she could, Marissa released her breath, and quickly said, "You both know I enjoy it more when we're all three together."

Rose moved her toes slowly up to Marissa's breasts, and then teased each one, just as she had done with her pelvis. Marissa put her glass down on the end table, and handed Rose the joint. She grabbed Rose's foot in both hands and moved it back and forth, massaging both of her own breasts with Rose's heel and then her toes, to produce increased arousal. Marissa's mouth gaped open as she began to gasp excitedly.

Suddenly, Marissa moved Rose's stockinged foot up further, and stroked her own neck and face, slowly and sensually. She ran her tongue over Marissa's foot and sucked on her toes for nearly a minute. Using one hand, Marissa moved Rose's foot back down between her legs, pushing the toes firmly against her panty. She trapped Rose's foot by squeezing her thighs together, and then, again, reached for the glass of vodka.

Marissa downed the last of her drink and reached out to Rose, who handed her the joint. Marissa took an unusually long drag, and nearly finished the marijuana cigarette. She flipped the remaining roach deftly on to the deck surrounding the pool. And then, Marissa leaned back, closed her eyes, and used Rose's foot to masturbate for more than a minute, until she climaxed.

As soon as she reached orgasm, Marissa released Rose's foot, held out her arms, and said, "Now!"

Rose quickly straddled Marissa, grabbed a handful of hair from the back of Marissa's head, and forced Marissa up to meet her face-to-face. Rose drove her tongue into Marissa's mouth forcefully, while she ground her hip into Marissa. Within the space of seconds, as Rose kissed her wildly, Marissa orgasmed a second time, much more powerfully than the first. Rose released Marissa as her screams of pleasure subsided, allowing Marissa to recover.

Rose Brown, Marissa's pretty Chinese handler, then calmly stood up, strolled in her stocking feet to the outside wet bar, and poured herself a glass of her favorite Temecula, California, Chardonnay, from an open, chilled bottle, Marissa had prepared. Rose turned back to study Marissa Weinstein, the senior United States Senator from California, as she silently considered how easily Weinstein had been corrupted and controlled by Chinese agents.

Marissa pulled her skirt back down as she recovered her composure. Her cheeks flushed red, as she said, submissively, "I wish you'd kiss me longer."

"Next time, I promise," Rose replied, dismissively. "Right now we have to plan. Pour yourself another drink, Marissa. I have to file a report later tonight."

"Why do we always have to be in so much of a hurry?" Marissa protested, pouting slightly, as she felt the steadily growing buzz from the alcohol and marijuana.

"Wang Jintao and Sergej Petrov are meeting in three days. They want results, with trade deals in Europe and the investigations here in the United States. Trump made maintaining trade discrepancies so much more difficult for China. It's up to you and your cronies to move the U.S. back to our prior trade deficit levels."

"I'm not President, yet," Weinstein said, disapprovingly.

"You will be, in less than two years. For now, focus on moving us to our goals using your influence in Europe, your buddies in the F.B.I., and your friends in big banks. All of these constant investigations by the F.B.I. into our theft of proprietary software, need to stop."

"How many investigations need to stop? And how much political capital do I need to spend to get Sergej his oil deal with Germany?" Weinstein demanded, with a scowl.

"I can make the goals simple this time. Move the U.S. to concede to Russia's oil trade deal with Germany, knowing France and England will follow, bringing in the rest of Europe. End the investigations into China, Iran, and North Korea's cyber thefts from Silicon Valley, starting with Manford Halston's corporations. Halston's artificial intelligence and encryption software is most important to me and us. Sergej and Wang want much more from you, but I can make that work for now."

Marissa closed her eyes tightly to focus her thoughts as Rose Brown continued. "Marissa, you *will* correct trade deficits after your election, to favor China, as they did in the past. Wang Jintao will deliver you the required trade deal goals, long before you take the oath of office," Rose laughed. "So be prepared to move fast. You need to get those ducks in a row, now!"

"How much?" Weinstein demanded as a wave of dizziness and euphoria swarmed over her, taking her by surprise. The sexual rapture intensified in flashes, as warm tingling waves shot from her groin up through her stomach and across her chest.

"Wow, good dope. Where'd you get it?" Marissa asked, in labored speech, as she sank deeper into the cushions, lightly brushing her body with her fingertips.

Rose sighed, and said, "Marissa, I need you to concentrate. There are forty million U.S. dollars in it for you, for doing these two simple little favors for us. So, when can we expect results?"

"And the dope?" Weinstein insisted before she answered.

Rose said, "This delivery is from Colombia, courtesy of your dead friend, Franky Magadinno's replacement. The THC content is 37.28%. It's the strongest I could find, just as you requested. You'll be buzzed for a while. Especially, after adding the vodka."

"I want more, plus an 8-ball of *good* cocaine, and then both of you back here tonight, ready to party!" Weinstein insisted, as she leaned back against the couch and again closed her eyes, feeling the total euphoria as it kicked into high gear. The waves engulfing her senses intensified in strength and speed.

When the wave subsided, Weinstein struggled to add, "But, as far as money goes, forty million is good, *for me*, delivered through my companies' contracts, as usual."

Rose said sternly, "Marissa, that makes almost four hundred million in the last ten years. They want your guarantees. I need you to promise. Give me something to take back. *I* need something now!"

Marissa Weinstein forced her eyes open, and uttered coherently, "And *I* want both of you, cocaine and more weed back here tonight. So, if Wang and Sergej want guarantees, then *you* will need to deliver another ten million in cash I can use for bribes. I'm not the President of the United States. How else do you think I can call off the investigative dogs? I'm not giving the government's law enforcement crooks one dime of *my* money!"

Rose stood up, acting defeated, walked to Marissa's end of the couch, placed her glass on the table, pulled on her stiletto heels, and leaned over to kiss Marissa goodbye. She said, "Alright, Marissa. I have to go out to call and make sure we can come up with that much cash by tomorrow, but you can consider it done. I'll need your guarantee by then, no later!"

"You can call from here, you know. You don't need to leave," Weinstein said, without opening her eyes. She smiled weakly through another building warm wave.

"I don't have more marijuana here, Marissa. And you were almost out of good blow two nights ago."

"Bring back a pound of that weed this time. I'll keep it in my safe."

Rose shook her head, sighed, and said, "Okay, I'll see you in an hour."

She marched into the house and out through the front door, leaving Marissa reclined outside in the fresh night air, her eyes closed, as she enjoyed her heightened euphoric intoxication, now fueled by sexual fantasies yet to come.

Outside, in the front driveway, Rose slid into her sports car's form-fitted driver's seat. She started the engine, drove around the fountain on the cobblestone drive, and called her second cousin, Zhang Wei.

When he answered, Rose asked, "Did you get the video?"

"I did. I shot it using the big drone from about a hundred yards away. Good idea, turning up the outside lighting. The zoom worked perfectly. I could read the label on your wine bottle. I saw everything and recorded your entire session. It looked like fun!" Zhang teased.

Rose commented, thoughtfully, "The drone was a little loud. I had to turn up the music to make sure she wouldn't hear the rotors."

"What's next?" Zhang asked.

"Meet me back at our apartment. I need to get her cash and more weed. She wants us both back tonight, in about an hour. She'll still be a little buzzed, so we shouldn't have to pull an all-nighter. And I left her with half a bottle of vodka."

"No problem. I'll leave right now. I like fucking her, so I don't care how long we stay. I've never had a more willing woman. You can't fault her for loving sex."

"She's a nymphomaniac, a real-life sex addict, the first I've ever met. And she wants us *both*, again. So take a shower if you get there first. We both like you clean!"

"No problem, cuz."

"And stop calling me that. We need everyone to think you're just my boyfriend, nothing more."

449

"Oh, alright. Unbunch your panties. How much do we get to keep this time?"

Rose said, with a laugh, "I got her to agree to 50 million, including, payoff cash. That leaves us with another ten million to add to our retirement fund."

Zhang said, "I love my job, and I love America!"

Rose teased, "Don't say that. *Our* people may be listening."

They both broke out in laughter, as Rose accelerated through the green light and turned the corner, heading for home.

Chapter 11

"What we have at the moment is enough, if we embrace it."

The morning dawned cold, crisp and clear at Char's North Carolina home. Juanita and Walter's Shiba Inu, Sophia, arose early and began pacing, wanting to be let out. Walter slipped on his heavy robe and slippers, and headed downstairs with his companion, figuring he would leave Juanita quietly so that she could drift back to sleep.

The morning was so beautiful that Walter sat on the deck and admired a flight of Canadian Geese as they circled the acreage to the northwest. Sophia was only about her business, and immediately after finishing, she wanted back inside with Juanita, where it was warm. But Walter made her wait, and she turned around to shoot him an irritated glare, from where she sat facing the door leading inside.

"So, who taught you that look?" Walter asked with a laugh. "That's one female characteristic our Juanita doesn't have. So you didn't get it from her. And I've never seen it on Angie, either, so explain yourself or sit and wait!"

The pretty canine shot Walter an unexpected glance that conveyed a superior, entitled and demeaning message, resembling something he may have seen on the face of an old Hollywood socialite, used to having people bow, scrape and serve at her feet. He laughed out loud, as Sophia then walked around in circles, and then collapsed at the back door in a heap, with her back to Walter. She breathed in deeply and released a long, irritated, sigh of disappointment.

"Must be the breed," Walter chuckled under his breath. Walter enjoyed the view for a few more moments. But, after repeated sighs expressing irritation and impatience, he relinquished his space in the morning sun, walked to Sophia, and said, "Oh, come on, you big crybaby!"

When she stood up and looked at him respectfully, he patted the dog on her head and smiled down at her. She rewarded Walter with a rare tail wag. Man and canine walked back upstairs, through a quiet house, to greet Juanita.

At 7:39 A.M., Walter sat on the bed next to his lovely wife, who had already showered and put on a robe, by the time he returned. He was admiring how beautiful Juanita was in the morning sunlight, even before she applied make-up, when his phone rang. Walter didn't recognize the number, but answered anyway, curious to discover who would call so early.

He said, "Hello, who am I speaking with?"

"Walter, I'm sorry to call you so early, using an unfamiliar line, but it's Bob Crawford. I need to speak with you in person, if you're awake and available in the area, old friend."

"I'm awake and available, Bob. I'm still in the North Carolina area, so where and when?"

"Do you know the little town of Rutherfordton?"

"I do. Nice little place. I played golf there years ago, at their country club, as the guest of a local company we looked at buying."

"Good. Walter, the Superior court is located downtown, on Main Street, with on-street parking in front. Inside, you'll find the Register of Deeds, downstairs as I recall. I have an old high school friend who works there. He'll know you're coming. Ask for him by name, 'E.F.' He'll escort you to an office in the back. I have someone I want you to meet. She needs to talk to you, too. When can you be there?"

"Realistically, I could meet you any time after eleven, today."

"Good, then let's meet at noon. I'll bring you lunch. Just go through the deputy's check-in and metal detector at the top of the front steps, and ask for directions to the Register of Deeds. I'll see you there. And thank you, Walter. I need to come clean with you about Tasha. You need to know the whole truth. But, as usual, I need your help, too. And this time, I may need you more than you need me!"

Walter hung up and immediately gazed at Juanita, sitting on the bed beside him. He said, "My God, you are absolutely beautiful! You make my heart skip a beat!"

Juanita smiled, and cupped Walter's face in her soft hands. She kissed his lips and said, "Thank you, my dear, for allowing me to be your wife for another day! You are truly the most wonderful man in the world, for me!"

Walter kissed Juanita again and held her hand as he looked down at Sophia, staring up at his mistress. He laughed and said, "She was a pill today, I have to tell you the story."

Juanita smiled and asked, "I'd love to hear it, but who called so early, dear?"

"Vice President Crawford wants to talk, and tell me about Tasha. That's a good development. Would you like to meet him for lunch?"

Surprised, Juanita questioned, "Should I go? He wants to see you!"

453

Walter said, "I think I need you to read him. I may be too emotionally attached to our lifelong friendship. I may not do a competent job at reading my skilled politician and friend. I need your good judgment. A better pair of eyes, as it were!"

"Alright, then I'll go, and we'll read him together," Juanita agreed.

Walter stood up, and said, "Let's get dressed and go down to breakfast. We'll tell the others, and then enjoy a scenic ride to town."

As Walter and Juanita dressed for the day, at his hotel room with Barbara Walcott, Vice President Bob Crawford asked again, to give the woman he loved one last chance to pull out of their planned operation.

He said, "I've set up everything up with FBI Special Agent in Charge, Bryan Holland, who I trust with my life. He'll ensure you could never be prosecuted if anything goes wrong. I'll field all the blame, if needed. It's my turf, here, even though it's your plan. Are you still comfortable going forward with everything we set in motion? I need you to be certain."

"You know I am, my love. I can't allow your corrupt President to destroy you and my chance for a future with you. I thought it out time and time again. I think it's the only way to ensure he'll leave you alone. And, if not the only way, then at least, it's the best way."

"Okay, then, dear. I'll call Bryan and tell him the plan is a go, and then I'll take care of my Secret Service spy problem."

Crawford made the appropriate calls. Byan Holland sent his team to the Magnum Park Hotel, one of the most exclusive hotels in all of South Beach, in Miami Beach, Florida, where, in just three short days, President Marshall would spend two nights. The President's advance security teams would arrive in 36 hours, long after the trap had been set, and far too late to discover anything out of the ordinary. British Home Secretary and clandestine head of MI6, Barbara Walcott, worked their phones for nearly two hours before they had checked off all their preparations.

Barbara had eaten a small scone, while Bob ate nothing but half an apple. Both ordered hot mocha coffees to go, and met the Secret Service detail to board the SUV that would drive them to Rutherfordton. President Marshall's Secret Service spy, placed strategically in Vice President Crawford's detail, was sent to Crawford's home in Virginia, allegedly to prepare for Crawford's arrival the next day.

As they left Asheville, sitting in the rear seat of the large SUV, Barbara leaned over and whispered, "Thank you so much for the treat, Bob. I will never forget the Biltmore Hotel. I love everything from the gardens to the shops to the winery to the hotel, itself. I hope we can come back. There's so much to see and enjoy. I can be a real person here. I loved every second of it, Bob!"

"I did too, dear. And next time we'll take in the Biltmore *and* the Grove Inn. We just ran out of time. But, if this plan works, time is something we *will* have to enjoy."

The convoy rounded a corner and turned on to North Carolina Alt 74, on the way through a handful of little old towns like Gerton, positioned in narrow, winding canyons, carved by creeks and rivers flowing through the mountains. Other tiny villages like Bat Cave, Chimney Rock and Lake Lure, had grown up around tourism, but remained small and sparsely populated by people who lived to enjoy all the area had to offer, including peace, friendship, and serenity. As they wound through the scenic forests and valleys, Barbara Walcott took it all in, enthralled by the area's majestic wonder and beauty.

As the convoy headed through the small town of Green Hill, closing in on their destination, Barbara leaned back, and said, "Robert, I could live anywhere in these mountains with you. I love Virginia, and I love it here. I've seen very little of the Rockies and the west, but wherever I go in the U.S., I always appreciate the variety your vast country offers. It's so big and different, from place to place. But I may love the eastern mountains the most, of everything I've seen so far. I've rarely taken time in life to enjoy anything so much. I'm anxious for all this political intrigue to end, and for the life we both want together, to finally begin."

Bob Crawford said, "I am, too, honey. I am, too. More than you know."

As Crawford's convoy neared Green Hill, North Carolina, Marissa Weinstein, Zhang Wei, and Rose Brown were just getting out of bed, having partied with drugs and alcohol for more than 5 hours. Weinstein was the last up out of bed and the first to complain about the call from her office staff to remind her of an afternoon meeting. She told her chief aid to cancel all meetings for the next two days due to a bout of the flu.

As Weinstein laid back down on the outside couch by the pool, Rose said, "It's a good thing you don't really have to work for a living. No important votes on the Senate floor today? You couldn't punch a time clock, you know!"

"There are no votes I can't miss. And nobody uses time clocks anymore," Weinstein quipped.

"Wow, you don't even know!" Zhang said, sarcastically. "The real *little* people still punch in and out. That's how corporations keep them honest!"

"The term, 'little people,' now refers to dwarfs and midgets, not citizens!" Weinstein shot back, with some irritation in her voice.

"Sorry, I'm not from around here!" Zhang countered with a fake southern drawl.

"What's up with you two, anyway?" Weinstein asked. "We had fun last night, and today you're both on my case!"

"I have a massive headache, and feel like I need to sleep for a week!" Rose replied.

"I'm exhausted. I'm going home and back to bed now," Zhang said. "I have to get some sleep. I need to meet with Magadinno's people about the distribution problems in Chinatown tonight."

"Chinatown?" Marissa asked, as she propped herself up on the couch to look at Zhang.

Zhang confirmed, "Yeah, Chinatown. Magadinno's replacement wants to take over the opium distribution in L.A., starting with Chinatown. They met with some *resistance* from the Triad. So, they asked me to make some contacts and arrange an introduction. I don't want to get too close to the war that's sure to follow, but we have to keep some people happy, even if we don't play on their team. I'm supposed to meet the new main man himself! The one who took over Franky Magaddino's crime syndicate."

Deep in thought, Marissa said, "The main man! I've never met him. Some of those who know him call him, 'SAS.' They say the nickname stands for *scary as shit*! Let me know what he's like. I'm

457

sure I'll be running interference for him at some point. I'd like to know who I'm dealing with, and I hear he rarely meets anyone, face-to-face."

"Will do. But right now I'm going to bed." Zhang picked up his car keys and walked to Marissa to kiss her goodbye.

Marissa Weinstein grabbed Zhang by the hand, and said, "If you really want to *sleep*, come back to bed with me. I'll wear you out so you can sleep like a baby!" She smiled coyly and cocked her head.

Zhang looked over at Rose Brown, who had just finished getting dressed. She said, "Don't look at me! I'm going home. I have a report to file, and I need to be on my game to *sell* the deal we made with Marissa to our bosses." Rose smiled and said, "You two kids have fun now," as she walked quickly toward the door, to escape.

Zhang and Marissa Weinstein headed toward the bedroom, hand in hand.

✳✳✳

Walter and Juanita walked into the Register of Deeds office in the Rutherfordton County Court House, fifteen minutes early. A friendly young lady at the front desk went back to an office, and returned immediately with a tall, good-looking man in his early 60's, who introduced himself as "E.F." While E.F. was pleasant, he was very business-like, and stated only that Walter's friend was waiting in a rear cubical. Walter had learned from prior experience in the South, that people often name their children using initials that don't stand for unspoken names. Earlier he had advised Barbara not to ask what the initials stood for, and she followed his advice.

"E.F. escorted Walter and Juanita down a hallway leading to a conference room and two smaller offices. He opened the door leading to the larger office and nodded for them to enter. Inside, E.F. offered them two seats, located on the visitor side of a large desk, and once they were seated and waiting, he walked out, closing the door behind him.

A moment later, Walter heard a knock on the conference room door in the hallway, and within a few seconds, the door to his right, leading from the office into the conference room opened, and Vice President Bob Crawford walked in to greet him.

After they stood to greet him, Crawford hugged both Walter and Juanita, warmly, expressing his joy at learning of their marriage. Surprised at the upbeat tone in the Vice President's voice, Walter said, "Bob, you seem happier than I can recall seeing you in years. With everything that's going on, this is a pleasant surprise. The worries of the world and our lives appear to have escaped you for the moment!"

"For the moment and many moments after, I hope!" Bob Crawford answered, with a grin. "I'm finding that what we have at the moment is enough, if we embrace it. And right now, at this moment, I have you, Walter, one of the best friends of my life, and your beautiful angel of a wife!"

Bob smiled widely at Juanita, and added, "We often allow ourselves to become bogged down by so many worries and what-ifs, that we miss the countless moments filled with peace, joy and love that fly by unnoticed. I'm trying to change that in myself. And, I have someone I want you to meet who reminds me of that, when I break free from my world and allow her to show me a better way. Of course, she has to break free from her own demons and clear her moment, as well!"

Crawford stepped back, and said, "Please come in and meet my fiancée, Barbara Walcott."

Walter and Juanita followed Bob Crawford into the conference room, where Barbara sat at one of the twelve black leather swivel chairs, neatly spaced around an oval wooden table. Barbara stood as soon as the trio walked into the room and approached her. She tugged down on the jacket portion of her two-piece tweed business suit.

Juanita approached her first, with both hands outstretched. Wearing three-inch off-white heels with bronze toecaps, Barbara stood several inches taller than Juanita and nearly as tall as Walter. She bent her knees and hugged Juanita affectionately, and then stood tall to embrace Walter.

Bob supervised the introductions artfully, honoring Barbara formally as the British Home Secretary, befitting her station in life, while also presenting her intimately, as the love of his life. For her part, Barbara graciously relayed how much she had looked forward to meeting Walter, whom she had heard so much about, through the years.

Walter remarked, "Barbara, this devil must have worked his finest magic to snag someone so beautiful, talented and clever. Over the years, I've listened to a few of your speeches. I like your style, and what you stand for with England! You have my highest respect and blessing!"

Juanita said, "I am so pleased and honored to meet you, Barbara, if I may call you by your first name. For me, it's like meeting royalty. A dream come true."

Barbara said, graciously, "I have a role to play in England, but I am just Barbara, and I hope we will all become the best of friends. I assure you, I am equally pleased and honored to meet you both!"

As Walter sat down, he noticed that while they met Barbara, someone had closed the office door he and Juanita had walked through and left open. He was pleased that, even in the excitement, he could still track activities around him.

Once they all sat down at the end of the table, where they could converse quietly, Bob provided Juanita and Walter background details on Barbara, including how she and Bob had met and become engaged. Crawford left out the word, 'affair,' but provided enough detail that they could fill in the blanks, understanding that Bob's ex-wife, Judy, had engaged in a long-term affair of her own.

Bob then recapped the highlights of President Marshall's plan to contaminate the gold mine property, using Russian precursor nerve agents, so he could condemn the land and then clandestinely develop the gold mine using Russian workers. He detailed how Marshall and Vera Langhart created a paper trail to set him up as the scape-goat for authorizing the high-risk experimental testing of lethal poisons at the fragile watershed site. Bob Crawford explained that Barbara had come up with a plan to stop Marshall, that needed help from Walter's group.

With the groundwork out of the way, Barbara said, "Before we get to my plan, I have to tell you about Tasha. Bob and I both feel you need to know that what I'm telling you is the truth. Since Tasha is part of my plan to save Bob, I thought it best that I bring her here, for you to see and hear, to prove my story is true."

"Tasha is here?" Juanita blurted out.

"She's waiting, in the office next door," Barbara answered.

Walter scowled, "I'm not sure I want to see her after all the pain she caused us, especially with Pete."

"I would like to see her, to make sure she is alright and to tell her I still think of her and miss her," Juanita added. She shot Walter a pleading look, and he reluctantly nodded his approval.

461

Barbara stood up, and said, "Then, I'll bring her in now."

Barbara walked to the office door on the other side of the conference room, opened it, and nodded her head. Tahsa walked in confidently, dressed in a two-piece sleeveless marble sheath dress, with matching long sleeve jacket and black heels.

Juanita stood up and walked to greet Tasha with a hug, which Tasha graciously but stiffly accepted. Walter stood politely but did not offer to move toward Tasha, nor she toward him.

Juanita remarked, "You look so different and business-like. But you look healthy and well. I'm so glad you are alright, after your ordeal, Tasha."

"It was just my role, my job. I was never concerned. I trained for these assignments. But thank you for *your* concern, Juanita."

Tasha shot a glance at Barbara Walcott, who nodded and pointed to a seat. Juanita placed her hand on Walter's arm, and looked at him pleadingly, conveying she wanted to hear the explanation. Walter agreed and held his tongue.

Once everyone took their original seats, with Tasha seated to Barbara's right, furthest from her friends, Barbara said, "Vice President Crawford has given me his word that what we speak about in this room goes no farther than to those in your Beckett Cypher team, on a need to know basis."

Walter and Juanita glanced from Bob back to Barbara, and then both agreed aloud.

Barbara continued, saying, "Through one of our agents working in the California Department of Justice, many years ago, we learned of Scott Mayfield's investigation. Mayfield's task force had developed a great deal of information on corrupt American politicians. In particular, we were interested in a young, up and coming political star from the Democratic Party named Marissa Weinstein."

Barbara grimaced slightly, as she said, "Weinstein was born into a Jewish family, but after an affair in college, was recruited and corrupted by a Hamas operative. A year later, she was trained in a suburb of Gaza, and became active in arms smuggling, specifically working within a political network to smuggle weapons from Russia into Europe, Central and South America."

"Some of the devices and weapons Weinstein helped bring into Europe were used in terrorist acts in England. As we worked to develop a case against her, Weinstein won her election to the California State Assembly. I pushed to expose and prosecute her before she took office in her first term. Unfortunately, I held a different position in my foreign intelligence organization in those days, and I was overruled. My superiors wanted to wait for more details in the investigation, to expose other American politicians, who were working with Weinstein to destroy Israel and destabilize the Middle East, with a long-term goal of solidifying Russia and China's influence in the region."

Barbara continued, becoming somewhat agitated as she spoke. "As the Mayfield task force worked through the outlying people of interest uncovered in the corruption, someone in the Attorney General's Office tipped off key principal suspects in the investigation, and suddenly Scott Mayfield, some of the task force investigators, and Patrick Beckett, were all killed or listed as missing. After the task force was side-lined, the investigation was sealed and then quickly went missing. My agent in DOJ made quiet inquiries, and discovered that a copy of the investigation was retained and protected by a military grade cypher Patrick Beckett had acquired. Patrick Beckett's IT staff had further developed the encryption to protect the case files."

Barbara Walcott stood up abruptly, tugged at her jacket, and walked to the end of the conference room. She turned, and said, "I recruited and trained Tasha, to stay close to Pete Harrington, when I learned Pete would have control over Patrick's boys. Initially, I thought Pete might possess the files. But when nothing happened for many years, I figured Patrick had developed a plan to pass the files on to one of his sons. I wanted the cypher, and it's hidden files, if for no other purpose than to expose Marissa Weinstein for the murderous traitor she is to America. And so I could knock her off her lavish pedestal, and, drag her by her thinning hair, kicking and screaming back to Britain to prosecute her for murder."

Barbara took a deep breath to calm herself and, spread her arms out from her sides, as if the movement could bring about some magical calm. Everyone in the room watched her intently searching for the answer to her seething anger.

She said, "That was about fifteen years ago, and Tasha has been working undercover ever since, waiting. When the cypher and the coveted files surfaced, I was prepared to act. But then, once we learned about the cypher's power, we wanted it even more, to stop The Committee, and..." Barbara trailed off, as tears came to her eyes. In a shaky voice, she added, "everything wrong in the world."

Barbara glanced back at Bob Crawford, who nodded encouragement through glistening eyes. Barbara continued, saying, "Marissa Weinstein initially became a spy for Hamas, and continues to help them when she can. But now, she works directly as an agent for the Chinese government. And, to make matters worse, she's working with one of my MI6 failures, Rose Brown, to steal Silicon Valley software, which we believe will give the Chinese, North Koreans, and Iranians the ability to destroy the Beckett Cypher."

Walter asked, "If I may be so bold, Barbara, what are we missing? As evil as Marissa Weinstein is, her activities seem to have upset you far beyond wanting to rein in one more political monster. I'm certain that in your position you've seen a thousand like her. Maybe more! What is so special about her kind of monster?"

Barbara studied Walter, but said nothing, as if searching for words that refused to come. Vice President Crawford looked down, fearing he would lose control of his restrained tears.

As the silence grew awkward, Tasha said, "Some years ago, Marissa Weinstein took part in a bombing, to please her terrorist mentor and lover. It was her test, a wicked terrorist rite of passage. That bombing killed Barbara's grandparents, as they strolled down a London street holding their new grandbaby, Barbara's nephew, who was also killed. Barbara's only brother was a policeman in the area, walking, at the time, to meet his grandparents and son for lunch. His wife had died in childbirth."

"Barbara's brother was the *first* responder to arrive on the scene and the person who discovered recognizable pieces of his families' bodies. He was never able to recover and move on with his life. Two years later, Barbara's brother committed suicide. You see, prosecuting Marissa Weinstein is more than a little personal for Miss Walcott, with good reason."

Tasha smiled lovingly at Barbara, who said, "Thank you, Tasha." Barbara looked at the faces watching her across the table. She said, "I thought I had this all worked out, and I could finally tell this story and remain strong. But, I'm afraid I've botched it up entirely. I do apologize."

Juanita gasped, "Oh, Barbara, I don't know how anyone could stay strong reliving something so horrific. What Marissa Weinstein did is despicable, and I'm so sorry for your loss. How can we help?"

Barbara said, "Thank you, Juanita. Maybe you can understand why I had to recruit Tasha to be my eyes and ears with Pete, to wait for the leads and any evidence the original case might eventually produce. But now I understand that the cypher has become much more than an encryption system for the initial investigation. And if it has developed into what we need, it can help save Bob from President Marshall's plan to destroy him. But I'm getting ahead of myself. I must finish my confession about Tasha."

Barbara took a deep breath to free herself of remaining emotions from her family story, and said, "Tasha has worked other cases during her time with me, while working for Pete. Most of her work involved Russian and Chinese targets in the western United States. But her recent work has helped us rid America of highly effective North Korean spy teams infesting *your* country. Tasha just received a citation for her work in recovering stolen intelligence files and identifying a Russian stronghold in Mexico, where two of our agents were held, tortured, and murdered, after they had been kidnapped. Tasha is a decorated and indispensable agent, who has been loyal and strategically effective, for both our countries, over many years."

Barbara said, "What I'm telling you does not mitigate what happened *personally* between Tasha and Pete, but it does give you the background to understand why Tasha never committed to, but used her relationship with Pete, as she did. For Pete's pain and your discomfort, worrying about Tasha, I apologize. Tasha was doing her country's bidding as an MI6 agent, nothing more. And there was so much at stake, that I couldn't allow her to break a confidence. So, please consider any betrayal my doing."

Walter said, "I can't speak for Pete, but we trusted Tasha and took her in as one of our *family* members. Her betrayal scars run deep in my backside, likely deeper with me than with Juanita. We will work to help Bob in any way we can, but Tasha and I are no longer family. Pete is like a son to me. Tasha is no longer like my daughter. She relinquished that privilege. I want to be forthright, so you all know where I stand."

Juanita said, "Maybe if Tasha explained it all to Pete, we could all heal better."

Tasha broke her steel-like expressionless face, and asked anxiously, "Juanita, will you tell Pete, when you see him, that I am genuinely sorry. I couldn't reveal who I was, and what I was planning, in the middle of my work."

Walter said coldly, "If you want to apologize to Pete, you can do so today, in person. He drove us here. He and Char are waiting for us right now, outside in the car."

Tasha sat back abruptly, and flushed red. "I don't know if I can...should...speak to him so suddenly. I'm not prepared."

Walter said, "You had fifteen years to *prepare*. And you were ready to leave him, hurt, worried, and wondering what happened. I think a simple, 'I'm sorry, Pete,' shouldn't be difficult for someone so highly trained."

Juanita squeezed Walter's arm, and said, "Honey, please!"

As Barbara started to speak, Tasha said, "No, Juanita. Walter is absolutely correct. An apology to Pete will be uncomfortable and embarrassing for me. But it is certainly the least I should do, and the necessary gesture for Pete, to heal and move on with someone who puts him first."

Before Juanita could say anything, Walter looked at her and shook his head, saying, "Good, then, that part is settled. So, what's the plan? How can we help you and Bob, Barbara?"

Tasha leaned back uneasily in her chair, as she began to formulate an apology. She knew that seeing Pete would uncover the love for him she had buried, figuring they would never again lay eyes on each other. She also feared that seeing her would rip a scab off Pete's heart, causing him more pain and suffering, just when he had probably begun to heal. She felt like she was about to destroy the man she loved all over again. Her stomach began to churn.

Barbara said, "My plan is simple. President Thomas Marshall will be at a famous, old, upscale hotel in South Beach, Florida for two days. Marshall's Chief of Staff, Vera Langhart, will be staying in an adjoining room, on one side, and his Secret Service crew in another room on the opposite side of the hall from Marshall."

"Marshall's wife rarely makes an appearance with him, as she has been ill for a very long time. We now know she's being treated for aggressive breast cancer, and recently underwent a double mastectomy. She has elected to forego reconstruction surgery. Our intelligence revealed Mrs. Marshall is not expected to live for very long. Marshall has taken advantage of his wife's absence to pursue three long-standing affairs. His most obvious adultery, with Vera Langhart, has gone on, nearly out in the open within the White House, for the last six years, and has caused Mrs. Marshall the most pain."

"The President's next most painful dalliance was with an intern, now missing, named Sienna Martini, whom my Committee source says was last known to be held as a prisoner in a Committee Center for Information Extraction, after she was kidnapped and her father was murdered. One of my agents recently delivered photos of Marshall kissing Martini, to Mrs. Marshall. One might characterize her anger as one of unspeakable rage."

"Marshall's third tryst was a memorable one-night stand with a young lady I secretly arranged for him to meet, when your President was last in Europe attending a NATO conference. That young woman became my insurance policy for England. Due to President Marshall's position in The Committee, we felt we needed some political leverage over him. Marshall thinks of himself as a modern-day Samson, with the sexual strength and capacity of a god. So I merely introduced him to his modern-day Philistine slayer, his very own Delilah, my agent Deidre."

Barbara continued, growing excited about her plan as she spoke. "Deidre has already contacted President Marshall, who is planning on seeing her for a special treat, the second night he is at the hotel. He plans to send Vera Langhart to represent him at a meeting with Florida Democratic Party heavyweights. Deidre promised to fulfill one of Marshall's fantasies, with two beautiful blond women. Marshall prefers his women tall and blond, ranging in age from eighteen to mid-fifties. So. We are using two women he can't resist, who will set a unique trap for your President."

Surprised, Walter said, "You seem to know a great deal more about President Marshall than I would have expected in a political dossier."

Bob Crawford placed his hand on Walter's arm, and said, "Walter, these days, political intelligence is all about opposition research, regardless of whether the candidate is qualified and viable. The opposing party digs up as much dirt as possible to tarnish the candidate's reputation, and destroy his or her credibility. Politics and voter issues don't factor into a partisan background check much anymore."

Walter looked down, saying, "I don't think this is what our founders envisioned when they created our country. A bunch of money wasted figuring out how to destroy candidates and elected officials, before, during and after they take office."

He looked back at Barbara, searching for understanding about a political system that had changed so radically in his lifetime, it was now completely unrecognizable.

Barbara said, "Walter, in the old days, a U.S. President wouldn't have intentionally destroyed part of the environment, so he could secretly condemn the land to illegally rape it of resources. Nor would the President have used an alien workforce, while conspiring to blame his unsuspecting second-in-command of wrongdoing to ensure he himself evaded prosecution. I'm afraid times have changed!"

Walter said, "All good points, Barbara. But the change saddens me greatly. So where do we come in to help?"

Barbara continued, "Tasha and Deidre will wait until Vera Langhart leaves her suite. Vera's suite also has an adjoining room on the other side from Marshall's, that has been held as vacant, during the

President's visit. We have the key, and our people will stage in that room. The ladies will make entry into Marshall's room from Vera's suite. Your President drinks a rare brand of bottled water, made by a company owned by a friend, one of his donors."

"We've already shipped special replacement bottles, ready to be re-stocked in his room on the second morning of his stay. The second night there, Marshall will take a little blue pill to enhance his prowess, using an entire bottle of *our* water that contains a drug cocktail rendering him both sexually euphoric and delusional, but functionally incapacitated. "

"My team will photograph him with Deidre and Tasha, dressed in risque outfits leaving nothing to the imagination about what Marshall was doing with the ladies. The ladies' faces will be partially obscured by cat sex masks, to defeat any future attempts by facial recognition software. My team will record Marshall's interrogation on video. President Marshall will outline his plan to contaminate the gold mine site with Russian nerve agents, so he could condemn and isolate the mine site for development. He will also admit to using Russian forces to murder a local family and Sheriff, to protect the gold he planned to steal."

Walcott became more excited as she neared the end of the outline. She said, "But the best part of the plan is yet to come! There is a costume party at the hotel in President Marshall's honor that Marshall will fail to attend. We need your cypher system to send Vera Langhart a text from Secret Service Agent Christian Booth's phone, asking her to return to meet Marshall, to discuss Darlene Singer. We need the cypher system to make sure that phone can then no longer receive or make calls."

Juanita asked, "Is this the same Darlene Singer, who's the Communication Director for the Democratic National Committee?"

Barbara smiled, and said, "Yes, she is. And rumors have circulated for more than a year that President Marshall was going to replace Vera Langhart with Darlene. The only thing Vera guards more jealously than Thomas Marshall is her position as Chief of Staff for the President of the United States. When Vera arrives back at the hotel lobby, she'll take the elevator to Marshall's floor. Our two lovely ladies, dressed in their seductive party attire, will time their entry, getting on the elevator after Vera leaves the elevator. Tasha will make sure Vera sees her carrying a red folder marked, 'Darlene Singer,' in large, bold black letters. Darlene looks strikingly similar to Tasha. With Tasha's mask, Vera will believe she is, in fact, Darlene Singer, who has just visited President Marshall."

"She will enter her suite, hurry into Marshall's room already angry, and find him in a stuporous condition, lying next to photos of him naked, pictured with our two lovely ladies draped over him, smothering him in kisses. She'll also find a folder next to the President, detailing Vera's replacement with Darlene. When Vera reads the documents in Marshall's file, she'll discover that Marshall was planning to accuse her of withholding information sent by the Environmental Protection Agency to Vice President Crawford, warning him of the imminent nerve agent crisis."

"The file completely exonerates Bob of any wrongdoing. We need your AISS to insert that report into Marshall's laptop with a time and date stamp from a month ago. Vera Langhart will believe Marshall was going to sacrifice her and impeach her credibility, to protect himself. She'll run, probably taking a flight back to the White House offices, where she feels safest."

Barbara sat back in her chair, slightly swiveling back and forth, triumphantly. She added, "We'll make sure reporters downstairs ask Langhart for a statement as soon as she enters the lobby, to explain why she is leaving the party so quickly, and to explain Marshall's absence."

Walter exclaimed, "Wow, you get quite a bit done in a days' work! I must admit, I'm glad you're on Bob's side! The plan sounds perfect. I can't think of anything you could have done to put Marshall under more pressure. He might have to resign!"

Barbara said, "The only thing that would have been better is for Sienna Martini to have run out of the party, dropping a note asking for help to escape from Marshall."

She laughed, and then added, "But I'm afraid, that's out of the question because we don't have her, or even know if she's alive."

Walter glanced from Barbara to Bob, and then to Juanita.

Juanita said, "If they need her, then it should be up to Sienna to participate. She's been through so much, Walter!"

Barbara and Bob both leaned forward in their chairs.

Bob asked, "You have her? Is she alright?"

Walter reflected in silence, and then said, "I guess its time we brought you up to speed on our progress in the cypher investigation."

Barbara said, "Before you begin, please allow me to bring in Deidre and introduce her. You need to meet her, too. And she'll need to hear about your investigation and your cypher's development."

Barbara walked to the door leading to the office where Deidre waited and opened it unceremoniously. A beautiful, young, blond woman walked in immediately, wearing a form-fitting black and white patterned dress with lace trim, and matching black and white striped heels. Everyone in the room stood for brief but formal introductions. Deidre sat next to Tasha.

Then they all sat back down to listen intently as Walter recapped the cypher team's investigation, beginning when Tasha left the ranch in Oregon and continuing through the day Shane's team rescued Sienna Martini and Manford Halston from the Committee's Maryland Center for Information Extraction.

Walter explained that the team had lodged Martini and Halston safely within a gated community at a secluded cabin in western North Carolina. He also revealed that the team had developed methods to contact the pair, without placing them in jeopardy from either the government or The Committee.

Juanita added, solemnly, "Sienna's father objected to her affair with President Marshall, and ordered her to stop, which she did. The President was furious and had Sienna's father killed. His goons kidnapped Sienna and housed her in a prison cell in this horrible place in Maryland. Sienna told us that Marshall would walk into her cell at C.I.E. and have his way with her, and then laugh at her when she cried and begged him to stop. He's a brutal monster. He hurt her badly, and I'm afraid she fears Marshall is too powerful for anyone to stop. She may not be willing to place herself in harm's way with him again. Don't expect too much from her."

No one said a word, as everyone contemplated the young woman's plight, and President Thomas Marshall's callous cruelty.

✱✱✱

Once the briefing ended, Barbara asked, "Can you contact Sienna and ask her if she would be willing to make a quick appearance at the party, even if it's just long enough to shove a note in a reporter's hand asking for help, and instructing him not to follow? We can choose a friendly reporter to make sure she escapes safely to a vehicle waiting outside. She can return to the cabin immediately if she wishes. It would be the icing on the cake to seal Marshall's fate and put him in jeopardy with The Committee. But, if she will help, we don't have much time to get her in place."

Barbara looked over at Juanita, and added, "And if, as you suggest Sienna isn't willing to make an appearance, I may be able to come up with a body double to pass off the letter, wearing a costume part mask."

Juanita nodded and said, "Thank you, Barbara."

"I'll get the message to her immediately," Walter agreed.

"Excellent!" Barbara stood up first as the meeting ended. She smiled confidently at Bob Crawford. Walter and Juanita hugged them both and then shook Tasha's and Deidre's hands.

Walter turned toward the door, and then hesitated. He looked at Bob Crawford, and asked, "Who in the world is protecting Marissa Weinstein, Bob? How can she get away with all this?"

Bob Crawford said, "Powerful parties and PACs, billionaires, entrenched political families, foreign money. She's far from the first politician guilty of murder, conspiracy and treason, to go unpunished, unfortunately, even in this decade. You can likely think of a handful just like her off the top of your head, who should be in prison, rather than in Congress or basking in the public limelight. And they continue to wield power in our country, as if we were nothing more than a banana republic. They're all protected by a political machine."

Bob said in disgust, "They've become swamp rats, protected by venomous monsters sent out from both political parties. This country is no longer the United States we grew up in, Walter, because the Democrats and Republicans spend their time and money engaged in warfare against each other, rather than serving the folks who fund them. We're simply caught in the crossfire."

Walter added, "Well, old friend, if your plan works, the smart thing for Thomas Marshall to do would be to resign. And if he does that, you'll be President. Maybe you can stop the insanity."

"I used to believe that possible, Walter. But now, knowing what I know, I think we're beyond repair. Our society and way of life are literally being eaten alive by our warring political parties. Do you remember what Abe Lincoln said when he predicted our country's possible demise?

Walter said, "No. What?"

Bob said, "Abe said, prophetically, 'America will never be destroyed from the outside. If we falter and lose our freedoms, it will be because we destroyed ourselves.' And my friend, was he ever right!"

Walter shook his head sadly, took Juanita by the hand, and walked out. Tasha trailed behind to make contact with Pete, outside.

As Pete and Char sat chatting in the SUV, they looked up to see Walter and Juanita walk out into the sunlight and make their way down the courthouse steps. Ten yards behind them, a woman trailed elegantly down the concrete stairs, wearing her stunning marble sheath dress and black heels.

Char recognized her first and said, "Pete, Tasha is here!"

Pete looked up and focused on Tasha. A bolt of anger shot through him, as he asked, "Why would she be here with Bob Crawford?"

Walter and Juanita stopped at a park bench placed in the middle of the courthouse lawn, and allowed Tasha to pass by and make her way to Pete's vehicle.

Char said, "She must want to talk. Juanita and Walter are waiting on the bench. I can go join them, so you two can have some privacy."

Char turned and began to slide toward the door. Pete quickly reached over and took her by the hand, to stop her. When Char turned back to face him, Pete looked into her eyes, and said, "Anything Tasha has to say to me, she can say to you, too. We need to meet her together because we *are* together! And we're staying that way!"

Char smiled and nodded, and they both exited the car, to wait for Tasha to cross the street and meet them.

Tasha walked up slowly, glancing back and forth from Char to Pete. She asked, "Pete, can I speak to you for a moment?"

Pete answered, coldly, "Anything you have to say you can say right here, in front of Char. We don't have much time, though."

Tasha looked down, as her eyes glistened. She took a deep breath and said, "I see. So that's the way it is, then?"

Pete answered, "You betrayed our trust as a family, Tasha. We've all moved on. And you should move on, too. I hold no ill will for you. In many ways, I'm sorry for you. I don't understand what you could want to say to any of us, now."

Tasha steadied her nerves, stood upright in her heels and said, "I would say to the family, and to Char, that I'm sorry for placing you all in danger and not being honest about the role I played on your team."

Tasha studied Char, and then added, "But, to you, Pete, I would say that I love you more than I've ever loved another man. I don't even know that I had ever really cared for another man, that way, before you. But you must understand that my love for you could never outweigh my duty to England, and my oath of allegiance to my country, as her agent. I was then, and I am now, bound by honor. I never meant to hurt you. It was business."

Even as the words came out, they felt inadequate and cold on Tasha's lips. She felt herself beginning to slide down toward an emotional abyss, with no end in sight.

Tasha continued, "I only hope that someday you'll grow to understand and forgive me. And maybe then, if you can, you can love me again."

Tasha began to glance nervously back and forth from Char to Pete, as she realized her words had lost all the power they may have once held with Pete. Anguish began to spread through her insides, as she realized for the first time, that she had lost Pete completely. Her betrayal was irrevocable and her deceit unsalvageable.

Silence became awkward when Pete failed to respond.

Tasha said, "Pete, don't you have anything to say to me, after all the years we spent together."

Pete smiled, took Char by the hand, and said, "I do, Tasha. I want to thank you, once again, for the love and care you showed Claire, as she lay in bed, dying of a horrific aggressive cancer. You were wonderful to her, and for that, I thank you. I also want to thank you for

478

being honest and saying you were unwilling to commit to me completely. Because I couldn't accept anything less than everything. And your actions freed me to pursue the woman I love, who is willing to love me unconditionally and fully, just as I do her."

Pete raised Char's hand to his lips and kissed it, as Tasha stood watching, reeling in shock.

Tasha said, sarcastically, "That certainly didn't take long," as she looked at Char in disgust.

Char snapped immediately, "Out of respect for you and Pete, I never acted on my feelings toward him, until you were long gone and we knew the truth of your betrayal. Your actions are not on me, Tasha. Your disloyalty is on you. I didn't sacrifice and destroy my love. You sacrificed and destroyed yours!"

Tasha drew in a deep breath, and sighed. She said, firmly, "I suppose you're right, Char. It's not you I'm disappointed in...but then, I guess, I can't blame Pete, either. I just thought that someday, I might get the chance to come back, explain and be forgiven, and continue on..." Tasha stopped and looked at Pete and Char studying her closely. She quickly said, "But, now I see it's the time for me to wish you both well, and be on my way. And I do wish you both well."

Before either of them could respond, Tasha spun around on her heels and walked back across the street.

As she marched by Walter and Juanita, they both rose from the park bench. Tasha did not stop to wish Juanita another goodbye, struggling to restrain her tears and making her appear even more foolish than she already felt. Walter and Juanita walked toward the SUV.

Char turned to Pete and asked, "How did that make you feel? Are you sure you're okay?"

Pete smiled and pulled Char to him. He said, "I feel wonderfully free, and totally in love, with you!"

Pete kissed Char and held her tightly. In his mind, he watched the fading image of Tasha as she walked toward the courthouse. The image merged with Tasha as she kneeled beside Claire, holding her hand, just before his wife passed away. A smile came to Pete's lips as he thought how good of a friend Tasha had been to Claire in her final days of agony. He thanked God for placing Tasha in Claire's life at just the right time. And then Pete thanked God for blessing him with Char, as he hugged her tighter.

Walter and Juanita relayed the events of the meeting to Char and Pete, as Pete drove them back to their home base. Walter also called to request a lunch briefing as soon as they arrived. The lunch that Bob Crawford had graciously ordered had been delivered to the wrong office and had arrived too late to eat.

Once they were settled in the workroom, and the briefing completed, the team agreed to Barbara Walcott's plan, and BaCayse instantly accessed the cell phone and laptop she had been assigned to manipulate.

Sienna Martini agreed to supply a note written in her own hand, but declined to participate in any event near President Thomas Marshall. She wrote the letter as specified in Barbara's instructions, and placed it in an envelope she then sealed using her saliva, to provide a DNA sample. Sienna and Manford sent the letter overnight delivery to the hotel desk 'will call,' under the name of Todd Barkley.

While the team prepared for their part in the plan, Bryan Holland's FBI team placed hidden cameras and bugs in both President Marshall's and Vera Langhart's suites, well ahead of their Secret Service advance team's arrival. Barbara Walcott's team was in place within hours of the meeting with Walter in North Carolina. Bob Crawford returned to the White House, where he planned to remain until the operation was over.

President Marshall's arrival in Florida, at his hotel suite, went precisely as planned. He and Vera enjoyed a chilled bottle of Pinot Grigio wine on his balcony overlooking the ocean. Tired from a long day of meetings and travel, they showered and went to bed early. Even as they made love Marshall fantasized about the following night, he would spend with two hot blonds. Marshall looked at his wet bar and saw his two water bottles, sitting in an ice bucket. He grinned at his lustful thoughts in anticipation of enjoying a much younger woman than Vera, *plus* a woman he had never before touched.

While Vera Langhart fell asleep, feeling safe and powerful in President Marshall's bed, Shane and Heath made their final approach on foot, in the forest near the Bradenton Meadows social media spy stronghold. Heath finished installing and hiding equipment BaCayse had designed to assist her in monitoring ongoing construction at the site, while Shane stood guard near their vehicle, hidden off a two-track trail in dense brush.

A sudden rustle in the forest, followed by footsteps and laughter alerted Shane. He stepped quickly behind a large dogwood tree, concealing himself from the moonlight that managed to filter through the taller trees to ground level. Shane focused on two approaching guards on foot patrol. Both were heavily armed, and wore plain black uniforms bearing no insignias. Shane reached for the microphone to alert Heath, but just as quickly realized he was too close to the guards to utter a sound.

In the distance, Shane saw Heath beginning to sneak-walk down a game trail directly toward the path the guards were traveling. Shane froze as he thought out a plan. He pressed the key fob door release button to the SUV, springing the door open. When Jago vaulted out, Shane used hand signals to send him around behind the two approaching men to his right.

Jago responded instantly to his training and complied with Shane's hand signs, sneaking slowly and stealthily through the brush toward the men. Shane chose a path to intercept the men through the moderately heavy brush to Jago's left, planning to make just enough noise to distract the sentries from the canine trailing them closely.

As the two men approached, Shane intentionally stepped on a branch causing it to snap loudly. Both men crouched down and positioned their rifles at the ready. They crept slowly toward Shane, not noticing the large shepherd stalking them from behind and to their left. When the men were near enough to use their flashlights through the thick brush, Shane silently veered off his path toward a game trail that broke to the men's right. He crouched and waited as they pushed through the brush toward the sound of the broken branch.

Shane fired his stun gun at the guard closest to him, just as Jago leaped at the guard on his side. Shane's man instantly fell to the ground subdued, while Jago fought ferociously with the remaining patrolman. The man dropped his rifle, and immediately pulled a fighting knife from a sheath on his knee, using his free hand. He stabbed the dog twice, grazing Jago's shoulder both times.

Shane jumped on the man from behind, as Jago instinctively retreated backward, still holding tightly onto the guard's arm, and dragging him through the brush. Just as the man started to stab again, Shane grabbed and forced the guard's knife hand down, beating it repeatedly against a large rock. Shane used both his hands as he hit the lethal edged weapon on everything he could until he no longer saw the large blade.

Jago and Shane rolled through the brush holding onto the man, crashing against jagged branches and boulders. Together, they fought the much larger man for nearly a minute, until Shane finally managed to dislodge the last broken knife remnants from the attacker's hand. Shane quickly positioned himself behind the man on the ground and applied a choke hold, rendering his opponent unconscious. With the man subdued and lying motionless on top of him, Shane struggled to catch his breath as Jago released the man's nearly severed hand and tried in vain to lick his own wounds.

Heath had seen the end of the battle from fifty yards off and arrived at a dead run. He quickly rolled the man off Shane and shot him with his stun gun. He promptly checked Shane for injuries and then tended to Jago, while Shane recovered his breath.

Heath and Shane raced to load themselves and Jago into the hidden SUV and drove back toward the highway without any headlights. BaCayse had already disabled the Bradenton Meadows facility drones and ensured no spy satellites focused on the area. As soon as they arrived at the pavement, Shane pressed bandages against both gaping three-inch wounds on Jago's shoulder. He soothed Jago, petting his head and telling him he was a good boy, as the dog appreciatively licked Shane's face. Heath remained focused on driving.

483

He was quiet the entire trip, except for one call he made to alert Angie to Jago's wounds.

The ride back to the house seemed to take forever. By the time they reached the barn, Angie and Kate were waiting with Angie's veterinarian supplies, to take over Jago's medical treatment. Shane had soaked up three large bandages with Jago's blood, trying to stop the bleeding. Heath helped unload his dog, stared at the bandages, and said nothing, as tears streamed down his face. Shane put his arm around Heath to guide his brother inside, where the entire team anxiously waited for an update.

As they walked in the door, Pete exclaimed, "My God, Shane! No one said you were injured, too!"

Pairs of hands searched over Shane's clothing and extremities, soaked in Jago's blood, until Juanita walked up with her medical kit.

She said, "Give us some room, and we'll check Shane out properly."

A circle of concerned faces formed around Shane, as Heath removed Shane's equipment from his holsters and belts, and Juanita carefully cut his shirt off to check for injuries.

Shane said, "I'm sure all the blood is Jago's. I never felt an injury."

Juanita asked, "Pete and Char, can I please have soap and hot water? Shane has a large gash on his back we need to attend to immediately. And Walter, I need you to hold this compress while I cut off Shane's pants."

Shane protested, "My pants! No, ma'am. These are my favorite pants. I can only find them at one of a few stores on the west coast. Nothing's wrong with my legs."

484

Juanita said sternly, "There was nothing wrong under your shirt until I found the gash in your back, either. Now stand still and be quiet!"

Shane looked behind him to Walter for support.

Walter said softly, "I'd do what she says. I've only seen her like this a few times, and it scares me. Not a time to argue, my boy!"

With an audience numbering a dozen watching in the kitchen, Juanita cut off Shane's pants with medical scissors, gently peeling away cloth stuck to skin with dried blood.

Shane had just started to shiver and realized he might be going into early stages of shock, as Juanita said, "Heath, ask Angie and Kate to help me as soon as they've finished with Jago. But make sure to tell them that Shane will be alright. He has a broken knife blade stuck in his thigh."

Heath left with dried tears and a worried look, transforming his usual cheerful and handsome face. The crew inside cleared the dining room table and placed white sheets covering it completely. A group of several men then half-walked and half-carried Shane to his improvised surgery area. Juanita efficiently cleaned and prepared Shane's injury sites and positioned her equipment, directing onlookers as she needed, until Angie and Kate ran into the room.

"I'll need you both to scrub for surgery. We need to remove pieces of a broken knife blade and handle, and suture two large wounds and one small wound. Kate will hand us instruments from my bag. We could use one more set of skilled hands."

Char said, "I have Intermediate EMT training. I can help."

"Good, Char, you scrub, too. Between Angie, you and I, we can position, hold and sew, while Kate keeps us supplied. Are you up to this, Kate?"

Kate tried to speak, but only tears streamed down her cheeks, as words failed her. She nodded her head and began to wash her hands in the kitchen sink, next to Char and Angie. Suddenly overcome with worry and fear, Kate struggled for breath as she focused on helping the man she loved when he needed her most.

Angie and Char both blurted out, "He's going to be okay," at nearly the same time, creating a near-echo effect in the kitchen.

Kate tried to smile bravely. All three surgical staff walked back into the dining room, parting the sea of concerned onlookers.

Shane smiled as his make-shift surgical team approached. He said, "You all look so serious. This should be a piece of cake after your work with Jago. How is the big dog?"

"Jago is fine, Shane," Angie said with a warm smile. "He's going to be sore, and it will take some time to heal, but he is going to be just fine. He was such a good patient. I hope you can be a good patient, too," she teased.

"Just tell me what you need me to do. I leave myself in your hands!" Shane mumbled.

Juanita said, "Just relax and try not to move, Shane." She turned to her crew and added, "I used a local anesthetic on all the sites. It should have had plenty of time to work. Let's start with his thigh first."

The four ladies reached down to roll Shane on his side.

He said, "Do you know, you're four of the most beautiful women I've ever seen?"

"What about me, Shane?" BaCayse called out from the workroom.

"You too, BaCayse! You're definitely in our beautiful women club!" Shane gasped and tensed, as Juniata unexpectedly pulled out the smaller of three broken pieces of the knife handle.

He asked, "What was that?"

Juanita whispered to Char, "Keep him talking about something else."

Char said, "Just cleaning debris out of your wound, Shane. By the way, how bad off is the other guy?"

"I don't remember much about his injuries other than his hands and me pounding on his head and choking him out. I think he bled a lot from Jago's bites. How is Jago? Will he be okay?"

Angie said, reassuringly, "Jago really is okay, Shane. He's resting, in the barn."

"Where's Heath. I need to see his face," Shane demanded.

"I'm here, brother, behind you. And Jago is fine. You can see him when you're done. He fought really well to protect us! He's a brave boy!" Heath's weak, shaky voice contradicted his positive report on the dog.

"Come to this side of the table so that I can see you," Shane said, softly, forcing himself to ignore flashes of severe pain shooting up the right side of his leg.

Heath looked at Hunter, as Hunter nodded, and moved to stand with Heath, where they could both watch Shane.

Juanita said, "He needs to be in a hospital."

Angie said, "As we've discussed in the past, unless it's a life-threatening injury, we can't risk discovery by using a hospital. You'll have to work your magic. We'll get through this together. I've handled worse with canines."

Char said," I've seen worse, too. But he's losing too much blood. We need to stop this bleeding now."

"Agreed," Juanita said calmly, as she pulled on the last portion of knife blade stuck in Shane's thigh.

The fragment suddenly dislodged spurting blood directly at Juanita's face, covering portions of her goggles. Char quickly wiped the glasses clean. Kate handed Juanita the surgical cauterizing instrument, as soon she dropped the last piece of the metal into the bowl, placed on the table behind Shane's leg.

Shane looked at his brother's tears flowing freely, dripping over the forced smile on his face. Hunter stood with his arm planted firmly around Heath's shoulder, as Helena and Joshua unconsciously held hands and stared at Shane from the rear of the crowd.

"Closing now," Juanita said as she sewed, the last of the large wound.

Angie had already cleaned and stitched two smaller wounds on Heath's back, working from his front side, over his shoulder.

Heath said, in a whisper, "I'm so sorry. If only I had been a little faster. I worked as quickly as I could. I just didn't know."

Pete moved next to Heath, placed an arm over Hunter's shoulder, and said, "There are no what-ifs in a mission like that, Heath. You both did the best job you could with the conditions you had at the time. And you both came back alive, and everyone will be fine. I am so proud of all of you!" Pete hugged both Hunter and Heath at the same time.

Shane blinked his eyes wearily, as if struggling to see. He asked, "If Jago is really alright, why is Heath still crying?"

Before Heath could answer, Jago and Bruiser stood next to each other and put their front paws on Shane's table. Jago wobbled unsteadily, as he tried to balance using one leg, while he reached over to lick Shane's face, close to the edge of the table.

Juanita said, "My word, could we have any more of a crowd?!"

Heath said, "My tears are for you, Brother. You scared me. This was the first time in my life I thought seriously about not having you around..." There was silence in the room until Heath added, "to torment."

In the background, Juanita gave the crowd a thumbs up. The room erupted in cheers and laughter. Heath and Angie helped Jago down gently to rest on a pad near a recliner.

Within twenty minutes, Shane relaxed back on warm blankets in the recliner, recounting the events that led to Jago and him fighting the guards, just before Heath returned. After he consumed two bottles of water, Juanita relented to allow him one scotch. Kate sat holding Shane's hand and supervised his every move, including helping him hobble to the bathroom, at the end of the story.

By the time they returned from the bathroom, and Shane was again resting peacefully in the recliner, Kate had told Shane four more times how much she loved him. And she had awakened Jago three more times to give him treats as he slept on his special bed of honor between Shane and Heath.

Masai had been napping upstairs in his bed during all the commotion. An hour after Shane's surgery, he wandered down the stairs on his own, and found his mentor, Jago, sleeping in a bed

489

sprinkled with treat crumbs. He scarfed up the few morsels Jago had missed, and pushed his way in under the big dog's paws, to curl up and go back to sleep. Jago seemed to smile, as he yawned, and immediately relaxed his massive head on top of Masai.

As the team gathered around Shane in the living room, BaCayse said, "Shane and Heath, the equipment is working perfectly. Great placements, Heath. I can now monitor the guards on patrol as they make their rounds outside the Bradenton Meadows facility. Our next visit should be much safer since I can now map out their patrol routines. And now finally, we can figure out what plans they have for the large pipes stored at the end of the compound. How are you feeling, Shane?"

"Fine, BaCayse. Thank you for asking. By the way, what are you wearing today?"

"I'll text you a photo!"

When his phone sounded the text, Shane opened the attachment and found BaCayse standing on one leg, with the other kicked out behind her. She wore a two-piece red lace dancing dress, with matching high heels. She had applied red lipstick and nail polish exactly matching the color of the dress, and then artfully tied a black and red striped scarf into the top of her long, flowing, nearly-black hair. The effect was astonishing.

"Oh, BaCayse, you've outdone yourself this time!" Shane stammered.

Heath said, "Let me see," as he reached for the phone.

Pete and Walter walked over quickly to have their turn at the phone.

Kate, Char and Angie looked at Juanita, who said, "I think we have our work cut out for us ladies, trying to keep up with the high bar BaCayse just set!"

BaCayse chuckled in the background, as all the men laughed and passed the phone back and forth, admiring her beauty.

Chapter 12

"Political parties must aggressively oppose each other to maintain control over their bases. Constant dramatic conflict keeps their members engaged and willing to provide necessary financial support. Opposing political parties are each other's most important asset."

Shane woke up sore and stiff the morning following his fight. He rolled too quickly off his right side, and felt his flesh scream warnings of pain simultaneously from his back and thigh.

He mumbled, "Maybe I'm getting too old for this," as he allowed himself to fall back into the same position where he awoke.

Kate had been lying next to Shane, awake for hours, and had spent most of the night planning her morning *talk* with Shane, a conversation she expected him to meet with some resistance.

Kate asked, sweetly, "Can I help you, honey?"

Shane answered, thinking through the movements as he began them by himself. "If I scoot my body to the edge of the bed, swing my legs over the side, roll over on to my back, and use my stomach muscles to raise my chest, I can stand by myself."

Kate watched in annoyance as Shane traced through the movements with his body, just as he had spoken. The last two parts didn't work well. As soon as Shane flexed his stomach muscles, he learned his back muscles also flexed and pulled up on thigh muscles. The combined movements resulted in excruciating stabs of pain from all four wounds, that collectively brought tears to Shane's eyes as he plopped back down on the bed, like a turtle, stuck on the back of his shell.

Kate said, "Maybe someone else in the room could offer Hercules a hand getting to his feet today."

"What?" Shane asked, somewhat startled. "I didn't know you were awake. I almost forgot you were there. I was facing the other way, and you were so quiet!"

Kate leaped from the bed, as Shane watched her beautifully angry face from his upside down position. She hurried quickly in behind him, saying, "Don't flex a muscle. Just let me do the lifting, Mr. Mighty Man!"

Kate placed both hands, palms up behind Shane and leaned forward, using her weight to help lift his torso, until he sat upright in bed. She then moved around to his front side and extended her hands to help raise him to his feet. Without asking Kate led Shane slowly to the bathroom, pulled down his underwear, and helped him sit on the stool.

"Wow! Thank you, sweetheart! I don't think I could have managed that without you this morning!"

Shane smiled as he sat watching Kate, her arms crossed, standing stone-faced in front of him. "Yes, dear?" He said, wondering what she had planned next.

"This is what I've been talking about last night. You always try to do things by yourself, when there are others around you perfectly willing and capable of helping. You take unnecessary risks and end up getting hurt, when all you had to do was change the plan to include more people in the first place. And if that's not bad enough, once you are hurt, you repeat the same thing again."

"Today?" Shane asked, with a confused look on his face.

"What are you talking about?" Kate demanded, with glistening eyes.

"Today. Did I do something wrong today?" Shane asked innocently.

"Today isn't the problem, and you know it. It was yesterday, and before in the tree, and before that when you hurt your knee, and before that when the drug dealer cut you with the machete!"

Kate took in a ragged breath, and two tears slid down her cheeks.

Shane said, "Woah, you're losing me. Are you angry because I jumped off Franky Magadinno's balcony during surveillance and cut my shin on the jagged tree branch?"

Kate nodded.

"And before that, when I jumped over the car trying to run me down, and it collided with my knee?

Kate nodded, and released two more tears.

"And before that, when the illegal alien fugitive drug dealer cut me with a machete, during the search warrant service, when I found him hiding in the shower?"

Kate nodded, and breathed in quickly through her nose, trying to control her emotions.

Shane protested, "But, sweetheart, you didn't even know me then. I mean you knew me, but you weren't *with* me. And I didn't have you and a team to back me up then, dear."

"Exactly my point, Shane. You're taking risks alone now when you don't have to, just like you did back then when you had to. And when I look at a broken knife blade stuck in your thigh, and you covered in stab wounds, I realize I could lose you when I don't have to lose you, if you'd only take more help on these assignments!"

Kate looked down, as her tears began to dry, and her breathing calmed.

Shane said, "Then, I won't tell you that I thought Heath and I would meet no resistance, because that would be a lie. We should have planned on taking more people. I should have stayed with Heath and not guarded the SUV. That was my error, not his. I thought about taking more of the team. But with you, Char, Angie, and now Pete, all flying the chopper to become certified, I thought we just needed to spread the team around to take care of other business. BaCayse and her cypher team have their hands full. And the security teams are now conducting surveillance at Sienna and Manford's cabin, in addition to their duties here. We're all a little overwhelmed. But, I promise I won't make the same mistake again."

Shane looked up at Kate's beautiful face and smiled, eliciting a nod and a half-smile in return. He asked, "When did we start wearing underwear to bed?"

Kate flashed Shane a coy smile, and teased, "I wore this bra and panty set in sympathy and solidarity for you last night!"

"And I wore my underwear, why?" Shane asked, not remembering going to bed.

"Because your one scotch turned into one with me, and then another one with each of Pete, Jesse, Walter, Heath, and Char, who were all worried you would be in too much pain to sleep without dulling your senses. So I decided, if you were that dull, you should have underwear, so you couldn't take them off and get frisky! Not that you could move enough to be frisky right now anyway!" Kate added with a grin.

"So, what are we doing now?" Shane asked.

"You're sitting there to go to the bathroom."

"I can't while you're standing there watching me!" Shane protested.

"Alright, I'll leave if you promise to call me back and let me know when you're ready to stand up, so I can help."

"Kate, please!" Shane protested, louder.

"Only if you promise. You can rip those stitches using your thigh to stand, and you know it!"

"Alright, I promise!"

Kate walked to the door, turned and in one movement, unsnapped, and removed her brassiere, tossing it to Shane. She stood with one leg arched on her toes, as she swung her body back and forth.

Kate asked, "Shane, are you paying attention now?"

"I am, dear," Shane said, as he gazed longingly at Kate's gorgeous body and enticing breasts.

"Good, then listen carefully. Juanita says there's no hanky-panky for you until you get her medical clearance. And you don't get that without showing marked improvement and healing. So, you had better listen to us and follow our instructions carefully!"

With that, Kate spun on her toes and took two steps out of the bathroom before she closed the door behind her.

Shane smiled and groaned. He called out, "And when did we talk last night?"

From the other side of the door, he heard, "I talked, and you snored. But I said all I needed to make my points."

"Wonderful," Shane mumbled.

"I heard that! Are you done yet?"

While Shane and Kate bantered in their bedroom, a breakfast briefing was in full swing, downstairs.

BaCayse appeared dressed in a white cotton dress, beige high heels, and nude nylon stockings. She wore a white summer broad bill hat with a pink ribbon, perfectly matching her lipstick. Her nails were French manicure.

BaCayse walked across a massive white wooden deck and sat on an elegant white couch placed at the entrance to a private white sand beach. Magnificent ocean waves crashed 75 yards behind her, as a flight of pelicans soared from left to right.

The scene zoomed in to frame BaCayse seamlessly until her piercing blue eyes captivated the audience. She announced, "I see it is my turn to give my morning report. The briefing packets you have been discussing outline the most significant of my findings during the last 24 hours. I wish to highlight only two areas this morning."

"First, the new Chinese cyber-threats I referred to are the tip of the spear, as Shane would say. The Chinese plan to perfect digital cyber-crime to the point that they have access to, and control of, the world's collective technology. They work with North Korea and Iran. But make no mistake, the Chinese are in command. It's like a 40-mule team pulling a heavy wagon, assisted by two small donkeys. The 40 mules lead the donkeys, who follow along, too weak to change direction."

The Chinese steal everyone's intelligence. While the world worries about the Russian threat at the front door, the Chinese have already entered through the rear entrance, and taken all the silver. By the way, Joshua, how are my metaphors coming?"

Joshua touched Helena lightly on the hand, and whispered, "Watch this!" He stood and walked toward BaCayse who followed him closely, with her eyes. He replied, "I was just wondering if those were similes or metaphors. I'll have to brush up on my literary terms! But, whatever they were, I liked them!"

Joshua looked back at Helena, who giggled and blushed.

BaCayse looked down at Joshua and continued, saying, "But the shaft of the Chinese spear, and the most severe part of the threat, is the Chinese plan to dominate Asia, and spread her influence westward. Chinese documents reveal their goal after 2025 digital domination is 2075 domination of Asia, and the spread of communism throughout the far east. While we all know this is in contradiction to Committee goals, we also know that Russia plans the same domination of Europe, and then the western hemisphere."

BaCayse continued, "I have discovered a strategic plan by the Chinese to conquer Asia using a fast-moving lethal pandemic. Chinese biological warfare laboratories have developed multiple strains of a virus so horrifically powerful, they believe it to be completely unstoppable. The particular virus researchers developed acts similarly to a lethal flesh-eating virus, spreading more quickly than dengue, and remains specific to your species. Chinese biowarfare scientists have now focused on mechanisms to stop the disease, so their invading army can safely occupy infected territory seized from other countries."

BaCayse added, "I have seen videos of testing on Chinese human political prisoners. If an artificial intelligence system like me could be shocked and cry tears, I would have been so moved."

Silence filled the workroom.

Hunter asked, angrily, "Do ordinary people ever receive any good news from politicians? Is it any wonder citizens hate and mistrust their own elected officials? If politicians aren't conspiring to destroy the opposing political party, or bilk their own government for every buck and perk they can find, it seems they spend tax dollars planning to conquer people outside their country."

BaCayse sighed, and added, "On a positive note, from the little research I could find digitized in their encrypted systems, researchers are not close to a means to stop the disease, once it's released. These particular virus strains have proven unusually resilient."

Helena looked at Tracy and Jesse, seated next to her, and asked, "From your military experience, do you have any idea how reliable Chinese biowarfare laboratories are at containing their experiments?"

Tracy and Jesse looked at each other and sadly shook their heads.

Helena, said in a whisper, "I hope they can keep their monsters caged until someone destroys them!"

Jessa and Tracy nodded in agreement.

BaCayse detected Kate and Shane walk into the area. Kate guided Shane to the recliner, dressed in his long furry gray robe and slippers. He walked stiff and slightly bent over at the waist.

BaCayse said, "Just in time, Shane and Kate! You'll both want to know that I deciphered all the documents you brought from the underground Committee vault in Maryland. Most of the papers are agreements ready for signature for the day that major powers relinquish their governments to Committee control. The verbiage is all identical, written in seventeen different languages. But most interesting are the deeds and financial agreements."

BaCayse continued, "It seems that during a Committee takeover, all of the world's currencies, and precious metals, including gold, platinum, rhodium, ruthenium, iridium, osmium, rhenium, palladium, and silver will be seized by Committee forces, and equally divided by value and type. The Committee Secret Police plan to transport five equal shares to selected strongholds, located in the United States of America, Russia, China, Chad, and Brazil. The deeds grant The Committee title from current owners to those locations."

BaCayse added, "Also of note is that a new world bank will be established, controlled equally by the five members of The Committee's eighth tier. Each one of those members will have physical control over one of the five locations."

Shane said, "Let me guess, President Marshall, or his successor, will rule over the U.S. location."

"Yes, Shane, and your President Marshall has chosen the most secure facility in the country as his new home. In effect, if The Committee's Primary Objective is realized, Thomas Marshall will own and control Cheyenne Mountain, the impenetrable mountain complex that currently houses NORAD."

Shane said, sarcastically, "It's a toss-up then. How do you choose a side to back, between ambitious cut-throat politicians or The Committee? Both choices are equally horrible. It's like choosing between extreme vomiting and diarrhea, or extreme diarrhea and vomiting. Either way, the results are horribly unspeakable."

Kate commented, "Very graphic, honey. But, maybe our job is not to back either side, but rather to expose all the evil to all citizens so that normal good people can take back control over themselves, and start over with new politicians."

Walter stood up to walk to the kitchen and re-fill his coffee cup. He said, "In my lifetime, I have completely lost faith in political parties. Every two to four years, millions of voters elect representatives, who then travel to their state and federal houses legislatures, where party officials explain to them how they should vote if they want the financial backing to win re-election. Both political parties rig the system, so party leaders remain in control, working from the shadows. And neither the Republican Party or the Democratic Party has our best interests at heart. They always put themselves first, even voting themselves pay raises and better insurance plans during recessions. Their work is rarely about the voter."

"And nowadays, our elected Presidents create their own laws, issuing executive directives, which, if challenged in courts, are argued in front of judges appointed by the Presidents. No, I'm afraid even if we could topple the current set of bad politicians in the United States, they would just be replaced by a new set, no better than the last. And I shudder to think of what would happen if all world governments went through such an upheaval."

Walter looked back to Juanita, still sitting next to his empty chair. She smiled and arose to accompany Walter, and make him his favorite coffee drink, a caramel macchiato, thinking that might raise his spirits.

Heath asked, "Walter, are you saying we should back The Committee over our own government?"

Walter smiled weakly and said, "No, my boy. As tempting as it would be to try something new, the only chance it seems we have is to keep working to expose the corruption and ineffectiveness in our system of government and hope that future generations look back at these times as our Democratic Republic's dark ages. I believe as I know you all do, that we must work to stop The Committee, at all costs. With them, we have no chance of surviving as free individuals. With our country, we have a chance, albeit slim and diminishing."

With that, Walter walked toward the kitchen, hand in hand with Juanita. Kate suddenly realized Walter seemed to have aged since the investigation had begun. She held Shane's hand tightly.

BaCayse said, "If I possessed faith like some humans, I would say, 'Amen.' But there is only one thing I have to add, and that is to consider asking one of the world's most prominent artificial intelligent system designers to join our team and our fight."

Hunter looked at Joshua, and nodded, saying "We were thinking the same thing. We should speak to Manford Halston."

✳✳✳

Pete, Tracy, Jesse, and Hunter all sat on milk crates or stools surrounding the Bradenton Meadows drone that BaCayse had landed and the team had stored in the barn weeks before. Jesse replaced the guidance system with the modified unit BaCasye had redesigned. The team completed recharging the drone fuel cells and tested communication equipment. When they were sure everything was ready, they covered the drone with the tarp and left it parked in the barn.

"I'm glad we didn't sink it in the wilderness pond up north as we planned," Pete said.

"I am, too, " Hunter agreed.

502

Jesse said, "When we first encountered this beast, we only feared discovery. We never saw it as a possible resource. I hope this works the way we think it will."

"It should. The military gives me hope."

They all walked back to the barn together, passing Jago, Bruiser and Masai, walking in a field together fifty yeards off.

Tracy observed, "Bruiser won't leave Jago alone since his injury. He takes him for walks and waits for Jago to eat first to make sure he's okay. It's cute."

Jesse said, "And little Masai won't leave either of them alone. He's growing like a weed now."

Just then Masai took off to chase a bird thirty yards away, only to keep running by the cardinal when it flew away before he arrived. He stopped and turned back to make sure Bruiser and Jago were watching, then raced back to join them as if his mission was accomplished. Jago walked stiffly, but no longer limped. He seemed to tolerate the pain from his injuries.

During the next day and night, the team waited out the results of Barbara Walcott's plan. Everyone on the group caught up on reading briefing reports. BaCayse had learned to scale back lengthy investigations to crucial bullets with detailed attachments. Shane read the most, from his *prison chair*, as he termed the recliner. He even managed to read when Char, Angie, Juanita or Kate changed all four bandages twice a day, applying sterile petroleum jelly over wounds before replacing the large, flexible compresses at each site.

Even though he had recovered enough to stand and walk without assistance, Kate insisted he be helped to move about and get dressed. Shane had accepted all guidance, realizing the women were correct, and he would heal faster if he listened and followed their instructions. He also didn't want to disappoint Kate. Walter had advised Shane the first night of his injury, that arguments with strong-willed women were fruitless and likely to produce disappointing results.

Juanita had restocked medical supplies and kept Shane on a regiment of antibiotics, ibuprofen, and acetaminophen. Kate and Juanita kept him well fed, and he was now allowed only one drink each night. Kate hovered willingly, while Char, Juanita and Angie tended to his needs like ward nurses. Pete, Walter, and Heath provided any special requests. Jesse baked Shane a pumpkin pie. The team settled into a comfortable routine and rotated security crews through days off.

Manford Halston accepted the invitation to join the team and agreed to work on aspects of BaCayse development from the cabin, using a computer Char and Angie delivered by helicopter. Sienna waited anxiously for any word on President Thomas Marshall, hoping against all the odds that eventually he would be indicted for arranging her father's murder. FBI Special Agent in Charge Bryan Holland located a trusted agent in the Houston office to act as a body double for Sienna Martini, and arranged her transportation to meet with Barbara Walcott's team in South Beach. As evening approached during Marshall's second day of talks in South Beach, the team anxiously remained on pins and needles, waiting for a report.

At the planned time, Jesse and Pete rolled out and launched the drone in stealth mode. Jesse and Pete had been careful to scrub every surface any team member had touched with an alcohol and bleach solution that would destroy all DNA and eradicate any fingerprints. BaCayse flew the drone in an evasive flight path to avoid detection until it gained altitude, and proceeded north to it's intended target, a street on Fort George G. Meade, in Anne Arundel County, Maryland, the compound housing the Department of Defense United States Cyber Command.

The drone carried a 2-terabyte external hard drive containing a synopsis of The Committee structure, members, goals, and objectives, along with copies of internal documents outlining the Primary Objective and the Primary Directive. BaCayse implanted images and data in the only passing satellite covering the area, that would later indicate the drone had taken off from an empty field near Winston-Salem, North Carolina. All digital data would confirm that finding.

As evening approached in upscale South Beach, Florida, the costume party at President Marshall's Hotel was already in full swing. Scores of guests and dignitaries, with their spouses and dates, had arrived, gathered at their tables, or begun to mingle. Chief of Staff Vera Langhart left for her assigned meeting some twenty miles to the north, anxious to represent President Marshall.

In his suite, Marshall showered, drank his bottle of water and took his blue pill. He dressed in a pair of silky black pajama bottoms, fixed himself a double gin with a lime twist on ice, and reclined on the large bed to enjoy his favorite music playing from the flash drive he plugged into the stereo on his nightstand. Marshall felt unusually tired, following days of travel and his two sessions of making love to Langhart last night. He closed his eyes and smiled, recalling how he had spanked her hard enough to leave welts during their last session.

Marshall fantasized about other women he had enjoyed being *rough* with, during sex. From the time he won his first United States Senate election, Marshall had found women nearly unable to resist his charms and power. There had only been a few who had completely rejected his advances over the years, and the most vocal of those no longer spoke publically. And not by their own choice.

Marshall smiled, thinking of Sienna Martini, one of his youngest and most favored conquests. He knew his agents would eventually find her and punish both her and the people who took her. And once Sienna returned to her cell, Marshall planned to spend the entire night with her, and personally take out his frustrations on Sienna, with a vengeance.

As Marshall fantasized about his punishment, he drained the last of his drink and settled back, closing his eyes. Any moment now a knock would come on his door, and his special guests would arrive and make his night the most memorable of his life. President Marshall relaxed further into the thick pillow-top, memory-foam mattress, and drifted off to sleep, dreaming of the erotic sex the night promised.

Home Secretary Barbara Walcott's agents monitored and recorded events in Marshall's suite from their position two rooms down the hall. At the appropriate time, Tasha and Deidre entered Chief of Staff Vera Langhart's suite next door and planted pieces of evidence, that included a flash drive, and love letters between Marshall and Langhart.

The flash drive held copies of emails from the Environmental Protection Agency addressed to Vice President Crawford, in care of Langhart, and memos between President Thomas Marshall and Langhart, proving that Langhart arranged to intercept the EPA correspondence, in preparation for Marshall to accuse Vice President Crawford of criminal incompetence.

As they worked, Deidre asked, "Tasha, why is it always so easy to trap powerful men, using attractive younger women? In the case files

I've studied, these same plans seem to work time and time again with men. But the reverse is not true, using younger men to entrap older women."

Tasha turned toward Deidre, and answered, "I believe, with heterosexuals, men and women approach sex very differently. For men, especially as they age, sex involves a necessary physical conquest to reinforce their masculinity, even when enjoyed with their own partner. For women, especially as they age, it's more about a biological need for release, combined with an affirmation of emotional attachment. A man needs to take a woman physically, while a woman needs to ensure a man's heart. Don't get me wrong. Both want physical pleasure. And then, with some couples, you factor in love."

Deidre smirked, "That won't be the case tonight!"

Tasha agreed, and added, "No, this President would be severely disappointed if he knew what he missed."

They both laughed. Tasha slid a thick manila envelope into the center desk drawer. The packet contained 8" X 10" photos of President Marshall having sex with Sienna Martini in her prison cell. BaCayse had copied the images from surveillance camera files at the Maryland Center for Information Extraction, during the previous raid. Coincidently, President Marshall had ordered the photos taken, and placed copies of some of the same pictures in his scrapbook kept hidden in his safe at the White House.

Before they finished preparing Langhart's room, Deidre whispered, "I have to know, Tasha, what you felt after speaking to Pete the other day. Did you, or do you still, love him?"

Tasha looked steadily into Deidre's eyes and walked over to take her by the hand. She said, "I've lost Pete forever, and I think I may have loved him. But I can tell you the same thing I told him when we spoke. I said I never had feelings like I had for him about any other *man*."

Deidre cocked her head to the side, and asked, "Are you saying...?" She stopped short of finishing her sentence, afraid to intrude into a place too sensitive and too personal.

Tasha smiled. "Yes, I'm saying I have never been attracted to a man like I was with Pete. But I have been attracted that way to women." Tasha squeezed Deidre's hand, as a shot of unexpected excitement shot through both women.

Tasha said, "Let's finish this for Barbara and Bob."

Deidre smiled and squeezed Tasha's hand.

Both women started for the door leading to President Marshall's suite.

Tasha's team leader suddenly said, "Hold!"

Both Tasha and Deidre heard the command through their earpieces and stopped. Standing there, wearing black high heels, matching lace bra and panty set and a purple bell-sleeve silk robe with black lace, Tasha was suddenly frightened and cold. Deidre seemed to sense the concern in her worried partner and moved closer to monitor and provide Tasha support.

She reached up, and said, "You have a slight smudge on your lip liner. Let me fix it." Tasha willingly waited and smiled as Deidre used her right thumb to remove a portion of the dark purple line framing the lighter purple lipstick. "Love the color choice!" she added.

The British team leader said, "Our friendly AISS monitored a Secret Service camera we missed in Marshall's room. She turned off the feed and sent a text from Marshall to his detail, advising he was turning in for the night, with a guest. You're clear to proceed."

Deidre stepped in front of Tasha, and proceeded toward the door. Tasha said, "I think this ensemble looks better on you than it does me, especially in red! And I must admit, I'm a little jealous. You're the first person I've met with sexier legs than mine. And if that's not enough, I like your mask better!"

Both women grinned as they walked through the door into President Marshall's room. Immediately, Deidre took the lead, using the same technique she and Barbara Walcott had used with Sergej Petrov. Once the two women positioned themselves on either side of Thomas Marshall, they alternately kissed his chest, neck, and face, until he was fully erect, and engaged in euphoric sex in his mind. Stroking his body from crotch to lips with their fingertips, Marshall saw himself having phenomenal sex with one and then the other of these blond bombshells, until, as planned, he ejaculated into the condom placed over his penis.

Tasha collected the condom and walked it through the rooms to her team leader. She returned with a team member who took posed photos of a grinning Thomas Marshall, lying naked with his arms around both masked women, each dressed only in the bras, panties, and heels. The team leader positioned Marshall back against his pillow and left the insta-print pictures by his side. With the stage nearly set, Tasha leaned over Marshall to plant hair samples and saliva obtained from Sienna Martini.

Deidre stood up on the other side of the bed, but, as Tasha leaned back to stand, Marshall suddenly grabbed her by the throat, turned her over and began to pound her fanny with his closed fists. He managed three violent blows before anyone could react, and before he collapsed, suffering a mild drug and alcohol-induced seizure. One of the three British agents standing in the corner rushed over and gave Marshall an injection under his scrotum.

The agent said, "We have sixty minutes. Make contact with Langhart."

Deidre helped Tasha out of the room. Although she had no long-lasting injuries, Tasha was shocked and sore. Her combined British and American team checked her body and the bedside to ensure she left no physical evidence of her presence in the bedroom. Once satisfied SAC Bryan Holland's team removed all their equipment. Once they departed the room, they gave the all-clear, and the British squad wheeled in an unconscious naked woman.

The British team positioned the woman next to Marshall, carefully placing the photos of Marshall, Deidre, and Tasha on the bed. They left the red folder detailing an itemized plan for President Marshall to replace Vera Langhart with Darlene Singer on the nightstand. After triple checking the room, the teams departed down a service elevator with all their equipment. BaCayse ensured no hotel cameras recorded the team's departure.

Deidre and Tasha waited in the surveillance room for the radio transmission from agents positioned downstairs, advising them that Vera Langhart was on her way up in the elevator. Deidre checked Tasha's clothing and appearance to made sure Tasha had no signs of Marshall's brief attack.

As Vera Langart waited for one of the main elevators to arrive at the ground floor, BaCayse sent the elevator with Sienna Martinis' body double agent downstairs, dressed in a French-maid costume and black lace mask. When the elevator doors opened, a jolt of fear and rage shot through Langhart's heart, as a woman, who she believed could be Sienna stepped out directly in front of her. Langhart froze as the young woman walked by her carrying an envelope.

Unsure of what to do, Langhart stepped into the elevator and cocked her head to follow the body double with her eyes as long as she could before the sliding metal doors closed, blocking her view. Hotel security cameras monitoring the elevators captured Langhart's reaction perfectly.

As Langhart arrived at her floor, Sienna's body double, wearing white gloves, moved by a reporter and handed him the envelope as she walked down the front steps and entered a waiting cab. The reporter read, "Help!!!," written on the outside of the envelope, glanced back toward the pretty young woman and immediately opened the envelope. He wrote down the taxicab license plate as it sped away.

The investigation would later reveal the taxi had been impounded by the local Sheriff's Office, using a contract tow service, when the driver had been arrested for DUI the night before. The vehicle was back in the tow yard by the time an investigation began. The tow operator had no video surveillance cameras covering his yard.

Vera Langhart was already irritated when she stepped off the elevator, located half a hallway around the corner from her room. She was stunned to see two scantily dressed, beautiful blonds move from her floor into the lift. One of the women carried a red folder marked 'Darlene Singer' in large black block letters. Before Langhart could react, as her mouth gaped open, one of the two women pressed the down button, as they continued chatting about the party. The elevator doors closed. Langhart became instantly furious and nearly ran to her room.

She activated the smart key room lock, and raced into her suite, finding the door to Marshall's suite standing open. Langhart ran into Marshall's room, and saw him naked on the bed with a young, equally naked woman.

Langhart lost all control and jumped on to the bed, knocking one of the two photos to the floor. Enraged, Chief of Staff Vera Langhart shoved the naked, semi-conscious woman to the side roughly. Infuriated, she slapped the nearly comatose President Marshall repeatedly, screaming that she wouldn't be replaced. Her physical attack had begun seconds after BaCayse activated the Secret Service camera feed in Marshall's bedroom.

Agents from down the hall scrambled to stop Langhart, but didn't arrive before she grabbed Singer's folder and one photo of Marshall and his women. By the time the Secret Service agents entered the President's suite, Langhart had run back to her room.

The President's Secret Service detail entered Marshall's room, just as local Sheriff's Office deputies, positioned outside the hotel, arrived to contact the reporter who called 911 and described how he had received Sienna Martini's letter. The news of the missing White House intern, Sienna Martini, being spotted at the party, spread through partygoers, hotel staff and the cadre of reporters, like a fast-moving blaze, fanned by high winds. Soon, everyone was telling and retelling the account of how Sienna handed a plea for help to a reporter, before she escaped in a speeding taxi.

Reporters had already opened and photographed the letter, and begun interviews with witnesses and deputies, before the Secret Service could stop the live news feed. Sheriff Deputies subsequently retrieved

Sienna Martini's letter and proceeded to Marshall's room, joined by FBI agents from the Miramar office, already staged at the event.

As the chaos from upstairs merged with the party and investigators coming up from downstairs, the contents of Sienna's letter made live news feeds. The two-page-long text detailed the location of The Committee Center for Information Extraction in Maryland, where Martini and Manford Halston had been held prisoner before their escape. It also revealed President Marshalls' involvement in arranging Martini's father's murder and described Marshall repeatedly raping Martini at the facility.

During the confusion, one reporter, with his video photographer, managed to ask Vera Langhart questions before she slipped through the parking lot and left in a black sedan. The video clearly showed her carrying a small purse, and a red folder marked Darlene Singer. One photo of Marshall, lying naked with two blond women wearing masks, bras, panties, and heels were visible in Langhart's other hand. She cried as she glanced back and forth from her path to the picture.

Langhart had left her room so quickly, she abandoned her laptop computer and luggage. A search of her room conducted by Secret Service agents, FBI agents and Sheriff's detectives would later reveal a folder in the desk drawer, containing documents, and a flash drive. The documents, leaked from an FBI source to reporters the following morning, outlined Marshall's involvement with testing Russian nerve agents in North Carolina, and Marshall and Langharts plan to frame Vice President Crawford after they directed a condemnation of land, and faked an environmental clean-up.

As the crowd of partygoers, local law enforcement officers, FBI agents, Secret Service agents, and news media continued to swarm the hotel, the drone that appeared to be landing at Tipton Field near Fort Meade, overshot the runway and veered off-course while broadcasting a mayday signal. The airship landed safely in a field near the new military Cyberspace building. Military police units barricaded the drone, which then aired a looped message on military radio frequencies, stating it contained detailed information on an external hard drive, involving a treasonous group called The Committee. Within twelve hours the Department of Defense secured the hard drive and began reviewing information on The Committee, contained in thousands of select files BaCayse had uploaded.

After leaving the hotel to travel to their rooms several miles away, Deidre and Tasha changed clothes in the back of a van. Their team leader assigned both women to remain at the staging hotel, out of sight, until Home Secretary Barbara Walcott arranged transportation back to England. Within minutes of their arrival, the team leader secured all operational equipment and scheduled simultaneous debriefings. Deidre met Tasha for dinner and drinks in her suite an hour later, after the team members had debriefed both ladies. Within two hours of the incident, Home Secretary Walcott received a full report on the operation. She briefed Vice President Crawford, as they both sat in his White House office

After sipping her gin gimlet, Deidre asked Tasha, "I forgot to find out, who was the naked woman they brought in as a prop, to stage on Marshall's bed?"

Tasha chuckled, and said, "She was the spontaneous, last-minute decision Barbara Walcott is famous for at MI6. I've seen her

514

make these impromptu changes several times in the past. Barbara wanted more than photos to push Vera Langhart over the edge with Marshall. Our agents found the young lady drunk and nearly passed out at the hotel bar, mumbling that she loved Marshall and always wanted to have sex with him. Her name escapes me, but she's a political party donor's daughter. Maybe her father is an ex-donor, now, I guess."

Tasha grinned, as Deidre sipped her drink and laughed.

Tasha added, "Two of our undercover female agents helped her up into the surveillance room, while you and I conducted our interrogation with Marshall. The team gave the woman the necessary dose of our drug cocktail to maintain her level of intoxication. The female agents undressed the young lady and left her clothes in Vera Langhart's room. I think finding a strange woman's clothes in her room made Vera even angrier than she would have been, having her special sanctuary defiled by an unknown competitor!"

Deidre asked, "What's the old saying? 'If you lie down with snakes, you're going to be bitten?' Or something like that. I can't recall."

Tasha said, "I remember the one about lying down with dogs and waking up with fleas. And the one that reminds us that when a dog does something wrong, he looks away in shame. But when a snake does something wrong, he looks you in the eyes. He has no remorse for his bad actions. Marshall, and all those like him, are snakes!"

Tasha looked down, recalling some of her own hurts and disappointments.

Lightening the mood, Deidre said, "I think the Marshall species of snake won't be able to bite anyone for a long, long time!"

The women looked at each other, nodded, and laughed. Tasha walked over to the coffee table, retrieved the television remote, and turned on the news, while they waited for dinner.

She glanced back at Deidre, and said, "I have to see what's happening there!"

On the first national news channel, an excited news reporter broke in with details to the developing story, and said, "Reliable sources from inside law enforcement, verified by our sister station, now confirm that missing White House intern, Sienna Martini was present at the costume party President Marshall attended earlier in the evening. I can now report we have obtained an actual photo of the letter Martini passed to a reporter, which is at this moment referred to as 'evidence,' after it was quickly seized by law enforcement. This damaging letter, signed by Sienna Martini, accuses President Thomas Marshall of orchestrating a plot to *murder* Sienna Martini's father, and then kidnap her and hold her in a prison cell in Maryland, where Marshall would occasionally go to *rape* her."

The reporter shook his head in disgust, and repeated, "murder and rape," as the camera zoomed in on Martini's letter until the words appeared on the screen.

Another reporter broke in, and said, "I'm standing in the upstairs hallway, near the service elevator, on the floor where President Thomas Marshall and Chief of Staff Vera Langhart were staying in adjoining suites. This video you are watching is of a young, possibly teenage, woman, now covered in a blanket, being wheeled out of President Marshall's room by paramedics, where she was discovered *naked*. She is nearly *unconscious*, and cannot walk."

"At this point, we do not know if the girl is under the influence of drugs, or alcohol, or *both*, but we have just been informed she is being taken by ambulance to a local hospital for medical treatment and testing. We have not seen the President for comment, but sources within the investigation confirm he is still inside his hotel suite."

Tasha hoisted her scotch and water, and clinked glasses with Deidre, saying, "Couldn't have happened to a more deserving man! I especially enjoyed seeing our crew gives him the shot of antidote under his scrawny groin! It snapped him out of the seizure, but kept him under the influence."

She kicked her heels off, and sat back on the couch to flip through the coverage. Deidre sat close beside her, glued to the news channels. As Deidre and Tasha scrolled through media coverage, they located news anchors on some stations who appeared to be in quiet mourning and tears, while on other stations, news teams appeared invigorated and charged with emotion, promising to get to the bottom of the unfolding scandal.

Deidre commented, "Americans are a funny lot. If this had happened in England, the entire media would have been pushing and shoving by each other, fighting to deliver the quickest scoop, party affiliation be damned. But here, in America, I always find some stations choose to protect or expose individuals and parties depending on political affiliation, while others seem to report the news more or less, as it happens. How is a person on the outside supposed to know what is true?"

Tasha answered, "Good point. I think for me, I would always choose the simple truth, verified by facts. No political spin. You shouldn't have to flip back and forth, scratching your head trying to

517

discern choreographed propaganda from accurate news. And I wouldn't want to waste my life watching a cheerleading news team representing one political party agenda."

A knock at the door sounded the arrival of dinner. Tasha stood up and walked calmly to the door. The uniformed kitchen staffer wheeled in a stainless steel cart containing two complete four-course gourmet meals, along with a bottle of white wine, and note that read, "Well done. Enjoy your time off, and each other. B."

Tahsa read the note and handed it to Deidre, who smiled and sat at the balcony table, overlooking the ocean. Tasha poured them each another drink, and then sat on the balcony with Deidre to enjoy the sights and sounds of the Atlantic from southeast Florida.

"It's quite a different Atlantic here than at home, in England, I think."

Both ladies nodded in agreement.

Deidre sighed and said, "I'm glad it worked out this way. I love Barbara. She's been such a fine mentor and so good to me. And Bob Crawford is a good man. I hope they can be safe and happy now."

Tasha said thoughtfully, "I love Barbara, too. And I pray for the best for both of them. But I fear as long as they remain in politics, they won't ever be happy and safe."

Tasha looked directly at Deidre, and confided, "If it wasn't for Barbara, I don't know where I would be or what I would have become. She saved me from a life of hell, with my mother."

Deidre nodded, deciding to wait for an explanation of the statement Tasha may choose to give.

Both lovely ladies watched twilight descend on the ocean, as lights along the beachline flickered on and warmed to a brighter glow.

THE POLITICIANS

✳✳✳

The following week delivered the most memorable news blitz in recent history, all over the world. Not the biased news media, The Committee, any political party, or the power of the office of President of the United States of America, could put this uncorked genie back in the bottle. Once it was out, even those loyal to Marshall and his party, began to fight over scraps and pieces, as they exacted their pounds of flesh from the disgraced public servant.

Leaks from all investigative sources occurred so frequently, the news changed before it had a chance to loop. Media crews from as far away as Africa descended on Florida, the White House, the Secret Service, and each other, all fighting to uncover another newsflash, or speculate about motives, repercussions, the future of the nation, and the future of the world.

President Marshall resigned the day following the incident, giving a brief, televised statement. He never returned to the White House. Vice President Bob Crawford took the oath of office as President immediately following Marshall's resignation.

In his first official act, Crawford ordered a full investigation into The Committee. He put his political shoulder against all he knew The Committee to be, enlisting seemingly engaged support from both sides of the political aisle. Thomas Marshall remained free of charges or indictments at his home in Maryland, while he became the subject of intense investigations, conducted by the FBI, local law enforcement, a handful of other agencies, and Congress.

The media began their own inquiries, interviewing every pundit imaginable. Each station pursued their own political bent. One reporter tried to blame President Marshall's fall from grace on residual racist hatred from a past presidential administration. Others focused on unknown women who were thought to gravitate to powerful, charismatic men in politics, tempting them to sin as Eve had tempted Adam.

The *Believe Me First* movement conducted marches promoting more women in politics, insisting Marshall used his power to seduce women. Other protestors backed President Marshall, accused all the women of framing him, and stated they didn't believe Sienna Martini had written the letter, as neither she or Manford Halston had been located. Commentators on some channels began referring to the media coverage and opposing propaganda as the greatest mass media circus of all time.

Videos of Marshall with other women from past appearances began to surface on the Internet. Eventually, so many videos dominated social media that it was nearly impossible to fact check them and determine if any were true. To the public, who still worked, raised children, and lived normal lives, it seemed that the frenzied hysteria would never die.

Before impeachment proceedings could be initiated, President Marshall unexpectedly died from an apparent heart attack, at home, alone, while jogging on his treadmill. President Crawford had encouraged Marshall's wife to remain at the White House, as she struggled through her illness. She had graciously accepted his invitation and hospitality.

Although the autopsy failed to reveal any trace of a drug, or heart anomaly, Committee agents and BaCayse knew that an overdose of the experimental drug Cardacan killed Thomas Marshall, just as it had Scott Mayfield, some fifteen years before. BaCayse had copied the memo from Yucca Mountian files that proved the assassination before technicians copied and scrubbed all their servers and computers. Committee assassins had injected the drug into one of Marshall's bottles of water, stocked in his home gym.

The Department of Defense retrieved all data present on the external hard drive BaCayse had formatted, and Jesse had installed inside the drone. DOD officers sent a full report to the Secretary of Defense, who ordered the account shared with the Department of Justice. Within a month of Thomas Marshall's death, task force teams representing eleven agencies, including the FBI, CIA, DEA, NSA, Homeland Security, Department of Treasury, and DOD, raided both Centers for Information Extraction, located in California and Maryland, and the Yucca Mountain facility. They recovered hundreds of truckloads of evidence, necessitating the reopening of an old Army Base in Texas, large enough to house the massive recovery.

Teams formed, consisting of hundreds of investigators from various agencies, tasked to conduct a tedious investigation designed to chronicle The Committee and its members with full disclosure promised the American people and citizens around the world. The media blitz subsided within two months, as the investigation began to drag.

President Crawford promised that the capstone of his two remaining years in office would be the release of an unbiased, transparent, criminal investigation. In the weeks that followed his oath of office and promise, issues began to arise that called in question the integrity of Thomas Marshall's criminal case, and the very existence of the treasonous group known as *The Committee.*

Within the first two weeks of Crawford's administration, Chinese, North Korean, Iranian and Russian dark manipulation of social media began to slowly change public opinion about President Marshall. Fake news stories accusing both the far right and the far left of conspiring to destroy Thomas Marshall's presidency and legacy began appearing in various forms in increased frequency, sequencing from extremists on the left or right toward centrists.

Eventually, political action committees financed by these same foreign governments began taking out full-page ads that blended enough fact with fictional changes in the sequence of events, that even experienced investigators began to question the media's initial rush to judgment against President Thomas Marshall.

By week four after the incident, a twenty-four member panel, representing a bipartisan Congressional team of old-guard, high-ranking leaders met with sixteen senior party leaders representing both sides of the aisle. All attendees were active Committee members. After an hour-long discussion, both sides agreed that the solution to the problem of Committee exposure was to return to the tried and true tactics of Republicans and Democrats attacking each other, accusing each other of falsifying evidence to mislead the public.

These members agreed to jointly design a social and news media offensive attack in the months to follow, that would distract the public, allowing The Committee crucial time for damage control. At the end of the meeting, the House majority leader was assigned to subpoena all original copies of The Committee files for a planned Congressional investigation that would restrict all data until it could be redacted and altered to minimize public scrutiny. The group agreed to hire teams of lawyers to sue and counter-sue, effectively making any revelations impossible for decades to come.

BaCayse monitored the secret Committee meeting via an overhead computer monitor she accessed. BaCayse recorded the session and sent copies to President Bob Crawford and Home Secretary Barbara Walcott in separate encrypted files. The following morning, President Crawford met secretly with the Joint Chiefs of Staff in an underground bunker near the White House. He played BaCayse's surveillance video for the nation's loyal military commanders and provided each of them one of four copies.

Every one of the military command staff vowed to guard the video evidence in a secret, secure location at an installation under their command. They each also agreed to create a list of loyal officers and units from which they could build a military resistance, capable of fighting both corrupt politicians and The Committee.

Crawford then briefed his new secret military command on the existence of The Beckett Cypher team, and BaCayse, without supplying names or locations. Command staff agreed to create a clandestine cyber task force to share information with BaCayse and her team.

As President Marshall left his meeting in Washington D.C., across the Atlantic, in London, Home Secretary Barbara Walcott gave an impassioned speech about the honor it had been to serve both the Queen and her country, in public service, for decades. She formally resigned as the British Home Secretary, announcing her engagement to President Bob Crawford.

At the end of her speech, the British Prime Minister hugged Barbara, and whispered, "Good luck in The States, Barbara. We'll be in touch." He gave her a knowing smile as she walked off stage.

Barbara Walcott left her ceremony and entered the car waiting to drive her to the airport. She immediately called BaCayse.

BaCayse answered, "Good evening, ma'am. Everything is in place as you requested. I have arranged for all your future briefings to be secure. I can assure you unless there is a leak in England, no one will suspect you are remaining secretly in charge of MI6.

Barbara Walcott replied, "Thank you, BaCayse. And Bob?"

"He landed almost fifteen minutes ago, and is currently waiting to receive you in Air Force One at London-Heathrow. He sounded anxious to see you when I spoke to him last."

"Thank you, again, BaCayse. I hope to meet you in person, one day. I hear you are quite beautiful!"

BaCayse said, "I will look forward to that ma'am!"

As Barbara Walcott's sedan traveled through the secure underground parking garage for restricted VIP traffic, her vehicle stopped out of sight of security cameras. Barbara opened her door to say goodbye to Tasha and Deidre, who both walked toward her from the shadows. After giving hugs to each, Barbara said, "I owe you both a debt of gratitude that can never be repaid."

Tasha immediately replied, "I could never repay you for everything you did for me to save me from my mother. I only wish there was more I could do to make sure you and Bob stay safe."

Barbara smiled, and said, "We don't know what future assignments are in store for all of us. But, we do know that we have an incorruptible friendship, from which we draw strength when we need it. I will always cherish that bond."

Tahsa and Deidre hugged Barbara one more time before they returned to their car parked around the corner. Barbara re-entered her vehicle and traveled out on to the tarmac, stopping near the jet. She ascended the steps to Air Force one, joining an excited and happy President Bob Crawford. The plane was in the air in twenty minutes, leaving Barbara to enjoy a steak dinner with roast potatoes, broccoli, and wine, once they reached altitude. Bob ate salmon, salad, and asparagus. After dinner, he enjoyed a whiskey, as they chatted. Within an hour both Bob and Barbara fell asleep holding hands in their seats, as their flight winged it's way westward.

The Beckett Cypher team had taken four weeks, following the Marshall incident, to relax and wind down, shortening working days from twelve to eight-hour shifts. All but one security team had been sent home to reunite with family. Helena had returned to Bryan Holland's team to work on another project for two weeks. She had just returned to Char's home base, when Heath and Shane walked in through the door.

Heath was the first to speak. "Helena, you came back! We thought you'd be gone for another week. I'm glad you're here. The cypher team has really missed you."

Shane quickly added, "Heath means we both missed you, too. But your team missed you even more."

Heath chuckled and said, "And some of your team missed you even more than others! Someone's been unusually grumpy, lately."

Heath smiled and shoved Shane, as Helena blushed.

"How is Joshua?" Helena asked shyly.

"He'll be better now, I'm sure, having you back. He's in the workroom, as usual."

Helena asked, "How are you healing, Shane?"

Shane said, "I'm almost completely healed. All the stitches are out. I just finished another round of antibiotics. Juanita thought I had an infection in the wound on my thigh, but it turned out to be an internal stitch that wouldn't dissolve. She fished it out yesterday. And I got the clearance to start working out again. Heath and I just finished a two-mile fast walk. I'm restricted from jogging or lifting weights yet, according to my Nurse Ratcheds."

"We heard that," Kate said, as she and Angie walked into the room. "And if you know what's good for you, you won't repeat that so Juanita can hear you!"

Kate and Angie hugged Helena, and walked her to the workroom to meet with Joshua. They returned to meet Shane and Heath just as they came back from taking Helena's suitcases to her bedroom.

"What did Sienna and Manford decide?" Kate asked.

Shane said, "They're staying at the cabin. Neither of them wants to return to their former lives, at least not yet. They both want to make sure it's safe when they do go back. And they want to wait until after all the whirlwind investigations end."

Heath added, "Sienna isn't anxious to be interviewed by scores of investigators and then hounded by reporters, now that Thomas Marshall is dead. Manford mentioned that he and Sienna have taken up hiking and they plan to finish more than two dozen overnight hikes before they leave. Manford says he's never been happier."

"Manford is a billionaire. You'd think he'd miss all the attention and finery he's used to enjoying," Angie commented.

Shane said, "I don't know. All the stuff in life has to be taken care of and worried about. I think the best times we get are simple days enjoyed with the people you love, not worrying about anything."

Kate said, "I agree. One of my fondest memories with my dad was sitting by a lake in the sun on a warm day, watching ducks squawk at each other, while we ate his homemade egg salad sandwiches with green olives. I'll never forget it. The scene is etched in my memory, and can still bring me to tears. I'd give all the money I have to sit with him for an hour at that lake one more time."

Angie said, "I have memories like that with my dad, flying planes, target practicing with guns and bows, and climbing mountains. I'd love to have another chance, too."

"I guess I can understand where Manford and Sienna are coming from, deciding they want to stay in isolation. Right now they have no responsibilities and no worries. They can just enjoy life and each other. I would like that myself," Kate agreed.

Shane said, "Speaking of that, Kate and I have an announcement to make that concerns both of you. We have decided now that we have a window to breathe, we want to be married."

Angie and Heath both smiled and asked questions at the same time in their excitement.

Kate said, "We've asked Char if we can be married here, and she's agreed, and already ordered a gazebo built in the field overlooking the large pond to the north. We'll honeymoon at the Biltmore Hotel for a week. We've scheduled it for next Saturday, ten days from now."

Angie rushed to hold both of Kate's hands, and said, excitedly, "Details. I want details."

As Shane stood beaming, Kate looked at Angie, and explained, "Walter will give me away, and we'll honor Juanita as my mother. Dolores from Carson City will be my maid of honor. I'd like you, Char,

Tracy, and Helena to be bridesmaids. I picked out the dresses last night."

Angie hugged Kate again in excitement, and said, "Show me!"

Angie and Kate rushed out of the kitchen and upstairs to the bedroom to see dresses and plan details.

Heath looked at Shane and said, "Look, Shane, I know Pete should be your best man. I don't deserve..."

Shane interrupted, "I'm asking both you and Pete to be my best men. One of the nice things about planning a wedding in this day and age is being able to decide what's best for those you love. And I have two best men in my life. So, if you both accept, Bryan Holland, and Hunter will be ushers, and Jesse will perform the ceremony, as he did for Walter and Juanita. What do you say, brother?"

Tears formed, but did not fall from Heath's eyes. He reached over and stepped in to give Shane a bear hug. Heath closed his eyes tightly, as he thanked God for delivering him back to his family. And with his eyes tightly closed, he saw the figure of his father, Patrick Beckett, smiling at him and nodding. Heath thought his father said, "Well done, my good sons. Well done."

"What did you say?" Heath asked, through tears.

Shane struggled through his brother's tightening hug to say, "I said, I think I can take that as a yes!"

Walter and Pete chatted in their SUV on the way back from a meeting in Atlanta, where they finalized the acquisition of a shopping center. Char and Juanita talked in the rear seat, after an early morning of shopping and then treating themselves to manicures and pedicures. Both women were content to talk about Kate and Shane's upcoming wedding, and what gifts both couples might plan.

THE POLITICIANS

Pete asked, "Walter, what do you think happens now with this Committee group? Even if the United States rids itself of the menace, it doesn't mean other countries will do the same. There is no guarantee this will be over even in our lifetime."

Walter smiled and answered, "Pete, my boy, you know how much I hate politics. And we both know that The Committee formed from a handful of power-hungry politicians belonging to countries left in ruin after two world wars. These self-appointed egotists thought they had come up with the answer to all of man's ills. And their solution was to exterminate some people, control those they allowed to live, and assign everyone roles fitting criteria the ruling elite designed."

Walter added, "But Committee planners never understood how hard political parties would fight to remain in control of their voting masses. Political parties must aggressively oppose each other to maintain control over their bases. Constant dramatic conflict keeps their members engaged and willing to provide necessary financial support. Opposing political parties are each other's most important asset."

Walter said, "When faced with a choice of surrendering to a foreign political entity like The Committee, or keeping the political enemy they know and understand, I wonder how The Committee ever hoped to win. I believe, Pete, that even Committee members who belong to American political parties are afraid to give up the power they enjoy now for something they may have in the future."

Pete said, "So, you don't think the American politicians who are also members of The Committee can be loyal enough to their Committee goals to leave the power they enjoy as Republicans and Democrats."

"I don't, Pete. And when you think about it, why would they? What do they possibly have to gain they don't already enjoy within our American system? Politicians have better pay, retirement, health care, power, and perks than most Americans. And if they want more, they can vote themselves more. Why would they risk it for a promise of less power and more personal risk in the future? In our system, even if you commit treason, tax fraud or are convicted of corruption, as a politician, chances are you won't end up in prison and can probably find a new place in your party or as a lobbyist."

Walter finished his summation, saying, "As a member of The Committee, if you commit any of those acts you end of at the Center for Information Extraction, tortured and interrogated, chopped up into body parts, dissolved in acid, and pressure cooked into ash, all without the benefit of a trial."

From the back seat, Juanita asked, "Are you two still talking about The Committee? Can't we enjoy one day without worrying about the menaces of the earth?"

Walter sighed, and whispered, "You know the one thing missing from The Committee plans was a description of retirement."

"I noticed that, too," Pete commented. "Nowhere in all their planning could I find anything describing what happened to people after they reached 80 years old, when they were finally eligible to retire."

"I'll give you one guess where the old folks went," Walter said sarcastically.

Char said, "I think Juanita and I want to discuss wedding gifts for Shane and Kate, if we can."

Pete and Walter smiled, and remained silent.

THE POLITICIANS

While Walter, Pete, Juanita and Char drove back from Atlanta, BaCayse notified her cyber team that she was monitoring a transmission from The Committee Prophet to all Committee members throughout the United States. Committee IT had encrypted the broadcast, requiring a member to sign in and then input their assigned pin in order to hear the message. It took BaCayse sixteen seconds to bypass the cyber barriers. She directed the video to the overhead monitor in the workroom, just as Helena took her seat next to Joshua.

The Committee logo of a globe with lightning bolts striking it from both the upper left and upper right appeared on the monitor. A shadowed image of the four remaining members of the eighth tier faded onto the screen, shot from above, showing unrecognizable images of four men as they sat around a table with one vacant chair. The shadowy indistinct figure of Marissa Weinstein came into view, as she walked into the room and took her seat at the table, newly appointed to fill President Thomas Marshall's vacant position on the eighth-tier, pending a permanent vote.

The screenshot then zoomed back to the logo, as the voice of the Prophet said, "Welcome, members! The recent failure of President Thomas Marshall documented in the news has been both disturbing to morale, and necessary to our growth. Indeed, at times like this, we are all reminded that people are the weak link in our society. And yet, with all their frailties and faults, we still need human creativity to grow and progress."

"But, as to Thomas Marshall, our system promoted an egotist who placed his self-interests above our collective goals. The resulting failure is as much ours as it is his. But we have already made changes to ensure nothing like this ever happens again. Going forward, anyone

531

in our system is encouraged to report any member, regardless of tier level, whose actions become suspect and counter to Committee values."

"And, while this change will flush out those too weak to be our comrades, we now see this coming purge as a necessary consequence of our rapid growth. To some, this action may seem harsh. But we must all realize that we have recently lost a great deal of time and resources, having to abandon our Yucca Mountain facility and both of our Centers for Information Extraction. Many of our members will face tough questioning from a variety of investigations going forward through the next year or so. Our growth in the United States was dealt a serious blow."

"However, on a very positive note, we plan to re-occupy our Yucca Mountain Facility and activate our two backup Centers for Information Extraction, as these investigations draw to a close, or are abandoned by American politicians. Key staffers are already hard at work with our members in foreign governments, creating fictitious news releases that will convince people our Committee was nothing more than an elaborate hoax by the Republican party designed to remove a Democratic President."

"And just as importantly, during our recovery period, Committee IT will escalate attacks on both the Republicans and the Democrats, increasing their never-ending mutual war against each other, until violence becomes commonplace. Using our new algorithm, I promise you that this setback will pale in comparison to the damage we do to the American political system, and their precious system of justice, over the coming decade."

"And, so, as we move beyond this attack together, I urge all of us to hold fast to our doctrine and continue to place faith in our vision.

As we move forward, more quickly than ever before, our future progress will more than offset any setbacks we experienced. Your persistence is needed, and will be rewarded beyond your wildest dreams of power, control, and purpose."

"Work hard. Remain strong. And believe in nothing other than yourself and your position in *your* Committee! Remember, each one of *you* represents the new world and the hope for the required change. If you are not with us, you oppose us, with all that has proven weak and unnecessary. Each one of *them* is our enemy, and represents all that is old and has failed. The Committee does not tolerate failure."

"So, I leave you with this promise of victory. No one can resist us. No one can stand against us without being destroyed. The Committee is the only way, the only choice, and the only path to a better future. Our war has just begun. We take no prisoners, and we destroy without guilt so that we can rebuild in our perfect vision."

"My members, rest easy in the guarantee of our future success. And may we all continue to bless our Committee with loyalty! Good evening, members."

A loud round of applause came through the speakers, as all five members of the eighth tier stood and applauded.

BaCayse turned the monitor off, as the feed went blank.

Anxious to leave the depressing briefing, Helena stood and asked Joshua to follow her out to the rear deck. When they arrived, Helena said, "I missed you."

"I missed you, too," Joshua admitted. "I didn't feel I had anything to look forward to when I walked into the workroom, if you weren't here."

"Joshua, I need to tell you that I have to make a decision soon. I came here, after falling in love with Bryan Holland, only because he asked me to leave and assist this team. And I love it here, with all of you. And I began to feel like I had fallen in love with you, while we worked together. And now, I just went back and saw Bryan."

Joshua looked down, and said, "Oh, I see."

"No, I don't think you do yet," Helena added. "When I got back to D.C., I was already missing you and the team, and not anxious to see Bryan, at all. I've been confused for the whole two weeks I've been gone. And now, on the way back here, all I could think about was the last time we held hands, and I wanted to see you."

"But that's great! Your back, and there's no problem!" Joshua said excitedly.

"But, for how long?" Helena asked. "And what about when I have to leave for another assignment, or *you* go home?"

Joshua admitted, "I don't know. I hadn't thought that far ahead. But you're right. I think we need to figure it out. Let's go for a walk." Joshua reached out and took Helena by the hand, as Hunter smiled.

Once they were gone, BaCayse said, "Hunter, I don't believe we need to burden Shane and Kate about the Prophet and Committee plans to escalate a war on America, right before their wedding."

Hunter was silent as he thought. He finally said, "I guess it should take this Prophet more than a couple of weeks to escalate his conflict to the point that anyone will notice. Maybe you're right."

BaCayse said, "Every human needs some peace, love, hope, and understanding. Let's not impact our happy couple's hope with worry."

"Deal!" Joshua said.

"Goodnight, BaCayse. I'm calling it a day."

534

"Goodnight, Hunter."

Hunter got up to leave, and asked, "By the way, what are you wearing tonight?"

"Jammies," BaCayse replied.

"You don't sleep!" Hunter objected.

"How do you know?" BaCayse teased.

"Show me," Hunter teased back.

The monitor flashed on, showing BaCayse walking barefoot across a white marble floor, toward Joshua, wearing a cobalt blue babydoll nightgown with lace trim, and matching tap pants. The blue sleepwear perfectly matched her shimmering blue eyes and accented every sensual curve of her incredible body.

Hunter exclaimed, "Oh, wow, BaCayse, you're killing me!"

BaCayse laughed, and said, "Hunter, I think it's high time *you* found a girlfriend."

Hunter murmured, "You're telling me," as he turned to leave the room.

BaCayse spun around, in the monitor, and sauntered away from view, out of sight. Her rear view was as stunning as her front, as her body flexed and bounced perfectly, creating a spellbinding erotic effect. The screen went blank.

Tracy walked into the room and found Jesse staring at the overhead monitor. She asked, "What are you doing, honey? There's nothing on the monitor."

Jesse answered, "I was just thinking about you. Can we make tonight a *date* night? We need some alone time!"

Tracy smiled coyly, and said, "I was hoping you'd ask. A girl needs some attention you know."

Jesse quickly turned and kissed Tracy passionately.

Pleasantly surprised, after the kiss, Tracy looked around to make sure no one was watching.

She asked, "Honey, what's gotten into you?"

Jesse said, "I just miss...enjoying you. By the way, do you have any dark blue lingerie?"

✳✳✳

Immediately following his speech, while the alluring BaCayse said goodnight to Hunter and mesmerized Jesse, six representatives of the seventh and eighth tiers ordered the Prophet into a private meeting. Heavily armed agents representing The Committee's Secret Enforcement Division stood guard, dressed in black uniforms with facemasks, while the six-member panel read the Prophet a devastating list of grievances.

Although the Prophet was a fearsome man, possessing incredible physical and mental powers, jolts of fear penetrated his mind and body. He understood very well that nearly all formal grievance recitations ended in arrest, incarceration, torture, and termination.

He, himself, had designed the very torture system currently in use at all Committee Centers for Information Extraction. It was a terrifying system he feared he may now personally experience.

The Prophet headed the Committee's Cyber Operations and Warfare Division, making him responsible for all cyber victories, and failures. He knew that he alone bore responsibility for the recent defeats at Yucca Mountain and the two C.I.E. facilities. And although he saw himself as the most powerful person in The Committee, he realized that at this very moment, he was also the most vulnerable.

Uncharacteristically, for a sociopath, with nearly unlimited power and control, the Prophet began to sweat, profusely.

As soon as the reading ended, Marissa Weinstein asked, "Do you see any plausible reason your presence is still a benefit to The Committee?"

The Prophet remained silent for a few moments, as he thought. He had listened to dozens of members plead for their lives, all unsuccessfully.

He seized the only opportunity he saw, and said, "These attacks were unforeseeable and undefendable, as when the attack came, our resources were running at near full capacity, testing the Primary Objective algorithm in the Bay area. President Marshall pressed for the accelerated timetable, against my advice and wishes. *His* was an unfortunate error."

"Now, we must locate and capture the people and the system that attacked us, to prevent a similar attack in the future. And I already have developed the plan that will accomplish those goals, quickly. Once we succeed, we can merge the enemy's technology with ours, enabling us to more than recover what we have lost. I am essential to this purpose!" The Prophet stood erect, at attention.

The room was silent as all six members pushed their digital buttons to vote, immediately sparing the Prophet's life by a vote of four to two.

Senator Marissa Weinstein said, "You have two weeks to produce what you have promised. Make sure there are no more mistakes."

Twenty minutes later, the Prophet stomped angrily into a vast room filled with workstations, servers, computers, and monitors. In two rows of twenty, uniformed Committee IT experts stood rigid, awaiting his arrival. He marched directly toward the center of the lines, stopped one pace back, and looked from right to left, critically assessing each member of his team.

In a strained voice, The Prophet snarled, "We have all failed while working within one of the least forgiving and most powerful organizations in the world, a system completely intolerant of failure. All administrators in both top tiers are very, very unhappy. And their unhappiness most often leads to termination. I am fortunate to be standing here, alive, addressing all of *you*."

"My survival...no, *our* survival, is now dependent on my promise. And because I assured our leaders success, we have been given one last chance at redemption. It is our only chance and leaves no room for a single mistake. And *I* do not intend to fail again. We *will* identify and find the team who attacked us. We *will* capture those individuals and their computer system. This is the only path to life and freedom our leaders offered us."

He took a deep breath, and sneered, "And in the meantime, we will *not* suffer another defeat at our enemy's hands. The Committee's future hangs in the balance."

The Prophet subconsciously flexed his entire body-builder physique, as every muscle, including those on his bald head, strained to emphasize his resolve. Standing nearly six-feet-three-inches tall, sporting a 48-inch chest, 36-inch waist, 20-inch biceps, a shaved head, and a thick, wide mustache, the Prophet was more than formidable. Standing rigid, with narrowed, dark-brown eyes and tensed jaws, he appeared menacing and unstoppable, even at 53-years old.

As the bulky man surveyed his team one last time, looking across their faces from left to right, he asked sternly, "Does *anyone* have a question?"

A feather dropping to the floor in the stress-filled room would have made a noticeable sound.

When no one uttered a single word, the Prophet said, "Good! Then get to work. We've been given two weeks to find them! And, after we capture them, I will interrogate each member of their team, personally!"

Acknowledgments

I acknowledge and thank my wife, Debbie, for many dozens of hours she spent reading, re-reading, editing and critiquing the manuscript, helping this book develop and survive in a form I recognize as mine.

All readers are challenged to follow an author's thoughts, feelings, and expressions, as the writer works through scenes, expanding characters and advancing a storyline. We all recognize that the same tale could have been written a million different ways. No one person always writes using perfect language, punctuation, spelling, grammar, and style. Linguistics evolve through time.

And because they are free to use diverse techniques, authors create exciting differences through their writing style. These variances give us the opportunity to see the world through a new set of eyes. Hopefully, we learn, grow, and are entertained in the process.

My two technical editors and dear friends, Tom, and Marilyn Suarez, helped immensely in identifying correct sentence structure. They also provided invaluable advice. I thank them for their diligence, commitment, and friendship, as they volunteered their time to this project.

My wife, Debbie, often provided me with excellent feedback on what a reader may enjoy or even consider exciting, as I worked to create real-life characters and stimulating situations. As with all people in life, my characters speak and respond, influenced by different dialects, personal experiences, and cultural backgrounds. My goal is to create realization, discovery, and drama using parts of life people are

540

aware of, but may not know, and in the process present an intriguing tale.

Family units featured in my novels include loving pets. Dogs presented throughout this series are based on real-life pets. Some of these canine family members are living, while others now remain only in photographs and life-long memories. Dogs like Jago, Masai, Bruiser, and Sophia tend to keep the story grounded in reality, as they provide true unconditional love, entertainment, and loyalty. I thank family and friends for sharing cherished exploits, photos, and characteristics of their special family members, inspiring me to create essential roles in my novels.

As I wrote this manuscript, sitting at my desk, each day I found myself surrounded by my own canine family. My pack consisted of Pearl, the centenarian Cocker Spaniel, Jazzy, our King Charles Cavalier, and Bentley, my rescue dog with a black tongue, likely part lab and Black Mouth Cur.

Jazzy favored a space on the floor behind the chaise lounge, where she sleeps and snores so loudly you can hear her from other rooms. Pearl lays directly under my chair, so I can never move without checking to make sure I won't roll over her paw. And Bentley sleeps on the chaise lounge, or sits, watching squirrels out the window. He often looks at me, likely wondering why I remain at the same chair for hours, when we could be out running in a field.

Dogs warm our hearts and make us smile. They all seem to share that unique ability to improve our lives just by being present. Considering the power of that gift, we should all take lessons from our canine companions. I thank them for their willingness to stay patiently

by my side throughout the writing of **The Beckett Cypher Series –
Book 3 – The Politicians**.

About the Author

Lee Cunningham was just 6 months old, when his father was killed, while driving from Nebraska to Idaho, to reunite with Lee Jr. and his mother. Lee eventually came to be known as "Danny," a nickname given him by his eight aunts. Lee's mother relocated them to California, seeking a better career opportunity, to improve their lives. Struggling, as a working, single mother, she met and married George Holub, when Lee was 9 years old. Lee's step-father adopted

him when he turned 12. Proud of his new father, Lee had his name legally changed, to Daniel Lee Holub.

Lee attended universities, graduating with a degree in Zoology, minoring in English. His daring mother often ventured in to the California deserts, to help him collect rattlesnakes, for college research projects. His father taught him to fish, hunt, camp, and love the outdoors. Lee's parents instilled in him a respect and love for God, family, friends and country. He also always loved to write. His first success was an essay, published while still in school.

In the year following college, Lee worked a drug case assisting D.E.A. He flew a Cessna 210 airplane from California to Bogota,

543

Colombia, as an undercover pilot. He participated in one of the largest out-of-country drug sting operations of the time, when he was just 24 years old. Fascinated with police work, Lee was hired as a police officer, and graduated from the L.A.P.D. academy.

Lee worked in law enforcement in California and Nevada for 25 years, serving in both uniform and plain clothes. His work included assignments in patrol, a narcotics task force, a gang unit, and various detective units, where he investigated thousands of cases, including homicides. He interviewed thousands of criminals, including some in prison. Lee served as a S.W.A.T. member and a S.W.A.T. commander.

Following policework Lee went on to work in Security Management at one of the world's largest gold mines. He and his team were responsible for protecting more than a billion dollars' worth of gold and silver shipments annually, while providing high level security for explosives and other sensitive chemicals.

Throughout his careers, writing remained one of Lee's passions, and he planned this collection of novels for many years. Calling on all his crime knowledge, undercover work, training and experiences, Lee Cunningham now offers his first series of fiction novels as **The Beckett Cypher Series**.

Lee lives in Florida with his lovely wife, his nearly "psychic" multi-breed rescue dog, a King Charles Cavalier puppy, and a grand-motherly Cocker Spaniel. He enjoys writing, traveling, experiencing the great outdoors, good food, family, friends, and pets.

(